Thieves' Castle

Dean Hamilton

TyburnTree Publishing
Toronto, Canada
MMXIX

While some of the events and characters are based on historical incidents and persons, this novel is entirely a work of fiction.

www.tyburntree.blogspot.com

"The Jovial Tinker" or "When Joan's Ale was New" lyrics originally registered as a ballad with Stationers' Company by John Danter 1594; re-published 1838-40 from "A Collection of National English Airs." Chappell, W, courtesy of Pennsylvania State University online.

ISBN: 978-0-9939174-4-8

Cover Design by Marko Paajanen, www.chosenidea.com
Photography by M. Vecera
Interior Design by D. Hamilton

Give me the scorn of the stars and a peak defiant;
Wail of the pines and a wind with the shout of a giant;
Night and a trail unknown and a heart reliant.

For Jarold Rae Hamilton, 1937 - 2018

Thanks Dad, for everything.

The Tyburn Folios

The Jesuit Letter
Black Dog (novella)
Thieves' Castle
Sorcerer Street (work in progress)

Acknowledgements

How do you say thanks to all the people that contribute to making a project like this soar? There is a very long list of people who have provided support, advice, encouragement and hope in helping bring this book to life.

Special thanks as always go to my wife Deborah and my son Zach, my parents Rae and Glen, and all my extended family for their continuing patience, assistance and support through the entirety of the ups and downs of the process of writing a book.

Special thanks to my editor Karen Conlin, who, as always, spots my missteps, helps keep me on the straight and narrow, and argues Elizabethan word usage with unmatched passion, humour and fortitude.

A huge note of thanks to all people who supported my publication fundraising endeavors, which made this book possible! You are all uniformly fabulous and your support helped make this happen. I hope you enjoy the read!

Thanks again,

Dean

Indie GoGo Patrons

This page is small attempt to acknowledge the impact and assistance that everyone listed below provided through their kind donations and support for my IndieGoGo publishing project. They truly helped to bring *Thieves' Castle* to life.

For that, they have my profound appreciation.

Stephany Babson	Susan Jobbins
Steph & Mike Barrett	Gail Kyrzakos
Connie Costa	Paraic Lally
John Cunningham	Andy Lank
Terry Edmonds	Greg Paisley
Dave H	Warren Paisley
Devon Hamilton	Sandro Perruzza
Glen Hamilton	Nicola Richardson
James Hamilton	Linda Thompson
Stephen Hartley	Timothy G Utting
Kirsi Henry	Linda Sukk
incspot613	Harvey Wolfe

THIEVES' CASTLE

"Ah, gracious lord, these days are dangerous:
Virtue is chok'd with foul ambition,
And charity chas'd hence by rancor's hand"

- William Shakespeare, Henry VI.

Chapter the First

THE MAN'S FEET slid in the muck as he crossed the open space of the laneway, the darkness yawning moist and thick around him. He leaned against the corner post, panting. Only his harsh breath broke the silence. In one hand glinted an unsheathed dagger. The man glanced around, eyes straining at the darkness.

Ivy Lane stank. The smell was a mix of urine, dung, and the foul, rancid stench of offal drifting down from the butcher's yards north of Newgate Street.

The man pushed himself away from the corner and turned hastily down the lane. The night was heavy and the darkness near complete, lit only by a sprinkle of candles fluttering in the tight confines of casement windows and the dim yellow light of a small lamp hung outside one fathomless doorway. Although the lane was cobbled, the stones were greasy with the accrual of filth and the endless tread of daytime commerce. The man paused, hearing the faint echo of feet behind him.

He cursed to himself and began to move down Ivy Lane with as much speed as the darkness and the uncertain footing allowed. He held the dagger at arm's length in front of him, as though to hold the night at a distance. The sounds seemed closer.

He glanced around. The laneway was narrow, a typical London thoroughfare, overhung with jetties that exiled the sky into a narrow strip and made the already oppressive darkness of the night into a stygian gloom. A flare of torchlight sent a set of shadows racing away as someone passed the corner he had vacated. The light sent the man scurrying, no longer mindful of the slippery cobbles. He caught a faint gleam of a bare blade in the glowing light of the torch.

"Find 'im, lads, winnow him out." The faint voice sounded amused.

The man cursed again and ran down the street, one hand outstretched, bumping along the irregular walls of the laneway. Another flicker of light in the distance ahead of him, coming from Paternoster Row and the distant bulk of St. Paul's Cathedral.

"Coads." The man muttered and pressed himself into the wall, shaking. The men were getting closer.

"Stay still." The voice was soft but firm. A dim yellow light emerged from the doorway to his right, carried by a young woman. Her hair was short and dark. She stepped out and hung the lantern on a sign bracket above the narrow doorway. She pointed at the darkened alcove to the left of the door, almost hidden by the thick corner beam of the house. "Go there."

The man wiped his face and nodded, sliding into the welcome darkness of the alcove as into a lover's embrace. He listened as the sound of footsteps grew more distinct. He could see the red flicker of the torch against the wall as they drew near, the shadows dancing back and forth with drunken abandon. He shrank back, feeling the rough timber frame digging into his spine. He listened.

"Bit late for punk trade, isn't it?"

"Codso, you lot out looking for sheep?" the girl said in a tired voice. "What's this rag and tag?"

"You seen a man? A blood?"

2

She laughed. "Likes of them in Ivy at this time of night? Not tonight. Any of your rufflers in coin?"

"Piss off, cunt, we're busy."

"Fuck you, you buggering cockless bastards, go find yourselves some rent-boy's arse." The torchlight flickered and began to move away. The man hidden in the alcove let out a long sustained breath of relief as the footsteps faded away. The girl continued to berate the trio's retreating backs until they disappeared.

"You can come out."

The man emerged cautiously, his eyes flinching as he scanned the length of the street.

"That lot's gone." The girl said. She canted her head at the man and surveyed him up and down with a practiced eye. "What'd they want you for?"

"No idea, love. They came at us when we left the tavern." The man shuddered at the recollection. He had stood mute and stunned as he watched his two friends beaten into the mud, and only when the steel had gleamed red did his drink-befuddled reflexes send him careening away as fast as his legs could carry him. He coughed as bile choked his throat.

"Here." The dark-haired girl handed him a wineskin. He tilted it back and gulped a mouthful of thin, acrid wine. As he wiped his mouth, he looked at the girl again in the lantern light. Her hair was dark and short, barely past her ears. She wore a long dress with the bodice bare and loose, the swell of her breasts clearly evident. The stays on the dress were untied, allowing the top to flare open, giving the man a tantalizing glimpse of a lean length of untrammeled flesh. The girl tilted her torso back and one nipple slid out from underneath the thin fabric.

"Why don't you stay with me for a time, until your hunters wear themselves out?" The man felt one hand brush along the front of his breeches, pressing against the hardening length of his member. His breath caught. His eyes closed as her grip tightened.

"That may be the wisest choice ..." the man breathed. Her hand slid around his waist and she slowly turned him, her dark eyes locked on his, her mouth open like a wet promise. He slid his hand down between her thighs where the thin material left little to the imagination. Maybe it was due to the terror of being hunted through the nighttime paths of London, but the girl's touch made his pulse hammer and his desire quicken. She smiled, a brazen smile of anticipation and lust.

It felt like a thump and a sharp tightness against his right side. He stopped in puzzlement. The girl continued to look at him and gave a slight half smile as hot pain coursed through him.

"I ... what ...?" The girl continued to smile. He felt her brace herself for an instant and then push her right hand against the handle of the long poniard that protruded from his side. He staggered, one hand grasping at the girl. He felt his numbing fingers trail over the hardening nipple of her breast, but his lust was overtaken by overwhelming weakness that made the dark alley swim. A sick feeling of horror flooded through him as he reached for her. She laughed and easily deflected his hand, tugging on the handle of the dagger, steering him, lurching, away from her. "You ..." His thought was incomplete, lost in a red wave of searing pain.

"Over here, come with me." She crooned in an encouraging voice, one guiding hand on his back and one on the dagger handle, as though driving a farm animal to market. He took a staggered step and then the girl grasped the dagger handle tightly and twisted it. The man felt a tugging sensation and his insides turned to liquid, as though he had drunk a skinful of hot spiced wine in one swallow. He could feel the cold length of the steel perforating his flesh, ripping into his bowels and belly. His breath roared in his ears and his eyes filled with tears. The lantern wavered and blurred.

He was on the ground, mouth tasting of blood, fingers grasping at the thin layer of muck that coated the cobbles. The torchlight flared again and he stared upwards at the girl's intent face. She wore a pleased expression like she had made some fresh discovery.

"Want me to finish him?" One of his hunters stood beside the girl, holding the torch and looking down at him with a bemused expression.

"No, I want to watch him go. You would spoil my fun, Bent." She smiled. Bent's eyes flickered at the girl with a measured look and then back at the dying man stretched across the muddy stones of Ivy Lane.

Bent nodded in careful acquiescence. "Can't have that." Bent reached down and ripped the blade free. The man felt a calescent, diffuse sensation spreading through his body, as though he had pissed himself. His blood was dark as night in the glow of the torch. He watched it puddle across the greasy cobbles. "Leave this on him when he's done." He handed her a small object. She nodded absently and lowered herself over the supine man's groin, settling herself upon him, eyes fixed on his face, knees on the wet cobbles, unmindful of either dung or bloody rivulets, her expression almost rapt in the flickering torchlight, watching his eyes as the man cried in pain and fear and bled to death in the dank confines of Ivy Lane.

Chapter the Second

THE SHIP WAS squat and shapeless in the fading light, backlit by an unfriendly autumn sun.

"*Het schip*," the man said. "That one." The speaker pointed at the vessel, a stolid, clinker-built trading cog resting quietly at anchor. Built for cargo and to withstand the mercurial Channel wind and waves, the two-masted ship was small and rotund and sat like a stone in the cold, flat waters of Bergen op Zoom.

"She's flagged Dutch, but English-owned." His words, which hung in the damp air, were directed at a short, dark-visaged man with an angular face and a beard that hung long, grey, and scraggling to a point well down his chest. "*Enn Engels schip*," he repeated in poorly accented Dutch to the two uniformed customs men who stood, bored and uninterested. One man scraped mud off of his boot on a convenient edged rock.

The bearded man scowled at the vessel. "This is the fourth vessel you have directed us to, each time claiming it was the one."

"This is the ship, I am certain of it. I recognize it now. The *St. Jan Baptista*. Look at the figurehead." Projecting from the bow was a poorly carved representation of a bearded man, staff held across his chest and one hand outthrust.

The grey-bearded man scowled again and gestured at the customs officer. A lengthy tirade ensued. The man who had pointed out the ship slipped past the argument and walked out onto the short wooden quay, where several boatmen were playing a desultory card game on an empty crate. With a few words and gestures he made his intentions known. One of the boatmen climbed to his feet and clambered over to his skiff.

"Here!" the man called to the still-arguing customs men. With an abrupt gesture, the grey-bearded man made a slashing motion with his hand and ordered the men into the boat. The customs agents, their irritation plain on their faces, clomped out onto the dock and with practiced ease slid into the craft. The bearded man, less experienced with small boats, eased himself carefully into the vessel and the boatman cast-off, rowing them away from the quay with powerful, practiced strokes of the oars.

The grey-bearded man turned his head and regarded the English ship with baleful eyes. "If it is as you stated, the vessel will be impounded until the cargo can be thoroughly searched and inspected. If it is not ..." The man let the implicit threat hang in the air.

"She's the one, Master Story, by God's truth. Carrying at least a thousand Geneva Bibles, printed in London. Supposed to be carrying just woolcloth and wine, but those bastard heretics can't be trusted."

Story grunted and offered a few quick explanatory words in Dutch to the customs men. The taller man, whose lank blond hair hung long under his flat-brimmed hat, snorted with impatience to get out of the damp wind and find a warm corner in a tavern. The man who had pointed out the *St. Jan Baptista* gazed out across the dark water. The waters of the estuary were calm and placid, though the tide was nearly high. Beyond the *St. Jan Baptista*, a score or more of ships were at rest, their bare masts looking like a forest in December, securely anchored in the deeper offshore water, immune to the sandbanks and shoals obscured by the rising tide. Oared boats flitted about like water striders, darting across the surface of the water. Several large fluyts loaded with cargo were being carefully warped through the shallows to the canal for unloading at the town of Bergen op Zoom itself, its red-tiled roofs bright with the last rays of the setting sun. Bergen op Zoom was a fortified town, secure, snug and stolid behind a natural defense system of marshes and polders backed up with an extensive moat surrounding the town.

"The English would be fools to come here, trying to turn loyalties with their heretical preachings," Story fumed. "This isn't Brill. The Spanish and the League now rule the Scheldt."

"I thought the Spanish had abandoned Zierikzee?" The man rubbed at a thin scar that tapered along his left jawline and hooked up onto the cheek, giving his face a sardonic, almost mocking look.

Story regarded the man with eyes like flint. The recent Spanish mutiny in Zeeland had forced the abandonment of a large portion of the Dutch province, and the Spanish *tercios* had withdrawn to the region surrounding Antwerp. Two years without pay had finally come to a head. "Temporarily, only temporarily, I assure you. Once coin is paid to the troops, they will resume their occupation of Zierikzee and drive the heretics from Zeeland."

"By God's Will, it will happen thus." The man replied and turned to watch their approach to the *St. Jan Baptista*. As they drew closer the vessel towered out of the water like a dank layered wall. A line of barnacles and weed hung just above the waterline, a telltale sign that whatever the ship's cargo, it was not fully loaded at present.

A watchman hailed the approaching boat in Dutch and the bored blond customs officer bellowed a reply. A rope ladder with thick wooden slats was hooked over the side and dropped down. The oarsman backed water until they were steady beside the ladder. The two customs officers swung onto the ladder and mounted to the deck above. Story followed, somewhat slower, and the scarred man came last. The oarsman released the ladder and drifted away from the *St. Jan Baptista*, occasionally sculling the water with the oar to stay close.

Story clambered through the entry port and stood on the deck. The watch officer was already speaking to the shorter customs officer, gesturing and pointing towards the sterncastle. A rotund man, wearing a flat-brimmed hat with a small feather emerged from the forecastle.

"I will speak with your captain." Story's voice was sharp and cut through the muttered Dutch conversation. "We will inspect your manifests and ship's papers. You will open your cargo for examination."

The heavyset man in the hat cleared his throat. "Hold there! By God, who are you and by what authority are you—"

"In the names of his most Catholic Majesty, Phillip of Spain, and Don Juan de Austria, Governor-General of the Low Countries."

The man paused. "I don't care if you are the pope himself, you don't demand on my ship. I am William Rogeres, captain and master of this vessel. We've all our permissions and writs."

"You are Dutch flagged," noted the scarred man, pointing at the masthead where a white flag crossed with two red laurel branches hung. The Lord of Burgundy's flag from the House of Hapsburg flew across the seventeen Dutch provinces, with the exception of the rebel-held areas of Zeeland and Holland, who flew the flag of the Prince of Orange. "That means these men"—he pointed at the two customs officers—"have the authority to inspect or impound this vessel."

Captain Rogeres face was red. "See here—"

"No. You see." Story moved forward, his face only inches from the captain's. "By personal appointment of the governor-general, I am empowered to strike down heresy and treasonous action in the Lowlands, to seek out and proscribe any and all heretical documents, books, or sundry manuscripts that I encounter, in the name of his Holiness the Pope and before the Divine and Worshipful presence of God." He placed one finger on the man's chest and jabbed it hard for emphasis. "I. Am. Appointed. The authority as to whether your ship is permitted to ply these waters rests with me, and with the degree of cooperation that you display."

He turned away from the captain. "These men will inspect your cargo. Should they find a page of a diabolical tome, any heretical nonsense or Lutheran documents ... you will burn alongside it." Story's face was bathed with satisfaction, his eyes bright.

The captain's face shone damp with perspiration. "Before God, we are always happy to cooperate with the authorities, but I cannot be responsible for what some Precisian sailor might have dragged aboard with him! Our cargo is above reproach, have your men search the holds, speak with my supercargo!" He gestured for the watch officer.

"Dr. Story, perhaps we should inspect the captain's papers?" the man with the hook scar said.

"When I want your recommendations, I will request them. Your veracity remains unproven, and if it stays that way you will find the stocks at Bergen op Zoom most uncomfortable." Story's voice was harsh but the look on his face as the scarred man quailed was one of supreme satisfaction. He turned and issued a slew of directives to the two customs officers. The two men nodded and gestured for the supercargo to take them below to inspect the cargo.

"Now, Captain, your papers ... and pray my men don't find anything amiss in your cargo, or you and your vessel will be wintering on the Scheldt, possibly as permanent residents." The captain, his face pale, nodded a reluctant acquiescence and led Story and the scarred man to the sterncastle. Half a dozen seamen watched from the upper castle, perched along the rail like a row of starlings.

They ducked as they entered the sterncastle, and the scarred man closed the door behind them. The room held a large chart table and a handful of chairs. A tall sideboard stood on one side of the room. The captain gestured at the two men to sit but Story ignored the courtesy, stepping up to unroll one of the charts piled on top of the scarred and worn surface of the table.

"I shall fetch my papers." The captain stammered and opened one of the two interior doors on the opposing bulkhead and disappeared within. The thumping clank of a capstan turning made Story turn his head in momentary puzzlement.

"When you find the Bibles, what will happen to the man and the ship?" the scarred man asked, pulling a chair away from the table and turning it to straddle it, looking at Story with quizzical eyes.

Story gave the man a snort of contempt. "Rather late for Judas to have recriminations. The captain will be held and questioned by the Spanish ecclesiastical authorities. Probably hanged, and his ship impounded."

"A harsh punishment," the man observed.

"He should burn. All heretics should burn."

"You've seen a man burn?" Something in the scarred man's voice made Story glance up from the chart of the Dutch coast.

"God has blessed me with the opportunity to burn more than a dozen heretics. It is worth observing, the purification of a man's soul in cleansing flame. It is what awaits all heresy in the bowels of Hell. The sharpness of the sword and other corrections bring forth what gentle remonstrance does not. I had the rare privilege of helping condemn and cleanse Thomas Cranmer at Oxford." He gave a thin smile. "That cursed heretic was Archbishop of Canterbury under Henry and Edward. ...." He sighed. "What a joyous day that was."

"Yes, I suppose burning a man alive would be a feather in your cap."

"He burned for the greater glory of God and the Church, as all heretics should be punished." Story gave the seated man a sharp look as the interior door opened. The man that emerged wasn't the captain. He was wide and round-shouldered, with a broad, fleshy face and barbed eyes. The scarred man felt the deck under his feet tilt gently, and he smiled.

"Where is the captain?" Story said. "These contrivances grow tiresome. Before God, you will pay dearly ..."

"Underway?" the scarred man asked.

"Just warping her out. Can't set off until the moon is higher, even with the pilot we have."

Story's face was suffused with fury. "I gave no permission to sail." He tore the chart in his hands. "Where is the captain? You will be gaoled for these actions! *Officier! Officier!*"

Story yanked on the door handle. It was locked. Story froze.

The scarred man rapped his knuckles on the table hard to get Story's attention. The face that turned towards him was white and drawn with anger and fear.

"John Story? Doctor John Story?"

Story nodded in reflex response to the question.

"Dr. John Story, in the name of her Majesty, by the grace of God, Queen of England and Ireland, you are charged with treasonous offence against the Crown."

"Treason? Who are you to charge me?" Story's voice rose to a shout. "Who are you to charge me? Servant of that faithless whore of Babylon, a heretical bitch that fornicates with the Devil." He turned to the heavy door and pulled at the latchbar. It did not budge. "*Officier! Officier! Help! Moord!*"

"Moored?" asked the stocky man. The man's name was Edward Woodshaw, and he served as Francis Walsingham's eyes and ears in Antwerp. He watched Story pound on the door with pitiless eyes.

"*Moord*. It means murder," Christopher Tyburn replied. "I thought your Dutch was better than that."

Woodshaw laughed. "We move in different circles. Ask me about Antwerp's financiers, venturers, and mercers. Those I can speak to. Murderers, rogues and cutthroats I leave to you."

Tyburn smiled without humour. Christopher Tyburn was another of Walsingham's men, a small circle of intelligencers that carried out the Crown's secret war in defense of the realm. Tyburn had been seconded to Woodshaw due to his familiarity with the region and the Dutch. Four years fighting with Thomas Morgan and Sir Humphrey Gilbert's expedition to Holland and Flanders had given him an intimate knowledge of the muddy Dutch polders, damp market-towns, and the coppery scent of blood that seemed to hang over the ravaged countryside.

Story slumped against the locked door, his hands covering his face. A whispered, despairing prayer in Latin began. Woodshaw and Tyburn exchanged a glance. The prayer finished and Tyburn watched as Story wiped his wet eyes and stood, his face steeled.

"You will release me at once. You have no right under the laws of God or men to hold me. I am a citizen of the Spanish Netherlands and under the righteous protection of the Catholic Church."

"Right has nothing to do with it." Tyburn's voice was flat. "You aren't here due to your work for the Spanish or for burning Cranmer or any of your other ecclesiastical murders. You are here because seven years ago you conspired with Westmorland and Northumberland in their treachery and rebellion against their sovereign. You helped foment the Northern rebellion, encouraged and preached sedition and treason, and actively attempted to promote the overthrow of your rightful sovereign. It's treason, not heresy you'll swing for. There's a subtle distinction."

"It is not treason to overthrow the Devil's spawn when it usurps the Church! Blessed Mary of Scotland is the true Catholic heir. Who are you to judge me?"

Woodshaw interrupted Story's tirade. "We aren't judging you, just delivering you."

"Minions of a diabolical lord ..." Story sneered.

"Irritated and bored minions now," said Tyburn. He stood and banged twice on the locked door. With a clack, it opened and two sailors entered. Tyburn gestured at Story. "Secure him below. Gag him for now but don't hurt him."

Woodshaw reached out and grasped Story's upper arm. "This way, Doctor, your quarters await." Story pulled back, turning as his left hand shot upwards towards Woodshaw's face, a faint metallic reflection visible, flickering in the air. Story's upper arm smacked hard into Tyburn's hand as the scarred man intervened. He pulled Story's arm over hard and twisted.

The thin, short-bladed knife clattered onto the chart table. Woodshaw was pale as his eyes dropped to the weapon. Story spat at

Tyburn. Tyburn bent the man's arm and levered him away from the table and into the waiting arms of the sailors. They pulled his arms behind him and tied his hands.

"The good news, Dr. Story, is that I doubt you'll burn. God's judgment on you is superseded by the Crown's at the moment. You might hang, but you won't burn."

The look of baleful hatred on Story's face spoke volumes. "You will. You and all of your friends, verily your heretical kingdom itself will burn, with all the flames that perdition can stoke. You will burn in a Godly fire, heretic bastard, your flesh consumed in purifying flame. You will scald ..." His voice was a low hiss.

The door closed behind him and Tyburn listened to the muffled litany continue unabated as the men took Story below. Woodshaw shuddered and moved to the sideboard, where he took up a leather-wrapped bottle and uncorked it. He pulled out two pewter mugs and poured a generous allotment in each.

"Here" he slid a mug over to Tyburn. "Bene bouse. Sauced gin."

Tyburn drank and grimaced at the harsh taste, not alleviated by the mix of pepper and spice that had been added.

"A good end to a bad one." Woodshaw said, draining his mug.

"Story thinks he's on the side of the righteous and the Godly."

"Well he's bloody not." Woodshaw snorted and poured himself another mug. "Bastard man of God just tried to carve up my face ... 'You will all burn.' What a load of tripe."

"How long until the Channel?"

"It's a bitch, that estuary with its tides. At least two, maybe three days beating down river and we'll pass Walcheren."

Tyburn rubbed his beard thoughtfully. "Be at least a day before anyone notices Story and his customs men are missing, probably another day to track them to the *Baptista*."

Woodshaw snorted. "The Spanish are too busy now to chase after some vagrant English traitor."

"What do you mean?"

"You hadn't heard? Word came in a few hours ago. The Spanish *tercios* rose. They're plundering Antwerp as we speak." He gestured in that general direction. "Now that it's nightfall, you can probably see the fires from here, it's only twenty miles."

"Dear God."

"I doubt God has much of a hand in this. The Spanish Army of the Netherlands is now looting, fucking, and thieving its way through the richest port in Northern Europe. Good luck for us and ours, bad luck for the mercers of Antwerp and their daughters."

Tyburn thought for a moment. "We'll be at the front end of a flood of merchant ships and refugees fleeing the port. No one will be looking for Story in the middle of this disaster."

Woodshaw nodded. "Barring the misfortune of a Spanish patrol, we shouldn't have any problems. We might be able to deliver Walsingham that 'clean and simple' result he's perpetually seeking."

It was Tyburn's turn to snort. "I don't think we're fated for clean and simple results." He drained his mug. Despite the harsh peppery flavour, the gin left a warm, pleasant burning sensation in Tyburn's throat. He reached for the bottle and then froze, listening.

"Hear that?" A din of voices arose on the deck, intermixed with shouts in Dutch.

"God's bones, what now?" sighed Woodshaw. The two men ducked through the narrow opening and headed for the deck.

The *St. Jan Baptista's* main deck was ringed by a small circle of sailors. In the centre of the ring the shorter Dutch Custom's officer was shrinking back, eyes frantic. The taller officer with the lank blond hair lay in a crumpled heap by the scuppers, a dark and widening puddle trailing away from his body. In the gathering dusk it had the oily look of black paint, pooling along the gently tilted deck.

"What in the bloody hell do you think you're doing?" Tyburn's sharp voice rang out across the deck. The Dutch customs officer stared at him in a mixture of hope and trepidation. Tyburn pushed his way through the circle of the *Baptista's* sailors and, grabbing the man's arm, pulled him away from the crowd, pushing him in the direction of the sterncastle. The man's face was bloody.

15

"Check him." Tyburn said, gesturing at the other man slumped on the deck. Woodshaw bent and turned the man. The blond man's eyes stared sightless at the deepening sky.

"Dead." Woodshaw's tone was laconic but Tyburn could hear the undercurrent of anger skating below the surface of the one-word reply.

"Dead, you say." Tyburn's voice was cold. Woodshaw glanced up and felt an atavistic shiver run down his spine. The scarred man turned to face the *Baptista* crewmen, his movement slow and deliberate.

"Who did it?" Tyburn surveyed the men. His grey eyes had all the emotion of a fleck of ice. The crew had been recruited in Brill, a seasoned mixture of Watergauzen Sea Beggars and merchant sailors, intermingled with some English deserters and Scottish coastal pirates. They were a mélange of talented and capable seamen and the dregs of a bitter and vicious war, come to roost in the makeshift fleet nominally loyal to the Prince of Orange. Beyond the chink of coin and the desire for drink, there was little uniting them except an abiding hatred of the Spanish.

"Who?"

"*Godverdomme Engels* ... I did it." The man was shorter than Tyburn, one side of his face mottled with a spray of dark smallpox scars that had left it pitted and crusted like bark. He wore a crumpled, short-brimmed hat and a typical sailor's costume of jacket and pantaloons. "He was a *verrader* bastard that sucked *Spanjaard* cock." The man hawked and spat in the direction of the corpse.

Tyburn looked at the man. "You didn't hear my instructions that none of the Dutch officers were to be harmed?"

The man smirked. "*Ja,* I heard. I shit on you and your instructions, *Engelsman.*"

Tyburn nodded to himself. He dropped his hand to his belt and, keeping his gaze fixed on the sailor, unbuckled his sword. He rolled up the belt and sword with deft hands and without turning his head spoke to Woodshaw. "Hold this for me."

Woodshaw took the proffered sword and hissed, "We don't need more corpses to explain to Walsingham..." Tyburn nodded and stepped forward, his eyes on the Dutchman. The remaining Watergauzen backed away.

The Dutchman, his flat, pocked face unmarred by any semblance of an expression, drew a long blade from his belt scabbard. Tyburn ignored the man and instead unbuttoned his cheap embroidered doublet. He shrugged out of it, folded it with care, and handed it to Woodshaw who took it with a bemused expression. As Tyburn untied his oversleeves, the Dutchman stirred with impatience.

"Come on you fucking *smeerlap*, let's finish this. Bastard *Engels* ..."

Tyburn gave the man a brief glance and then folded the oversleeves and handed them to Woodshaw.

"Done undressing, you cock-sucking shit?" The Dutchman stepped forward with ready blade, but Tyburn raised one hand, motioning the man to wait. The Dutchman paused as Tyburn stretched out his arms and rotated his shoulders. He raised one arm high and leaned sideways, giving a brief grunt as his muscles stretched. He repeated the motion on the opposite side. The Dutchman stared in disbelief.

"By Christ, are you ever going to be ready?" The Dutchman gestured with the knife. "Do you need to take a shit or have dinner before we start as well?" Several of the watching sailors laughed, but Tyburn moved into a set of leg stretches, alternating sides. The Dutchman turned to his fellows. "This *Engelsmann* must be stupid, or maybe someone sliced off his *klootzak*. Fuck you, *Engels*, time to ... huhrk!"

When the Dutchman turned to speak, Tyburn pivoted and slammed his foot into the man's groin. As the man doubled over, Tyburn was already moving. His left hand caught the wrist holding the knife and twisted it to one side. His right hand hooked over the back of the Dutchman's head and pulled him forward as the agent's knee rose to meet him.

Tyburn enjoyed a flaring, unholy sense of satisfaction as the man's jaw slammed into his knee. He felt the bone-jarring impact and heard the crunch of broken bone and popping cartilage. The knife fell to the deck as he pulled the man's head back and hammered it down into his knee a second time. Keeping his hand buried in the man's hair, Tyburn stepped backwards, dragging the almost insensate crewman with him. Glaring at the remaining crew, who stood in mute collective astonished silence, he raised the man's head and then slammed it onto the deck.

Tyburn exhaled with a hiss. "Anyone else care to contest my instructions?" He stepped forward and bent to pick up the fallen knife. "Anyone at all?"

The stupefied silence was broken by steady cackling laughter from the forecastle. Someone, Tyburn thought, had just collected some coin.

Tyburn heard a faint scraping sound behind him as the Dutchman tried to move away. He turned to the fallen man. Tyburn pulled the man's right hand out flat on the deck, raised the knife and slammed it down, pinning it to the deck just below the knuckles. The man gave a gargled scream and writhed, his free hand trying to pull the knife from the wood.

"The next *stuk vuil* that crosses us doesn't live through it. And no one collects their gelt." At least twenty pairs of eyes refused his gaze. A ragged cry indicated the knife had indeed been pulled free. "Now get to bloody work." Tyburn picked up his doublet and oversleeves from the deck and plucked his scabbarded sword and belt from Woodshaw's unresisting hands. Behind Woodshaw, Captain Rogeres stood gaping, open-mouthed. Tyburn pointed at the Dutchman who now sat on the deck, moaning and clutching his hand, his face a mask of blood.

"Secure him below. He'll be going ashore with our customs officers. He'll hang for his crime." The captain nodded a hasty acquiescence and Tyburn turned away to the rail. He could taste the bile in the back of his throat, a burning reminder of present and past. He swallowed hard, suppressing the urge to spit, and took a steadying breath. He could feel them, flickering away on the edge of his thoughts, the ghosts that threatened to rise up, screaming. The flickering lights of Bergen op Zoom were drifting away as the ship edged out into the main channel. The flat landscape of the Netherlands was already fading into dank obscurity, the grey-black of the land melding into the shimmering ripple of the water as the moon began to rise. Far to the south, a red glow reflected off low clouds. Antwerp was burning.

Woodshaw stood beside him at the rail. "Was that strictly necessary?"

Tyburn shrugged. "Rogeres is a thin reed and the Watergauzen play a hard game. They smell weakness and they're like to step in for an opportunity. It's a long way back down the estuary and I didn't want anyone, especially his friends, getting the idea that they could make more coin off selling us to the Spanish."

Woodshaw nodded. "Now I know why they sent you with me." He laughed. "Walsingham's pet wolf, or so I've been told."

Tyburn gave the man a sour look, one that reflected the acrid taste in the back of his throat. "I can't see him too pleased at this turn of events. It was supposed to be uncomplicated. A dead Dutch customs officer didn't enter into his plans."

"So no clean and simple results?"

"Not tonight," the scarred man said, watching the darkness gather over the land. "Not tonight."

Chapter the Third

"DEAR GOD, I give you the simple task of lifting a man no one, not even the Spanish, particularly care about, and you complicate it." Francis Walsingham's brown eyes were harsh as he leafed through the papers that lay thick across his desk. The principal secretary had a lean and angular face, with dark, almost brooding features. Nicknamed "the Moor" by the Queen and her immediate circle, Sir Francis Walsingham had been appointed to his position three years before, but his title failed to describe his more acute role in handling the realm's network of informants, agents, provocateurs, and intelligence operatives.

Christopher Tyburn kept his gaze fixed on the wall hanging visible over Walsingham's shoulder. He didn't recognize the scene depicted but given the look of beatific prayerful supplication on the figures on the tapestry, he guessed it was some applicable lesson in humility.

"The crew had explicit instructions."

"And that worked out marvelously well." Walsingham found the papers he was looking for, a long, dense written sheaf of script. He glanced through it and gestured to his secretary. "Lisbon packet." He handed the papers over. The secretary nodded.

"The Dutch have complained." Walsingham's voice carried no edge, which indicated how little he truly cared what the Dutch thought. Tyburn made no reply.

Walsingham paused and lifted his head. "This is the point where most of my operatives fall over themselves in justifications, protestations and promises."

"I miss cues regularly, according to Master Oldcastle."

The secretary re-entered, another sheaf of yellowed papers in his hand. Walsingham glared for a moment at Tyburn and then shuffled through the correspondence. "Malaga report—the Spanish packet, please. No more monies for him I think, for a time. His reports are nonsense. And find me the latest missives from Antwerp." He grimaced. "The Spanish may have turned it into a smoldering pit, but I still need to know what is happening with our Dutch friends." The secretary nodded in affirmation and disappeared again. "You need to go to ground for a season. I may have some work in the spring but not before. Too many questions have been raised concerning Story, and the Spanish Fury seems to have failed to rouse court as I had hoped. Rather the opposite. They are thoroughly cowed in fear of where the Spanish may next turn their eyes. Despite his treason, Dr. Story has ... adherents in court, and they are displeased. You should rejoin Worcester's Men."

Two years before, when Tyburn had returned from the bitter war in Flanders and drifted into Walsingham's orbit, the spymaster had arranged for his appointment as a play-actor to The Earl of Worcester's Men: a playing troupe, one of a number that plied their trade in London, at court and the immediate environs. The appointment served Walsingham's dual purpose of providing Tyburn a steady income that didn't come from the Exchequer or Walsingham's pocket and allowing his agent the social mobility to mix with both the high and the low. Play-acting, though regarded as lower than vagrancy in social status, was one of the few professions that by their nature mixed freely with both court and commoner.

"I doubt Oldcastle will be forthcoming." Oldcastle was the troupe leader of Worcester's Men. In the two years Tyburn had been a member of the troupe, Oldcastle had developed a healthy dislike for him that he was not shy about sharing.

"Master Oldcastle will do what is requested and required of him, as he always does." Walsingham gave the player a baleful glare. "Would that you did as well." The principal secretary turned back to his letters, cracking the wax seal on a packet and giving Tyburn a dismissive wave. "Absent yourself, and try not to stir the hornet's nest."

Tyburn cleared his throat. "There is the matter of my pay."

Walsingham's dark brows lifted and his frown deepened at his employee's presumption. "Robert, if you please, settle our accounts with Master Tyburn."

"Yes sir." The man gestured for Tyburn to follow him back out into the anteroom. The player gave Walsingham a quick bow, receiving in turn an irritated glare. He followed the secretary into the anteroom.

The man fished around an open drawer and removed a handful of coins. He counted them twice and handed them to Tyburn. "Sign the receipt." He spun a thin leather-bound account book around and presented it to the player. Tyburn counted the coins.

"You're short." The player's voice was flat.

"You have received your full accounting, minus the requisite deductions." The secretary sniffed.

"You're short." Tyburn repeated.

"Sign the receipt or you receive nothing." The secretary sounded exasperated.

Tyburn reached out and with exacting care, closed the account book. "London is awash with rogues and vagabonds. Good men like yourself would be wise to walk careful when you are about your business. It is easy to find oneself in perilous company."

He tapped the account book for emphasis. "God willing, you avoid such peril."

The secretary froze.

"You're short." Tyburn repeated.

The secretary licked his lips and nodded. "I shall recount." He carefully tallied the coins, adding some additional silver to the handful. He passed the monies to Tyburn, who counted it without expression. After opening the account book, the player dutifully scrawled his name and the date below a ragged X where the last recipient had signed. The words "Robert Barnard, his mark" were written beside it in neat slanted writing. Tyburn wondered how much he had been shorted on his payments.

The player nodded his thanks and exited.

Tyburn was annoyed. Not with the secretary; that type of petty thievery was commonplace and expected. Walsingham's network of agents crisscrossed the Continent, a mélange of merchants, ex-priests, thieves, diplomats, thugs, smugglers, and cast-off nobility, with their one common element being a venal cupidity in submitting their expenses and disbursements. Walsingham's parsimonious strategy hinged on keeping his informants barely above water, making them hungry for more and always alert to juicy tidbits they could pass along to justify a request for additional coin. His thrifty strategy undoubtedly included the salaries for his small army of assistants who sifted the steady flow of parchment and correspondence that drifted into the fine house on Seething Lane. Shorting the payments worked fine with distant correspondents, but to essay it with the payee present demonstrated a profound lack of judgment.

Tyburn stepped off the entryway and into the street. The November skies were grey and hurried, but for the first time in more than a week, dry. The noise and stench of London rose to meet him. The player turned right and threaded his way through the tumult of Seething Lane's commerce, considering his ongoing penury as he pushed his way through the foot traffic.

The coin in his purse would settle some of his debts, but with Walsingham putting him at loose ends until the spring, he would need to source another income. The spymaster had instructed him to rejoin Worcester's Men but Tyburn knew that Oldcastle had recruited a replacement when he had left for Flanders seven weeks before. The old man would be loath to reinstate Tyburn until the troupe finished their current round of performances at the Boar's Head. The player turned onto Hart Street, trudging past the squat bulk of St. Olaves which sat on the corner like a fat, grey, stone matron. Oldcastle was likely at the Boar's Head and, given that it was barely forenoon, probably still sober, the player thought, we'll see what shape his mood is in.

--

"Why, by God's holy buttocks, would I want you darkening my door again?" Tyburn's wince did nothing to slow him. "I've got Colle as Vice now. He's a drunkard and a wastrel and a whore-mongering snipe but at least I know what gutter he's rolling in. You? You disappear for months on end and stroll in without so much as a by-your-leave or a sack of wine to show for it and whine like a mangy dog about rejoining your position. Ha! What I say to that! Fie!"

"Walsingham suggests—"

"Walsingham! God's blood! Why does the principal secretary to the Queen give a gold-encrusted shite for a wayward player ... or, for that matter, a third-tier playing company like ours!" Oldcastle paused to retch a thick wad of phlegm onto the rush-covered floor. "Been coughing for the entire month of October," he observed, his voice glum. "Can't abide the wretched snot I've been spitting up. I'd kill for a clear head." He glared at Tyburn and continued. "If his high and mighty Master Walsingham truly gave two shits about your employment, he'd have dropped you a missive and right now I'd be reading it and cursing and you'd be smug and smiling. He didn't, you ain't, and I'm happy with Colle as Vice ... for now."

Tyburn sat stone-faced as Oldcastle drained his tankard. He wiped his mouth and hawked and spat again, shouting at the barmaid for a refill. Oldcastle waited in silence until his fresh pot arrived. He took a long appreciative gulp, peering over the rim as he drank.

"But, if its work you're looking for ... I might have someone that could avail themselves of your particular skills, not on the boards, you understand."

"I'll not be spending my time as your tallman," Tyburn said. "You chase your own debtors."

Oldcastle waved away the thought. "Not for me, you coxcomb, but it would serve me well enough if you provided the help. Help Worcester's Men and our position." Oldcastle squinted at Tyburn. "You recall last year when word came that Burbage was fixing to build his self a permanent theatre."

"In Shoreditch."

"Aye, in Shoreditch. He started building this summer past— you being absent abroad on your ... business, you wouldn't be knowing much—but Burbage got a lease at Holywell Court, at the Priory." Oldcastle nodded to himself. "Burbage is a canny bastard. Shoreditch is outside London's jurisdiction, so the aldermen closing the inn-yards to plays 'cause of the plague, as they done this summer, don't signify. It's a purpose-built playhouse, not some bloody inn-yard. Lots of room for groundlings and cushions."

"Sets up good for Leicester's Men," Tyburn observed.

Oldcastle glared at him at the mention of the rival troupe. "Course it does. But I know Burbage and he's as crafty as a Jew and twice as treacherous. If we help him with his current difficulties, he's promised Worcester's Men a dozen performance dates, provided we split the gate with him personally, not with Leicester's Men."

"Leicester's Men don't have a share in the theatre?"

"No, he's partnered with his brother-in-law, Brayne."

"Owns the Red Lion, doesn't he?"

Oldcastle nodded and gulped another mouthful of ale. The Red Lion had been the site of a previous attempt for a permanent theatre but it was stymied mainly by its location on the outskirts of Whitechapel. Few people would trudge through winter mud to visit the Lion, when the inn-yards at Ludgate and Southwark were readily available.

"What does Burbage need?"

"Gelt. His coin's drying up. Burbage and Brayne's mortgaged their properties for the funds, but ..." Oldcastle laughed "construction was slow on account of Burbage swapping out materials on the joiners. Heard he was buying the expensive stuff, then swapping it out for cheap work and selling the other on the side. He's a skivvy bastard. Now the summer's done, winter is coming and they're running out of ready coin. Can't open for performances until the work's done, so if he misses out on half the season, he'll come adrift."

"So he opens up for a partner or an investor." Tyburn responded.

"Burbage? He don't want anyone else having a piece. He'd bury his brother-in-law if he could afford it, but he needs his pull for the lease and the coin. No, they had a goldseller backing a loan for them. And he's missing."

"Missing?"

"Dropped out of sight two weeks ago, taking Burbage's papers and account books with him. No coin, no writs, no loans. All gone, along with the goldseller." Oldcastle's thin smile bespoke more cruelty than amusement. "Burbage is tits-up if he don't get his coin or his paper."

"Burbage needs him found."

"Aye, and he needs his paper and monies belike, but that won't be your problem. You find the man for Burbage; what Burbage decides to do to him is his business. Well, him and the bailiffs, I reckon."

"Why did Burbage come to you?" Tyburn gave the troupe leader a pointed look.

Oldcastle laughed. "He didn't. I went to him. I heard rumors he was in a bate, and I heard you were back from Flanders. I know you have a talent for turning over rocks and setting everything under them running, so I thought how I can use that." He shot the player a glance. "You want back in Worcester's Men, this is your cross to bear. You get us in good with Burbage and get us access to the theatre, and Colle can go back to humping Winchester geese and drinking his pots."

"That doesn't put coin in my pocket." Tyburn observed.

"You deal with your compensation from Burbage your own self. Charge him what you think he can bear, but if you can't come up with the goldseller, don't expect any coin." Oldcastle drained his mug and gave a prodigious belch. "And don't be throwing sheep eyes thinking you're back with the troupe. Walsingham don't pay our freight, Worcester does. Mayhaps he'll pitch you back in but I can make your life a bloody, God-fucked misery if you don't come up right with Burbage. We need access to the Theatre. Inn-yards won't suffice, not with those Precisian bastard aldermen shuttering our doors every time some poxed yeoman drops from the plague."

The chair scraped across the floor as Oldcastle stood. "You'll find Burbage at Shoreditch. He'll fill you in on the details. Come back and see me after you've found his goldseller and you can help Jack and Willens toss poor Colle into the dung heap." The troupe master gave Tyburn a derisive salute and disappeared through the tavern door.

--

"Venetian tile, did I mention?" Burbage pointed at the edge for the staging with an air of impatience. "And the sky vault will be blue with golden stars—gold leaf, mind you, not some tricked out yellow paint." Tyburn nodded yet again, as he listened to Burbage once more list out the variety of accoutrements with which he was bedecking the Theatre. He glanced again at the reddish tiles that a laborer was carefully cementing in place. They looked like they had never been closer to Venice than Tyburn.

Despite the mounting evidence of James Burbage's parsimoniousness, Kit was impressed. The Theatre, modeled loosely after the tiered inn-yards that the troupes traditionally used, was a very much still a work in progress. The building was shaped like an octagon, almost eighty feet across, with three high towering galleries surrounding the open pebbled yard. It most resembled, Tyburn thought, the bear-baiting rings in Southwark, except they seldom rose above a single tier. The stage area thrust out into the yard and was partially surmounted by a gabled roof supported by carved wooden pillars. The stage roof was still under construction, rendering Burbage's commitment to painting the underside of the sky vault moot. The high galleries lacked siderails, benches, and in some cases flooring. Half the interior was still bare framed wooden beams, reeking of pitch and resin. The upper gallery was open to the sky, as no roofing materials beyond the skeletal timber framing were evident except a lone sheet of canvas flapping loose in the damp November air. A pigeon fluttered away and outward. Bird guano spattered the yard in dozens of locations, including the stage where the glazier was applying edging tile. The tiering house, the backstage area for the actors to change and move about, was a vacant shell.

The player turned his attention to Burbage. James Burbage had a narrow, foxlike face and a dusty reddish beard that looked like it had been left in the rain for a season. The eyes were sharp and astute, and kept sliding sidelong at Tyburn at random intervals, as though weighing the player's credulity in between momentary assessments of his lack of character. It made Tyburn feel self-conscious and ill at ease, which, he realized, was intentional.

From everything that Tyburn had heard of Burbage, the man was a consummate manipulator, one who had migrated from a successful joinery enterprise into one of London's most influential troupe-operators. It was Burbage who maneuvered Leicester's Men into their premier position at court, Burbage who cajoled venues and prime inn-yards when the London aldermen had closed off performances, and Burbage who deftly managed the often incongruous demands of the Master of Revels. And now it was Burbage whose flight of ambition and imagination was being hammered together out of timber and coin at Holywell Priory.

There had been several efforts to establish a permanent theatre in London in recent years, including the effort by John Brayne, Burbage's partner and brother-in-law. The London aldermen had quashed efforts within the city and distance and winter mud had squelched the efforts outside the gates. If anyone could make a permanent theatre work at Shoreditch, it would be Burbage.

"It seems a little quiet," Tyburn noted drily, nodding at the single glazier fitting tiles. Burbage scowled.

"A momentary setback, a hiccup, a fart, it's nothing!" he waved one hand in impatience. "Three weeks. We open for performances in three weeks. Maybe four..." he amended. The scowl deepened. "It's coin I lack, not workers, nor materials. We've all our supplies sitting the Great Barn waiting. Groats! Angels! Even pennies would suffice, but I can't draw anything from our bankers without the accounts and the writs. Stokely has them. That gnat, that irredeemable, insufferable, pox-addled, bastard son of a whore, Janus-faced cunt!" James Burbage's face was red and the last burst out of him as a rapid spray of profanity. He drew a deep breath. "You find Charles Stokely and you find our theatre alive and well."

"When did you see him last?" the player asked.

"Two weeks ago right here, arranging transfer of the remaining lease monies, and paying for that God-rotted tile." Burbage grimaced. "If I had known, I'd have taken all the coin then. Never would have expected Stokely of cozenage."

"Why not?"

"Because it was small beer, it was nothing. Stokely's a goldseller and a factor. He deals in monies that make this job look like a dung heap. He works with court. He's got offices and position, which is why we went to him in the first place. Six hundred God-cursed pounds this place cost, and Stokely's business shits that much offhand."

Burbage turned and looked at the unfinished galleries. His face was calmer and when he spoke, his voice was quiet. "Think on it, what we could do here? This space, a good troupe, a stirring piece of work … you'll hear them howling like Bedlam for more."

Tyburn turned and looked, imagining the galleries populated with spectators, the yard swelling with the bustle and noise and catcalls of groundlings, the stage alive with excitement. For a moment he could see it in his mind's eye, the clamor and the chaos stilling as the play began and that strange hush that would steal over a rapt audience being pulled into a different world fraught with its own dramas and particulars.

"This is my St. Paul's, my very own cathedral." Burbage laughed. "But it needs coin and I'm no pope, so selling indulgences is right out. But I can offer Oldcastle some performance spots, I can do that much."

"That's fine for Oldcastle, but by God's pity, I need to eat."

"You know how much coin Oldcastle stands to take in if I allow Worcester's Men performance dates?"

"No. I do know how much I'll likely see from Oldcastle's largesse, if he gets his performance dates. Which is none. Oldcastle sent me to you because I am good at what I do. I'll find your goldseller, and then you can turn him upside down and shake him until your coins fall out. But my time and talents are valuable, so you pay me. And then I go do what I do."

Burbage's scowl returned. It seemed to be a semi-permanent fixture. "For twenty pence I can hire a pair of rufflers to dig out Stokely and have them beat you into the ground for good measure."

Tyburn turned and faced Burbage. "No. You can't."

Burbage's face went a shade paler at the expression on the player's face. "How much?" he blustered.

"Ten shillings up front for the search, another ten when I find him."

"Five," Burbage countered.

"Good luck with your cathedral." Tyburn turned to leave. "I'm not bartering. You decide what this ambition of yours is worth."

"Fine then, ten shillings now and ten when you find the purblind wretch!" Burbage reached into his doublet and removed a large cheveril purse, took out a fat gold coin, and handed it over. Tyburn handed it back.

"Unclipped, if you please." The coin's edges were ragged and torn on one side where someone had clipped off small pieces of gold. Clip enough coins and you had extra cash in hand. Burbage made a noise deep in his throat but fished around and pulled out an acceptable coin.

"Where did he do his business?"

"Off Cheapside, in Maiden Lane around the corner from the Goldsmith's Hall."

Tyburn nodded. "I'll start there. What else can you tell me about him?"

Burbage sniffed. "He's named Stokely, but if he's not half Jew, by God I'm the king of Rus. The man makes his gelt loaning out to merchants and venturers and managing investments from court. I know Burghley's[1] into him for the wool trade, and he's tight with the Steelyard."

"You said he had offices?"

"He clerks for the tariff. Has a Crown license."

"For who?"

"Earl of Rutledge, I think."

Tyburn nodded in thought. Crown licenses and patents for trade, tariffs, and commerce were often awarded as a court privilege, providing a lucrative income for the holders, although

---

[1] William Cecil, 1st Baron Burghley served as Secretary of State and chief advisor of Queen Elizabeth I. He was appointed Lord High Treasurer in 1572.

they rarely actively had to perform any work in administering or managing the license. That task fell to various third-party intermediaries or agencies hired for the purpose, like Stokely. Crown monopolies were highly sought-after appointments, as they provided a steady stream of profitable coin independent of land holdings or dubious investment ventures. If Stokely was managing a license or monopoly for the Earl of Rutledge, then Burbage's comment about the theatre investment being small beer was accurate.

"What's he look like?"

"Stokely? Got a face like boiled mutton, grey and mottled. Dark hair and round nose. Raspy beard, like Lanahan from Warwick's Men. He's a chary bastard, a bit twitchy." Burbage glanced around impatiently.

"Burbage!" The shout echoed across the hollow shell of the theatre.

"God's mercy, that doddypol," Burbage cursed. He locked eyes with Tyburn for an instant and gave a short, emphatic shake of his head.

Two men pushed their way past a loose-hanging canvas tarp. The shorter man spotted Burbage by the stage and shouted again. "Burbage, you cozening bastard, where are our men? We should have five men working. At this rate we won't be done for two months!" Tyburn had frequented both the Boar and the Lion often enough to recognize the man by his thick mane of hair and the tapered beard. It was John Brayne, Burbage's brother-in-law and titular investment partner. The second man wore the blue smock of an apprentice but it was the man's size that drew the eye. He was a full head taller than Tyburn.

"Coads. No men working. No progress on the galleries. Just some God-damned tiling being done? Care to explain, James?"

"As I told you last week, we are progressing and—"

"What kind of a wretched fool do you take me for? You're a scheming bastard, you got some close packings about? Who's this

32

doddering idiot?" He turned his attention to Tyburn, squinting at the player. "Well? Loose that tongue of yours."

Tyburn gave the man a ghost of a smile and turned to leave.

"Hold it you bastard, I want to know what's about." Brayne's face was bright red and he gestured at the blue-smocked man. The man stepped past Burbage and gripped Tyburn's left arm. The player reached his right hand across, locking the man's hand onto his arm and then pivoted to his right. The apprentice was pulled off balance and Tyburn twisted the man's gripping hand up and out, using the man's arm as a lever. The man gave a hissing gasp of pain as his arm was yanked back. Tyburn reached over and gripping two of the man's fingers, applied pressure. The hiss turned to a deepening gasp and a curse.

"Down." Tyburn said, his voice flat. The apprentice nodded, his eyes tearing as he sank down onto the pebbled gravel of the yard. Tyburn looked at Burbage and Brayne. Brayne had a shocked look on his face. "Are we done here?" Burbage nodded. Tyburn leaned down to the apprentice's ear. "I'm going to let you go now. You are going to stay there until I leave. If you lay a hand on me again for any reason, I will start breaking things. You will not enjoy it. Do you understand?"

The man nodded, his face pale in the shaded light of the theatre yard. Tyburn released the man's hand, nodded to Burbage, and strode out of the theatre. Burbage stared after him, with a bemused look on his face.

"Who was that James?" Brayne grated, "We're partners in this forsaken venture, and I need to know."

"Hopefully, that is the solution to our problems." Burbage said, "God willing."

Chapter the Fourth

THE ROOM SMELLED of incense and sex. A small brazier on the fireplace mantel supplied the incense, a sweet cinnamon and floral musk that sent thin white tendrils of scent wafting into the dark recesses of the high ceiling.

The light in the room flickered and wavered as the naked girl prodded at the fire. In the ruddy firelight, her body was supple and lean, with no hint of blemish or scarring. She stood and stared at the lambent flames, watching them dance and gutter, flaring occasionally as a new piece of fuel ignited.

"Come back to bed." The man lay across the canopied bed, watching the woman in the firelight.

"Have you ever watched fire? Watched how it moves?" Her voice was soft and barely audible. "It dangles and frolics like a morisco, seethes and flares ... destroys everything it touches. Reduces all to ash." She smiled. "Just like people—all ash in the end, no matter how hot or bright they burn. Just cinders and dust."

"You are fire to me. Come here, girl." She ignored him and continued to gaze into the flames. "Come here, girl." His voice hardened in command. The woman paused in her sojourn and for a brief moment the glow of the fire reflected in her eyes. She breathed out soft and then turned back to the bed, her face placid and composed. She strode over and pulled the thin sheet covering the man aside. She looked up and down the length of his body. He was a young man, barely twenty, thin and slight of build.

"You aren't ready," she said, allowing her gaze to linger.

"I will be in a moment." He reached one hand up to pull her onto the bed. She deflected his grasp and leaned over, her breasts dangling tantalizingly low over his face. She watched and as he reached again, she stepped back, teasing.

His face tightened into a look of angry petulance. His hand whipped out and grasped the back of her neck. "You need a lesson in obedience."

Her eyes splintered for an instant as his hand tightened on the back of her neck. She reached out with her left hand and grasped his hardening member, her fingers trailing upwards. His breath caught and the fingers around her neck loosened. The girl paused, toying absently with the thought of reaching around the base of the bedpost with her free hand, taking the short hooked blade she had secreted there, and slicing him asunder. She could picture the blade in her hand, feel the cool heft of its pommel in her palm.

It wasn't time, she reminded herself. Instead she pulled herself astride the man's naked torso and set to work. It didn't take long before he was gasping and writhing to a climax, although she found her patience diminishing with each tortured plunge. When the moment came, she decided, she would make it worth the wait. This, now, would be too easy—and her goal would be harder to accomplish with this bed drenched in blood.

He flopped back into the down pillow, a faint sheen of sweat visible. "Ahhh. I swear you are a witch, a succubus, or no! More a naiad like Melite, cleaved unto Hercules."

She smiled and stroked the side of his face. "Was it not to your complete satisfaction, milord Thomas?" Her voice was pitched low and suggestive.

He pushed her hand away and sat up. "Fetch me some wine." He swung his legs over the edge of the bed and began to dress. She stood and walked past the fireplace to the sideboard and poured a generous portion of dark red wine into a wineglass. She brought it to him and stood watching as he gulped it down and carelessly tossed the empty glass onto the bed. He scowled into the darkest corner of the room.

She frowned at him. "I thought I had distracted you from your problems?"

"You cannot appreciate the magnitude of my issues," he snapped at her. "The Court of Wards will not release my settlement so I am shackled to that bastard Audley. My lands and incomes are sequestered and stolen, the Queen hesitates to release the wardship on Burghley's advice, and that villain Rutledge publicly berates me. Me! That son of a whore, that base shit-borne bastard ..." By the time he finished his brief tirade, his voice was shaking.

She wrapped her arms around him and cradled his head against her bare breasts. "Shush, my darling. They will pay! They will pay! Remember what we planned, what you've planned. Imagine how they will suffer for their actions. Think on their humiliation and fear ... they will come crawling for your favour, supplicants cowering at the feet of the Earl of Asquith, begging at your feet. Nothing but dogs to be kicked away as you please."

"They slew three of my men, butchered them like cattle in the street, for no reason."

"They fear you, milord. They fear your power, they fear the nobility of your purpose. They are rats facing a lion, so they attack on a tangent, too afraid to approach direct. But we have their measure, we have their weakness, and we will strike them down even as we raise you up."

She felt him mouth her nipple and his breathing calmed. She held him tight and leaned into him. "Yes. We will cast them into the pits of Hell and make them pay for all their crimes against my house." He lifted his head and kissed her lips.

She laughed and pushed him away. "No more! You are a monster." She stood and shrugged into a thin silken gown, tying the two sides together loosely. "My men will see you safe home to Audley House."

"When will we have word?"

"Soon," she promised, her lips curving into a smile. "Soon. Everything is coming together in time. Be patient, my love." She strode to the door and knocked twice. The door swung open. "Bent, have your men see Lord Asquith home safe."

Thomas tugged on his boots and picked up his fur-trimmed brocade mandelion overcloak. He stepped past her and through the doorway without a backwards glance. Bent gave the girl a curt nod and followed Lord Asquith into the candlelit hallway and down the stairs.

She closed the door and laughed, shaking her head. She stretched, a long languorous movement and turned back to the flames. A few minutes later the door swung open and Bent entered the room.

"Two of my boys are on him. He'll be safe back to Audley House, though why we don't just slit his throat and dump him in the Fleet, I don't ken."

"You are so impatient, my Bent. Good wine takes time to age, as do our devices."

Bent grunted. He had heard this argument multiple times and was indifferent to her reasoning. "Slice 'im up and leave his body for the crows. It'll have the same result."

She patted his cheek. "Don't think, there's a good Bent. Just kill what I aim you at, when I tell you to, and you will be rich with gold and wine and pheasant and whores. Once our Lord Thomas is well primed and tindered, we will light him up and watch everything burn. But for now, we focus on the ledger. You have men watching the house?"

"The house, his wife, his business, and his whore. He's gone mole on us, nary a sign."

She pursed her lips in a momentary pout. "That's very churlish of him. Keep hunting. He's a fat goldseller, not a magus. He has connections, friends, acquaintances. He will make an appearance, if only to preserve his business interests."

"Doubt it. He knows the Castle's looking for him."

"He suspects, he doesn't know."

"Hard to keep a search like this on the quiet. He knows. Less he wants to get paunched, he'll hide deep or run far. Thieves' Castle ain't one to trifle about with."

"He hasn't run. He's in London. He has too much at stake to run."

"We'll keep on him."

"And keep an eye on Rutledge's men, on the off-chance they're cannier then we think."

"We're spread thin," Bent said in warning.

"Use the beggar boys and the filchers."

"Means no more coin coming in," he replied.

She waved off his cautioning. "We've banked enough for a few weeks, and they can work while they watch can't they?"

"Roaring Boys see us shifting turf, they might get restless."

"You pass my word to Pollack and the upright men that it's temporary. They'll stay their hands."

"You don't know that."

"Course I do. They're afraid of me, Bent."

Bent was silent. He could brook no disagreement with that statement. She waved him out the door and shut it firmly behind him. He heard the faint sound of her laughter echoing hollow through the thick oak door. For a moment he stared at the scratched surface of the wood, the unsettling reverberations of the sound still in his ears. He nodded to himself, turned, and disappeared into the darkened hallway to talk to the filchers before they set out in the pre-dawn darkness.

--

London was noise and stench.

It began before dawn, with the harsh squeal of market-carts and shouts of drovers piercing the quiet dark. The tramp of early foot traffic crescendoed as the sun edged above a yellow and grey horizon invisible to most city-dwellers. With the light came a cacophony of trade and commerce, a cadence both familiar and discordant as the city woke to the new day. Strident cries warred for attention, hawking baked apples, cabbages, fish, milk, bread, and pie. The distant percussion of hammers on metal was overlaid with the sounds of shouts and greetings, dogs barking and howling, pigs squealing, and tinkers and knife-sharpeners bellowing.

It was the bells that woke him. They rose in a chorus, first St. Clements with a brassy clangor that sent birds skyward and silenced the yelping cries of the neighbourhood dogs. Then came St. Martins, lighter in pitch, a plangent tenor that hung a beat behind the nearby St. Clements like a thin sibling. The sound spread like ripples in a pond, the echoes flitting down alleyways and thoroughfares, as more bells joined in the daily refrain.

Christopher Tyburn lay in his bed, eyes closed, listening as the bells spoke. "Oranges and lemons, say the bells of St. Clements," he whispered to himself. St. Clements' bells, a bare hundred-odd yards away and three streets to the east, were almost close enough to feel. "You owe me five farthings, say the bells of St. Martins." St. Martins was another hundred yards away but the lighter tone of its bells made their sound distinctive in the morning bustle.

Tyburn paused and listened but could not pick out the remaining bells of the morning rhyme, lost in the cacophony of London's dawn commerce. Out of habit, he recited the rest of the rhyme to himself.

"When will you pay me? say the bells of Old Bailey. When I grow rich, say the bells of Shoreditch. When will that be? say the bells of Stepney. I do not know, says the great bell of Bow." He hesitated over the last couplet. "Here comes a candle to light you to bed ... And here comes a chopper to chop off your head."

Christopher Tyburn sat up and swung his legs over the edge of the bed, feeling a dull aching pain radiating in his left thigh, a bitter reminder of Haarlem, courtesy of some unknown Spanish harquebusier. The player rubbed his sore thigh hard, feeling the lumpy ridge of the scar running under his fingers, trying to bury the memory of blood splashed across snow. The memories tugged at him, pulling at his waking thoughts, just as the torn, scarred muscles whispered a steady trickle of pain when the weather was damp and cold.

Some things are best forgotten.

As always, the small stack of folded letters seemed to beckon from the table. He stared at the papers, with the neat curlicued handwriting and the cracked red wax seal embossed by a signet. One hand reached for the topmost, hesitated and then fell. *Best forgotten.*

As he pulled on his clothes, he considered what rocks to turn over next in his search for the wayward goldseller. For the past two days the player had prowled, cajoled, and questioned Stokely's acquaintances, family, and associates, making a nuisance of himself up and down Maiden Lane. He had drifted through the Exchange, digging into the limited contacts he had within London merchantry, plying them with ale and gossip, but to no avail.

The man's disappearance was a cipher, a blank. Stokely had vanished like a stone dropped into a pond, and any tantalizing ripples had long since faded. Neither his wife nor his business associates had any clear idea of what might have precipitated the man's disappearance. The wife in particular, a fat, matronly woman with thinning hair and a squalling infant on one arm, had appeared petrified. She had responded to the player's questions with the fixed stare of a rabbit faced with a slavering hound. Pale and drained, she had closed the door firmly in his face by his third question.

It was unusual. Tyburn had been fairly certain that the man's evaporation would be tied back to Stokely's life—sex and greed were the usual motives for rabbiting—but Tyburn hadn't found anything unexpected. Stokely had a mistress, a well-paid whore he frequented off Cheapside. He wasn't into the local upright men for dicing, monchance, or primero. He wasn't an aficionado of the rat pits or the cockfights, although he had attended both. He wasn't known for booze or perinades and didn't haunt the Southwark brothels. Stokely had a solid reputation with his guild and business associates and didn't have the appearance of a thief or an embezzler.

Tyburn dug into his small cupboard, scrounging through his small store of provender for a chunk of cloth-wrapped hard cheese that would be fit for breakfast. Stokely might, he thought, be dead; however, the watch hadn't reported anyone that fit Stokely's description in their daily tally of abandoned bodies, although their idea of a description often left much to be desired. The player recalled a conversation he had with three beadles outside the Boars' Head who had been seeking a man with a beard and small eyes. They would know him, they stated with confidence, by his air of miscreancy.

The player buttoned a leather buff coat on over his doublet and picked up his scabbarded rapier and belt. Settling the weapon on his left hip, he went down two flights of stairs. The draper, who was his landlord, gave Tyburn a vague amiable wave and nod as the player passed his front workroom and out into the street.

The weather was cold and damp and Tyburn's breath hung in the air. A thin skiff of ice crackled underfoot where puddles had formed between desultory sets of cobbles and thick, sagging expanses of mud. Tyburn gave a rooting pig a sharp kick to open up some walking space between the stony wall of a building and a heavily laden cart. The cantilevered upper stories of the timbered houses on Shepard Lane hovered overhead like an oppressive canopy, giving the narrow laneway the feel of a mountain defile. The player turned up St. Swithins to cut across Bearbinder Lane and onto the crowded, wider expanse of Cheapside.

The aromatic mix of spices and herbs from the apothecaries warred with the heavier stench of the Stock fish market, busier than normal due to it being Wednesday, a day when the consumption of flesh was forbidden by law. A distant shout of "Ware below!" came from the street ahead and Tyburn watched the throng suddenly diverge as a householder emptied a slop bucket from the overhanging window.

Tyburn passed the rectangular, reassuring mass of St. Mary Woolnoth Church, edged through the bustling traffic of the Stock market, and out onto the broader thoroughfare. Cheapside ran from the Stock market west to St. Paul's and Newgate. Jammed with hawkers and bustling with carts, foot and mounted traffic, and the occasional herd of cattle or sheep being ushered to the shambles, Cheapside thronged and hummed with trade, the beating heart of commercial London.

The walk to St. Paul's was a slow one. Anyone deigning to invade London, Tyburn thought wryly, would be well-advised not to do it on a market-day. St. Paul's Cathedral rose like a stony, intricate pile, plunked into the warren of streets and alleyways at the western end of the city almost as an afterthought, dominating all the buildings surrounding it. The truncated tower gave the building an oddly squat appearance despite its impressive height. The tall spire had collapsed from a lightning strike more than fifteen years before, the rebuilding of which was an annual London argument. As the player drew closer, he left Cheapside and ducked through the narrow hive of streets that led to the cathedral. He wove his way through the crowd gathering at St. Paul's Cross for a sermon. A man stood immobile in the pillory, a small group of youngsters catcalling and mocking him. As the player passed, he noticed the man's ears were nailed to the pillory, an extra fillip of punishment for whatever transgression he had committed. The usual practice was to cut off the ears rather than pry out the nails. The player passed by without a second glance and headed up the stone steps and through the open doors into the building.

St. Paul's Walk, the long, stately length of the cathedral's vaulted nave, was London's sounding board. It was here that the city came to gather news, exchange gossip, set assignations, broker deals, grumble and converse about the latest perfidies of the

Spanish, and complain about the latest affront from the Crown. Courtiers and merchants, venturers and money-lenders, students, promoters, gallants, booksellers, pickpockets and thieves, all came to St. Paul's Walk like moths to the flame. The hum and buzz of conversation filled the air and thrashed chaotically through the hollow arches of the open space, an aural wave filling the air and permeating the senses like heavy surf crashing onto a ragged coast.

The player threaded his path down the crowded middle aisle to the western end of the nave, ignoring the imprecations of the gaudily dressed prostitutes that solicited business among the walkers. He kept one hand on the hilt of his rapier and the other on his purse. Some of the most effective foists and draws in London worked the Walk and the churchyard. Jacob Willins, one of the permanent players in The Earl of Worcester's Men, refused to enter the Walk unless he had first lined his pockets with fishhooks to catch the inevitable sly fingers.

Tyburn paused as he neared the western end of the nave. The broad doors were plastered with handbills and public bills. Tyburn was looking for different prey. The player spotted his quarry near the convocation court: a young man with long, neat-dressed dark hair surmounted by a broad-brimmed feathered hat. He was elegant and well kept, his heavy cloak edged with fur and abraded gilt thread. The stains and tattered edges of his clothing were barely noticeable except under careful scrutiny. He was speaking very earnestly to a moon-faced older gentleman in neat, but rustic, clothing. Tyburn circled past the bulk of the supporting column to listen to the conversation.

"London is not a place for wayward display of your valuables."

The countryman waved one hand in airy dismissal. "These rogues and ruffians would not dare ..."

The elegant dressed man sniffed. "You underrate them at your peril. The sight of a moneyed gentleman such as yourself draws them like flies to shit. I have seen them deliberately start a riot in order to distract a gentleman while his purse is cut. That gold chain and sigil you wear are an invitation to disaster."

"I thank you for your kind advice, but I think it is safer around my neck than in a pocket."

"Indeed. But if I may, here is a trick even the cony-catchers of St. Paul's have not mastered." The young man undid the binding on his sleeve and slid out a handkerchief. "You wrap your valuables thusly, and tie them into your sleeve. No cutpurse or foist in Christendom can have your sleeve off without you noting it!"

The man nodded. "Good trick. You think it necessary?" At the young man's sidelong glance and short nod, and with a sigh of exasperation, the older gentleman reached up and opened the clasp on his gold chain. The young man held out a handkerchief as the man deposited the chain and sigil. He tied it into a tight bundle, but just before he handed it back to the moon-faced man he froze and stared down the middle aisle of St. Paul's, his face pale with shock. The older man turned his head and followed the other's gaze, but saw nothing unusual.

"What? What is it?"

"Your pardon sir, I thought I saw one of my acquaintances, a gentleman of ill repute and poor temper, a man best avoided." The young man handed the handkerchief over and the man loosened his sleeve and slid the small bundle up before tying the sleeve closed once more.

"You must allow me to thank you properly with a meal, my son." The older man began but was interrupted as the younger man held up his hand.

"Your pardon sir, but I cannot stay. *Tempus fugit*, as they say." He bowed his thanks and turned to leave but halted in mid-stride.

Christopher Tyburn was leaning against the side of the pillar, amusement flirting with his lips. "Hello, Chaucer."

"Kit. Well ..." He recovered and gave the player a quick nod. "Good to see you. I ... um ... I would stay, but I have an

44

appointment." He nodded again and started forward, his movements erratic.

"Chaucer." The tone was flat but the warning was unmistakable.

The young man stopped and gave a heavy sigh. He reached under the edge of his doublet and tossed a tightly knotted handkerchief to Tyburn. The player nodded and handed the bundle back to the surprised countryman.

"My chain? God's blood! What treachery!" The man unwrapped the kerchief and stared at his property in disbelief. Tyburn reached up and, gripping Chaucer by the back of the collar as if he were a stray puppy, turned away and pushed his quarry through the crowd and out into the churchyard.

"You cozening bastard! You fie-faced purblind wretch! You cullion! Do you know how long I waited for that bait to come along? I had to threaten to cut Foster and his doxy to get that cony for myself."

Unfazed, Tyburn shoved Chaucer against one of the stone columns of the portico that sheltered the western doorway.

"Shut it. You'll have another in your talons before the day is out." He narrowed his eyes as Chaucer sniffed and straightened his fur-edged cloak. "Where did you get that piece?"

"A contribution from a wool merchant from Kent. He got a nice luncheon with lots of canary and a ride from Molly. While he was hacking in the saddle, we helped ourselves to his coin and cloak. Poor bugger didn't even have enough on hand to pay off Molly, so they called in the bailiffs. I think he's still in the Counter."

Tyburn shook his head. "You are an evil little bugger at heart, Chaucer."

"Aye, but my services are in demand, ain't they? So why are you here and not treading the boards with Oldcastle and his lot?"

"I'm looking for information."

"You and the rest o' London, so join the walkers and the news-mongers. Why piss in my soup?"

"I've noticed your vocabulary drops right off when you aren't cony-catching."

"Only spent a year at Cambridge, Kit. Been four years working the London tricks. You'd be amazed how little I can recollect." Chaucer gave the player an icy glare. "Now I've business to attend, so what kind of bait you need?"

"Charles Stokely, goldseller, off Maiden Lane."

Chaucer shook his head. "Never heard of the bugger."

"He's in the wind, done a runner and I need to find him."

"What's it worth to you?" Chaucer gave the player a sly look from under his broad hat.

Tyburn reached out and grabbed Chaucer by the throat, shoving him hard against the polished stone of the portico's column. "I won't go to the bailiff tomorrow before he's drunk and swear out a writ on you that lands you in the Hole or Bartholomew Fair. You owe me for digging you out of that pit six months back, and this is your chance to pay out."

Chaucer made a placating gesture with his hand. "Fine, by God, fine! Truly I do owe you for your assistance, but try not to damage the material." Tyburn released the man's collar and Chaucer reached up with anxious fingers to smooth the crumpled lace and folds. The young thief gave the player a look of exasperation. "You need to cool your blood, my friend. You seem put out over more than usual over my recalcitrance. Mayhaps you should visit Molly? Very efficacious, she is. Relieve you of some of those humours."

"Keep your scabrous whores for your conies, Chaucer, just see if you can get a string on this Stokely. You come up with anything, there's a pair of groats in it for you."

"And you won't have me flung in the Hole."

"That too." Tyburn grunted.

Tyburn watched the young thief circle back through the churchyard and disappear into the crowded precincts of the Walk in search of new quarry. There was seemingly no end to the parade of hapless victims. London was a lodestone, and St. Paul's was the swirling vortex to which they all irresistibly were drawn, conies for the hawks of St. Paul's.

The player gave the book stalls around the Stationer's Hall a glance, half-tempted to lose what was left of the morning poking through the tracts, pamphlets, and books. He had heard that one of the stationers had printed a chronicle of England; however, he doubted it was an indulgence he could afford, at least not until he had found Stokely and collected his earnings from Burbage.

Burbage. Tyburn rubbed his beard thoughtfully. The impresario would not be pleased. So far Stokely was proving a more elusive fox than Tyburn had anticipated. He guessed he still had a couple of days before Burbage began to hound him for results, so it was best if he used the time well. The player turned north, cutting around a lottery seller haranguing an indifferent crowd with promises of wealth and fortune, and threaded his way through the alleyways back to Cheapside. He would take one more run through Maiden Lane and the Goldsmith's Hall to see what his luck might turn.

Chapter the Fifth

H E PICKED UP his stalkers at Foster Lane. Tyburn glanced up the street where the Goldsmith's Hall stood square and stolid, the entrance framed by a pair of wardens to keep out the unwanted. The lion face hallmark, a device used by the guild to certify the purity and veracity of their members' works, was carved into the double wooden doors. He tossed a penny to a dark-haired beggar with a drooped eyelid and foreshortened, palsied arm. The man nodded his thanks and tucked the small coin out of sight.

Tyburn tilted his head to glance back to where Foster Lane met Cheapside. Despite the steady stream of foot traffic, two men were standing holding a conversation by the overhang on the corner. They seemed deep in a concerned and animated dialogue. Tyburn watched for a minute and then moved, sidestepping a carter trying to maneuver his wagon through the crowded thoroughfare. He angled across the street, catching another glimpse of the pair slipping through the pedestrian traffic with the nonchalant grace of long practice. The taller of the two men wore a rakish feathered hat, under which hair the colour of pale straw was visible. He wore a long rapier and carried it with a practiced ease.

Tyburn smiled a humourless grin. His presence on the street the previous day had been noted by someone. This might be an opportune time to generate some answers, he thought. He turned down a side- street that intersected the lane. Just past a chandler's shop a narrow gap lay between two buildings, just wide enough for a man to fit through sideways. Tyburn ducked through the opening, grimacing as his feet slid in the mud. He followed the dank course until it opened into a wider alley bordered by several fenced gardens.

The player walked the short length the alleyway back. He emerged back onto Foster's Lane. His stalkers had followed him down the side street. However, their prey having vanished, the pair had split, each man covering part of the street like a pair of hunting dogs casting wide for a scent.

Tyburn watched the two men mill about, the taller one giving hand signals to his shorter, broader companion. The shorter man nodded and moved down to Gutter Lane. He strode to the intersection, ignoring the imprecations of a carter, and glanced in both directions but the player was nowhere in sight. He gave a theatrical shrug to his taller companion, whose irritation was plain writ on his face.

Tyburn laughed to himself. He stepped around the corner and saw the shorter man freeze at the sight of him. The player walked up the middle of the roadway, strolling past the taller man. Tyburn gave him a withering look of contempt as he passed. Ignoring the shorter man, he turned up Gutter Lane and sauntered past the Wax Chandler's Hall. A large alehouse stood square on the corner, and Tyburn went inside, stooping under the low-hanging sign. He emerged several minutes later, carrying a set of three tankards. Pointedly, he set two on the low stone wall fronting the alehouse and leaned against the gatepost, taking a long draught of the warm ale, the rich dank scent of the hops filling his nostrils.

The tall man gave his companion an exasperated glance and then shrugged. The two men crossed the laneway and approached. Tyburn tilted his tankard at the other two drinks and waited until both men had had a taste. The shorter man took a long, deep swallow and belched happily. The taller man looked at him and shook his head before locking eyes with Tyburn. Under his pale straw hair was an equally pale set of eyes of the faintest blue. His face was wide but cut with lines as though carved by a frost-laden wind. Tyburn's eyes flicked to the worn pommel of the rapier that hung with practiced ease on the man's hip.

"Your name is Tyburn." The player did not respond. "I thought I recognized you." He turned to his shorter companion. "This one was at Bruges…and Middelburg, if I recall." He turned to Tyburn. "And Goes?" The player nodded. The man's lips curled slightly. *"No habras mas Flandes."*

The words sent a chill unrelated to the brisk air shivering down the player's spine. "There is nothing like Flanders." Tyburn agreed, "But you have the advantage of me. I don't know you."

"Covington is my name. My silent friend here is Bristow. Don't ask him for a conversation, he's more a listener than a talker. Of course, the Spanish divvied his tongue a number of years back, so that might explain his lack of verbiage." Bristow smirked and drained his tankard.

"Where do you know me from?" Tyburn asked.

"You mean why were we following you about like a pair of hounds, or why I know you from Flanders?" He paused and took a sip of his ale, grimacing at the sour taste of the hops. "I saw you take the gatehouse at Goes. It was a nice piece of work. Three men, I think?"

"Four."

"Four? Indeed. Try to stay on his good side, Bristow, will you?" The shorter man snorted and took another draught.

Tyburn took a sip and gestured for Covington to continue.

"Imagine my surprise, when word comes through that someone is asking questions up and down Maiden Lane, trying to winnow out a certain Master Stokely, who's done a runner on his wife and his business partners."

"Why is that a concern of yours?"

"There is a purpose emerging, a crossroads of intent, so to speak, that my patron would have words with you about. He requests the gracious attendance of your person upon this business, as soon as we were able to track you down. I was not expecting to find the redoubtable Master Tyburn from old wars in Flanders to be the inquirer. Nor was I expecting a drink out of it."

"What were you expecting?"

"Someone more suitable for Bristow here to thump over the head and drag back in coffers." Bristow beamed. "I expect we will take the simple route and ask you to come with us." Covington's eyes narrowed and his hand moved a fractional inch towards the hilt of his rapier. "I would commend you towards agreement to this proposal."

"And will I be leaving of my own accord once this interview concludes?"

The blue eyes were rimmed with frost. "One way or another."

"And who is it that seeks this ... interview?"

"A man used to getting what he wants. Which is why he employs Bristow and myself. He is not someone that fails to achieve his wishes."

"Your master has a name?"

"Lord Cecil Benton, the Earl of Rutledge."

"Suddenly I move in lofty circles." The player gave Covington a sarcastic smile. "And why would the esteemed Lord Rutledge want to bother with a minor play-actor or a missing factor?"

Covington's glacial eyes reflected little humour. "His lordship does not share his confidences with me direct, but I would venture that the factor in question has absconded with considerable funds in tow."

"Recovery of which would warrant a significant reward?"

Covington smiled slightly, his face amused. "Or a painful and drawn-out punishment in the event of any collusion with the thief."

Tyburn grunted and drained his tankard. "Best finish your pots then, gentlemen, and we'll go see your lord and master." The player tapped one gloved hand on Covington's chest. "Not because you threatened." Covington glanced down at the hand and looked at Tyburn's face. He nodded.

Covington drained his drink and set the tankard back on the stone wall. Bristow gave a cautioning whistle as four men detached themselves from the passing crowd and positioned themselves in front of the trio.

Covington looked at the men and gave an exasperated sigh. Bristow rubbed his hands together, his face alight.

"Well, what do we have here? A set of Rutledge's little pretties a-roaming the streets? Looking for more men to bleed out in alleyways?" The speaker was a heavyset man wearing a short feathered cap and a thick set of unkempt whiskers that fell away on one side, giving his face an angular and unfinished look. He carried a long stave and wore a short sword that rode awkward, high on one hip. "By 'slud, you prats will get yourselves a taste."

"Bowen, isn't it?" Covington said. "Best get yourselves back to your sty and resume licking out Asquith's arse."

"Very full of yourself you are, master cunt? Let's see how clever you are when we've beaten you into the cobbles. How's that smile going to look when we finesse out yer teeth?"

Covington turned to Tyburn. "Would you suffer a momentary delay?"

Tyburn gave the four men a pitying look and stepped back, his hands raised. "Your quarrel gentlemen, settle it how you will."

Bristow, tired of the posturing, hammered his fist into the side of the head of the man nearest him, a slack-jawed young fellow with the barest fringe of a beard decorating his chin. The man dropped like a tree into the cold muck of the street. Passersby squeaked and darted aside, leaving the stretch of the street suddenly bereft of traffic.

Bowen bellowed and swung his long stave at Covington. The blond man leaned back, avoiding the strike and stepped in before

Bowen could reverse it. His booted foot hammered into Bowen's knee and his hands grasped the stave, pulling it down and twisting it. Bowen's grip was tenacious, and Covington used that to his advantage, hauling the heavyset man off balance.

Tyburn winced in sympathy as Covington released his grip on the long stave and slammed his fist into Bowen's face, sending him staggering backwards to the accompaniment of the crack of broken cartilage and the spray of blood.

The man facing Bristow yanked a dagger from his belt and lunged. Bristow had a wide smile on his face as he batted the man's thrust out of line with his body and caught the man's jerkin with his left hand. Bristow pulled the man close. Tyburn couldn't see what the shorter man did, but the assailant fell back from the melee weaponless, with his arm bent at a decided unnatural angle. He staggered across Gutter Lane and fell to his knees, his wails echoing against the tall buildings. A handful of blue-smocked apprentices, drawn by the noise of the melee, shouted and cheered the fighters.

Bowen drew his sword. Covington looked at him and it was as though dark clouds had occluded the sun. The shouting apprentices fell silent. The fourth man in the group took one look and fled down Gutter Lane, the sound of his footsteps diminishing rapidly.

"I'm going to feed your guts to the pigs," Bowen grated, spitting a mouthful of blood into the mud. Covington stepped to the left, one foot crossing over the other, the gliding gait of a practiced swordsman, his foot only fractionally above the surface of the street. Covington kept his gaze fixed on his opponent and continued to circle. He drew his weapon, the scraping metallic sound as it left the scabbard plainly heard in the now silent street. Bowen pivoted, his eyes locked on Covington. The crowd was wire-tense, watching this mortal drama play out on the muddy roadway.

The crack of the pewter tankard on the back of Bowen's skull made the crowd visibly start. Bowen gaped, one hand sliding up to the back of his head in surprise. The second blow sent his eyes rolling back and the man toppled onto the mire-coated cobbles. Christopher

Tyburn inspected the empty tankard in his hand. A sizable dent marred one side. The player caught Covington's eye and tossed him the mug. The apprentices laughed, cat-called, and booed the player before turning back to their work. One knelt beside one of the prone bodies and appropriated the man's dagger, waving it at his friends as they moved away.

Covington sheathed his sword and nodded at Tyburn, who shrugged.

"If you killed him, we'd be here forever dealing with the Ward beadles," the player explained. "I have things to do."

Covington laughed and watched as Bristow helped himself to the assailant's purses, weighing each one with a progressively happier smile before tucking them into his coat.

"What's their quarrel?" Tyburn asked.

"They serve that shit-faced cullion, the Earl of Asquith, a runty, bare-out-of-swaddling babe whom my Lord Rutledge publicly humiliated two months ago at the Queen's reception." He grinned. "Called him a puppy. He's trying to get his wardship with Lord Audley annulled and thought he could twist Rutledge's arm with some empty threats. Rutledge served him up cold in front of the entire court." Covington shook his head. "Now he's hired himself a crew of miscreants as retainers. They've been messing about, burned a barn full of hops down in Westminster, beaten some servants, raped a maid. Couple of them got shivved in an alleyway last month and Asquith publicly blamed Rutledge's retainers. Us." He grinned.

"Did you?"

Covington snorted. "I would have gladly sent that pair footing their way to Hell but it wasn't any of my men. They're smart enough to not to leave bodies lying about if they did need to send them into eternity. Rutledge is no fool. He'll crush Asquith the way the peers always do—money and humiliation and buying up his debts until he is as poor as a dog and dies in shame."

Tyburn gazed down on Bowen who was stirring feebly on the cobbles. "You might consider a new vocation," the player said drily as the three men moved away. The beggar with the palsied arm watched from the corner and Tyburn tossed him another penny as they passed.

--

Rutledge's London house lay off the Strand, just short of Charing Cross. It was an expansive walled London mansion, with a gatehouse hard by the road and the house set well back, with nothing but a small grove of picturesque apple trees and an elaborate, well-maintained knot garden lying between the building and the Thames. A stone stair and private landing gave the occupants egress to the river which, in warmer months, provided ready access via boat to Whitehall and Westminster.

Tyburn and Covington waited in the gallery hallway. Broad windows gave the hall an open, airy feel. The late-afternoon sunshine filtered through the window at the end of the hall, the reflected light wavering off the polished wooden parquet tiles. The door to the sitting room opened and a servant wearing the crossed poleaxes and collared unicorn livery of the Earl of Rutledge spoke to Covington without turning his head. "His Lordship will see you now."

Covington grunted and stepped past the liveryman into the sitting room. Tyburn followed. The room was broad and surprisingly bright, consisting of two adjoined chambers divided by a pair of decoratively carved whitewashed columns. The walls were covered with what Tyburn at first thought were wall hangings but on closer inspection was a type of wallpapering decorated with white and yellow flowers entwined with thin green ivy. Blue curtains surrounded the large bay windows and gold leaf provided a glistening outline for the carved wooden moldings that edged the room. A man sat at one of the tables, peering at a chessboard with thoughtful intensity.

"Master Christopher Tyburn, late of Sir Gilbert's brigade of Flanders, milord," Covington said by way of introduction. "Now a player for The Earl of Worcester's Men."

"And apparently a hunter of men on the side." said Rutledge without taking his eyes off the chess board. "Do you play, Master Tyburn?"

"Not well nor frequently, milord."

Rutledge nodded. "You know the pieces though?" The player nodded. "Which piece is representative? How do you see yourself?"

"Milord?"

"Are you a pawn, Master Tyburn? Moved about the board and sacrificed at another's whim? Or mayhaps a knight, careening down the tilt. Do you see yourself as a castle, a sturdy bulwark against troubles?"

"A wayward bishop milord, tacking my way through life."

Rutledge laughed and looked at Tyburn for the first time. The man had a knife's gaze, edged and direct, but it felt more conveyance then reality, a façade for a poor masque. "A devious piece, Master Tyburn, forever sliding out of Fate's path and attacking from the unexpected quarter. Not," he noted, "the most powerful of pieces but an apt choice."

The earl rolled one of the pieces between his palms. "Has Covington granted you any explanation for this summons?"

"That we seem to share an interest beyond the chessboard, milord."

Rutledge chuckled, an indulgent, false laugh that set Tyburn's nerves on edge. Or perhaps it was the locale, he thought. Kit had a long and bitter experience with the soft-spoken men who sat judgment in well-appointed drawing rooms, parsing out fate and death without consideration for the lives they disbursed like clipped copper pence.

"You are seeking a man."

"I am, milord."

"Charles Stokely, factor and goldseller. My factor, by point of circumstance. And the man appointed to manage my offices with the Exchequer."

"Which offices are those, milord?"

Rutledge set down the piece and waved one hand dismissively. "Various sundry tariffs, of little import I expect to a man like yourself. Why," he continued, "are you seeking Master Stokely?"

"Stokely vanished in possession of certain writs and accounts required for a venture. My patron is seeking redress of this situation."

Rutledge leaned back in his chair. "Your patron is …?"

"Busy, milord. May I ask why you have summoned me here?"

Rutledge's indulgent smile tightened imperceptibly. "I need to determine whether it serves my interest that your enquiries continue, or if they should be brought to a halt. Covington, any thoughts on this matter?"

Covington stirred. "Short of killing him, doubt you can bring him to heel. I've seen his ilk before, he's hard-schooled and not as like to stop."

"We should kill him? By Jesu you are a blood-thirsty cur, Covington. The poor man has done aught but ask about a missing man and you'd have his corpse littering the Thames."

Covington shrugged offhand. "Didn't say that was by preference. I suggest an accommodation."

Rutledge turned, his pale rounded face beaming. "An accommodation! What a splendid consideration. Would you reflect upon it, Master Tyburn? Or is your preference to try the skills of my Covington." Out of Rutledge's view, Covington rolled his eyes in exasperation.

"What form of accommodation did you have in mind?" Tyburn asked.

"Seek your wayward goldseller. Winnow him out from whatever crack he has ensconced himself within, and when you find him, shake him until your writs fall out. Upon which, you pass him *virgo intacta*, to Master Covington, without question or compromise, with his accounts, books, and papers untouched." He looked at the player, his eyes a ferrule of hard brown. "It would grieve me shamefully to see one of Worcester's Men never walk the boards again, or for your patron—Burbage would be my guess—to see his theatre fall before it ever opens."

Tyburn felt a brief frisson of unease. His preference was to keep men like Rutledge at arm's distance. *There is nothing like Flanders* whispered in his ear like a flickering haunt, a transitory resonance from the corners of this gilt and papered room. Rutledge was a smooth-faced, oily bastard. Whatever Stokely had done to earn Rutledge's sharp vengeance was not Tyburn's problem, and Tyburn had no desire to cross a man with Rutledge's influence. Ignoring God was one thing, but crossing a peer was a short trip to a very bad place.

"I have no issue with tossing Stokely to your hounds, once I have what I need from him. Any writs, papers, or accounts not pertinent to my patron can be Covington's affair. If Stokely's hidden or burned those papers, though, it's not my problem. Have your lads keep out of my path. I'll sing out when I have Stokely, but I'd rather not have them dogging my tracks. And you need to pay me."

"Pay you? You are already being paid by your patron."

"Being paid to find Stokely for him, not for you."

"Paid twice for the same job?" The earl chuckled. "You should be a factor yourself, Master Tyburn. Very well. Your price?"

"Twenty shillings. Half in advance."

Rutledge raised one eyebrow in mock astonishment. "I could hire all of Worcester's Men for a command performance for less."

"And a brilliant performance you would receive, milord, but not one that ends with Stokely in your hands."

The thin smile reappeared on Rutledge's face. "I think we can agree to those conditions but you receive no monies in advance. I pay only for success. I will expect regular reports on your progress through Covington. You can make your own arrangements as for when or how." He waved his hand and turned back to arranging the pieces on the chessboard. "That's all. Covington, please ask my next appointment to join me."

Covington tilted his head, indicating the door. As the player reached out to pull on the carved handle, Rutledge spoke again. "I trust I don't need to emphasize what happens if you fail?"

Tyburn spoke without looking back. "We'll see how that Wheel turns." He pulled open the door and stepped out into the hallway.

Francis Walsingham's head rose as the door opened and his dark eyes locked on Tyburn's. The principal secretary was seated on a settee, a small cup of sugared water in one hand. Tyburn had spent enough time with the man to recognize the look on Walsingham's veiled and composed features, despite the man's iron control. It was a mix of surprise and then tightening suspicion and growing anger at the sight of his agent. The player bowed his head in acknowledgement of the other visitor and turned down the hallway.

"His Lordship will see you now." Covington said respectfully. Walsingham set his cup down with a sharp click that made the player wince inwardly. He could feel Walsingham's reproving stare on his back as he walked down the long gallery to the entrance hall.

"Come in, come in, my dear Master Walsingham." Walsingham turned his hawk gaze to his host who had arisen and was gesturing for him to enter the room. The principal secretary took one last look at Tyburn's retreating back and stepped into the room.

"Milord, it is good to see you again. Are you planning a performance?" Walsingham inquired. The earl took Walsingham's outstretched hand and gave it a firm shake.

"What? Oh, you know Master Tyburn and Worcester's Men?"

"I was acquainted with them last year at a performance in the Midlands," Walsingham said. "I am not fond of plays but they seemed to provide adequate service. You should be speaking with Master Oldcastle, however. I don't believe Tyburn is any more than a player."

"Truly? Well, he seemed to know his business. I trust he will acquaint me with Master Oldcastle in due course. Would you care for some wine?" Rutledge clapped his hands and a retainer entered with a tray bearing two glasses and a decanter.

"I thank you, sir." The servant poured two glasses and set them on the side table. He bowed and withdrew.

"To your good health, Master Walsingham." Rutledge nodded and raised his glass.

Walsingham bowed his head in acknowledgement. "To you and yours, milord." The two men drank.

"Have you by chance, had the opportunity to try this *herba Regina*? Hawkins recommended it to me for my headaches and humours. Apparently the savages of the New World partake of it in both food and drink and, extraordinary as it sounds, by burning it in small quantities and breathing in the fumes."

"I try to avoid such affectations milord." Walsingham replied.

Rutledge tutted. "It is supposed to have some mind-cleansing effects. In your business, that might be seen as helpful."

Walsingham gave a thin humourless smile. "'In my line of work mind-cleansing may be an impediment. It is precisely my line of work that brings me to you today."

Rutledge leaned back in his chair and took a sip of wine. "Yes, Lord Burghley has spoken with me. He noted that you had some reservations about my assuming a more prominent role in dealing with"—he waved vaguely—"these foreign plots and intrigues."

"More cautions, than reservations milord. It is an unrelenting and thankless task, ferreting out these machinations, parsing fact from falsehood, the trivial from the weighty. Knowing of your lordship's current burdens with the wool tariff, the Privy Council, and the Star Chamber, I would be loath to burden you with a single hour of this overwrought position."

"The Earl of Leicester has suggested it would be better to have this burden divided, together with the associated costs and travails. Would you not agree?"

"As much as I admire the earl's acumen, of all the particular offices and places of charge in this state, there is none more subject to variability than my office. You have no warrant or commission in matters of greatest peril save the virtue and word of our sovereign." He looked at Rutledge. "This is not a position of note, honour or repute, only of service."

Rutledge froze, and then set his wine glass down on the side table with the faintest clink. "You think me ill-suited for this role, Master Walsingham?"

"No one is suited for this role, milord. It is an ill-fitted jacket that wears uncomfortably no matter the number of times worn."

"And you will oppose my appointment." Rutledge's voice was soft, even in the quiet of the room.

"No, milord, not yours. I will oppose any ill-affected appointment that does not meet the needs of the Crown."

"You dance neatly around the edge of the blade, Master Walsingham, but Lord Burghley has indicated the need for the Crown to have more than a single set of eyes abroad and at home. If I recall, that Jesuit in Warwickshire slipped past your nets last year."

"Leicester's nets, not mine."

"An agent of the papacy was actively fomenting armed rebellion and you failed to apprehend him. And then there was this Story incident last month."

"Story, milord?"

Rutledge gave the secretary a look of exasperation. "You had your agents snatch the man from Flanders and have him locked up in Yarmouth. Hardly a brilliant act of statesmanship that will endear us to the Spanish or the French."

"I was not aware that the endearment of the French or the Spanish was a devout wish of the Crown," Walsingham replied.

"We cannot afford the continued enmity of Spain!" Rutledge's voice echoed through the ornate sitting chamber. He paused and Walsingham heard the man's breath hiss out through his nostrils. "Drake and Hawkins tweaking Philip's nose by raiding his ports and burning his ships might appeal to the mob, but we cannot continue to slight them in this manner. Supporting William the Silent in Flanders and taunting the League does not strengthen the Queen."

"On this we must disagree, milord." Walsingham rose to his feet and gave Rutledge a careful bow. "I will bleed the Spanish and the Catholic League at every opportunity and at every turn. I will bleed them from a thousand pinpricks if I must, but bleed them I will, for in bleeding them, I weaken their resolve, their strength, and their focus. For every Story I snatch, quarter, and hang, there will be one less fence-sitting Catholic likely to provide support to the next priest selling absolution for rebellion and treason in God's name. I will wear that jacket, ill-fitted as it is, every day I live."

Rutledge waved his hand in dismissal. "Thank you for seeing me, Master Walsingham, your discourse has been … illuminating." The principal secretary gave the man a careful bow and left.

Walsingham was escorted by a single liveried servant back to the great hall, where his assistant and guard sat waiting. As they exited through the broad-leafed doors and turned towards the Thames where their boat waited, Walsingham turned to his assistant.

"Find Tyburn."

Chapter the Sixth

W HEN WILL YOU *pay me? When will you pay me? When will you pay me?"* The bells of the Old Bailey reverberated across Ludgate as Tyburn trudged over the Fleet Bridge and through the flinty expanse of London's westernmost gate.

Tyburn barely noticed the late-afternoon traffic clogging the gate, preoccupied with the ramifications of Walsingham finding him with the Earl of Rutledge and the need to pin down some clue to the whereabouts of the goldseller. The November sky was steadily darkening, and the afternoon sun had vanished like a late sleeper pulling a blanket over its head. The stiff, chill and damp breeze from the south-west was actually welcome as it blew away the stench of offal that hung over the Fleet like a miasma. The upstream area around Smithfield was the locale for many of London's stockyards, butchers and shambles, with the Fleet being the illicit repository for blood, offal and the butcheries remains.

"When will you pay me?" the bells intoned again. Tyburn snorted, reminded that Ludgate was home to numerous prisons and the painful residence to numerous debtors. Newgate and Ludgate were literally steps away.

He paused.

Now that's a thought. Tyburn turned and looked north up Old Bailey. London's notorious criminal courts lay in close proximity to Newgate, Ludgate, and the Fleet prisons. You could pass through those forbidding gates for numerous offences, debt in particular being a vicious conveyance, as a writ could be sworn out by the debt-holders and, without any foreknowledge, a person could be seized and confined. Vermin-infested, dank, and malignant, the quality of your confinement would depend on the depth of your pockets. Money could see you confined in relative comfort, with food, ale and bedding. Penury saw you residing the Commons or worse, the Hole, often shackled and fettered, living on charitable crusts and scraps until gaol fever or the noose saw an end to it.

Tyburn shivered. Newgate in particular had a dark reputation; anyone who walked in its shadow felt the oppressive weight of the locale. No one would willingly venture into the jaws of that beast.

And no one would look for them there.

Stokely had vanished. Mayhaps he had gone where none would think to look. A slow smile crossed the player's face. Not Newgate—too dark, too dangerous, and too public. Not the Fleet nor Ludgate, God knows, they were just too close to Cheapside and home. Stokely would want to be somewhere less known, less visible to his everyday acquaintances, but close enough he could know what was doing in London.

Outside of the city authority. Tyburn turned and gazed towards the Thames. The city wall ran west from Ludgate, out to the Fleet, a stony obstacle blocking any view he might have of the river, but his imagination skirted the hindrances and the dark waters to focus on Southwark and Bankside. There, on land held by the bishop of Winchester, lay the liberty of the Clink. Not administered by Surrey and outside the authority of the London Corporate, Southwark was a notorious collection of inns, gaming houses, brothels, bear-baiting pits, and theatres. Worcester's Men performed at inn-yards in Southwark dozens of times a year, particularly when the inn-houses of London were closed to performance due to threats of plague. Most of the land fell under the ownership and ecclesiastical authority of the bishop of Winchester, making one of London's most powerful figures the nominal landlord for the dense, vice-ridden, pox-infested stews and brothels that lay at the southern end of London Bridge.

It also held a prison. The Clink.

The Clink was perfect. Far enough away from his usual haunts that Stokely might be able to purchase some anonymity from the keeper, for a usurious price to be sure. Tyburn, like all the players who passed through Southwark's vice-filled precincts, had a passing familiarity with the place, mainly from walking past the sunken prisoners' grill, a barred window that opened onto a shallow alleyway. It was here that you passed the pale, depressed faced wretches begging for scraps at the bars from a passersby or weeping with their families, huddled at the iron grate like moths around a flame. The Clink was notorious for its use of fetters and, being smaller than Newgate, the Fleet or the Counters, didn't offer the freedom of a common area. If you were in the Clink and lacked coin, the chains went on and rarely, if ever, did they come off.

It was also the prison of choice for Catholics and captured priests. Being under the auspices and authority of the bishop of Winchester, recusants and heretical prisoners were often relegated to the tender mercies of the Clink. Tyburn knew, from his work with Walsingham, if you needed to find a Catholic priest in London, the Clink was the likeliest spot.

Tyburn laughed. Tomorrow he would scout the prison, and with luck, pull Stokely out of his hide, deliver him and his writs to Burbage, then turn him over to Covington's tender mercies. The player threaded past a row of carts waiting to enter the city and strode under the dark shadow of the Ludgate.

--

The tavern was dark, dense, noisome, and filled with shouting bedlam as Tyburn ducked past the low-hanging sign embellished with an improbably buxom mermaid and pushed open the heavy wooden door. Legally signs in London had to be hung high enough that a mounted man could ride cleanly under them, but the law was not often observed and the opportunity to crack a head or for an unwary rider to be toppled into the muck was frequent.

Tyburn pushed his was way into the common room, scanning the crowd. The Mermaid was filled with apprentices drinking away their wages, clerks and chapmen dicing in the corner, a handful of Cheapside merchants and yeomanry trading barbs and gulping ale and cheap Madeira. The light was dim and lanterns hung along the serving table and at each corner of the room. It smelled of stale, unwashed humanity, wood smoke, bread, burned meat, and the ripe tang of ale and spilled wine. He finally spotted Burbage, seated with his partner, Brayne, and another man at a private table in an alcove in the back. The player slid through the throng but stopped short when he saw Oldcastle seated at the end of the table, a beatific smile on his face that abruptly vanished as he bent over in a fit of coughing.

"Not dead of that cannikin yet?" Tyburn asked, his voice caustic. Oldcastle raised one hand in reply, his face flushed as he hacked and wheezed, half bent over the table.

"Ahh ... Christ. You cock-sucking wretch, I—"

"What's happening?" Burbage cut him off, face and voice sour and irritated. "Have you found Stokely yet?"

Tyburn looked down at Burbage. Two bottles empty of wine and one half-full of dark red canary stood on the table. The three men were red-faced and Oldcastle looked inordinately pleased with himself. Brayne merely swayed back and forth slightly. It was clear that he had drunk more than his fair portion.

With his foot, Tyburn hooked a stool out from under the neighbouring table and sat down, taking Brayne's empty mug for himself and refilling it from the half-bottle. He gulped it, tasting the acrid fruity ripeness of the Spanish wine. For an instant he was back in the damp polders of Walcheren, drinking down the spoils of a Spanish raid. Clearly Burbage or Brayne was buying; this was far better than the normal swill that Oldcastle preferred.

"Well? Where's Stokely? Do you have him yet?" Burbage was red-faced but clear-eyed, his face intent. "I've paid good coin, I expect..."

"I have a line on him. If the fates favour us, we should have him for you tomorrow."

Oldcastle cocked an eyebrow. "I'm shocked. I was beginning to think you had been out-foxed and buggered by a bastard goldseller."

"He's been a hard one to dig out," Tyburn admitted. "Not to be found in any of the usual places, and no one seems to have a clear idea on why he did a runner in the first place. Any thoughts on that?" Burbage shook his head. "Why did you want me to meet you?" The player had found a note from Burbage waiting at his room. His landlord had described Burbage as "all hat and feathers," which Tyburn had recognized even before seeing the signature and opening the sealed note.

"A ten-shilling reason, that's why." It was a sign of Burbage's desperation that he did not dance around the issue. "You've been chasing your tail for near four days and nary a report or a note. I need my money. I have a theatre to complete and I can't carry it another two weeks or I'll be hung up by my creditors or tossed in the Marshalsea."

Tyburn snorted. "You may find him your own self if that were to happen." The player outlined his plan to visit the Clink and the reason he thought it the most likely hiding place for the goldseller. Burbage nodded thoughtfully and Brayne sputtered about how they would make Stokely pay for his insolence and thievery. Oldcastle simply laughed and poured himself another draught, filling his glass to the rim with the expensive canary.

"And you think you can find him in the Clink?"

"He may well be hiding in one of the Counters, but I expect the Clink fits the bill so that's my first stop. Besides, if he is as mercenary a factor as he seems, he's probably gotten debtors or filchers consigned to the other prisons at some point, so it seems he's more like to go where he's not known. The keepers are an avaricious bunch. Cross their palms with silver and they'd sell Christ himself into fetters. As long as he's in coin, they'll keep his secret."

"And how do you find him?" Oldcastle interrupted. "They aren't likely to find you appealing."

A musician began to strum a cittern and a group of apprentices shouted out a song and then, impatient for him to start, began to drunkenly sing it themselves.

> *"There was a jovial tinker, who was a good ale drinker,*
> *He never was a shrinker, believe me this is true.*
> *And he came from the Weald of Kent,*
> *When all his money was gone and spent,*
> *Which made him look like a Jack-a-Lent.*
> *And Joan's ale is new,*
> *And Joan's ale is new, my boys,*
> *And Joan's ale is new."*

Oldcastle hummed along, his thick hand bouncing on the tabletop, head cocked to follow the conversation. Tyburn leaned in to answer to Burbage, ignoring Oldcastle. "The keepers value their hides and their position more than any single inmate in their so-called care, even one paying them a year's wages for sanctuary. I drop the right names in the right ears, and they'll roll over on him." Tyburn paused. "Probably best to honey it with some groats. I'll need at least six shillings."

Burbage's face fell. "Six? What makes you think we have six shillings to throw away after the ten we've already invested? So far you've got nothing but guesses and wind."

"If I'm wrong, you can deduct the six shillings from the ten more you owe me, but I need silver to sweeten them. Pennies for the doorwardens and at least three shillings for the keeper."

"The tinker did he settle
Most like a man of mettle, and vow'd to pawn his kettle;
Now make what did ensue;
His neighbours flock in apace, to see Tom Tinker's comely face,
Where they drank soundly for a space,
Whilst Joan's ale is new,
Whilst Joan's ale is new, my boys,
Whilst Joan's ale is new."

Oldcastle bellowed the lines across the room, his hack rasping across the common room.

"You could always go yourself," suggested Tyburn, as Burbage hesitated.

"No." Burbage pulled out a small purse and counted out a handful of silver. "Here, but if I find no satisfaction, you get none of your remaining ten shillings."

Tyburn nodded, exuding a confident mien he didn't quite possess. He stood. "We'll have Stokely and your writs on the morrow." Burbage nodded.

"The cobbler and the broom-man, came into the room, man.
And said they would drink for boon, man.
Let each one take his due!
But when the liquor good they found,
They cast their caps upon the ground,
And so the tinker he drank round,
Whilst Joan's ale is new,
Whilst Joan's ale is new, my boys,

Whilst Joan's ale is new."

The song chased Tyburn out into the London night.

Chapter the Seventh

THE WATER WAS bruised and sluggish under grey clouds, looking more like a slab of wet clay than a river. Tyburn clattered down the stony staircase leading to the Hay Wharf and the waterman's stairs. The tide was coming in, so he didn't have to navigate the narrow wooden causeways and muddy flats to reach his transport.

The player scowled at the murky water of the Thames. He found the Thames a malevolent and indifferent river; dark, heavy and brooding, choked off and constrained from everyday life in the city by stone and wattle and walls. Always extant, the ebb and flow of the water pulsated like a secret heart. It was a place that hid secrets, and left one with the sense that old gods lurked beneath its murk. The mudlarks that plied the tidal flats, searching for lost coins and detritus, once found an ancient bronze figurine embedded in the silt. The legs and arms had been hacked off and twisted. The head had a long flowing beard and wild hair with vacant hollow eyes that seemed to bespeak a horror of the waking world.

Tyburn beckoned to one of the waiting watermen, who sculled his craft over to the stairs. The player stepped nimbly into the watercraft and the man shoved off even before the player had sat.

"Southwark, if you please."

"Two pence or fuck off." The man grunted. Tyburn nodded and handed over one coin. The second would be delivered upon arrival at Southwark. He sat and watched the London shore slowly slip away as the waterman sculled out from the wharf, angling westward against the flowing current. London Bridge loomed on the right, its nineteen arches and accompanying "starlings" funneling the water downstream into a quickening race that seethed and boiled into frenzy when the tide turned. Tyburn remembered a bit of bridge doggerel he had heard from a waterman, "wise men walked and only fools went beneath". The tidal race drowned dozens of people each year, caught up in the silent strength of the water and pulled downwards. The old gods of the river rarely favoured the foolish.

The river traffic was thick, dozens of wherries, barges, and lighters darting about, clustering at the various docks and wharves, carrying passengers and goods. One barge was filled with a dozen bleating sheep, the owner obviously trying to avoid the bridge toll in favour of a barge passage.

Tyburn had a healthy distaste for journeys over water, exacerbated by his various trips back and forth across the Channel. He had spent his first voyage vomiting up his breakfast on a storm-tossed troop ship to Brill. He could still recall the sickening slide of the ship as it crashed and tossed on the brisk Channel waves and the snickering laughter of the veteran Scots and Dutch sailors at the handful of English soldiery, slithering in the foul mess on the wet deck.

The Thames by comparison was calmer but cold. A brisk wind had brought darker clouds scudding from the south-west and the distant rumble of thunder. The waterman sniffed and crossed himself. "Weather coming, like as not. God's truth, ye'll best be walking back o'er the Bridge."

Tyburn nodded and watched as the oarsman deftly spun the boat to slide neatly to a halt at St. Mary Overy Stairs, the stony landing opposite Winchester House. It was only a block away from the Clink. The player tossed the man a second penny and clambered up the damp stone steps, crusted with ice.

Southwark.

Southwark was another world, a world apart from London. It was rife with vice, bedlam, and amusements. London's dark underbelly was exposed here, to the intense chagrin of the Precisian aldermen that dominated the city. The area was thick with brothels, inn-yards and betting houses. There was cheap nappy ale, wine, music, whores, and cards; bear-baiting and cockfights; thieves and malefactors, cony-catchers, beggars and minstrels. And playing companies. All of London's playing companies rolled through Southwark's inn-yards in a constant flow, playing Lewes and St. Augustine's, the George and the Castle upon the Hope. There was no lack of patronage for the players, with the constant flow of apprentices, merchants, yeomen, and students from the Temple crossing the river to waste their wages on sin, ale, gambling, and women.

Tyburn turned past the wide and stately girth of Winchester House down Clink Street towards the prison. A dark-haired beggar with a palsied arm sat on a stoop, one hand vainly waving for supplication. The player ignored him. A dog darted past, barking wildly, pursued by a small mob of filthy children hurling sticks and small rocks. A distant roar from down Bankside told him that either the bull-baiting or dog-fights had started.

The Clink was an unimpressive edifice. A large, iron-reinforced door was set into a windowless, thick stone and brick wall that towered four stories. A faded swinging sign marked with a fiddle hung above the entrance. Further along was a narrow alleyway that dead-ended in the Clink's infamous "grill". There, a handful of common prisoners could beg through the bars for bread, coins, or drink, or have a momentary, if painful and stilted, conversation with friends, creditors, and loved ones while rattling their fetters against the cold iron.

Tyburn yanked the pull-bell at the door, the clanging sound alerting the doorwarden to his arrival. A narrow slot opened.

"You got something?"

"I need to speak with the keeper."

"Bugger off cullion."

Tyburn held up a small coin. "I need to speak with the keeper."

"You a thief-taker? Or a beadle? You got someone for confinement?"

"Just get the fucking keeper or your coin goes through the grate."

"Alright, alright. Didn't mean no harm." The door bar snapped back with a crack and the gate opened. An unholy stench of rotten meat, shit and unwashed humanity flooded out through the opening, making Tyburn gag. The man grinned at the player's discomfiture. "You should smell 'er in the summer heat."

The player entered into the front landing, while the doorwarden slammed the heavy door behind him and slid the locking bar into place. The only visible daylight shone through two narrow slots above the door.

"Come on, then." The doorwarden turned and shuffled his thick bulk down the long hallway muttering to himself. The player followed. The stone walls were damp and sweating with a fetid miasma, the air thick and still. There was no discernible sound beyond a faint clanking and an indistinct subliminal murmur. The doorwarden cracked open another door and the flood of bright cool light from the open yard beyond shone with an almost tangible relief. The doorwarden's hand made a hungry gesture and Tyburn dutifully dropped in the small silver coin as he stepped out into the enclosed yard.

A smaller building stood on the far side of the walled yard. Almost half the yard consisted of a well-tended garden, now quiescent for the season, many of the plants tenderly wrapped against the gathering chill of the impending winter nights. A slight man sat on the stoop, carefully mending the straps on a device that made the player stiffen. It was a set of fetters designed to be strapped to stone or iron weights. A wooden stand with four timber legs and a narrow board that tapered to a wedge stood to one side. The player recognized it. Nicknamed the Spanish Donkey, it was used as a punishment device by some of the armed bands in Flanders. The malefactor would be tied astride the board and the weighted fetters attached to his feet, so that the angled board cut into his groin.

The slight man rose to his feet as the player crossed the yard. "How may ..."

Tyburn cut the man off with an authoritative gesture. "You need to listen with both ears, while you still have them." The keeper's expression darkened as the player continued, leaving him no room to respond. "Under the authority of the Earl of Rutledge, I am hunting a fugitive that is under your roof. He goes by the name of Charles Stokely. Mottled face, dark hair, round nose, raspy short beard, and no shortage of silver. He's paying good coin to lurk about your prison, but he's not staying with the commons or in the Hole. He's getting food, drink, and bed, and paying you well for the privilege."

The man's face was a mask.

"You might think the coin he's promised or paid is worth the risk of ignoring me. Or maybe you're thinking of having your boys fetter me up and dump me in the coal house, so you can pocket your gelt and milk him until his lour is gone. I am here to disabuse you of that notion. Stokely is more than just another sheep to be fleeced. He is a millstone around your neck and a promise that you will ride that wooden beast until you split, if you choose to defy our order."

The player kicked at the leg fetters for emphasis. "Or you can be the smart man I know you are. Rutledge pays his partners and his friends well, and always has need for a trustworthy man he can rely on to assist him in his hour of need."

Tyburn turned away from the man and glanced about the walled yard. "Silver or iron? It's an easy choice."

--

"I paid good money for that hide," the man grumbled, "fair coin. Twenty bloody shillings a week for the Knight's Side. Bastard should return it."

"Probably." agreed Tyburn, pushing the man bodily out the gateway and into the brisk afternoon air. Charles Stokely stumbled on the stone steps, his eyes squinting against the light despite the dark cast of clouds that occluded the November sun. Stokely was as Burbage had described—raspy beard, mottled face and a round, full nose with the look of an overly ripened apple left to rot on the tree. A full head shorter than Tyburn, the man was stout but ghost pale from his sojourn in the prison. His once-fine clothes were stained and greasy, and his hair a tangled mess. Despite his paying good silver, the room Stokely had been allocated had been damp and greasy with accumulated filth.

"We should hire a boat." The man's nasal whine set the player's teeth on edge.

"Do you good to walk. Been locked up a fair bit, and I don't fancy a wherry with weather rolling in. We'll take the bridge." The sharp rumble of thunder and a cold gust of wind lent weight to the player's words.

"And I have to carry this?" Stokely gestured at the flat lockbox he was carrying.

"Your stuff, you haul it."

"We could hire a cart."

"Do I look like I piss gold? Shut it and move."

Stokely glanced warily about the busy precincts of Southwark. Despite the encroaching weather, the road was alive with commerce. A steady stream of traffic was threading past the prison in both directions, jostling by on route to taverns, brothels, and dicing rooms. A group of street performers were juggling on the corner, faces covered with red, black, and white harlequin masks, their clothes loud and boisterous. Tyburn didn't recognize them as part of any of the licensed troupes, so they were probably in from the country, trying their amateur hand at Southwark. Venturing into London proper would be more problematic, as the London aldermen could arrest unlicensed performers. Licensed playing troupes like Worcester's Men looked askance at upstarts like these. If they settled in a local inn-yard or public space commonly used by one of the troupes, violent altercations were known to occur.

"I shouldn't be out," Stokely averred, "it isn't safe."

"Just walk. You try to piss off on me and I will thump you within an inch of your life."

"You think they won't find me?"

Tyburn turned to look at the unkempt man with puzzlement. "I found you. Who else is chasing you?"

Stokely's lips were taut, his face bleak and tight. He shook his head. "I should have stayed at the Clink."

"Not your choice to make." Tyburn grunted. "You didn't want to get pinched, you should have headed to the Cinque Ports, run for Brill or Calais."

"Twouldn't have made a difference."

"Burbage just wants his writs, he doesn't care about naught else."

"Burbage is an ass. He don't warrant hiding."

"You running from Rutledge?" the player asked, glancing at Stokely's face in curiosity.

Stokely's eyes slid sideways and he grunted in response. "The earl and I have a good understanding. I manage his license and tariffs, don't lift any ready coin, and he gets to keep it at arm's length and pocket his gold. He pays me, that's all you need know. Best not dig into the dung if'n you don't want to get rank." He shifted the flat lockbox onto one shoulder, steadying it with his free hand.

Tyburn stared at the man for a moment. "Why bury yourself in the Clink?"

Stokely merely shook his head.

"You ran from your family, abjured all your friends and guild, buried yourself in a stone hole deeper than anyone would have expected. I'm curious why?"

"Just take me to Rutledge. I've his accounts and your friend Burbage's writs in the box." He laughed, a sour sound. "If'n that shit bastard weren't skimming his own accounts, he'd have had his coin before I did a runner and his edifice would be done by now." The man's head was like a swivel, pivoting and turning to eye the growing crowd flowing to the south end of the bridge.

The bear-baiting had ended; the audience had spilled out and was now spreading through the various inns, taverns, and stews that lined the roadway. A group of drunken legal students from the Inns of the Court, easily recognizable by their dark gowns, pushed past, seemingly torn between the temptations of the low-bodiced whores lounging in the doorways and the need to get back to Chancery Lane before the weather turned.

Tyburn pushed the reluctant Stokely along the roadway, past the vaulted stone intricacy of St Mary Overie Church. The priory at the site had long since closed, its monks and nuns scattered in the wake of Henry's seizures, its rents and monies dispersed to the bishop of Winchester, and its lands rented out to brothels.

Ahead loomed the Great Stone Gate marking the southern end of London Bridge. Crowds of pedestrians and cart traffic were funneling into the gloomy arched mouth of the bridge. Jutting out above the Great Stone Gate, impaled on the ends of long pikes, stood a grim collection of traitors' heads, hanging round and black against the sky like carrion fruit. Traditionally heads were displayed at the Drawbridge Gate Tower, but the old and decrepit defensive structure was in the process of being torn down to make way for a new wooden building, so the traitor's heads had been relocated to the Great Stone Gate where they bid an ominous welcome to London's visitors from the south. Tyburn idly wondered if anyone he knew was staring back at him.

London Bridge itself was sheer spectacle. It stretched from bank to bank, more than nine humdred feet long, supported by nineteen stone arches constructed upon piled starlings embedded in the dark waters of the river. The bridge was surmounted along both sides by lines of buildings roofed in red tile, some rising up to seven stories high, with bridge traffic squeezed into a narrow twelve-foot passage.

The pair strode through the tunnel gateway, the echoes of their footsteps lost in the crush of people pushing along the narrow passage. Nominally the roadway was wide enough for two carts to pass abreast, despite the buildings that lined the side of the bridge. The reality was that piecemeal stalls, hawkers, musicians, and beggars combined with the high foot and cart traffic turned the passage into a slow ambling walk at the best of times. The sky was a rare glimpse along certain sections where the buildings had been tiered out or attached at the upper levels, giving the passage a darkened and tunnel-like ambience. It was said you could cross more than a third of the way before realizing you were on a bridge.

"Did you steal from Rutledge?" Tyburn asked the goldseller diffidently.

The man gave the player an exasperated glance. "I'm no damned draw-latch. I gave him an honest accounting, and served my office as I was instructed, by God's bones." He rubbed his red fleshy nose. "Are my wife and little ones well?"

The player shrugged. "Well enough, as much as I saw. She wasn't forthcoming. Seemed afraid."

Stokely nodded, his eyes distant. "As she should be. Out of the smoke and into the flame."

"You planning on speaking in oblique riddles for the entirety of our journey, or do you want to just say what you mean for a time?" Tyburn said, a touch of asperity in his voice. "You claim you didn't steal or defraud Rutledge and you aren't running from him or Burbage. Whose cart did you upset?"

The pause made Tyburn think the man hadn't heard him in the noise of the crowd. Finally Stokely spoke. "Rutledge is an ambitious man. Man of influence and reach. He has enemies, some friends even, that wouldn't think twice about grasping for leverage on him, same as he does to others." Stokely gave the player a sidelong glance. "He's on the Privy Council, sits in the Star Chamber, hands in the pocket of the Exchequer. And he's a bit of a vindictive bastard. He's a lavish enough man when it suits him, but God help you if'n you took him for a penny or failed to pay back in kind or coin anything he loaned out."

"How's he get on with Asquith?"

Stokely's laugh was deep and throaty , the nervous energy that had pervaded him since leaving the Clink gone for a moment. He shifted the strongbox, balancing it on his hip. "He hates the poncy bugger. They both tilted a lance at Arabela Howard, niece of the Countess of Lennox. Rutledge isn't a man that accepts losing, and word is she favours the cot-quean."

"Well sought is she?"

The factor snorted. "Got more land than Asquith and Rutledge combined. But Asquith is still under the thumb of his guardian, Lord Audley, so his revenues are into Audley's and the Crown's pockets. He can't get permission to marry without the Crown's approval, so Lady Arabela is still out of reach and likely to remain as virginal as the Queen. Maybe more so."

"And Audley?"

Stokely's eyes rolled. "He and Rutledge both shit from the same arse. Rutledge says, Audley does."

The buildings fell away and the river emerged into view for the first time as the two men plodded along in the line of traffic across the heavy wooden drawbridge. The Drawbridge Gate Tower was one of London's defensive bastions, although it had long since fallen into disrepair. Wooden scaffolding was hung along one side, preparatory work for the slow removal of the structure. Tyburn could hear the rush of water below as the tide and current boiled, the waters compressed and pushed into a seething cauldron by the massive stone starlings. They filed through the dim gatehouse tunnel, slipping past several laden carts halted by the bridge wardens assessing the toll.

A man on horseback thrust his way through the press, in the wake of a liveried groom who shoved people aside. "Make way. Make way," he intoned.

Tyburn felt a brief clutch at his left arm and Stokely half gasped, half retched.

The player turned.

Stokely was frozen in place, his eyes staring down the length of the bridge. His once-fine coat bulged, strangely tented above his left breast. Tyburn felt someone push past on his right as he watched the expensive material of the coat split asunder, the thin reddened tip of a long poniard emerging with sullen slowness, protruding outward from below Stokely's left collarbone. Stokely retched again and staggered, grasping at Tyburn's arm with nerveless hands. He fell to his knees and someone shrieked in horror. The hilt of the weapon protruded out of Stokely's back, the blade angled upwards into a neat and precise thrust to the heart.

The player spun around, eyes seeking. The flat lockbox was gone. Stokely slumped down into the roadway, blood dripping down the front of his now sodden coat. He toppled onto his side, emitting a deep groan that faded into a long hiss.

Shouts of alarm rose and the crowd split to both sides. Tyburn stared down the length of the bridge, looking for the assailant in the dense throng. Pale shocked faces stared back at him in a ring. The killing had brought the crowd around them to a dazed halt, opening space in the relentless bridge commute. Tyburn craned his neck and shoved his way away from the supine body for a glimpse.

The lockbox was in the hands of a man dressed as a harlequin.

Pushing their way through the crowd ahead of him was the group of garishly dressed street performers that Tyburn had observed near the Clink, still wearing their checkered red, white, and black masks. One wearing a half mask gazed back and caught the player's eye. Tyburn saw the face twist in a lazy, contemptuous smile and turn away as they vanished in the crowd.

"Shit." Tyburn heaved a gawping bystander out of the way and pushed through the crowd, ducking and sliding sideways, one hand on his sword and the other bodily thrusting people out of his path. "Make way, you bastards! Move!" He used his best sergeant's voice as he slammed past the man on horseback and his servant, dodging a food stall and slipping past a cart stacked high with produce.

The harlequins were gone. He clambered up on the cart, raising himself above the crowded traffic. He could hear shouts behind him where Stokely's body lay bleeding out on the cobbles. There was no sign of them ahead on the bridge. Tyburn glanced about but the traffic in front continued unabated and undisturbed. Anyone running or pushing through would have disrupted the surface calm of the crowd, but it was as placid and composed as a slow-running brook.

Only one place they could have gone, the player thought, his eyes drawn to an open wooden doorway in one of the buildings. He jumped from the cart, ignoring the wealthy rider berating him. The player charged through the open door, finding himself in a small entrance room, with a shop doorway opening to the right and a narrow staircase to the left. The bridge buildings extended out over the edge of the bridge, supported on heavy thick wooden beams and buttresses, but they were still relatively narrow. There was only one direction to run. Up.

The player bounded up the stairs, pausing at the first turn to draw his dagger. In this narrow space a sword would be more hindrance than help. He stopped to listen. The thump of running feet, felt rather than heard, reverberated through the stairwell. He cursed and resumed his pursuit.

Tyburn was angry. Not so much at the assailants, but at his own foolishness in not taking Stokely's nervousness as a clear sign that there was more afoot. He had been too pleased with himself for winkling out the missing goldseller. Should have paid more heed to why the man had secreted himself in the first place, he thought.

He paused on the third landing. He could distinctly hear shouts and a distant thud above. A woman emerged from the landing behind him and shrieked, startled, before ducking back into the adjacent room and bolting the door.

The wooden staircase turned to the left and reversed roughly every twelve steps, leading the way to the next landing and floor. The stairway was dark except for a long, narrow, barred window on each landing providing a dim slant of grey light. The floorboards creaked underfoot. The player paused at each landing for an instant to listen.

The attack came on the fourth landing.

He paused, listening. He could hear the distinct noise of voices and feet stamping above, now closer, probably only two more floors. The thought that he might be deliberately drawn in flitted through his mind just as he rounded the last turn on the fourth floor. The squeak of the wooden boards behind him made him pivot and duck. The dagger thrust intended for his back slid past on his left, more by luck than design, and a red and white clad harlequin crashed into him, crushing him against the wall of the stairwell. Tyburn grunted in pain as the man's shoulder slammed him backwards. The sharp edge of the wooden stair boards grated against his back. The man's left hand slid under his chin, pushing his head back, fingers grasping at his throat, but all Tyburn could think about was the location of that cold-edged blade.

Tyburn felt the dagger in his hand slide away, as though pulled loose by a furious wind. The player's left arm shot out and blocked the man's attempt to bring his own weapon into play. Tyburn leaned to his left, trapping the man's arm against the wall, the narrowness of the staircase preventing the harlequin from ripping the weapon across Tyburn's exposed throat.

The man hissed and hammered his knee into Tyburn's groin. Again the tight confines of the fight prevented the blow from striking home as most of the force impacted the stair. Tyburn hammered his right hand upwards, vainly trying to gain some space and traction. The man pounded down again with his knee and Tyburn felt the right arm with the dagger slicing across his upper arm as the man extricated it. He could smell the man's breath, fetid and reeking of onions. Tyburn drove forward, his forehead slamming into the man's nose. He felt a crack as the lacquered half mask broke, sharp-edged shards falling onto his chest as the man fell back. Tyburn kicked one leg out, catching the man on one shoulder, sending him spinning back into the wall opposite the stair. The player looked frantically for his dagger, seeing it lying out of reach on the open landing. The man levered himself off the wall and lunged.

Tyburn caught the man's wrist and deflected the thrust to one side as the man bore him back against the staircase. He grimaced in pain as the man's hand hit him in the face and scrabbled for his throat like a wounded animal, clawing and thrashing. His right hand fell on a narrow, broken shard fallen from the shattered mask and, grasping it, Tyburn drove it into the man's left eye.

The shriek must have been heard the length of the bridge. The man reared backwards. Tyburn reached out with both hands, twisted, and reversed the man's dagger, slamming it into his stomach. The man's hands fell away after that first thrust, and Tyburn yanked the narrow blade free and stabbed again and again and again, fear giving speed to his reflexes.

A guttural moan flowed from the man as he slumped on top of the player. Tyburn pushed the man's torn body away and leaped to his feet, both hands still on the weapon, eyes seeking new assailants—but the dark stairwell remained quiet.

"Jesus." He muttered, his hands shaking and wet with blood. With a hollow clunk, the dagger fell from his hands. He picked up his own weapon from where it had fallen, stepped over the prone body of his assailant, and resumed the climb.

Chapter the Eighth

THE STAIRS ENDED on the sixth landing, with a door opening into the long room that ran the width of the house. A dead man lay slumped in a heap on the floor beside a table piled high with papers and ledgers, probably only feet from where he had risen to demand the reason for the intrusion. The man's throat was slit from ear to ear.

The room was bright and well lit by the set of broad, windowed dormers and another set of glassed windows that opened facing the westward expanse of the Thames. Tyburn glanced around and then peered out the dormer window.

It was unlatched.

He shoved the window open, pausing to listen for a moment, alert to any sound or shift in weight that might indicate someone waiting. There was nothing but the distant rumble of thunder and the cold droplets blown into the opening, marking the edge of the fast approaching storm. Tyburn scrambled out, turned and clambered up to the peak of the sloping red-tile roof. His eyes took in the long length of the bridge undulating before him, rising and falling in steep waves of slanting rooftops, all of the same tile, and tall chimney stacks. London Bridge stretched out before him with the city beyond rising in the distance, stacked and piled upon itself in smoky splendor. The Tower stood sharp and stolid to the far right, like a watchful beast squatting in its den.

They were three rooftops away, climbing out of the steep inclined valley that lay between roof peaks. Tyburn swore in Dutch and half slid, half jumped down the roof and ran up the steep incline of the next one in pursuit.

The tiles were slick and damp, and Tyburn felt his feet slip with each yard he climbed. The tiles shifted and grated, occasionally skittering away underfoot as he moved, clattering down. The downslope was faster and easier to manage, but the incline was tricky. Worse still, there was a gap between two of the buildings—a long, narrow drop that was unseen until the player was almost upon it. Only a sudden leap saved him from a long slide into darkness.

The harlequins stopped and watched as the player crossed the gap. One of them snapped his fingers, pointed at two of the gaudily dressed figures and indicated their pursuer. They nodded and both men drew swords and moved apart, waiting on the apex of the roof. The remaining three, one carrying the lockbox under one arm, turned and continued down the length of the bridge.

At the peak of the red-tiled roof, the two men waited.

Tyburn had lost sight of his quarry when he descended into the defile of the next set of roofs. When he clambered up the next peak, he saw the two men waiting for him on the rooftop beyond. The fading light gleamed on the drawn blades. Tyburn paused and for a long moment the three men faced each other across the gulf between peaks.

Tyburn glanced to the right. The roof ended with the long drop onto the stony expanse of the bridge below. Prior to the drop, another dormer stretched out into the valley between roof peaks, like a letter T, extending a good six feet. Tyburn spun and ran along the spine of the roof, turning along the dormer and launching himself across the gap, landing just shy of the neighbouring roof peak. There was no way he would have been able to successfully climb the steep slope in the face of two swords, but now he stood on the same peak as the two assailants, but with no space to retreat or backpedal. Behind lay the fatal drop onto the crowded bridge, and ahead, cold steel. He drew his sword as the men danced along the narrow roof line towards him.

The blades met with a furious ring of steel. Tyburn deflected the lead man's initial thrust and countered, his weapon pivoting against the blade, the promise of thirty-four inches of razor-edge steel bringing the assailant to a sudden halt. Tyburn drew his dagger with his left and held it low by his side.

The long peak of the roof channeled the fighters into a single line of attack. Anyone sliding off line would have a difficult time clambering up the incline, sword in hand to attack. This allowed Tyburn to engage his opponents singly, but they had the advantage of more room to retreat. The empty promise of a fall to the bridge was all that lay behind Tyburn.

Kit lunged, trying to push the men back, to gain space and ground. The lead man, his face hidden beneath the mask, parried, sliding his blade along Tyburn's and pushing the attack out of line.

A mistake.

Tyburn stepped in, his left foot sliding forward and the dagger in his left hand slicing into the meat of the man's right leg, ripping deep before Tyburn darted back. The man shrieked with pain and, off balance, fell, sliding and spinning off the peak of the roof. He landed heavily and the impact sent his sword clattering away. The man lay on the slope, holding his torn leg and rocking.

The second man held back, sword ready. The man's eyes were calm and fixed, watching Tyburn. He had removed the mask and the face that looked back at Kit was lean and harsh, the tracery of stubble giving him a barren, stripped appearance, like a field shorn down to dried stalks.

The player moved. The sword parried and countered; steel flickered as the opponent feinted. Tyburn hammered forward, pushing the blades up, slamming his shoulder into the man's chest, but his opponent danced back with deft steps and both men slipped off the peak, Tyburn to one side, his opponent to the other. Tyburn felt his boots sliding on the clay tiles and he scrambled sideways to regain the summit. He reached up and hooked the dagger on the peak to pull himself up. His eyes were level with the crown when his opponent's sword whipped out, catching the guard and lashing across his gloved hand.

Tyburn cursed and his dagger skittered away. His hand burned. He flexed it. Fingers still working, he thought. The glove had protected him from the worst damage. He shifted backwards, sword ready, intent on ending this man.

Emboldened by his success the man lunged forward. Rather than parrying or deflecting the blade, Tyburn caught it on the forte and slid down to the guard. He pushed the blades high and slammed his left hand onto the man's wrist, locking it in his grip. The player threw himself backwards, yanking his attacker over with him, using the added force permitted by the slope behind him to pitch the man overtop.

The two men hit the roof with a thunderous crash. Broken tile grated and shifted, as Tyburn, head down on the incline, tried to turn and regain his feet. The other man was on his knees, bleeding from a cut on his face from a sharp-edged fragment of tile. Tyburn shook his head and rose, the bright length of the sword still in his hand. Ignoring his weapon, he spun and slammed a brutally efficient kick into the man's midsection, sending him staggering backwards, off balance.

The man took one step too many.

His foot stepped off the edge of the roof and with a horrified, strangled screech he disappeared. The sound of the splash into the Thames was muted.

Tyburn turned. Two rooftops away, the remaining three harlequins stood watching. Tyburn was surprised they hadn't moved, seemingly content to watch the struggle as if it were a cockfight or a game of bowls. The largest of the trio had drawn his sword, but the younger one that had caught Tyburn's eye on the bridge had one hand on his companion's arm, restraining him. The player wearily began to climb the incline. By the time he reached the peak, he saw that the younger one had climbed up and was waiting, sword drawn, at the far end. He wore an elaborate black and white half mask, designed to mimic the look of a skull, the upper half decorated with silver edgings.

"Just leave the lockbox. There's been enough killing," Tyburn said.

This seemed to amuse the youth. "There is never enough killing. No matter how the Wheel turns, there are always a few more that need to die."

"Leave the lockbox and you won't be one of them. Not today."

"You know what the problem is, all these monarchs, these rich lords and ladies. Barons and sheriffs, all these fat, bovine merchants and traders. All of this rabble, rag and tag … they are afraid." The youth raised his head and looked at Tyburn. "They fear death. They fear the grim onslaught of time, the hunger of fire and the red surge of blood. They don't understand. It is as inevitable as the tide. They will all die."

"Everything dies." Tyburn replied. The cold damp of Flanders seemed to hang in the air like a shroud. The slight, almost negligible patter of rain increased in intensity.

"Yes, it does." The youth practically shouted. "Everything dies. It all turns to ash, no matter how hot the fire. The angels themselves tell us that everything that walks the earth is doomed to dust. Dying is just another path to salvation, so I serve God's work. I take my lambs to salvation." He raised his sword. "Are you seeking salvation, swordsman? I can deliver you, if you wish."

"I'm already well damned, boy. Just leave the lockbox and be on your way."

The youth in the skull mask merely laughed. Tyburn advanced with deliberation and care, keeping the others in his peripheral vision, in case they moved to flank him, but they stood stolid and uncaring as the downpour grew stronger.

When the attack came, it was fluid and smooth and faster than anything the player had ever seen. One moment the youth had been waiting with languid ease; the next a razored edge of steel was thrusting high in a feint and corkscrewing low, a blow that Tyburn barely parried. The youth riposted and Tyburn found himself being pressed back in a flurry of steel.

The cold certainty that the boy was the finest swordsman Tyburn had ever faced coursed through him in an instant. He could feel it in the touches of the blade, the hungry intensity of the steel. Tyburn parried another, almost casual, attempt to end his life, catching the blade on his guard and shoving his opponent backwards to close the distance between them. The younger man skipped back, leaving Tyburn off balance and exposed. The steel flickered and Tyburn felt a hot, stinging pain on his side as the point tore the skin and flashed deftly away.

He spun, deflecting the next attack and riposting in viciously. The attack was turned with studied indifference, and the player found himself forced backwards, towards the inexorable drop to the dark, chill waters of the Thames.

A blinding flash of lightning flared and the crack of the thunder slammed into them almost in the same instant. Tyburn blinked and feinted, bringing the tip of his weapon up in a lethal, supple movement that slid past the boy's guard. The youth slapped the blade out of line with one gloved hand and a laugh.

"Close, swordsman, close!"

The boy's blade darted in once more, this time punching deep into the muscle of Tyburn's left arm. Before his opponent could rip it loose, Tyburn hammered the pommel of his sword into the youth's face, sending him reeling backwards, the immaculate white enamel of the skull mask cracked and broken. The youth cursed and stepped quickly back, reaching up and tossed the mask to one side.

Tyburn checked himself in astonishment.

It was a woman.

The moment passed in an instant as she drew a dagger with her left hand and her sword sliced upwards in a lethal thrust the player barely parried. The dagger, used as a main-gauche, drove in from the right. Tyburn skipped back as it cut the air. The woman crouched, left leg forward, sword high and dagger held low in a lethal pose. Her eyes were dark and fixed.

Holland, the damp polders of Walcheren and Flanders, had been a brutal and merciless killing field. Mercy was a state seldom observed in the war with Spain and neither side practiced restraint or quarter. Tyburn had seen them: the cold, unpitying husks of men who found no joy in friendship or gold or drink or women. No spirit of brotherhood, friendship, anger, hatred, or rivalry seemed to stir their attention. They seemed to animate only in the face of carnage, peril, or death, like insensate puppets, banked and slumped in repose, until the strings were jerked and tugged, and the dark energy coursed through them again. Her eyes were like theirs.

The woman lunged and Tyburn sidestepped. A mistake. He felt the thick clay tile crack and shift under his back foot, pulling his extended left leg out from under him. The blade came in on a hungry wind, glimmering in the cold rain. Frantic, Tyburn threw himself flat and rolled back. The weapon cut the air just in front of his face and the player felt his legs fall away, over the edge of the high-pitched roof. His sword fell into space with a clatter.

Tyburn gasped, the muscles in his arms straining, fingers clawing at the wet roof tiles, trying to hold. The sharp edge of the roof support cracked and crumbled, and he slid another few inches. Only his head and upper torso remained on the roof. The rest of his body was suspended in space, hanging over the yawning gulf.

He could hear the tide of the Thames frothing through the stone piles of the starlings below. His muscles burned with pain. He forced his eyes upwards. The woman stood staring back at him.

She looked disappointed.

"I was so looking forward to watching your eyes as you met God's judgment." Her voice was laced with an undercurrent of amusement. "Are you sure you don't want me to just cut your throat before you go? So much cleaner than a river death."

Tyburn slid another inch as his hands slipped on the wet tile. The sinews in his arms shook. He swung his feet back and forth, trying in vain to gain some type of purchase or foothold.

She knelt in front of him and tapped one hand with the tip of the dagger. Her face was twisted in a quizzical look. "If I drove this through your hand into the roof beam, how long do you think it would take your weight to slice it completely through?" She looked at the dagger and then at Tyburn, blinking the rain out of her eyes. Tyburn heard the rumble of thunder receding, intermingled with the distant peal of bells.

"Let's find out." She stabbed down and Tyburn released his grip, feeling the yawning space beneath him opening like a hungry mouth. She seemed to float away from him in slow motion, the rain droplets splashing around her, her lips nearly smiling and her eyes as empty as those in a hollowed skull.

It seemed both infinitely slow and utterly swift at the same time. The plunge seemed to take forever until the player smashed hard into a protuberance. The force drove the breath from his body and spun him in the air. Tyburn felt as though a giant hand had reached out and caught him, although he could see through the grey fog of his vision he was still falling.

A second impact sent a flaring apparition of colour across his sight. The last thing he felt before the black, hard final impact was the rough, ripping sensation of stone raking along his back, until he hit and everything collapsed into utter darkness.

Chapter the Ninth

ON BERNARDINO DE Mendoza, *Orden militar de Santiago,* ambassador and representative of his most Catholic Majesty, Philip the Second, King of Spain, stared into the mirror and adjusted his ruff, flicking a small speck away. His servant straightened the drape of the long silken embroidered cloak that hung over one shoulder.

Mendoza silently inspected his finery in the mirror and cursed the stupidity of the English workers who had cracked his full-length looking glass. Somewhere between the ship's landing and the long cart journey to the *residencia de la embajada,* the delicate and expensive Murano glass had been dropped, leaving him with less than one third of the mirror intact. Even after having the remains re-sized and re-framed, the mirror was still better than any replacement he could obtain in England or France.

He ran his fingers along the edges of his oiled mustache and gave the end a slight curl, nodding to himself. Let the English heretics gaze upon Spain's new ambassador with respect and awe, although he suspected that most of this court of sacrilegious bastards would be sneering, secure on their cursed little island.

The servant gave Mendoza's clothing one last light brush before opening one of the boxes and removing a pair of pale, silver-threaded embroidered gloves. Mendoza took them with the same frown with which he had greeted each part of his ensemble. He was certain that the styles had changed since his arrival in London four months past; however, it was impossible to stay current with the Spanish court from this benighted posting. He had arranged for his agent in Madrid to send him court models frequently, to keep him apprised of the most fashionable wear, yet none had arrived with the infrequent post. He cursed to himself. It made little difference. The English had no sense of fashion, wearing a mix of whatever notable Flemish, French, and Spanish trends wound their way into London's singular sensibilities. It made, he thought, the English court look like a group of antics desperate to astonish or impress a credulous audience.

"Enough." He gestured for the servant to leave. The man bowed quickly and slid out through the door as one of Mendoza's aides entered the room. Mendoza shot the man a look as he gave himself one last inspection in the glass. He adjusted the gloves he had tucked into his belt and grunted at his aide. "Any word?"

"A fat, round man that smelled quite revolting left this for you." The aide handed over a small folded letter, sealed with wax.

Mendoza took the letter, checked the wax seal, and then broke it, quickly scanning its contents. He chuckled to himself, a pleased look stealing over his face.

"Good news, milord?" his aide asked.

"It appears the Moor has been dealt a blow. According to our friend in court, he will be forced to accommodate a new bird in his cockpit."

"Which bird? The one we have in hand?"

"Not in hand yet. This puts Walsingham in a difficult position. Share his spy networks and choice information, or hide it from his own Privy Council, Burghley, and Leicester. He does not have ready coin of his own to expand his nets, so if he opts to cut out our little bird, he forces his nets to become smaller and less effective. If he accommodates our friend, then his network is revealed to us and slips from his control. Either way, the Spanish Crown gains."

"Milord, I fail to see what this minor functionary can do that can trouble the might of Spain. We sit at the right hand of God. His Majesty rules Castille, Leon, Aragon, Navarre, Naples, Holland, Zeeland, Sicily, Jerusalem, Majorca, Sardinia, and the Indies. England is ripe for his plucking and no clerk can stand between Phillip and his rightful destiny."

Mendoza gave a thin smile. "*Non sufficit orbis.*[2] And yet we must do our part to make this happen, for the glory of Spain, for Pope Gregory, and for the eternal glory of God in his Heaven. Crushing Walsingham is ideal. Hobbling him, less so, but sufficient for our purposes. His agents are effective. They snatched Story from Bergen op Zoom. You think Europe did not notice and take heed? The exiles are all nervous as virgins on their wedding night, starting at every sound for fear they, too, will be abiding in the Tower and facing the justice of English heretics."

"When do we receive word if our bird is secured?"

"When the woman sends it." He grunted. "I find reliance on this Huguenot bitch troubling. She is effective, but so unpredictable."

"We use the tools that God wills us," said the aide.

Mendoza rolled his eyes. "I would that God willed us a more stable tool. I suspect her own agenda may eventually conflict with the interests of Spain."

"On that day, a misfortune may afflict her," the aide replied.

---

[2] The world is not enough – Philip II motto

Mendoza laughed. "Pray I don't send you to deliver that judgment. You have not the years or experience to handle that she-witch. No, when the time comes, we will reach out to her own people to deliver her from this world. Only one close to a Caesar can strike a truly mortal blow, and thus until that day we will abide and hope she can deliver our little bird, along with the gilded cage to chain him in. On that day, we will turn Walsingham's net into our own, and bring his heretical bitch-queen down in a blaze of hellfire." He looked at the aide. "For the glory of Spain and the True Church, of course."

The aide smiled and held open the door as Mendoza took one last glance in the looking glass, reassuring himself that everything was pristine and perfect, exactly as he had intended.

--

Francis Walsingham scanned the letter from Bordeaux for the fourth time, trying in vain to decipher the blotted writing. Rueful, he set the letter aside and rubbed his tired eyes. It was late, and reading by candlelight, even using the expensive beeswax candles that gave good light, was hard on his eyes.

The principal secretary was not happy. Both Lord Burghley and the Earl of Leicester had privately expressed reservations about the proposal to shift some of his responsibilities onto the Earl of Rutledge, but both men were publicly supporting the change. Walsingham knew they had valid political reasons for providing support to Rutledge's efforts—Burghley wanted Rutledge's and Audley's support on the Privy Council, and Leicester wanted Rutledge prevented from deepening his hold on the Exchequer and the purse. If these things had to be accomplished at the expense of Walsingham's spy network, well then, so God willed it and Master Francis had best look to his own matters.

"Charles."

"Sir?"

"Any word from Tyburn?" Walsingham asked.

"We sent a man around with a note, but no reply yet."

Walsingham frowned, a very slight deepening of his usual tight-lipped expression. "That is ... unusual. Did they check the Boar's Head? Is he with Master Oldcastle and Worcester's Men?"

"No sir, apparently not. I had Robert checking. No sign of him."

Walsingham gave a huff of exasperation. "That makes it four days."

"Nearer five, sir, given the hour."

"Anything unusual in the daily reports?"

"Nothing outstanding sir. Italian gentleman beaten and robbed near Aldgate, pair of knifings out Bishopsgate way..." He shuffled some papers. "Man apprehended passing Catholic screeds in Southwark. Fishwife nabbed for poisoning her husband. Some apprentices had a set-to outside the Lantern on Maiden Lane. Couple of dead men fished out of the Thames at Wapping, and three murders on the Bridge, near the Gate Tower."

Walsingham stared at the desk, lost in thought. The player had always been one of his most reliable agents. He couldn't fault the man for chasing new employment or pursuing some other opportunity. Walsingham had told him to make himself scarce until spring, so he could hardly blame Tyburn for his absence.

But it was troubling.

"Send a note to Oldcastle and query after Tyburn. Go yourself and don't leave without a reply."

"We could ask the Earl of Rutledge? That is where you last saw him."

"No. We won't trouble the earl with this inquiry. He has no inkling of us having any connection with Master Tyburn and I would prefer to keep it that way. Check with Oldcastle, he has his nose in everyone's business."

"You don't think he is in the earl's employment?"

Walsingham snorted. "Tyburn and Rutledge? Given the one man's stubbornness and the other's cupidity, can you see that lasting past a turn of the clock? No. If Tyburn is absent, it is some other cause. However, we may need him here, so best track him down and pull him in for a time."

"Yes sir."

"Any more correspondence?"

Charles smiled. "Nothing that cannot bide until morning, sir."

Walsingham nodded wearily. The uneasy sensation persisted that something unseen and malevolent was swimming past, just below the threshold of perception.

"Reach out to our London net. I want anything and everything they can ferret out that might be unusual or exceptional."

"Everything? That may prove to be quite a pile."

"Then you had best start on culling through it as sharp as possible. I don't know what we are seeking, but I suspect we will know it when we see it."

Chapter the Tenth

DARKNESS. NOTHING BUT damp, racking cold and thick, gluey splatters of half-frozen mud caked over boots and cloaks, sodden and clinging like a desperate child. Flanders was mud, damp, and desperation roiled into a furious blend of fire and hate. The charred scent of burning hung over the landscape like a dour cloud, seemingly immune to the brisk, wet, sea-tinged wind that locked fingers and froze toes.

The land was dead, strewn with half-rotted corpses, putrefied and decayed except for their eyes. They followed you as you walked, sharp and filled with intensity, remorse, fear and accusations. They stared as you threaded past their torn bodies, perpetually frozen in a state of rot.

They never spoke.

The dead locked your gaze as you passed. There was naught said, but the words echoed in your thoughts anyway. *There is nothing like Flanders.*

Tyburn felt himself moving. Each plodding step was heavy with glutinous mud despite the frozen ground. No matter how you averted your gaze, you lighted upon those eyes. He had tried to look up, to gaze on the encroaching darkness that surmounted the vault of the sky, but his eyes would inexorably drift downward, at the carrion-strewn field.

One set of eyes arrested him. Clear blue, vivid as a summer's day, they hooked his gaze. He drew nearer, one reluctant step at a time. The shape of the torn flesh and the half-rotted smile of greeting sent a shiver down his spine, whether of terror or gladness he could not say.

"Annika." The whisper slipped out of his lips as he saw a pale sliver of long, gold hair cascading down the shattered skull. The eyes glared back at him, impossibly blue and luminous. The mud of Flanders rose up to claim him as he slid away from the apparition. He thought he saw the gleam of a tear before the icy cold tugged him away into its embrace.

--

The dull clanking of a cattle bell woke him. He blinked and stared at the bars of sunlight that angled across the room. Dust motes spun and pirouetted slowly in the still air, caught by the long rays like dancers on a stage. The cattle bell clanked again and a squeal of a laden cart came faintly from outside. A dog barked frantically in the distance.

Christopher Tyburn winced as he turned his head. It ached abominably. He blinked. His eyes were gritty and sluggish. One hand rose unsteadily and fell back. He turned his head to take in his surroundings. He lay in a large, canopied poster bed. A low side table with a blue pitcher, bowl, and cup stood stolidly beside the bed alongside a padded chair. A fire burned low in the hearth on the far side of the room, and a heavy set of curtains framed the diamond-patterned glassed windows rimed with curlicues of frost. A large carved wooden cabinet stood in the corner.

100

A thump on the bed made him start. A large grey cat with matted fur and baleful yellow eyes sat on the end of the bed, giving him a slant-eyed glance. It picked its way carefully along the length of the bed, remaining just out of arm's reach before settling down and giving the player a look of indifferent irritation.

"Piss off," Tyburn muttered. The cat ignored him.

"I don't suppose you know where I am?" he asked the animal.

"You are where you are supposed to be. Where you belong. In my bed."

Tyburn turned his head sharply, taking in the tall, auburn-haired woman that leaned against the doorframe, her arms crossed. Clair Carey regarded the player with steady eyes, her lips curved up in a slight mocking expression.

The hair was the same. Pinned back but spilling out in artful curls and twists, framing her face and a long graceful throat. Tyburn felt his breath catch at the sight of her.

"After eight months' absence, I would have hoped for a better response," she observed.

"God's bones! What..." Tyburn paused. "What am I doing here? Where is 'here', and how did you get here?"

"You are in my London house near Cripplegate. I found you at your room. Your landlord was convinced you were about to die and was trying to decide if your books could be sold for enough to cover your burial."

"He sold my books?" Tyburn's thoughts were muddled and confused. "Why ..."

"No, I have your books. Along with your spare clothes, linens, some nasty sour wine, and your buff coat." She sat on the cushioned chair that stood beside the bedpost. "And my letters. Unopened."

Tyburn felt his chest tighten. Her pale eyes were locked on his, but they gave no trace of emotion.

"You know what I do."

"Like no other."

"I can't tar you with that. I almost caused your death once. I'll have no part in bringing that pall to your door."

She gave him an almost wistful smile. "You don't rule the Fates, Christopher, any more than I do. If you recall, last year in Warwickshire you saved my life. It was my brother and father that leavened the landscape with blood, not you."

"I killed your brother."

"And he well deserved that killing, one he brought upon himself. He had a number of souls to answer for, and you justly served God's will. I do not begrudge you that action."

The silence that followed was broken by the thump of the cat dropping off the high bed onto the floor. Tyburn tried to sit up, but his breath caught at the sharp pain that lanced through his lower back. "Jesus." He winced.

Clair leaned in and helped him struggle to a seated position, placing a thick pillow to support his back. Tyburn could smell her familiar scent and feel the touch of her arms as he struggled to pull himself up. Another momentary stabbing pain made him freeze.

"How did I get here?" he asked, his teeth clenched.

"I found you at your room. As I said, your landlord thought you were dying." She paused, frozen at the memory of his fever-racked body, shivering under thin, sweat-soaked blankets. "I can't say I disagreed with him. I had you brought here five days ago. Your fever broke early yesterday. I had a woman from Fore Street tending you, and a barber-surgeon stitched up your wounds. You've at least two cracked ribs and a swollen lump on your back, athwart your spine. Now that the fever is gone, you should mend, but you won't be in any condition for dancing for a time." Her eyes were mocking. "As for the rest, you do talk in your sleep."

"What did I say? I remember ... falling." His breath hissed out. "The bridge."

"Your landlord said a waterman helped bring you home. He spoke of fishing you off of one of the starlings."

Tyburn remembered the freezing cold rain pouring down and edged stones of the pilings against his face, covered with a slick skein of thin wet ice. He vaguely recalled the querulous face of a young boy staring down at him, eyes as wide as the moon, asking if he was dead.

"I fell off the bridge."

She nodded. "So I gathered. Fell or were thrown unwillingly, would be my assumption, but you are a bit daft at points." The corners of her lips curled up in the slightest of smiles.

"Coads." Tyburn tried to push the heavy blankets off and sit up.

"What do you think you're doing?" Clair pulled the blanket back up and pushed him back into the bed without any discernible effort. The player hissed as the stabbing pain radiated upwards from his back and side. "Christopher, you aren't in any shape to go anywhere. If you try, by God's truth, I will have you tied down. Stop being a fool." She smoothed the blanket. "After ignoring my letters, disappearing for months on end, and then making me think you were about to die, I think you owe me a bit of your company before you run off and do something foolish." Her gaze was barbed, and Tyburn, feeling the stabbing shaft of pain in his back fading, reluctantly nodded.

"Now get some rest. We'll try some mutton soup later, see if you can start keeping some food down." She stood up and Tyburn caught a momentary flash of relief in her expression, her eyes darting away as though reluctant to linger on him. Tyburn nodded, feeling the ache of his muscles pulling at him. He watched her turn to the door. Just before she passed through, he called out.

"Clair." She paused. "I didn't open the letters because I didn't want to let myself fall into that hope again."

"As I said, stop being a fool. *Amor, ch'a nullo amato amar perdona* ...[3]" She gave him a smile and vanished from the doorway,

---

[3] "Love, which absolves no loved one from loving" - Dante

leaving only the lingering scent of her perfume floating on the winter air.

--

It was three days before Tyburn was able to swing his legs over the edge of the high bed and hobble to the chamber pot without assistance. He pulled off the nightshirt and took an inventory. His left side was a vivid arrangement of bruised and abraded flesh. A short set of neat black stitches marked the spot where the harlequin's blade had torn into his side. He ran his hand over his lower back, feeling the half-healed scabbing of torn skin where his back had raked along the stony face of the bridge starling when he fell. Another set of stitches trailed down from his right hip, marking where he had been torn open by the fanged stones. Gingerly he examined the swollen lump on his lower back with his fingertips. It had begun to shrink but any sudden movement left him with an excruciating flare of pain that radiated into his side.

Tyburn cursed. Stokely's death on the bridge nagged at him like a sore tooth. He had dragged the poor man from his hide for the sake of a handful of shillings, and then marched him to his death like a calf to a shambles.

"Well enough to start fretting, I see."

Tyburn turned his head. Clair stood in the doorway. "Your barber seems to have been adequate at stitching. No rot, that I can see."

"You can thank the mid-wife for that. She took one look and slathered on the poultices. They seem more effective than most of the other doctoring."

Tyburn shrugged his nightshirt back on.

"You're thinner," she observed.

"Couple of weeks living on shipboard food does that to you." He looked at her. "Should I even be here? Won't your neighbours talk?"

Clair shrugged. "Let them talk. I'm a respectable widow. Whom I take into my home as a boarder is my business. They may buzz about it at church, but I provide enough coin to the bishop to gain surcease from any nonsense."

"I need to leave soon."

"You don't."

"Clair ..."

"You don't. You can barely hobble across the room, you've no coin, no clothing, and no roof over your head. They'd find you dead in a laystill within three days, and I for one, have no overwhelming desire to pay extra for digging a grave in still-frozen ground. You stay."

"I had forgotten how God-damned stubborn you were."

"And I'd forgotten just what a ten-shilling fool you could be when you think you're responsible for something." She flared. "Since you are now my guest, you can spin me the tale of how you ended up tumbling off London Bridge, and of your grand adventures in the Lowlands that you so carefully failed to mention."

Tyburn sat back with a rueful expression on his face. He should know better than to brook an argument with her. His memory flashed back to the tangled, scarlet-sheeted visage that had greeted him at the estate in Warwickshire, at the bloody denouement of her father's plot. His preference was to remember her face in the ruined Charlecote barn, eyes tightly closed, her body rocking against his, her breath and lips locked on his.

He pulled himself away from the dangerous territory his thoughts were straying into and began to talk.

It took a surprisingly lengthy time to spin his tale. By the time he finished, recounting what he remembered of the fight with the harlequin on the bridge, and the fall into blackness, Clair's face had passed through a dozen expressions, ending with a thoughtful, far-away gaze.

"Do you have any idea who these people were?"

"I have my suspicions."

She tapped her leg with impatience. "Clearly they knew you were coming to pull this man out of the prison. How could they have known beforehand?"

Tyburn shrugged. "Only two ways—they could have picked me up when I was roving Maiden Lane, the way Covington did, and followed me. Or someone told them where I was going and they were lying in wait."

"Who knew you were bound for the Clink?" Clair asked.

"Oldcastle, Burbage, and Brayne were the only people who knew, but God knows who they might have sounded off to in conversation."

"Anyone else?"

"Naught that I can think of." He paused, trying to recollect the events of the day, and closed his eyes, trying to think. "Dark hair."

"Dark hair? And she was pretty I suppose?"

"Not a her. A clapperdudgeon, a beggar. Dark hair, palsied arm. I tossed him a penny by the goldsmiths' hall ... and I saw the same man near the Clink."

"You're certain? I could walk out the door and find three dark-haired, palsied beggars within any two streets."

"That's my watcher. Beggars don't shift. They work particular spots, particular crowds. This one was watching Maiden Lane for anyone hunting a certain missing goldseller. Not likely he would choose that time to re-locate to Southwark. He must have identified me to the harlequins when he spied my arrival at the Clink. They were waiting when we emerged."

"So there you have it!" Clair clapped her hands together in mock triumph. "You just need to find the one dark-haired, palsied beggar in London and have a word with him. Your Sisyphean tasks are resolved."

Tyburn snorted. "I know who the spotter was. I still don't have any idea how they knew and who they are, but I know someone that might." He rubbed his hand over his unshaven cheeks, feeling the heavy stubble of the last week and the thin, ropy scar that hooked up the left one, courtesy of a Spanish blade.

"It can wait." Clair's tone that brooked no disagreement.

The player nodded. "Given they dropped me off a bridge, it might be best if I stayed dead for a time. Does anyone know I'm here?"

Clair shrugged. "My servants, the barber-surgeon, and the mid-wife, but none of them know your name or the circumstances. I haven't passed any word to Oldcastle or Master Walsingham, if that's your concern."

Tyburn winced at the thought of having to unravel his current circumstance under Walsingham's implacable gaze. "Let's leave me a corpse for a time, at least until I get an idea of how all these rivers run."

"Good. It's settled. Now get back into that bed and rest. You're as pale as a shroud." She opened the cabinet and fished out a book. "This should help keep you occupied. How's your Italian?"

"Non-existent," the player responded drily.

"A shame, it's much better in the original. But have no fear. God willing, I will translate and we shall see if that ridiculously hard head of yours survived its drop from the bridge."

"I'm trapped in this bed with a madwoman for a nursemaid," Tyburn groused.

"It's seems quite odd that the only time I can get you stay in my bed for any period is when you are too injured to flee." She pretended to frown, but Tyburn thought he detected a bare flash of steel in her voice. He settled back into the pillows and gestured for her to continue.

"Since you revel in your ignorance of Italian poets, I am going to introduce you to my personal favourite." She settled herself onto the chair and thumbed open a well-worn volume. "*Nel mezzo del cammin di nostra vita* ... Midway upon my life's journey, I found myself astray in a dark wood, having lost the true path."

"Are you trying to make a point?" the player asked.

"You were whipped regularly by your schoolmasters, I expect," Clair noted. "This is the story of a man's journey through Hell, Purgatory, and Paradise. It may provide you with some necessary guidance in your circumstances."

"By truth, it may." Tyburn grinned. "But God and I aren't really on speaking terms."

"At the rate you heal, we will have barely passed Hell by the time you are up and about."

Tyburn gestured for her to continue, content to listen to her voice rising and falling in a slow, hesitant cadence as she translated the work.

"What was this savage forest, rough and untamed, in which fearful thoughts renewed? So bitter is it, death is little more …"
Tyburn closed his eyes and let her soft voice carry him off to sleep.

Chapter the Eleventh

COVINGTON DIPPED THE thick crust of bread into the pottage and pushed the sodden portion into his mouth, pausing to pick a small piece of unidentifiable gristle out of the bowl with his fingers. He flicked it away onto the rush-covered floor and took a deep draught of ale.

He sat in a back-alley ordinary near Sermon Lane, hidden away from the bustle and hubbub of St. Paul's. The ordinary catered mainly to the apprentice printers, bookbinders, and sellers that jammed the streets around the Stationer's Company. At this time of day, most of the apprentices were still hard at work, but given another hour, the little ordinary would be dense with blue-smocked apprentices eating, drinking, and carousing. Until that time, its darkened recesses were a welcome refuge.

He pushed the wooden bowl away and leaned against the wall, feeling the uneven timber pressing against his back. In the weeks since Stokely had turned up dead on London Bridge, he had watched with caution as Rutledge began to disintegrate before his eyes. The earl had always been arrogant, over-confident, and controlling, someone who walked in certainty of the divine benefice of his power and influence.

And now the ground had tumbled out from under him.

Rutledge's fury at the news of Stokely's death had been breathtaking. He had spent that fury hurling abuse on his mistress and his queans, leaving Bristow with the unhappy task of escorting the bruised and blackened girls back to their stews and placating their masters with gold.

Rutledge spent more rage damning Tyburn, to the point of ordering Covington and Bristow to hunt him down, castrate him, and let him bleed out on the streets. Covington sighed in exasperation. He eventually pointed out to the earl that the player hadn't been seen or heard since and was probably dead at the bottom of the Thames, so any vengeance would be better directed at finding Stokely's disastrous paper legacy rather than hunting the wayward actor.

Covington drummed his fingers on the table in thought. He was surprised that Tyburn hadn't been successful. The player had struck him as competent and sharp. He had seen him in action at Goes; the man was a deadly and efficient swordsman. None of the street rufflers that Asquith hired were anything but back-alley thieves and roaring boys. Either the player had been taken by surprise, or something else was lurking in Asquith's back pocket.

The door to the ordinary opened with reluctance. An abundance of cold wind danced through the yawning opening as two men pushed their way inside. Covington sat up, his eyes sharp. His right hand slid under the table and hefted the ungainly wheellock pistol that lay across his knees. He cocked the dog and slid his finger along the trigger, careful to keep the barrel elevated. The shot was wrapped in cloth to keep it from rolling back out the end of the barrel if the weapon was tilted down, but he took no chances. Best if the shot sat firm and tight against the charge.

The men walked across the ordinary with the swaggering exaggerated gait born of false confidence.

"You got our gelt, cullion?"

With his left hand, Covington tossed a leather bag onto the floor beside the table. It landed on the rushes with an audible thump and clink that would have turned heads had the ordinary not been deserted.

"Two hundred angels, fallen from heaven. Don't be banting about."

"Do we need to count it?" The speaker had yellowed, uneven teeth that sat in his face like a poorly cobbled roadway, framed by a dark, unkempt beard that ended well below his neck.

"I have my doubt that you could manage the sums once you ran out of fingers. Why don't you trust to our agreement, take it, and absent yourselves."

The sound of the man's blade being tugged from its sheath faded into silence at mid-draw. Covington had tilted the hexagonal barrel of the wheellock upwards, resting the dark open end of the barrel on the table edge. "You can draw it. I've seen shot at this range tear clean through a man. It's a sight."

"There's two of us. You might get one, but t'other will settle your guts before you can draw."

"That's why I invited a friend." The harsh metallic snap made the two men stiffen. Bristow stepped out from the shadows, a squat grinning menace with a cocked wheellock in one hand and a tankard of ale in the other.

"Pick up your coin, you bastards, and bugger off or I will shoot you in the stones and laugh while you bleed."

The man cursed and nudged his companion. "Scarp it up, you bullock. Let's go. We'll see you in again soon for another," he added to Covington, lips drawn back in a humourless smile. The two men retreated out the door of the ordinary and Covington carefully eased back the dog on the pistol until it was resting again.

"The boys on 'em?" Covington asked Bristow as the stubby man pulled a stool over to the table, setting his pistol and ale down with care. Bristow nodded and flashed three fingers, pointed at his eyes, and then made a rapid walking motion with his left-hand fingers.

Three watchers, following in turns.

Covington nodded. Bristow pointed at the bowl of pottage inquiringly. When Covington nodded, the man tore a thick chunk of bread off the loaf and began wolfing down the remaining pottage with gusto.

This was the third payment they had been forced to hand over.

It was odd, thought Covington. He could understand someone using the leverage obtained from Stokely's books to extort Rutledge, but he couldn't understand why it was such an insignificant, petty amount. Two hundred angels came to only about one hundred pounds. It was more than Covington earned in a year, but Rutledge spent that much on wine. Rutledge would cheerfully lose more in an offhand bet on a tennis match or how a throw of bowls would turn.

It was strange. Every contact, every payment increased the danger to the blackmailers. A clever man would demand one or two very large payments, and then run or vanish into the ether to avoid Rutledge's inevitable retribution. Either whoever was behind this blackmail had no comprehension of Rutledge's true worth, or this misadventure was moving in an unforeseen direction.

Covington shook his head, remembering Rutledge's ashen face when the first letter arrived, accompanied by a single page torn from Stokely's ledger. If the blackmailer was looking to drive the man over the thin edge of reason and temper, he was proceeding down the right path.

Covington took a long pull at his ale, uneasy. For a moment, he thought he saw a hint of design, a skeletal thread suggesting that maybe the purpose was not money but some other plot, with Rutledge being only part of a larger enterprise.

Whenever we find out, there will be blood in the streets for certain.

Chapter the Twelth

"THAT BRAZEN-FACED, beggarly bastard."

Clair choked back a laugh. "Don't mince your words, tell me what you think."

Tyburn leaned back in the saddle and surveyed the construction of Burbage's Theatre. The exterior of the building was almost complete, barring some additional plastering that remained to be daubed on the thick lattice of wattle panels walling the areas between supporting posts and crossbeams. A small gang of nimble-footed workers was busily tying and layering thick bundles of thatch over the steeply angled frames and crossbeams roofing the galleries. Their casual movements at dizzying heights made the player wince.

A hammering din from within the structure bespoke more workers laboring to complete interior fixtures and staging. By the entrance lay a pile of crushed ragstone, used to gravel the performance yard for the groundlings.

"I thought you said Burbage was having money problems." Clair's voice was impassive but with just the barest hint of amusement.

Tyburn grimaced sourly. "It appears that tide has reversed itself."

"Could Burbage have been responsible for the attack on the Bridge?" she asked.

Tyburn shook his head. "Not his style. He's all wind and whistles. But I am curious how he's managed this turnaround. With Stokely dead and the accounts gone, his purse was empty."

"You're certain?"

"If Burbage decided to drop me, he'd hire some tavern rufflers. Cheaply. These people were an entirely different quality." He tugged on the reins and turned the horse towards Hog Lane. The two rode in silence until Hog Lane opened up beyond the tall bare elms that lined Curtain Road. Clair angled her horse to the left, spurring it across the ditch and up the low slope into the frozen patchy sward of Finsbury Fields.

Tyburn felt a momentary stitch of pain that stiffened his lower back as his horse followed. It had taken another week of bed rest before the player had found himself able to move without wincing at every movement like some ancient cart-man. They had, as Clair had threatened, barely completed their Italian literary journey through Hell. Purgatory and Paradise would have to wait, Tyburn thought. He had spent enough time abed.

"Do you think Oldcastle might have told someone?" Clair asked.

"Oldcastle's been cogging and foisting for years, but strange as it may sound, he doesn't backstab a friend."

"He detests you."

Tyburn grinned, the first genuine smile Clair had seen since he had arrived. "He doesn't like being told what to do. When the earl dropped me into Worcester's Men, Oldcastle did his level best to drive me out. It didn't work. Now he treats me like the neighbourhood cur. I may be the dog he likes to kick, but I'm his dog. No, Oldcastle wouldn't turn me over. It was almost certainly Burbage. He's flush, where before he was skint. But I need to know more before I have a conversation with our theatre impresario. I need to know about the harlequins."

"Where do we look next?"

"The hawks of St. Paul's."

--

The woman eased her path through the dense crowds that thronged in the western entrance to the nave of St. Paul's. She paused for a moment in the entryway to scan the handbills plastering the tall, curved wooden doors. Legal notices warred with advertisements, tracts and pamphlets, treatises and meeting notices, and the ragged remains of a Catholic screed, torn bodily from its nails, a quarter page dangling like a lonely autumn leaf.

She was tall and graceful, wearing an expensive dress of simple design and a black widow's hood over her hair. A sprig of rosemary was pinned to one sleeve, advising the world in general of her widowed status. She walked through the portico into the nave, the high vaulted ceiling soaring above. The woman stared about, wide-eyed at the vast, spacious interior and the bustling passersby.

It took Clair two long, meandering trips through the crowded stretch of the nave, fending off the advances of several overdressed bravos and merchant-traders, before she spotted her quarry. The young man in question wore a broad-brimmed feathered hat, tilted to a rakish angle. A short, blue-dyed lace ruff encircled his throat and a fur-edged cloak hung over the dark red, yellow, and pearl jacket, all of which had the dilapidated look of a decrepit building, softening around the edges, wilting from time and boggy ground.

Clair paused near the young man, lingering with a look of utter confusion on her face. As expected, the momentary pause drew the man like a hound coursing a fox. She could almost feel his eyes widening.

"Milady, you look like you are in need of some assistance. Mayhaps I can provide you some aid?"

Clair glanced at him for the barest of an instant before turning away. "Thank you, but I can manage on my own." Even in that brief pause, she could see the vulpine look in his eyes as he noted the quality of the cloth, the widow's hood, and the rosemary sprig.

"Please, milady, it is not seemly for a woman of quality such as yourself to be bereft of assistance on St. Paul's Walk. How can I help you? Do you seek a particular merchant or gentleman?"

Clair stopped and let her face fall visibly. "I am seeking a man named Infortunas Hastings. He is, apparently, holding a number of accounts on behalf of my late husband, a part of his investment in this Muscovy Company. This—cur," she sputtered, "has refused to acknowledge my letters or respond to my imprecations. I have taken it upon myself to venture from Sleford to London, to beard this scoundrel and take possession of my husband's ventures. Only I cannot find him."

"Unfortunately, cads and scoundrels thrive in St. Paul's Walk. Did your late husband describe the man? By the light, I would be pleased to assist you in your endeavor."

Clair turned towards him, allowing a moment of hope to lift her expression before she turned away. "La, you mock me sir. You are one of these ruffians of St. Paul's I have been warned of so oft. You do not care what fate becomes a widow in the harshness of the world."

The young man drew himself up, bristling. "Milady, you wrong me. God's blessed will has brought me to you today. I never frequent the Walk. It is Fate's turn that has brought me here today, nothing less. If you scorn my assistance in your pursuit, then that is your choice." He pulled his fur-trimmed cloak over one arm.

Clair reached out and grasped his hand. "Your pardon, I am distraught and unmanageable in my grief." She took a deep breath. "I ... do wish your assistance. I do need help. London is so ... full. I know not where to turn. Please, tell me your name?"

"I am Reginald Percy, at your service."

"What would you advise, Master Percy?"

His hand slid down to cover hers. His touch was warm and reassuring. "I do know a man—well-connected with the trading companies—who undoubtedly is familiar with your Hastings of the Muscovy Company. He also wears the coif at the Inns of the Court and can place any necessary legal actions. He would be best to meet with directly ..." He hesitated and glanced downward.

"What?"

"He is not a man of generous nature. He would require payment for his actions and his advice."

"Oh." Clair pulled her hand away. "I have my jewelry still. It would fetch a decent price, probably more than thirty shillings I would expect. Would that suffice?"

The young man's expression remained utterly unchanged, but Clair could see that the hook was well set.

Clair spun out the lengthy and rather grandiose tale of her late husband's reckless spending and profligate investments for the better part of twenty minutes, leading the young man out of St. Paul's down the streets to within a stone's throw of the Thames to Barkley's Inn, an unimpressive, run-down inn-yard that had seen better days. She paused on the doorstep.

"Perhaps you should wait here. It would not be seemly to have you entering my private room." He nodded his assent and waited while Clair disappeared up the narrow staircase.

His smile of anticipation froze as the sharp blade pricked the skin just above the wilted blue ruff.

"Hello Chaucer." Kit Tyburn stepped out of the darkened alcove near the door, the long blade balanced easily in one hand. Chaucer could feel the tip of the blade delicately tracing a shivering path before coming to rest adjacent to his ear.

"Christ ..." he whispered. "Thought you were dead."

"I rose. Upstairs." Tyburn gave the young thief a push and Chaucer stumbled up the uneven wooden steps. By the time they reached the upper landing and a smiling Clair opened the door to the room, he had recovered some of his composure.

The young thief tumbled into a chair as Tyburn bolted the door behind them.

"Glad to see you upright, Kit."

"You're sweating, Chaucer. You unwell? Caught some flux?" The pale face darted from Tyburn to Clair and back again. "You should uncover for the lady." Tyburn snatched the rakish hat off Chaucer's head and tossed it into the corner of the room.

"Easy, Kit."

"Where did you hear I was a corpse?"

"That's not on me and you know it!"

Tyburn leaned over the table, tapping the long dagger blade on the scarred wooden table surface, his eyes locked on Chaucer.

The man flinched. "Word was that you took a blade and went off a bridge jetty into Thames."

Tyburn pulled out a chair, the legs scraping against the rushes on the floor. He sat. "Who passed the word?"

"Kit ..."

"Who passed the word, Chaucer?"

"I can't be blowing on this—"

"Who?" The shout made Chaucer freeze, his face stricken.

"It were the Castle." The whisper was barely audible.

"The Castle? You mean the Tower?"

Chaucer gave an audible snort of derision. "No, you geck. Not the fucking Tower. The Castle. Autolycus and his crowd. Thieves' Castle."

Tyburn sat back, regarding Chaucer with curious eyes. "Who are they?"

"That'll take more than just your poxed threats. Anyone winnows out I crossed the Castle, I'm caulked."

A pair of silver coins spun across the table. One caught in a groove and spun towards Chaucer, who snatched it up in reflex. Clair smiled down the length of the table. "No threats. Just answer the questions, please."

Chaucer regarded Clair with a wary glance and then nodded at her, throwing a quick glare at Tyburn. "There's some that ought learn some regard and manners in how they ask."

Tyburn sighed wearily. "Answer the questions, Chaucer, or I swear I will shove those coins down your gullet and you will be pawing through your shit for a week searching for them."

"The Castle runs the west thoroughfares—Newgate and Aldgate, holds Smithfield and clear to Holborn Bridge. All the filchmen, the beggars, priggers … everyone on the vagrant or the sly pays their tax."

Tyburn leaned back and sheathed the dagger. "That's news. I thought I knew most of the Roaring Boys."

"You been out of London a lot this year past. The Castle used to just run the filchmen and beggars out of the Saracen's Head, but they've been … expanding."

"Expanding?"

"The Castle was run by this Huguenot exile, owned the Saracen's Head Inn, without Newgate. Name of Benoît Thieves. He blew off like a north wind about three years back, nary a sign or a hint where." He paused. "And she took over."

"She?"

"Name's Suzanne Martaine. They call her the Harlequin."

"And?"

Chaucer grimaced, his face waning in the dim light. "You don't cross the Harlequin. Not for love nor silver. You can find out what you need about her on your own, don't rook me in, Kit, s'truth."

"What would Thieves' Castle want with Stokely's books?"

"By Christ's Bones, how should I know? I don't mix with that lot. I pay my gelt and they let me ply my trade. All the hawks of St. Paul's pay the Castle."

"And the rest of the Roaring Boys?"

Chaucer gave a sour grin. "They hate the bitch, but they're afraid of her. And you should be too. Unpredictable. Feral. She's the butchering kind."

Tyburn gestured towards the door. "Keep your mouth closed about me being alive, Chaucer."

Chaucer nodded, bending to retrieve his fallen hat. He picked the remaining coin off the table and waved a thanks to Clair. He turned to the door and stopped. "Don't let the Harlequin know about your friend there. Bitch goes where you're most vulnerable and she'll draw anyone close to you."

Tyburn gave the thief a skeptical look.

"How do you think she grabbed so much prime turf in such a short time?" Chaucer spat. "She's done at least three I know of, maybe more. Don't underestimate her. She's not ... what anyone should ever be. Don't be pulling on me anymore, Kit, we're done."

He closed the door behind himself.

"You do have the most peculiar friends," Clair observed.

"Met him at Cambridge, before I left for Flanders. He spent most of his time cony-catching everyone in earshot."

"What did he mean by 'she'll draw anyone close to you'?"

"As in 'drawn and quartered'."

"Ahh. A light dawns. Now what?" she asked.

"Now I chase down the Castle."

"Why?" Clair demanded. The blank look on Tyburn's face in response increased her ire. "Why do you care? Stokely's dead but Burbage obviously received his due—from the Castle, clearly, but he has what he needs, so why bother to chase down these thieves? You don't give a tuppence for Lord Rutledge. You are alive, when you clearly shouldn't be, but I doubt the Castle will care as you aren't relevant to them anymore with Stokely dead and his books in their hands. So I ask it again—why?"

Tyburn visibly paused before responding. She could see she had struck a nerve. The scar on his cheek was a thin, questioning white line against the red of his controlled anger. "He was in my care when they killed him. That has to be answered."

"Why? Stokely won't care, he's moldering in a pit by now. Is it pride? They beat you, tossed you off a bridge and now you're angry? Humiliated?" Her face looked wind-blown and her eyes as sharp as needles. She reached out with one hand. "You don't need to do this. You don't. It's pointless." She kept her hand extended. "You can stay with me. We can be together. You don't need to go on rolling stones uphill. Just don't. Don't."

Tyburn sat down and took her hand, his fingers gripping her warm palm. "I asked you if you knew who I was and what I do."

"You did."

"I don't do this for Walsingham. I do this work because I'm good at it." He gripped her hand tighter. "I left people behind me in Flanders, some living, most dead. And I swore not to allow myself to be bearer of that burden again. I've too many bloody haunts tailing me, too much weighing on what's left of my soul. I'm too damned to let this kind of murder go unmarked. Stokely's gone. But I'm not. And his death was my fault. It marks me."

"You are a fool," Clair observed, her tone bleak.

"Yes. A verifiable antic, a poor one, by Oldcastle's measure." This brought the slightest of smiles to Clair's face.

"So now you chase down the Castle."

"Yes."

"But not at this moment. It needs planning ... and new clothes. You go straight at these people and you will be back in the river before nightfall."

"I also need a good sword." Tyburn smiled.

"That I can help you with." She leaned in and kissed him hard on the mouth.

Chapter the Thirteenth

CHRISTOPHER TYBURN LEANED against the cartwheel and gazed along the crowded, slop-coated roadway. A recent spate of warm rain and intermittent sun had temporarily loosened winter's iron hold on the ground, turning the once near-frozen mud and offal into a malodourous trap for the unwary. He let his gaze drift through the mass of people that ebbed and flowed along Snow Hill and Cocke Lane. Holborn Bridge funneled much of London's west commercial traffic through this intersection. Cattle and sheep were bound for Smithfield Market and the shambles, while merchantry and fashionable goods trundled down Snow Hill past St. Sepulchre through Newgate and into London proper.

Holborn was thick with inn-yards and drinking establishments, and Snow Hill was dense with rambling tenements strewn through grimly shadowed winding laneways that branched off in myriad directions, twisting and turning back upon themselves. The stench of blood and offal hung in the air despite the season, wafting down from Smithfield and radiating off of the waste-thickened waters of the Fleet River.

Tyburn had spent much of his morning in the Three Tuns, casting about for snatches of overheard conversation or information. Weary of the dense air and denser ale and with little to show for his efforts, the player had changed tactics.

Kit shifted his weight and squinted against the uncharacteristically bright December sunshine. He was accompanied by a worn, squalling cart and an equally worn, ancient pony, borrowed from Clair Carey's modest household, along with two empty water barrels and one of her grooms. He had stopped alongside the Holborn water conduit, which lay a long stone's throw from his objective, the Saracen's Head Inn.

At first glance, the Saracen's Head was strange.

The inn had a stiff, decrepit look from the street, its relatively narrow frontage belying a much larger edifice that twisted, widened, and warped behind the neighbouring structures. It clambered upwards in a ramshackle fashion, gabled ends projecting outwards, each successive level or half-level overhanging the previous until the building loomed over its neighbours. Each subsequent floor seemed to be a victim of an almost cancerous growth, bulging at odd angles and directions, a haphazard assemblage of pieced-together materials that somehow, against all reason, had become a building.

The player had been watching the inn-yard for almost an hour, first from the water line at the conduit, waiting alongside other cobs to fill tankards and barrels, and afterwards, lazily leaning on the cart, pretending to drink from a wineskin and playing cross and pile with Clair's groom, like any of a dozen desultory apprentices within sight.

The inn-yard had the typical appearance and traffic of any inn on a busy London thoroughfare. The entrance to the yard was a cobbled gate between two buildings that led into the inn-yard proper, like a keep comfortably ensconced within its fortress walls.

A heavy wooden sign depicting a scowling, vaguely Moorish face topped with a winding turban hung above the laneway entrance.

Nothing appeared any different than with any other London establishment.

Then the sword caught his eye.

The elaborate tarnished silver basket and guard, topped by thirty-four inches of razor sharp Toledo steel was as familiar to Tyburn as his own hands. He could still see the expression of panic on the face of the young Spanish officer as Kit slammed through the open doorway of the Spanish guardpost at the head of the English assault on Goes, ripping the lethal blade of the shortened pike he carried through a scarred Spanish sergeant's throat with almost laughable ease.

There is nothing like Flanders.

The young officer died, despite his screaming protestations. The hungry silvered rapier had passed to a new owner; Tyburn carried it through the next two years of carnage, at first reveling in the lethality and balance of the weapon, before the slow, deadening of his soul gradually purged him of any sense of victory. The sword was now a scar, a memory long carried but his nonetheless, to be carried close, alongside the recurrent pain and nightmare-tinged sleep.

The blade lay on the hip of a tall heavyset man who walked with a familiar lope the player had last seen on a clay-tiled rooftop. This was the man that had carried Stokely's lockbox.

Tyburn watched as the man, accompanied by two others, strode past the entrance of the Saracen's Head before turning into a small nondescript doorway. The player waited patiently for another thirty minutes, but no one emerged. Gathering up the groom, he led the cart and horse back up Cocke Lane. They stopped just short of the bustling chaos of Smithfield. Tyburn tossed the cheap coverlet he was wearing into the cart and peeled off the blue apprentice's smock borrowed from one of Clair's neighbours. He pulled on an expensive-looking dark-grey sleeved doublet, embroidered with faded yellow stitching and reinforced with embossed tan leather panels. According to Clair, her late husband had favoured it while hunting, a fact that suited the player's predatory mood. A thick traveller's cloak and a flat, short-brimmed hat completed the look of a well-travelled merchant or factor.

The player reached behind the water barrels and unrolled a long, cylindrical cloth wrap to reveal a cheap *spada da lato* sidesword that James Carey had once owned. It was dull and shorter than the Spanish-style rapier that Tyburn preferred, but Carey had not been a man of swords. From the few times Clair had spoken of him, he seemed to have been a peaceable, kind man, one that rarely carried any weapon except when hunting or at public functions.

A good man, Tyburn thought ruefully, a sad day for Clair to lose a good man and gain a wastrel.

Tyburn waved the groom off to return to Clair's household while he turned back towards the Saracen's Head.

In his experience, people generally saw what you wanted them to see. In this case, it was another road-weary traveller ambling through the inn-yard gate and into the common room for a drink and a bowl of savoury pottage. The common room was busy, thick with conversation and discussion, rich with the smells of hoppy ale, unwashed visitors and smoke. Small groups sat huddled around various tables and benches, laughing and shouting. The day was wearing on, and for some, this was the end of a laborious road or an arduous workday. Tyburn sat at a bench at the end of a long trestle table, accompanied by a small set of Sussex merchants who, from their muttered attempts at conversation, appeared to deal mainly in clay and glassware.

The player had a clear view of the interior entrance to the inn and the narrow staircase that led to the upper stories. He sipped his ale, nodded blithely at the Sussex merchants' complaints, and watched the steady stream of custom ebb and flow like the tides.

Tyburn froze, his gaze arrested by the sight of a thick-set man hunched over a plate several tables away.

It was Bristow.

Covington's mute assistant was seated with his back to the wall, the narrow bench angled to face the same entrance and stairwell that Tyburn was watching, probably the only reason that he hadn't noticed the play-actor. Bristow tilted his head, eyes gleaming under the brim of a fat shapeless hat as three men descended the narrow stairs with clattering steps. A fourth man descended behind them more slowly, a richly embroidered blue and silver cloak hanging off one arm. The three men shoved their way past those standing in the narrow entrance. The first two exited while the third man held the door and gestured for the well-dressed gentleman to precede him. The gentleman paused on the landing and called back up the stairs, giving an ostentatious bow and a lascivious smile to an unseen party above before hooking his cloak around his neck and stepping out into the cold winter air.

Bristow was up and moving before the door had closed, head down, bulling through the crowd, following the group. Kit weighed the situation and drained his drink, following him. The player paused at the entrance and shot a quick glance up the staircase, catching a momentary glimpse of a sharp-featured, dark-haired woman in profile moving away from the landing. Tyburn turned away and followed Bristow through the door into the cold late-afternoon wind.

The well-dressed gentleman was mounted on an expensively saddled jennet, which stepped delicately through the inn-yard gate and out onto the road to Holborn Bridge. The three men preceded him and for the first time Tyburn noted that they were all armed, two with swords and the third, leading the procession, carrying a long iron-tipped pole. Tyburn watched as they threaded through the late-afternoon road traffic, with Bristow nonchalantly pacing thirty strides behind, slipping expertly in and out of the crowds.

The player followed the odd procession as it passed over Holborn Bridge and turned down Shoe Lane, angling south past St. Andrew Holborn Church. Tyburn guessed they were heading down to the Thames and whichever edifice the well-dressed gentleman called his own. Given the man's age and attire and the expensive Moorish horse, Tyburn guessed he had just seen the earl of Asquith, though what such a one was doing in a down-market ale-bush like the Saracen's Head was questionable at best.

So … keep picking at this particular clyster, or go back to the familiar? The player considered for a short time. Covington's man seemed to have this group well in hand, so Tyburn turned back to resume his watch on the Saracen's Head.

Grey clouds had swept in from the west, occluding the now wan and tepid daylight. The street traffic had thinned out considerably as shops were shuttered, makeshift stalls taken down or emptied and the dinner hour approached.

Tyburn headed past the inn-yard, angling down the road in the direction of Newgate, when he heard the voice.

"That's him."

Kit spun at the sound, recognizing Chaucer's distinctive slurred cadence. The young thief stood behind a stout younger man holding a drawn poniard. He was flanked by the two men Tyburn had seen disappearing into the Saracen's Head earlier.

"Well, cully, you got stones on you, to be banting about here." The man with the poniard leaned in, his breath sour behind ragged and blackened teeth. The long blade hung four inches from the base of Tyburn's throat. The look on his face was a mixture of unbridled satisfaction and a gleam of anticipation. "That poncy draw-latch says you've been asking about the Castle?"

"You know, you really need to be either closer in or farther out to be effective." Tyburn commented.

The man's face twisted in confusion. "What?"

The player slapped both hands together in a sudden motion, capturing the man's hand that loosely held the hilt of the poniard. Tyburn's left foot lashed out and down in a sharp kick to the man's right shin. The man's hand instinctively pulled back in response to the grab and the player twisted his wrist, reversing the poniard point upwards and sending it slicing back with both hands. The weapon ripped and gouged alongside the man's left cheek, flensing through skin and flesh. The man shrieked and fell backwards onto the muddy stone, one hand clutching at the sudden spurt of red.

Tyburn pivoted and ran.

He wasn't familiar with the neighbourhood, but he knew his only chance would be trying to lose his pursuers in the myriad laneways, alleys and turnabouts that lay scattered in the area bordered by the Fleet and the city walls. If he could angle south past the Old Bailey to Ludgate and leave his pursuers far enough behind, he could easily vanish in the maze of crowded streets.

He could hear the slap of feet on the roadway behind him as he ducked past an elderly woman carrying a laden basket. He barely noted her startled imprecations as he cut down a laneway, past a crowded ordinary milling with blue-smocked apprentices.

"Clubs! Clubs!" Tyburn shouted as he ran past the alehouse. "Prentices, clubs! Clubs! Clubs!"

It started as a trickle, with a handful of blue-clad apprentices stepping out into the laneway, glancing around in puzzlement at the shout. That small handful was enough to impede Tyburn's pursuers momentarily.

"Move, you cockless whoresons!" one of them shouted, pushing his way past, sending one of the smaller apprentices sprawling.

The cry that arose in response was one that many Londoners dreaded.

"Clubs!"

More of the apprentices came pushing onto the street, a shoving, eager, half-soused flood of young, drunken men, some barely old enough to have even a sparse spray of whiskers on their faces. Almost all carried short wooden staves or truncheons on their hips.

London was awash in apprentices. Every trade, every master of skill, hired apprentices to train for periods of often seven to fifteen years, depending on the work, age, and skill of the young men. London streets were filled with bare-faced, bare-headed young men in blue cloaks and gowns, shouting "What do you lack?" at passersby, filling the ordinaries and the taverns, drinking away their frugal wages, and banding together in the face of the Watch and the authorities. They fought in the streets, brawled, rioted, pulled down brothels on Bankside, and occasionally pelted theatre-troupes with mud clods if their performance was lacking. They came together at the drop of a hat and melted back again into the teeming throngs of the street. Forbidden to possess swords by edict, they almost all carried wooden clubs, which they wielded ferociously when called upon.

A dark-visaged young man stepped out of the milling group and hammered the butt-end of his short truncheon into the face of one of Tyburn's pursuers. There was a shout, and the heaving mass of apprentices eagerly began swinging. The player, well past the fray, paused for an instant to appreciate the sight as the three men chasing him vanished into a cursing, milling, arm-swinging pile of blue-clad youngsters. One shoved his way free and tried to find room to draw his sword, only to find his arm pulled away and back by one man, while another took careful and deliberate aim at the elbow with his club. The screech of pain from the blow elicited a bark of laughter and a bevy of kicks and thrashing as the blows rose and fell relentlessly.

Tyburn didn't stay to observe the aftermath. He continued down the laneway until it joined a broader avenue that the player recognized as Fleet Lane. Hurrying, Tyburn pushed past a torturously slow carter, heading towards Old Bailey and the short jog south leading to Ludgate.

The hilt of the sword hammered into his temple, the steel pommel sending him to his knees in the muddy street. Tyburn shook his head dazedly, one shoulder slumping almost into the soft, half-frozen muck coating the lane. He levered himself up and reached vaguely towards the weapon at his belt.

The second slamming impact sent him crashing backwards, one leg folded under himself. He could feel chill water soaking into his back and sides, a warm trickle of blood dripping down the side of his face. A fat red drop plopped into the puddle and Tyburn watched it dissipate into the muddy residue. His head lolled backwards, impelled by some unseen hand gripping his hair.

"That's the cullion. Bring him."

A pair of arms hauled him upwards, and he jerked as a stabbing lance of pain from his back convulsed him. His vision swam and focused on a pair of shabby boots. With difficulty he raised his head to take in the sight of the tall, heavyset man from the red-tiled rooftops of London Bridge. The man gave him a tight-lipped smile. The last thing Tyburn saw was the silvered guard of his own rapier hammering him in the face.

Chapter the Fourteenth

THE THROB OF his head seemed to pulsate in concordance with his breathing. Every exhale sent a cascading flux of pain through his skull, a sensation that pushed thumping sheets and spirals of colour across the lids of his closed eyes.

"*Es un problema? Mi principal tiene algunas preocupaciones.*"

"No. Tell your master, he need have no concerns." The voice was feminine, lilting soft but with a sharp, commanding edge. "Our timetable is unaffected."

"*Hay que matarlo?*"

She laughed. "In due time."

Tyburn heard a door open and close, and felt a warm hand ruffle through his hair. He flinched away from the fingers, and as his eyelids fluttered open, realized he was tied to a straight-backed wooden chair, his body slumped to one side. His arms were secured behind the chairback, pulled taut and up at a painful angle. As his awareness increased, he felt his chest and shoulder muscles ache, stretched sharp and tight by the knotted constraints. His legs were tied to the legs of the chair.

"What do we do with this offal?"

"We killed him once already." The source of the silken voice slid into view.

The dark, predatory gaze surmounted a pale, unblemished face, accentuated by sharp, symmetrical cheekbones and a full-lipped mouth that curled up in the corners with a feline blend of amusement and indifference. Her hair was dark and short, hanging in tight curling strands that clung to her head like an angry halo. It was a face he had last seen watching with amused curiosity as he plummeted towards the Thames.

This was the Harlequin.

"He did for Tobias and Nance on the Bridge. Carved up Swofford's leg so he's gone hoppity, and Nick … well, he ain't pretty no more." The man gave a dry chuckle devoid of any humour. "I can just slit his throat and drop him in the Fleet. Be quick."

The dark-haired woman showed a ghost of a smile. "Bent, you have no imagination. This one is unique. How many enemies that escape our reach ever willingly come back?" She ran one finger along Tyburn's scarred cheek, tracing the curlicue path of the mark. "This one's … interesting. He kills two of our men, tracks us down. Finds out who we –are. And then has the temerity to stalk us in our own abode." She gripped his chin and tilted his face upwards. "He needs a more—tempered death."

"Trim him up a bit, slit his throat, and drop him in the Fleet." Bent's voice was sour.

"Bring in the others." Harlequin stepped back and Tyburn lifted his head to glance about the room, ignoring the excruciating stab of pain that lanced though his skull. Bent nodded and left, closing the door behind himself.

The room was dim and shadowed, but Tyburn could see a canopied bed off to one side, and a tall ornate sideboard with its edges carved into a festive spray of curlicues and flowering roses. The fireplace burned low, casting a dull flickering light that rippled across the rush-strewn floor. The Harlequin bent, lit a long taper from the fireplace, and lit in turn a set of tall beeswax candles sitting on a low table. A pile of books lay haphazardly on the floor. She walked past the bound player with languid grace and seated herself on a small settee by the table. On it sat a flagon of dark red wine sat from which she poured a full measure into a finely cut glass.

"This the point where I'm supposed be filling air with queries"—she took a deep, appreciative draught—"but I don't truly care. I'll let Bent pursue that path. He's very inventive with pain and he likes to feel useful." She picked up one of her books and idly flipped it open. "I am curious, though. How did it feel to die?"

"Terrifying."

"Truly? You did not think you would be delivered into salvation, into the Heavenly Kingdom?" She leaned forward, her face intent. "What black sins lie on your soul that make you fear death so much? You a murderer? A thief? Adulterer? A heretic? Oh, I forgot, you are a play-actor." She drained the glass and stood. "A liar's profession. Putting on masks and assuming roles."

She walked behind him in a slow, deliberate gyre. He felt her arm drape across his shoulders. Her breath huffed in his ear. "What should I do with you now, play-actor?" Her hands slid down his chest teasingly. He could feel her pressing the length of her body against the back of the chair and his bound arms. Her teeth found his earlobe and bit down sharp for a second before her lips caressed against his throat. She slid around and swung herself astride his lap, locking her legs around him, arms tight around his neck, pressing his face into her throat, gliding her lissome form against him.

The prick of a blade under his chin wasn't a surprise.

She leaned back, surveying her catch with a critical eye. The player didn't move. He felt the sharp point graze his beard and then felt the chill metal of the blade as she laid it against his cheek.

"You know what this blade is used for? Castrating cattle. I use it for a similar purpose, but I don't keep beeves. You don't seem surprised."

"Your reputation precedes you."

"My reputation?" She snorted. "Tales and nonsense. What? You've heard of my flaying my enemies? Drawing and quartering?" She let the blade slide delicately down the length of Tyburn's neck. The player sat frozen as she reached the hollow of his throat, above his clavicle. She leaned in and he felt her lips part against his throat, her tongue delicately tracing a thin line along the base of his neck. "Useful stories to bant about. Tales to unsettle. You know London's upright men won't tally for a woman, unless she impresses upon them the consequences of resistance. I impress upon them as oft as I may, to keep their lessons fresh and sharp." Her voice was soft in his ear.

Tyburn winced as the blade slipped, drawing a thin oozing line of blood from his skin.

"Why Harlequin?" the player asked.

She smiled. "In England, it represents a clown, a buffoon. But in France, my father's home, the land of my birth, it is *Hellequin*, the emissary of the Devil himself, the one that drags the souls of the living to their everlasting damnation. Let these upright men see something to laugh about, to bait and gambol with, but I am truly the black-faced demon, the keeper of the gate to Hellfire and the realms of the dead." She laughed. "I spoke truly on the bridge. I can deliver you to salvation, if that is how God and fates will it. Or are you one of those that live in fear of damnation?"

The door opening precluded Tyburn's caustic reply. Bent had returned, along with two of his men escorting a sour-looking Chaucer.

"At last, at last, at last!" said the Harlequin with a winning smile that sent a cold ripple down Tyburn's spine. She reached up and grabbed Chaucer by his worn ruff, pulling his head level to hers. Still straddling Tyburn's bound form, she nodded towards him. "Is this him?"

Chaucer was pale and nervous, his breath ragged. "Od a' mercy, that's him, Kit Tyburn. From Worcester's Men. He soldiered in the Low Countries before that, a true killing gentleman, if I may say."

"And you know him how?" Bent asked.

"We spent a year at Cambridge together, before I went on the cozenage, and he went to the wars."

"Why'd you come to us?" Bent demanded.

"I pay my dues. I heard on the sly he was querying about the Castle. I figured you'd want to know."

"And you thought you'd see some coin in letting us know," the Harlequin said.

"Your pardon, milady, but yes. I was tol' you were paying bene for news on any that asked about the Castle."

The Harlequin laughed. "Indeed we are. Angels from heaven for our true friends." She let go of his ragged ruff and patted him gently on the cheek. "Pay him, Bent, pay him! We have to reward our associates."

Chaucer's face was flushed with relief. Bent fished out a small purse and retrieved three gold angels which he weighed momentarily in his palm, before depositing them in Chaucer's open hands.

"We pay all our friends," the Harlequin said to Tyburn, her eyes fixed on his. "Just as we pay out our enemies and malfeasors. And how"—the Harlequin's voice was a husky, almost sensual whisper—"did this penny-antic come to know about the Castle?"

Bent pivoted and punched Chaucer hard in the stomach, buckling the cony-catcher over, as the other two men grabbed his arms. The gold angels tumbled through the air, one rattling off the wine flagon with a singing tone.

The Harlequin smiled once more. "You told the play-actor about us."

Chaucer was retching on his knees, trying to breathe, choking on fear. "N-no. I tol' you, only you."

She slid off Tyburn and reached over to cup Chaucer under the chin, cutting off his frantic pleading. "Shhhh. Shush." Her fingers played over his lips, squeezing them closed. "Do you think I'm foolish? Do you think, because I'm a woman, I'm some prating dotterel? Do you believe him, Bent? What about you, Master

Tyburn? Is your friend a blower? You know he betrayed you for coin, why not us as well? Who knows what wind might spout from him next?"

Tyburn shook his head, a sick tight certainty clenching his insides.

She laughed. "I'm not sure you're a credible witness, play-actor! Bent, perhaps you should ask him nicely." Her face, which had been genuinely amused, became devoid of expression. "Card him."

Chaucer went into a paroxysm of thrashing and pleading, as the man on the right gave him a practiced kick hard to the back of the knee, forcing the young thief to kneel on the rushes. The second man knelt astride his legs, and levered Chaucer's right arm behind his back. The other man gripped Chaucer's left arm and forced it into extension, locking one arm around it, while Bent gripped the wrist and pulled the arm taut.

The Harlequin tapped her blade gently on top of Chaucer's head to get his attention. "I thank you—and I've rewarded you—for bringing me the play-actor, but if I fail to punish malefactors who noise about like so many crows about who we are and our business, then everyone gets to talking and, well, nonny-nonny-nonny!" She caught the stained and worn edge of Chaucer's cuff, slid the edge of the castrating knife under the fabric, and proceeded to slice the cuff and the long length of the sleeve, exposing Chaucer's thin, pale arm.

"You've probably seen the ladies wool-carding before." She lifted a thin, hand-sized wooden board. "My mother taught me how to card, when I was very small. You take the card and rake it through the wool strands before you spin them. The nails stuck in the card rake out the dirt and the dust, and straighten the strands. Makes it easier to spin thread. Dull work. Very repetitive. My father showed me a different usage."

She turned over the wooden card to reveal the backside was a delicate forest of thin blades, each no more than a half inch in length, set in a line like the teeth of a comb. The sight brought a fresh spasm of thrashing and pleading from Chaucer. She turned the card back over, gripping it firmly and set it, blade first, against his upper bicep.

"I'll ask again. Did you tell our guest here about the Castle?"

"Please don't, please by Jesu, by my troth, pleaseplease please*please* ..."

"Answer the question, cully," growled Bent, losing patience.

The Harlequin shifted the card slightly. Tyburn saw Chaucer flinch as a thin line of blood ran down the curve of his arm to drip onto the floor.

Chaucer's face was an ashen sheen in the candlelight, sweat dripping down his face. "YES! Yes, I told him. He forced me to ... I had no choice, you don't know what he's like. It wasn't my fault!"

The Harlequin smiled. "You see. That was easy. 'Pon my faith, but truth among friends is so much better than lying. *Veritas lux mea*! The truth is my light. No harm."

Chaucer sagged in relief.

The Harlequin ripped the bladed card in her hand down the length of the locked, extended arm. The razor edges of the blades were so sharp she had reached the elbow before Chaucer even began to react. Neither Bent nor his men had relaxed their grips but the hideous spasm of pain and fear pulled Chaucer's arm back for a moment, before Bent re-gripped it, allowing The Harlequin to continue the journey of the card all the way to the wrist.

From the youth's throat came a hideous high-pitched keening sound that Tyburn hadn't heard since the bloody forays of Goes and Middleburg. The hot stench of blood filled the room, overwhelming the musky scent of the candles and the incense stick that had been burning on the fireplace mantel.

The woman had a fierce, almost exultant look on her face, as she finished slicing her way down his forearm. Standing, she tossed the wooden card aside and ran one hand through her hair, pushing back her short ringlets. Bent released Chaucer's arm and the other two men let go of the hapless cony-catcher and stepped back. He toppled over onto his side, his breath panting and bursting in shrieks and wails as he clutched his shredded left arm. Blood poured down his arm and side, puddling on the floor and soaking into the rushes.

"Should we do the other arm as well, you think?" the woman asked Tyburn. The player felt the room blur and distinctly heard terrified screams in Dutch, smelled the stench of burning flesh and the thick acrid smoke of the burning barn. In his ears was the memory of the desperate babbling of the Spanish Dominican begging for mercy before Tyburn ripped his long blade through the man's stomach. His mouth filled with bile.

There is nothing like Flanders.

"He is a raucous one." She observed, giving Bent an airy wave. The man grunted, leaned over Chaucer and the sound died abruptly with a gurgling swallow as Bent rammed his poniard into the hollow below Chaucer's right ear.

The other two men dragged the dead cony-catcher from the room with practiced ease, one of them pausing to kick more rushes onto the blood pooled on the floor.

"Customarily we would send him on his way, as an example to others on keeping their silence, but I don't really have the patience for banting about, and he seemed... mercurial at best." She shrugged. "You should at least feel some measure of satisfaction at having your enemy dance on a trap of his own making. He didn't tell us much about you that we didn't already know." She paused, her full lips pursed. A splash of Chaucer's blood decorated one perfect cheek, arced upwards in a crimson half smile. "He couldn't tell us who the girl was. No matter. He gave us a very full description. I'm looking forward to a long conversation with her."

Tyburn felt the blood draining from his face. Bent's thin lips smiled.

"What do we do with this one?" He poked a hand at Tyburn, still secured to his chair.

"We'll keep him for now. He looks like the type who enjoys the dark. Our friend will relish the company. Put him in the Devil's Hole."

Chapter the Fifteenth

THE NARROW CONFINES of the stairwell were the only thing that kept Kit from crashing down the roughened steps when his escort gave him a particularly hard shove.

"Leave off, you coxcomb. He kills his self on the way to the Hole, you'll be takin' his place on the Harlequin's dining table." The guard carrying the lantern growled.

"You could always untie me," Tyburn offered helpfully. He received an open-handed crack to the back of his head in reply and they continued down the constricted, winding staircase. Dust was thick in his nostrils, his body was bruised and battered, his head ached and throbbed in tempo with each stride, but his steps were light nonetheless. Escaping the flat, basilisk stare of the Harlequin's eyes relatively intact seemed to make any other potential threat fade to insignificance.

The size and intricacy of the Saracen's Head was impressive. What looked from the street like an ordinary London inn-yard was, in actuality a complex series of inter-connected buildings that ran hidden, like a rat's warren, twisting and weaving through the maze-like structure, crisscrossed with narrow passages that seemed to hive off in all directions. As far as he could determine, at least one wing of the inn-yard was private, home to the Harlequin and her associates, with the attached neighbouring structures allocated for a range of purposes. One thin wall had blocked off what sounded like a brothel or a molly-den operating at full tilt, the rhythmic sounds and ecstatic mutterings fading rapidly as the guards shuffled Tyburn down several bare hallways and through multiple turns and two separate flights of stairs into a tight, stone-walled passageway that ended in the narrow dusty stairwell.

It went down. Seemingly endlessly.

Tyburn could smell the fecund stench of sewage and rotting offal long before they reached the bottom step. The stairwell opened into a pitch-dark room that seemed long-abandoned to light, until one of the guards raised his lantern. They were in a low-ceilinged, square-vaulted stone and brick chamber nearly thirty feet in length. The chamber was bare except for a few scattered staves, a collection of ruined barrels, and a broken pile of smashed crockery. A dark rectangular gap in the ceiling in one corner marked the vertical shaft for a hoist, the wooden platform of which was stacked with casks. Two doors exited the room on the far side, their dark, warped wood hanging askew in their frames.

Tyburn staggered off balance on the rough stone floor, catching his foot and toppling hard against the ruined barrels. The staves collapsed as he fell against them, sending him to his knees in a shower of rotted wood. He turned and slid to the floor with a muffled grunt. The guard hoisted him up without a word and shoved him towards the far doorway.

Tyburn slid the short rusted length of hoop he had palmed as far up his sleeve as he could reach, the jagged, broken iron cold against his skin.

The second guard unlocked the warped door and levered it open.

"What next?" the player asked.

The guard turned and punched Tyburn low in his side. "Shut it, cully." Tyburn sank to his knees, the pain radiating outward, joining the other injuries in a barking chorus. *Maybe*, he thought, *I should temper my tongue for a time.*

The second guard entered the room and lit several tapers, giving the room an oddly reassuring glimmer of warm light.

"Bring 'im." The first guard gestured. The man dragged the player unceremoniously through the open doorway and threw him against the wall. A pair of shackles joined by a long chain lay on the floor, strung through an iron circlet embedded in the wall. The floor was damp and slick, the air thick with the stench of feces and rot. The guard yanked Tyburn's right leg over and locked the fetters just above his ankle. He locked the left ankle and then ostentatiously pocketed the key.

The fetters were heavy and cold. Tyburn could feel their weight in his very bones.

"Look, cully," the first guard said, his voice dour but not unsympathetic, "yer in the Hole until her ladyship decides it's time to end yer run, so do us all a favour and don't fuck about. You piss off Thieves and he'll probably strangle you like he did the last two we've dossed him with. Enjoy yer stay and mind the dark." The man stepped over and blew out the thin rush glim burning a dull orange by the door. The two men levered the warped door back into place and Tyburn watched the bright light of the lantern flicker like a knife's edge through the gaps in the planks. As the two men turned back to the staircase the light faded out abruptly, a brief, narrow-arced sunset that vanished in a rush of stygian gloom.

It was pitch dark.

A voice drifted out of the black, like a moth fluttering around a flame, directionless and seemingly random. "It was a mercy, killing them. Better I leave them for the lovely *Hellequin*?" The voice chuckled. "Well, killing Thatcher was more a pleasure than a mercy. He was an annoyance, weeping all hours. You are not a weeper, are you?"

"Who are you?" Tyburn asked, his fingers tracing the fetters around his ankle.

"I am the keeper of this darkness. Once I ruled, now I lie in these cold grounds."

"That's not really an answer." Tyburn's fingers found the fetter pin, tracing its short, rusted length to the locking mechanism. He could feel a small keyhole in the lock, about a half inch from the end of the fetter.

The voice laughed and spoke again. "No, it is not." The voice was strange, almost mushy in its tone, half-finished and broken. "You will want a name, will you not? The dull ones always want a name to conjure with. In the waking world, I was Benoît Thieves, lord of west London, owner of the Saracen's Head, exile, advisor to the admiral, *robins* and *Noblesse de lettres.*"

The sudden flare of light made the player flinch. Another set of sparks flashed and the sullen yellow light of a burning rush candle sent the darkness scurrying away.

"Better, yes? We can converse as civilized men do, in the light." The figure turned towards Tyburn, the dim candlelight revealing a slantendicular smile cutting across a ruin. The left half of Thieves' face was a scarred and pocked nightmare, a demon visage of torn scar tissue surfaced by edged fissures, burned and blackened. "This?" The candle circled and dipped, indicating the damage. "Courtesy of my lovely daughter."

"Your daughter? Harlequin is your daughter?" The flat astonishment in Tyburn's voice echoed through the small chamber.

"You do not see the resemblance?" Thieves laughed again, a sound void of humour, deeply etched with bile and venom. He limped across the room, one leg dragging in a shuffling fashion. A low table sat in the corner, beside a thin sack of blankets and trash. The rush candle hissed and sputtered as he propped it upright in a clay cup. He sat heavily on the blankets and waved one hand genially at the player. All the fingers save one ended at the first joint. Thieves caught Tyburn's gaze and opened and closed the hand, the abbreviated digits giving it an eerie, perverse look. "A gift from last year. She has a temper."

"How long have you been down here?" Tyburn asked.

"Uhmm … Two … no, three years now, at least. Each year, she visits me. In August. And gives me another gift. The first year …" He tugged up his long, stained gown to reveal his left foot, the toes removed and the foot twisted, broken and left to heal crooked. "She also sliced the tendon. Did not need fetters after that. The second year, she took my face." He lifted his long, greasy hair back to reveal a missing ear. "And the ear. Because I laughed at her. She wanted to take the eye as well, but I think she was afraid I would fester and die. The third year …" He waved the maimed hand and shrugged. "For the same reason, she has not castrated me yet. She wants me to linger here, in this unholy darkness, a broken man. But I do not break. Not for her. *Superbe pute,* my Suzanne."

Tyburn stared for a long moment before turning his attention back to the fetter lock. "So why is she named Martaine, not Thieves?" he asked as he tugged the short length of rusted barrel hoop out of his sleeve. He slowly began to bend the hoop in half, breaking it into two equal lengths. Thieves watched in amusement.

"You do not like your adornments?" Thieves grimaced. "I fear you are wasting your time, but it hangs slow in these depths, so no matter. To answer your question, I never married her mother. She was English. A heretic, like you, but I'm Huguenot, so it was a small thing. Her mother was lovely and beddable, so I forgave her English. We lived in Paris, as I served the admiral—de Coligny, you know?"

He rubbed his finger stumps distractedly. "I was absent when it all went to Hell on St. Bartholomew's Day. She died there, in Paris. Badly, or so Suzanne claims. I thought both of them dead, but the little bitch reappeared a year later, here, in London, seeking vengeance on an old man who never did her harm. That is how she repaid her father." Thieves voice trailed off slow, as if in puzzlement at a past never clearly understood.

The silence hung for a minute. "You must forgive a garrulous old man. I have lacked good social company for more than a year now." He fished a small wineskin out of the fetid pile of his bedding and tossed it awkwardly to Tyburn. "Drink. And tell me your story? What horrid offence have you gifted upon my *belle étoile*?"

"I failed to die." Tyburn took a cautious sip of the wineskin and was surprised to discover a decent, if sour, canary. He tossed it back to Thieves.

Thieves pointed one truncated finger at the player. "The worst possible offence. Other than mine, of course."

"What did you do?"

"Aside from father the *Hellequin*?" He sighed. "She blames me. Blames me for all things. As though I could control fate and destiny. As though I could control kings and mobs. That bitch."

Under the thick plate of scar tissue, Tyburn could see hot, lambent anger burning in his eyes, just glints in the dim candlelight, like embers under ash. "I trained her. Taught her swordcraft and subterfuge, to think and plan and manipulate. I showed her how to lift herself out of the muck, to use the gifts that God and the Fates bestowed upon her. To use her body to pleasure the lordly and the influential, to take their secrets, their vices, and turn them back upon themselves. I taught her! I did, not that bitch mother of hers. Fucking *pute d'Anglaise. Maudit!*"

"Trained her for what?"

"To win. To control. She was my tool against *la famille Guise* and that bastard *Le Balafré*, the Duke of Guise. I crafted my Suzanne as a weapon of war, *un assassin séduisant*[4]. Calculated to bring him close, to serve the admiral and the House of Condé. *La Massacre* spoiled our plans."

---

[4] An alluring assassin

Tyburn looked at the man for a moment in distaste, soaking up the implications of his commentary. He turned his attentions to the short length of rusted iron and began to scrape it against the damp, greasy surface of the stone floor.

The St. Bartholomew's Day massacre four years before had torn France and Paris apart in a violent eruption of Protestant slaughter, just one more horror story in a vicious internecine conflict between Huguenots and Catholics that had been raging for more than a decade in France. Tyburn had been hip-deep in cold, glutinous Flanders mud at the time, but vividly recalled the broadsheets and missives that circulated among the small English force in the Netherlands. A Huguenot army under Louis of Nassau, the younger brother of William of Orange, had fought beside the English and Watergauzen forces at Mons in the spring of 1572, so news of the brutal massacre by Catholics had spread like wildfire among the Protestant soldiers.

Mass murder and rioting consumed Paris for days, with the Huguenot leadership under Admiral de Coligny slaughtered to a man, alongside thousands of Huguenot men, women, and children. Their bodies had clogged the Seine and fueled Protestant hate and Catholic glee across the Continent. The violence had spread throughout France, a brutal cascade of murder that had lasted for months. Walsingham had been in Paris during the massacre, serving as the English ambassador to the Royal Court (or so Tyburn had been told), but whatever dark experiences he had of the horror, he had not deigned to share with his servants.

The candle guttered out and darkness fell, as Thieves continued to mutter balefully to himself in French.

The slow hours passed. Tyburn worked by touch in the darkness, slowly wearing the iron down to half its width, testing the size constantly against the holes on the lock.

At some point, he slept.

When he woke, he resumed filing down the iron band, using a small stone he pried from the loose mortar of the wall. He fitted the narrowed iron band into the hole in the lock. Perfect. Tyburn slowly bent the tip and cursed when the brittle rusted iron snapped off in his fingers.

"I need to borrow one of your candles," he said into the darkness.

Thieves laughed. "Why should I loan my glims to a dead man?"

"You want the Harlequin to just carve me up like some trussed leg of mutton?"

"You know how many men get tossed into the Devil's Hole with me, and how many I have seen go out again? I have killed four myself over the years and seen another score get their throats slit and tossed into the drains."

"You like the tables, Thieves? You a gaming man?"

There came a long pause. "I have been known to toss the bales from time to time. What of it?"

"I will bet you five groats to obs, I can finesse my way out of this hole, if you help me slip these fetters."

"And if I win, dead man, what would you have me spend it on in this cesspit? You see any mercers or victuallers here? Perhaps I should spend it on a fancy sarsenet mantle so the guards and my dung-crusted daughter will be impressed when they next come down to lop off my extremities?"

"*Lex talionis*[5]."

The Latin phrase made Thieves pause. "You are a clever one, dead man. You think you can help me revenge myself on Suzanne? I am my revenge. Each time she comes down into this pit, this stinking dark place, and looks upon her father, she is reminded of my deeds and I am revenged. She will never be free of me, never be rid of what I shaped her to become. Her soul is mine, in its entirety." He snorted in genuine amusement. "She has become the *Hellequin* to avenge herself upon me, but in doing so she has

---

[5] The law of retaliation

condemned herself to become Hell's black-hearted servant, a bitch-queen like no other." He laughed again, a sound that hung in the black like a distant rumble of storm.

"Still," Thieves mused, "it would be amusing to see her face when she found you gone, another plaything denied her, the cat's toy stolen from the cat."

The silence that followed stirred Tyburn's hopes. There was a quiet rustle and a flicker of bright sparks. A rush candle sprang to fitful life, banishing the darkness into the far reaches of the fetid chamber.

"Very well, dead man. Here is your light. Much joy may it bring you." Thieves handed over the flickering candle and watched in silence as Tyburn held the thin-shaved iron band over the flame. He held it for several minutes until he thought the corroded metal was heated enough to flex, and then slowly bent the tip into an angle.

It didn't break.

Tyburn slid the hooked piece of metal into the hole in the fetter and twisted it cautiously, feeling the tip sliding against the locking pin. "Coads." He muttered to himself as he felt the thin iron of the band bending under his twisting. He delicately adjusted the position of the hook and tried again. The tiniest shiver of vibration heralded the movement of the pin. He increased the pressure and felt the pin slide aside with a barely discernable pop.

Tyburn gasped audibly in relief, sagging back against the rough surface of the stone wall. He quickly slid open the fetter and removed his ankle, rubbing it where the sharp metal had abraded the skin. The lock on the second fetter was easier, giving way to the makeshift pick on the first attempt. He drew both legs up, wincing at the pain that radiated through his aching muscles. The player clambered to his feet while Thieves watched, his face an impassive mask of torn, ridged flesh.

"Congratulations, dead man, you are no longer chained. In case you did not see, the stairs are bolted and barred at the top and the bottom, and the pulley chain is thirty feet up a vertical brick shaft. Are you Icarus, that you would soar away to freedom? You are stuck in the black with me. You are right. It will be amusing to see what happens when my sweet Suzanne comes calling."

"Didn't you say, she disposed of your compatriots through the drains?"

Thieves snorted in disbelief.

"From the stink and shit crusts on the walls, I assume this was used as a laystill for the inn privies. No car-men are going to muck out a basement at this depth. But they would shovel it out into a sewer. My guess, from what you've said, is there's a dunghole into the London sewers. That's my exit."

"You will die in a narrower hole."

Tyburn grinned. "Not by her hand, at least." He stooped and picked up the sputtering rush candle. "I'll need more of your glims—"

A sharp, short blade slipped under his chin. Thieves had moved with the supple speed of a snake, despite his injuries.

"I am reconsidering how angered my daughter would be, if deprived of your company. Enjoyable as it may be to watch her shriek with rage, I am unsure I want to be the one for her to vent upon."

"I thought you were the man that she could not break?"

Tyburn could hear Thieves panting in the dim light, feeling the strain of supporting his weight on his one good foot, the pain of holding the short knife in his one good hand.

"It would be better, I think, to kill you."

The player flicked the rush candle he held in one hand into the corner, immersing the chamber back into pitch darkness, and kicked his stiffened right leg backwards, catching Thieves in the ankle of his supporting leg. Unable to shift his weight, Thieves toppled straight down, the short blade in his hand ripping across Tyburn's shoulder, tearing fabric and skin in equal measure. Tyburn pivoted and dropped as well, elbow angled sharply down, onto the crippled man. A hundred and eighty pounds of impact sent the air out of him with a brutal slam, leaving him heaving for breath on the chamber floor, thrashing under Tyburn like a gaffed fish. Tyburn felt Thieves' arm flailing for the knife, which had clattered off somewhere into the darkness. The player locked his hands around the arm and bent it backwards. Thieves screamed as his arm audibly creaked under the force.

"*Non, non!*" he begged. "Enough!"

Tyburn reached up and grabbed a fistful of the man's lank and thinning hair, feeling it tear and part as he hauled Thieves to his feet. "Where's your flint?"

"The table," he yelped. "In the cup, with the glims." The player edged over, keeping a grip on Thieves with one hand, and felt outwards until he reached the wall and bumped the edge of the low table with his leg. He reached down and felt about searchingly, finding the rough clay mug and the long, thin, waxen rush candles. His fingers dug in the cup, closing on the small flint and steel striker and a small cloth spill. Tyburn shoved Thieves away, hearing him clatter and topple in the room with a cry of pain as he hit the floor. Tyburn struck the flint and steel, sending a bright cascade of sparks onto the spill, which smoldered and flickered. The player touched the candle wick to the small flame and breathed a short sigh of relief as the yellow light returned.

Thieves was sprawled across the dank floor, his breath billowing and sucking like a bellows. "That was foolish," Tyburn observed, scooping up the loose glims from the table and pocketing the steel, flint, and spill cloth.

"Better had you killed me," Thieves rasped. "I am tired of being snipped and nipped like a dressmaker's form. I do not have too much left for her to trim up."

Tyburn tugged at his torn borrowed doublet, ruefully observing the ragged tear that Thieves' blade had rent and the cut beneath. Blood was welling along the length but the wound was shallow and minor. Clair, he thought, would not be pleased.

"You said yourself that you shaped her into a tool. Consider yourself hoist on your own petard." Tyburn shoved the wooden door open, the trailing edge scraping along the stone floor. He closed it behind himself and glanced about the long entry chamber. As Thieves had noted, the pulley hoist was gone, vanished into the upper recesses of the vertical shaft. The exit staircase was closed off by an iron-shod door and grate. Just rattling it convinced Tyburn it would unlikely to be opened anytime soon. The player kicked in the second door at the end of the chamber, opposite Thieves' cell. The room was similar in size but the stench was markedly worse. A thick carpet of dried feces and nightsoil coated the floor, culminating in an abundant pile in one corner. A small narrow hatch interrupted the wall on the far right. It was wooden, about half the size of a normal door in both width and height.

"By Jesu." Tyburn gagged. The candle flared and flickered in the miasma. He stepped carefully, trying to avoid the deeper, glutinous piles, discovering that the nightsoil was mostly now dried and scaling. It had been several years since it had been deposited, doubtlessly mucked out of all the chambers by hired car-men when it was converted into a holding cell for the Harlequin's father. Tyburn knew that cesspits in basements were not an uncommon find in London. It was a rare house that did not have at least an outdoor privy, and the malodorous practice of piling sewage in basements until it became unbearable was a relatively common practice among poorer peoples. The horrific job of then shoveling out nightsoil and waste fell to the car-men, who would cheerfully fill barrels and haul them through the streets to ditches and pits surrounding London. Kit vividly recalled Edward Alleyn, one of the actors in The Earl of Worcester's Men, recounting with unsuppressed glee how his landlord's basement had collapsed and been swamped in a fetid flood of indescribable filth from a neighbouring property whose owner had neglected to muck it out.

The player reached over and tugged on the metal ring embedded in the door. For a second it resisted and then gave way with a sodden squelch. The puff of stale air that followed the opening door made the rush candle sputter and fume. A narrow brick passage that ended in a dark hollow greeted him.

Tyburn forced a grim smile and threaded his way past the door to the hole. The candle provided only a fitful, meandering light, not enough to illuminate whatever lay below. He sat on the edge, legs dangling.

"*Alea iacta est*. The die is cast. Right into the shit." He muttered and lowered himself into darkness.

Chapter the Sixteenth

"REMEMBER, WE CAN'T kill the little bastard." Covington had repeated the warning at least six times to the small collection of armed men sitting in an enclosed yard off Maidenhead Lane, near the Cordwainer's Guild Hall. The low chorus of mumbled agreement that came back left him unsatisfied. "You 'accidentally' kill the bugger and we all dangle, so watch yourselves." Covington's eyes were chill and even as he glanced over the small group.

The low gate that marked the alleyway entrance creaked open and Bristow stepped in, compact and silent as always. He gestured with his hands, fluid and quick.

"Three minutes. Five men. And Asquith." Covington translated for the benefit of the others. The men clambered to their feet, checking their blades. Covington had forbidden the use of any pistols as the danger of some handless fool blasting the earl of Asquith off his horse was just too problematic. They filed out of the yard in pairs.

Covington's crew were as fine a collection of brazen-faced boot-halers as he had been able to hire. At least half were former soldiers, while the rest were a variety of cheap swinge-bucklers and pothouse hangers-on. He had fitted them out as much as possible with decent steel and as foppish a collection of clothing as he could muster.

Covington had made the small group rehearse their positions multiple times before retiring to the yard to await their prey. The earl of Asquith passed through the street on a recurring basis, usually bound for an expensive brothel that operated out of a residence near Mary Le Bow Church, on the outskirts of Bread Street Ward.

The party scattered across Maidenhead Lane in loose pairs, each covering the various side streets and alleyways. Two men waited at the far end of Maidenhead, near the entrance to Pissing Lane by St. Margaret Moses Church, to catch any potential runners. Covington himself idled by the narrow entrance to Distaff Lane, which sat at the midpoint of the street. Bristow ambled slowly past, heading towards the western entrance.

They had not long to wait.

Asquith's group consisted of three men on foot and two outriders, flanking the earl. All were armed with side swords, and the three walking men carried long, iron-shod wooden staves, useful for shoving aside slow-moving crowds and prodding the occasional pig or dog out of their path. Covington edged his sword up and down in its scabbard, unconsciously checking to ensure it wasn't sticking in the cold winter air. He watched as one of his men, a tall, lugubrious man named Batten, casually set out across the path of the outrider, forcing the man to check his horse.

"Mind your way, you fool!" the horseman growled.

"Sirrah, are you speaking to me?" Batten stood and gaped.

"Move your bloody self out of my bloody way, you gob-smacked arse."

The mournful-looking Batten reached up and smacked the horse across the nose, open-handed, sending it reeling sideways, startled. Batten's partner quietly drifted up the far side, and while the second rider gaped in astonishment at his compatriot,

Covington's man reached up and yanked him sideways off his mount, slamming him down to the frozen cobbles.

The metallic rasp of steel being drawn sent the regular denizens of the street scrambling away as Covington's men closed on the small group. One rider was down and bloody, the other scrambling to check his panicked horse while the earl shouted and turned in his finery, confusion writ large on his face. Covington watched as the earl's footmen tossed their staves aside to draw their swords and intervene. Two of Covington's boot-halers stepped up behind them as they scrambled to intervene, but the footmen's eyes were locked on the disturbance in front of them.

The men died with brutal efficiency. One cried out, twisting as he fell, sending a spray of blood across the cold stones. The remaining footman scrambled away in a panic, sword drawn. Asquith drew his sword and spurred forward, lunging down at Batten, the blade narrowly missing his throat. Batten, his face now suffused with choleric anger, turned, intent on ripping his long blade into Asquith's back, just as Covington stepped in to deflect the attack with a crisp, ringing blow. "Not him." He growled and shoved Batten aside.

"Ride, sir, Ride!" he shouted at Asquith. The startled earl rammed back his spurred heels and his mount careened out of the melee and down the narrow laneway.

The first panicked horseman that had confronted Batten had now checked his mount. His eyes raked over the bloody fray and without a moment's hesitation, he turned his beast and fled in pursuit of his master.

The last footman was hammered down, insensate, his blood soaking the cobbles.

One of Covington's men lay on the stones, gasping and hissing in pain. One sword thrust had torn through his shoulder and another had laid open his stomach. Covington stepped over him, his blue eyes glacial and hard. "Sorry, lad."

The young man sputtered and wheezed, trying to speak, hands grasping air in panicked denial. Covington drew a short, sharp poniard and slid it across his throat, trying not to hear the hideous choking sound that abruptly stopped.

Covington glanced up and down the suddenly deserted confines of Maidenhead Lane. Bristow was gone, discreetly following the pale-faced Earl of Asquith in his flight. Hopefully, he thought, Asquith in his fear, leads us back to whoever is pulling his strings. Three weeks of payments and subtle back-tracking had only ever led them back to Asquith. Covington refused to believe that the foppish imbecile had any capability for fomenting blackmail and subterfuge.

He turned and paced back down Distaff Lane, closing the wooden gateway behind him. Rutledge had been in a fine fury for the past weeks, pushing, cajoling and finally ordering Covington to "teach the puppy a harsh lesson." The pale ex-soldier was not convinced that any action on his part would result in any abeyance of the blackmail, but he had settled on using the brutal ambush to hopefully spur Asquith into a reaction that might provide answers. Bristow would silently lope along after the earl, to see into what hole he rabbited.

Covington could hear shouting from the street as the Watch was summoned, but he knew that the response would be painfully slow. The Bread Street Ward beadles had been well paid in advance. Covington left little to chance.

In the confines of the enclosed yard, the remaining men were stripping off their borrowed finery, dropping cloaks and hats onto a blaze kindled in a small hearth. They pulled on cheap slops, apprentices' smocks and other nondescript clothing and filed out through the building. As they passed Covington, he deposited a small coin purse in each man's hand, before they stepped out the door and vanished down the alleyways to Bread Street and the crowded thoroughfares of London. Covington paused to shake an admonishing finger at Batten, who hung his head in sheepish apology, before sliding his lean frame out the door like a trout in a stream.

Covington shrugged into a long cloak, made one last check to ensure nothing compromising had been left, and followed. The hunt is up, he thought. Let's see what game we course.

Chapter the Seventeenth

THE DARKNESS WAS enveloping. The light provided by the cheap rush candle illuminated only the immediate vicinity in a fitful glow. Tyburn had dropped into an open tunnel about three feet wide. Flat, stone-bricked walls extended arrow-straight in both directions, vanishing into an opaque black that hung like a squalid curtain. The flat walls curved upwards into a supporting arch at the top, giving him a scant and stooped five feet of headroom. The floor was damp and thick with silt and grime, though thankfully not brimming with water or waste.

The air was cold and Tyburn's breath floated and fogged around him in the stillness. Surprisingly, there were no corpses or bones scattered about, so either Thieves had been lying about The Castle using the sewer tunnels as a disposal pit, or they had been dumping them elsewhere. Kit blew an inward sigh of relief. The thought of entering this sepulchre pit had been bad enough; having to clamber through the dead would have made it nigh unbearable.

He lifted the rush candle and peered into the black. What direction? He deliberated. If there were waste water in the tunnel, he might have at least gotten some idea of where it was flowing, but the thick layer of silt and grime that encrusted the floor of the tunnel, though damp, showed no indication of slope or flow. The air was still and cold, and only his own labored breath stirred it. The tunnel was as still as a tomb.

"Toss the bales." He muttered to himself and turned to the left. He paused and scraped a ragged X on the wall with the small steel striker he had taken from Thieves.

The player walked at a stilted crouch, careful not to move too fast and extinguish the sputtering rush candle. His feet squelched in the damp and his breath was ragged in the air. At some unfathomable distance, he thought he heard the rush of running water but otherwise the oppressive dark was soundless, leaving him with the unsettling sensation of floating in dark pitch, thick and cloying.

Every hundred steps or so, Kit stopped and scratched a mark on the wall. The walls themselves were smooth and well laid. Some ancient Roman mason had done a superb job. At one point, Tyburn saw some lettering etched into the tunnel wall, *Numini Cæsaris provincia Britannia,* and a worn set of dates too faded to be legible[6].

The sound of rushing water was distinctive now, mumbling in a dull undercurrent to the player's harsh breathing. The air seemed thin and constricted, as still as death and starved of oxygen. Tyburn pulled out another rush candle and lit it from the now shortened original. The cheap glims seemed to last between fifteen and twenty minutes each and the player counted only six remaining in his doublet's thin pocket.

The tunnel's end was abrupt. In an eyeblink, the bricked walls vanished and the floor fell away into darkness. For the first

---

[6] "To the deity of the Emperor, set up by the province of Britain"

time, Tyburn felt a breath of wind on his face: fetid, rising air, cold and thick with moisture and the stench of offal. He knelt on the lip of tunnel, peering into the darkness, trying to ascertain the depth of the drop. Fumbling with his cold hands, he relit the tiny remaining candle stub and let the small flame drop. It splashed into darkness almost immediately, momentarily revealing a sunken junction only four feet below.

Tyburn clambered down. The chamber seemed to be a cistern junction of some type, with at least three or four additional sewer tunnels feeding into it from different directions. Two of the tunnels were squat and narrow, each trickling a noisy stream of foul-smelling liquid. The liquid had pooled, leaving the cistern puddled with about a foot of watery, oily waste that clung to his boots with the persistence of a petulant child.

Tyburn lifted the candle, peering into the darkness and willing the candle to give him something more than the tepid yellow glow it provided. He grimaced. The oppressive stillness and the absoluteness of the dark were beginning to fray his nerves. The wastewater seemed to flow sluggishly down the second tunnel to the right. He stared down the shaft and sniffed the air dubiously. Guessing that downhill was probably a tunnel outbound for the Thames or the Fleet, the player decided to follow the tunnel with the slow trickle of flowing wastewater.

Kit scratched a ragged mark on the entrance he selected and continued into the dark. This tunnel was built of more ragged stone than the last smoothly bricked passage. He was constantly ducking his head to avoid jagged outcroppings of rough-hewn stone. The base was uneven, with a wide cut running along the left-hand side of the tunnel that was filled with the wastewater, a continual hazard for tired and wayward feet. Moisture dripped endlessly off the stones. He began to shiver as the dampness permeated his clothes. At least, he thought, I'm getting used to the stench.

The sudden shine of two red eyes in the tunnel ahead made him freeze. The eyes blinked and as he crabbed his way forward, a second and third pair gleamed in succession. Tyburn stopped. The eyes blinked and vanished and a low chittering sound of rats scurrying away echoed through the silence.

The player resumed on his stygian path.

The uneven stones of the floor were slick with dampness and decaying, slippery mildew that concealed ragged-edged traps for the unwary. Cursing from yet another barked and torn shin, Tyburn lit another glim. Only five left, he noted.

The candle guttered and flared unevenly. Tyburn paused, listening. A dull and distant roaring sound echoed faintly off the torn rock walls. In the din of a London street, it would have been overrun by a mere passing conversation, but in the echoing dark, it was blaringly discordant. Tyburn felt a brief flutter of hope, wondering if the noise heralded either a broader thoroughfare, a cistern, or possibly even an outlet. Though he reckoned he had been underground for only about an hour, it felt as if much more time had passed. He increased his pace as much as he dared, given the uneven footing and the continued blue sputtering of his candle.

It took another twenty minutes of slippery caution before the player emerged in another cistern junction. This one was wider, with more feeder tunnels, arched and bricked into a broad chamber. The distant roaring sound had evolved into a distinctive symphony of splashing water, draining in cold streams of effluent and steaming sprays from a series of pipes and conduits that drained into a broad cistern. The cold spray soaked Tyburn as he made his way along the lip of the tunnel entrance and climbed down the two-foot drop into the room. A dozen-odd rats scrambled away into the tunnels.

The water level was only just above a foot, but Tyburn thought he could feel the cold through to his very bones. The candle, which he had shielded so diligently, burned a bit brighter here, flaring and guttering in an unseen breeze. The player looked around the cistern, his eyes immediately drawn to a broader tunnel that seemed to serve as an outflow.

The candle guttered and popped and Tyburn glanced down to see an impossibly brilliant, perfect blue light that for a single heartbeat encompassed the entirety of the colour, an apex of blue sky under a sunlit, cloudless bowl.

He felt himself gripped by a staggering force that flung him bodily into the air, in a combined physical blast of sound and impact that he had only ever experienced when a cannon shot had punched past him at Goes. He felt it ripple through his chest, a harder, broader punch that sent his arms flinging out, his legs torn from the sticky mess of wastewater, heat scorching the very air.

That instant of perfect blue light vanished and the weightless split-second ended as he clipped the tunnel edge and cartwheeled into the cold wastewater and the iron-hard stone of the conduit surface. The thumping roar of the explosion echoed down the tunnels, sending the rats racing into side channels and nooks. The tunnels collectively moaned as air flooded back into the void left by the blast with ear-popping force.

"Jesus Mercy." Tyburn groaned. The explosion had tossed him like a rag doll across the conduit chamber and into a neighbouring tunnel. With one shaking hand he clawed silt and ordure from his eyes and face. His face felt red and hot, his hair was scorched and crisped to the touch. One doublet sleeve was torn completely away, shredded loose from its laces and tossed into the cold darkness. He blinked. And blinked again.

Nothing.

The player reached for the pocket of his doublet, frantic. The flint, steel striker, and spill cloth were gone, along with all the remaining candles.

Tyburn cursed aloud, first in English and then in his best gutter Dutch, something he usually reserved for special affronts. He became aware of sensation again, felt the rough stone of the tunnel wall against his back, the freezing cold wastewater he slouched in, flowing past into the cistern.

His ears rang like a bell, the cascading water muted and shrouded into a tinny, hollow sound. Dazed, he staggered upright, catching the top of his skull on the low, ragged rock of the ceiling. The painful crack seemed to help focus his balance. Tyburn cautiously extended both arms, feeling the flat, wet surface of the brick under his palm.

"God's bones." He muttered. The sound of his own voice was flat and muffled. He blinked again, still seeing the bright blue afterimage on his eyelids. He rubbed his eyes and checked his pockets again for the flint.

Nothing.

The player felt a horrid implacable weight settling on him. The frisson of fear that had begun when he had entered the tunnels had quickened into a solid and absolute dread. The tightness in his chest and the raw, grinding sensation weren't just an aftermath of that explosive blast, but an anticipation of his fate. A long, blind crawl through darkness and filth, and a slow, putrid death, far from a clear sky or sunlight or Clair or … Stop it. Tyburn's arms gripped his chest, hugging himself hard. Focus.

He forced himself to calm. Leveled his breathing. Panic was a foe. Panic would sow his destruction.

There is nothing like Flanders.

For once the mantra seemed to calm him. It echoed through his mind like a soothing balm. Usually shouted or muttered as a biting and sarcastic aside by soldiers of both the Spanish and the English armies, the cry had morphed into a screaming declaration of anger, fury, and loss, exemplified by the endless wet, the sullen cold, and the steady erosion of their sanity in the face of blood and war.

There is nothing like Flanders.

Cling to that, Kit thought to himself. This, this is nothing. A walk in the dark. A stroll through Cheapside. The player reached out again, touching the two edges of the tunnel, orienting himself to the sound of the water cascading through the cistern junction. He shuffled forward in the darkness, one hand trailing along the dank brick, the other outstretched. He shuffled forward until he could feel the spray of the cascading water on his face and his hand reached the corner edge of the brick. He paused, thinking. The cistern, in the brief glimpse he had before the blast, had several tunnels emptying into it, but only two that had the look of an outflow. He tried to imagine his position in the chamber. He knew he hadn't been blown back into the tunnel he originally exited from, as it had a two-foot drop down into the cistern. He thought he had been blown back into the tunnel that angled in to the left of his entrance. That mean the outlet lay to the far right.

Tyburn began a slow circuit of the chamber, one hand resting against the wet, slippery walls, the other outstretched, occasionally catching the torrent of foul-smelling wastewater draining from the pipes and outlets above. The first opening he reached was wrong. The air smelled foul and stale and, even with the tinny ringing in his ears, he could not hear or sense any flow of water outward from the cistern.

Kit stumbled across the yawning gap, in actuality only three feet of open space but in the ominous dark it felt like a hundred. With the reassuring rough cast of the brick cistern wall under his fingers again, the player shuffled forward, groping blindly like a man seeking salvation. The second tunnel gaped and Tyburn felt a brief breath of moving air on his face. He listened in fruitless attention, but could hear nothing in the beckoning depths. He dropped to one knee, splashing into the cold water and ignoring the screaming response of his stiff muscles. He wasn't sure, but it felt like an outflow. He reached out, feeling for the far wall. As he stood in the centre of the tunnel entrance he could feel the slight pressure of the water building up on his calves.

This way, he thought. This way is the outlet. This way is open sky. Tyburn levered himself up and began a slow, laborious shuffle, one hand trailing along the wall.

The darkness was absolute. And the tunnel endless.

Christopher Tyburn slumped in exhaustion against the wall. He had been walking in darkness for at least two hours, scraping and sliding in cold mud and dank silt. The relentless cold and wet were making his teeth rattle like dice in a cup. The tunnel he had followed had slowly curved to the left, narrowing as it went, forcing the player to turn his broad shoulders sideways in the confines of the space.

At one point, Tyburn discovered a partial collapse of the ceiling had necessitated a long, cramped crawl, his face barely above the smelly, bone-rattling cold water. Kit had to force himself to move forward, despite the horrible gnawing fear that the tunnel would shrink down to nothing and leave him trapped in some constricted passage, unable to turn around or backtrack, doomed to freeze or drown gagging on sewer water.

He saw his first ghost at the constricted bend.

In the absolute black, the first hazy flicker of light might have been his eyes playing tricks on him. He rubbed his face, feeling the deep layer of grit and muck that had coated his entire body. It felt thick in his hair, and tended to slither down in an itching cascade that left him constantly wiping an endless layer of grime from his lids and face.

The light flickered and teased, floating amorphous and unceasing, a dull twilight glow that illuminated nothing. Tyburn paused and stared at the light, but each time it drifted off to the periphery of his vision, tantalizing with a nimble promise of salvation from the darkness.

Ignore it, the player commanded himself, forcing his steps farther down the passage, his knees scraping over the edge of a rough protruding stone.

"... *Spelen* ..." Play. The word floated out of the tunnel and Tyburn froze in his tracks. Miriam had been dead almost four years now, lost in the chaos of the escape from Harlaam and murdered by the Spanish. The little four-year-old had liked to shout the word at Tyburn each time he visited the kitchens where Annika labored, asking him to play. The young blonde widow had spent considerable time ignoring the scarred English soldier quartered in the old miller's house, who smiled and brought a seemingly endless stream of stories, sweets, and wooden toys to her daughter.

Tyburn rubbed his grit-crusted eyes and stared hard into the black. The light drifted like a will-o-wisp or a firefly, just out of reach. When he extended his hand and skinned it bloody against the unyielding stone of the tunnel wall, the light vanished, only to reappear farther away, seemingly embedded in the hard stone itself or perhaps immune to its physical presence.

"Fuck this." The player muttered to himself. Bad enough they haunted his dreams with guilt and despair, damned if he would let them haunt his waking world. He levered himself to an upright position, still stooped against the low ceiling and narrow, constricted passage, and began wading forward. The glow subsided and died away, replaced by a darkness that seemed, if anything, more implacable than before.

A flicker of red hazed his vision. He could distinctly hear the voice now, cursing him in Spanish, damning him for his heresy and his murderous anger. The red flared into a torch, held in his left hand. The right held a long, needlelike Spanish rapier with a silvered guard, a dead man's weapon, taken in spoil. The voice cursed again and Tyburn felt himself staring deep into the red-flecked eyes of Silvio de Ignace Campillo, Dominican priest, murderer of children, Inquisitor and tormentor. The blade lunged forward for the thousandth time, ripping the man's throat asunder in a red spasm.

You are damned. The voice was cold and implacable and Tyburn felt hot rage boiling through him. He fell into the sewer water face-first, the shocking cold sending a cascade of shivers and cramps through his muscles. Slowly he raised himself back up, staring into the undefeatable shadow. "There is nothing like Flanders." The words were a mumble, barely discernable past frozen lips.

The player hauled himself upright again, catching his head on the low ceiling, welcoming the raw pain.

And still they came. A long trail of ghosts, some with voices, screaming and horror, some mute with nothing but pale, empty eyes like flensed skulls. Miriam returned, waving a wooden top, and Annika, her blonde hair trailing in a cascade from a rotted, half-fleshed skull; Alec Masterson, clutching a bunched cloak and laughing uproariously at jokes only he could hear; Roose, face torn and shredded as though by some bestial force; and dozens more, nameless and sometimes formless, only half-recalled through memory or nightmare. At one point a dog blacker than pitch trotted past, its red-rimmed muzzle down, intent on a scent only it could follow, giving Tyburn a wary glance from eyes that flickered and raged with fire.

"Can't do more. Can't. Sorry, Clair." Tyburn was slumped against the angled join of two tunnels, the brick sharp and ragged at his back, his breath wasted and panting. Tyburn felt his eyes closing. The darkness was rising. Even the cold was now more like a lover's embrace, pulling him insistently, ardently into oblivion. He felt himself start to slide away.

"When will you pay me?"

It thrummed through him like a distant drum.

"When will you pay me?"

What? Tyburn felt his consciousness push back, rising to the surface like a drowning man.

"When will you pay me?"

It wasn't a voice. The deep, distinctive sound vibrated through the tunnel.

"When will you pay me?"

"When I grow rich," Tyburn croaked in response.

"When will you pay me?"

"When I grow rich, say the bells of Shoreditch." The sound that he felt thrumming faint through the black tunnel was the bells of Old Bailey, St. Sepulchre-without-Newgate. The sound filled the player with a rousing warmth that helped fight back the ever-present cold.

"When will you pay me?"

Tyburn scrambled upright, muscles knotted and screaming but functional. "When will you pay me?" the player muttered to himself. "Oranges and lemons, say the bells of St. Clements. Fuck me." Tyburn muttered as he limped down the tunnel length, his feet splashing through the water and muck. "You owe me five farthings, you bastard," he croaked, legs moving like a broken metronome. "When will you pay me?" The player was shouting now into the darkness, striding along, head ducked, oblivious to the dangers and unknowns of the gloom. "When I get rich! And when will that be, you prancing coxcomb?" Tyburn staggered for a moment and froze. The tunnel ran arrow-straight and the player could see, hanging like a half-penny moon, the barest distant outline of rounded, silvered light.

"When will that be?" Tyburn's voice was a whisper. "By God's mercy, it'll be now."

Chapter the Eighteenth

STUBBES HATED THE Fleet. It was cold and exposed in the warehouse doorway facing the river, with a bitter wind that swept in damp and chill from the western reaches of London across the open, fallow fields of Covent Garden and Long Acre. He shifted his body slightly, feeling his companion stir. Gale was once a draper's apprentice, but debt, drunkenness, and an inability to stay out of the gaming dens of Southwark had brought his fortunes low, and now, like Stubbes, he slept rough and plied the mendicant trade as an unlicensed beggar.

Stubbes cursed the cold. They'd had a good spot near Aldersgate, until Gale made the mistake of mishandling the wrong mort. Before they had realized their blunder, the clapperdudgeon for the ward had chased them out. Aldersgate had been rare coin. All the travellers and merchants making their way to St. Paul's and Cheapside's robust markets rolled through Aldersgate in a steady stream. A couple of drooling Abraham-men, begging by the side of the road, elicited a slow but steady stream of sympathetic coin, more than enough to keep them supplied with cheap ale and sour wine. You would have thought Ludgate, with its steady traffic, would have been equally munificent, but no; it was rife with lawyers and students, churchwardens and parsimonious booksellers, all of them stolid and churlish, unwilling to part with a ha'penny. Nary a slip nor a bit, muttered Stubbes to himself.

Stubbes glared at the sleeping Gale. He remembered the sermon they had heard preached at St. Paul's Cross the previous week, which had likened the playing of bowls and gambling to "privy moths that eat up the credit of many idle citizens." Gale had lost their small hoard of funds playing shove-groat with some idle carters. That money would have given them some winter's shelter in a noisome, lice-infested shared room off Bread Street. Stubbes cursed again and pulled the communal blanket away from Gale to give himself more coverage.

A rusted clanking sound made Stubbes sit up. He stared outwards, seeing nothing but the dim, stinking expanse of the River Fleet, cold and morose in the pre-dawn light. The clank sounded again, a low, tearing screech of metal twisting. Stubbes nudged his dozing companion, who muttered imprecations and pulled the blanket tighter around his body. "Hsst. Gale. Did you hear that?"

Something heavy and slow was dragging itself up the steep, stone-edged bank of the river; Stubbes could hear it. "Gale, wake up you prat," he whispered harshly. Stubbes felt a slow nub of fear growing. All his grandmother's tales of gasters and bull-beggars, cacodaemons and foliots arose unbidden in his thoughts. He stared outward, seeing something shuffling towards them.

The noise stopped. The man-shape seemed to have vanished in the early morning haze. Stubbes pivoted his head back and forth. His breath caught as a grime-coated hand reached up over the edge of the stone wall bordering the road, where the bank dropped to the river. As something spectral clambered up and over the wall, Stubbes' nerves broke. With a panicked wail, he clambered to his feet and stumbled off down the laneway.

Christopher Tyburn stood in the cobbled-stone laneway and raised both arms upwards to the open sky. No longer full night, the pre-dawn grey cast presaged the new day, but for once, the usual thick layer of winter cloud had been peeled back. A handful of stars winked in the eroding dark. Kit stared upwards, his eyes drinking in the distant flickering lights that hung like jewels on a curtain of night. He took a deep, shuddering breath, savouring the fresh bite of free air. Even the usual miasma of the Fleet and the daily common stench of smoke, unwashed humanity and offal that hung over the city seemed to smell to him of green and life and the promise of daylight.

Tyburn turned and followed the course of the river southwards to where the Fleet Street bridge frowned over the foul, ice-flecked waters. The sky to the east was steadily lightening, casting the dark and morose clouds hanging in the west into full illumination, white and piled tall, a promised distant purity that was unreachable. Kit was exhausted but not so tired that the thought of taking the shorter route back to Clair's abode near Cripplegate didn't set off his internal alarm bells. Better to avoid Newgate and the Saracen's Head, and take a roundabout path that would avoid anyone possibly reporting his presence to the Castle.

London was slowly awaking to another winter day. Carts and horse-drawn wagons crawled through the narrow confines of Ludgate. The usual early morning clangor and bustle of commerce filled the air, accompanied by the inventive cursing, shouting laughter, and raucous cries of the street sellers and apprentices. Tyburn threaded a slow path through the crowds, his grime-coated appearance and stench granting him a slight extra allocation of space in the busier avenues.

It took him more than an hour to limp his way past the heavyset grandeur of St. Paul's and slip through Cheapside, then wind his way through St. Albans, Cripplegate, and St. Giles. He arrived at the entrance to Claire's London abode: a tall gated house with an enclosed yard that lurked in an unremarkable laneway off Chiswell Street. The gate was locked and shut, so the player hammered on it with a loose stone cobble until one of her porters finally deigned to open it. Tyburn pushed his way into the yard as the old doorwarden hobbled off to fetch her.

"God's truth, I thought you were gone again." Clair stood framed in the kitchen doorway. She had a thick blanket draped around her for the cold, and was wreathed in steam and aromatic scents pouring out of the household kitchens.

Kit just stared. Her hair was askew, curling tendrils winding down past her shoulders. Her brown eyes looked wounded and concerned but he just stared, drinking in the long expanse of elegant throat visible above the wrap, her full lips and sharp profile. He felt that same sharp sensation as when he first met her, a momentary touch of grace upon his very soul.

"It's been two days," she said. "I thought you were dead. Again." He nodded, unable to frame a reply. He took a slow step towards her but stopped when she laughed outright. "Oh dear Lord. You stink." She smiled and lifted a warning hand.

Tyburn nodded. "I do indeed." His voice was a dry croak.

"You are not—NOT—coming into my house in that state." Clair's voice was crisp and firm. She waved her hand at the doorwarden.

"I've …"

"Not. Coming. In. You need a wash."

"But …"

The near-freezing bucket of water caught the player completely by surprise. The shock of the cold momentarily stopped his shout and left him gasping and blowing in the yard, water streaming down in runnels through the silt and grime that coated his hair and face.

"Two more at least, Master Rumford." Clair gestured imperiously at the doorwarden who grinned and called to the stableboys to fetch more water. "Then strip him, burn the clothes, and wrap him in this." She unwrapped her blanket and handed it to the grinning warden. "Then see Master Tyburn inside. I'll see to a bath for our guest." She stopped Tyburn's objection with one arresting finger. "It's that, or you freeze in my yard." She held the position until the player gave a reluctant nod. "Good. You're learning." She gave him a long stare, directly into his eyes, and

Tyburn felt that sharp soulful tug once more, a sensation abruptly cut short by the arrival of a second bucket.

--

Francis Walsingham frowned across the desk, a look that hung like growling thunderheads. "What, precisely, are you trying to say?"

"That his lordship the Earl of Rutledge apparently arranged for a group of assailants to waylay the young Earl of Asquith in an ambuscade on Maidenhead Lane in Bread Street Ward two days ago."

"Yes," replied the principal secretary, rubbing his eyes, "you've noted that three times, but you have yet to provide me with any actual evidentiary proof of this claim."

"There are three dead gentlemen littering the street and one in hospital. And him only thanks to the immediate ministrations of a barber-surgeon. I would think that was proof enough."

Walsingham raised one eyebrow in mock astonishment. "Dead men are not proof. Any given day of the week, London births dead men by the dozen, a recurring malaise for which the city is known. Two groups of bravos getting drunk and brawling is not an unheard occurrence. While I can appreciate that for the Earl of Asquith this is a clear and immediate concern, I fail to understand why it should distress the office of the principal secretary. Our focus is generally further afield."

"Lord Asquith has brought the matter to the Queen." Walsingham's dark eyes narrowed as he turned his head to fix the man with his direct gaze. Sir Henry Willoughby was a court attendee of Robert Dudley, the Earl of Leicester, but despite that pedigree, he flinched under Walsingham's glare before recovering and continuing. "Or rather to the Queen's representative. Lord Asquith is still technically a ward of the court, under the wardship of Lord Audley. It is tantamount to an attack on the Queen herself." He finished loftily.

"I thought the Queen was at Hampton Court."

"Indeed sir."

"Then how, Sir Henry, is the Queen even aware of this affray?"

"Well ... I suppose she isn't, directly, but Lord Leicester was fully apprised by Lord Asquith. He insists that the matter be brought to your attention and he instructs, if I may take the presumption to quote him directly, 'Walsingham will deal with it. Best bring Rutledge to heel soonest.'" Sir Henry's ruddy face bounced with a vigorous nod. "And so I come to be here, a veritable Hermes, in service to the needs of the Crown, in this time of troubles."

Walsingham carefully laid aside the feathered quill with which he had been writing. He nodded gravely and intoned, "The Crown thanks you for your vigorous pursuit of your duty, Sir Henry. And did Lord Leicester provide any enlightened direction on how he wished these matters settled? No? Then I will, of course, set myself upon this problem in due course. Please convey my thanks and goodwill to his lordship when you return." The principal secretary glanced down at the paperwork strewn across his desk and gave a sharp nod. As if by magic, one of his assistants materialized, holding Sir Henry's feathered cap and long, fur-trimmed cloak, gesturing towards the door.

Flustered, Sir Henry stammered through an abrupt farewell and was bundled out of the office, down the hallway, and into the London streets almost before realizing it.

Walsingham felt the quill in his hand bend under the pressure of his grip and set it hastily aside, lest it join the daily allotment of broken or thrown quills his clerks collected. "Charles!" Walsingham called.

"Sir?"

"What's this business with Asquith?"

Charles fumbled for the domestic London report packets and pulled out a sheet covered in tight, crabbed handwriting. "Apparently he and five of his entourage were traversing

Maidenhead when they were accosted by a group of men. Three of Asquith's manservants were killed and one struck alongside his head. Lord Asquith, by the grace of God and a swift horse, escaped the affray and rode to safety. One of the assailants was killed."

Walsingham's frown tightened a fraction. "Any news on who the assailants were? Neighbourhood bravos? Apprentices on a spree?"

"No. But one of our brighter lads," Charles noted, "whom we placed with the Watch, thought the assailant's throat was cut after the fight had ended. He would have died at any rate, with a belly wound, but our man speculated it was done to prevent him from naming his employer." Charles handed the missive to Walsingham, who gave it a cursory look.

"Of course it was, by God's light. What do we know about this Rutledge and Asquith business?"

"Only that it seems to stem from a couple of sources. Lord Asquith's requests to be released from his wardship have been denied for the past two years. Lord Asquith blames Lord Audley, who claims that the matter rests entirely with the Crown and beyond his authority. It has been said that Lord Rutledge has repeatedly urged the Queen and Lord Burghley to deny the release from wardship. The reasons are somewhat vague."

Walsingham gave a quiet grunt of acknowledgement, which was for him the equivalent of a full-blown snort of amusement. "I suspect Lord Audley hasn't yet siphoned enough from Lord Asquith's holdings."

Charles allowed himself the barest nod in return. "Indeed, sir, Lord Audley is a gaming man, and, if you will allow me to combine some baser rumors into our enquiry, is deep in debt to Lord Rutledge."

"Rutledge ..." Walsingham rubbed his thin beard thoughtfully. "Where does Rutledge draw his income?"

"His incomes come from a number of ventures aside from his significant property holdings and enumerations. I believe he was vested in the Muscovy Company and active with the Hanseatic merchants. He also holds a number of tariffs in his position with the Exchequer."

"No sign of a Spanish pension, like Norfolk?" Thomas Howard, the Duke of Norfolk, had been tried and convicted of treason four years before, after stumbling himself into a failed plot to overthrow Elizabeth, marry the imprisoned Mary Queen of Scots, and, with the help of a Spanish army and the rebellious Northern earls, return England to Catholicism. The plot had died stillborn when the monies and letters had been intercepted by Burghley's agents. Norfolk's head was subsequently removed on Tower Hill. Ambition had ever been the bane of the foolish, thought Walsingham.

"Lord Rutledge has indicated no sign of interest in any Spanish ventures." The clerk hesitated. "However, we did receive a summary of the movements of our new Spanish ambassador and his men that seems to, how shall I say, cross paths with Lord Asquith."

Walsingham leaned forward, brows narrowing. "Tell me," he commanded.

"Mendoza has four principal aides and two secretaries—that we know of—in his embassy. We have Barnard and Phelippes on them, whenever they sally forth. On two separate occasions one of them, a gentleman named Sebastián López de Portolà, wandered somewhat far afield. The first time, he caught them unawares and they lost him near Lambert Hill. The second time, they dogged him to an inn-yard, the Saracen's Head, without Newgate. He was alone. According to the report, he was upstairs, not in the common room or the inn-yard. They waited for him to leave and not above an hour later, observed Lord Asquith arrive. The Don left after another twenty minutes but Asquith stayed for nigh on four hours, according to Phelippes."

Walsingham leaned back. "I suppose it has occurred to you that Asquith might simply have designs on some woman."

"Indeed sir, which is why we hadn't paid much attention to the report, but you said to reach out to our London network and report items of interest."

Walsingham was silent.

"There is one other rumor you might be interested in hearing, sir."

"God frowns on rumor-mongers, but I find them, however distasteful, a necessity in our line of work. Pray tell, Charles."

"There is a suggestion that the nefarious Harlequin might be working to assist Lord Asquith."

Walsingham waved his hand dismissively. "The Harlequin is a tavern tale. A woman, running the criminal activities in the west of London? Nonsense!"

"The Roaring Boys don't think so, sir. She apparently assesses an annual fee for all their activities west of Wood and Friday Streets. Paid in gold."

"So you suggest an alignment of forces—the Spanish, Asquith, and this Harlequin. But to what end? Why should the Spanish care about Asquith, a boy of no note, influence, or office? And this street malfeasor? You truly think a woman could manage the London rabble? They would joint her like a hare. No. Have Phelippes and Barnard continue on the Spanish. Second Milles to them, so they have a third man, but no extra coin. Barnard spends it on drink and licentiousness."

"And Lord Rutledge?"

The principal secretary grimaced in distaste. "Do we have any evidence Lord Rutledge was behind the affray in Maidenhead Lane?"

Charles shook his head. "No. Only this supposed escalating feud between the two men. We would need someone with direct knowledge to either inform or provide evidence. Barring any arrests, we have no witnesses."

"And we can't take anyone into the Tower and ask politely. Any word on why Tyburn was foisting around Rutledge?"

"No, sir. We've had no word of him in near three weeks past. Oldcastle's heard nothing either, though apparently he was taking on work for that Burbage fellow, the one building a permanent theatre in Shoreditch."

Walsingham leaned back, his fingers steepled in thought. "Tyburn vanishing concerns me more than Rutledge or Asquith's petty and farcical posturing. No word to us, no word to Worcester's Men ... I would have expected something from him."

"You think he was caught up in some scheme involving Rutledge's petty street war with Asquith?"

"No. But he has a bad habit of chasing stray cats and tilting at the empty air. He needs keeping at times." Walsingham closed his eyes, feeling the dull throb of a headache resonating in his skull. They had been coming off and on for several years, with increasing and irritating frequency. He sighed and opened his eyes, sharp and tight. "Put another two men on Asquith. If someone else takes a pass at him, at least we'll have watchers who can provide us a thread to pull from this clyster."

"And Rutledge?"

Walsingham smiled. "Rutledge wants to sit at this desk. He will need to learn to protect himself and chase his own troubles. I'll not have the Crown footing the bill for street antics and personal affronts. We stay on the Spanish. And Asquith, because of the Spanish connection, however loose and unproven it is. See what other threads we can pull." The corner of Walsingham's mouth quirked upwards ever so slightly. "Maybe one will lead to this mythical Harlequin of yours."

Chapter the Nineteenth

H E HAD FINALLY stopped shivering. It had taken almost an hour before the bone-rattling cold had retreated. The tepid bath had washed off the filth, and hot water and wine had rinsed away the dried blood scabbed across his chest and legs. Fresh, clean poultices had been applied and Tyburn had rolled, exhausted, into the same bed he had recently recuperated in, asleep almost before his head touched the pillow.

When he woke, the room was dark. The low orange flicker of the hearth crackling away on the far side of the room cast a dull, burnished glow, lending the shadows a tenuous breath of life. Tyburn sat up, feeling the coverlet slide down his chest. He could hear the wind battering against the diamond-paned windows, the faint pattering sound of snow or ice flecks dashing against the panes like spent shot against a fortress wall.

A shape moved in the stillness of the room and Tyburn's breath caught.

Clair Carey stood adjacent to the bed, a long, lace-trimmed robe wrapped about her. The robe was flecked with red and gold flowers stitched along the wide sleeves and across the front, arrowing down from her shoulders to the waist. She reached out and Tyburn felt her fingers laid gently across his mouth.

"No," she breathed. "Don't speak." She leaned down and he felt the warm touch of her mouth on his, her breath a gossamer caress. Kit's heart was hammering in his chest, a familiar tightness, a mix of hope, fear, and pounding desire. She reached up and untied the ribbons at her throat, letting the silken robe slide apart. It puddled down onto the floor and she stood for a moment, still as a deer in the forest, naked and gleaming in the light of the fire. Kit slid back the coverlet, reached up, and wrapped his arms around her, his questing mouth and lips sliding up her body, over the exposed nipples and across her breasts.

She gasped and lifted herself onto the mattress, straddling the player. Kit kissed her and felt the heated smoothness of her body arching against his nakedness. He slid his hands down the length of her and back up, cupping her breasts in both hands, feeling her breath, moist and hot. She kissed him and her tongue darted and curled against his own shaking mouth. The scent of her filled his nostrils, and he drew it in, in deep shuddering breaths, as though to drink of her.

Her hands glided down his body, fingers tracing the thin white lines of scars and wounds that ornamented his skin. His arms were taut and hard, lifting her across the tangled pile of bedding and locking around her as she slid against him. Clair's heart was hammering in her ears, her breath short and tight as his fingers caressed, flitted, and delved, slow and languorous. She felt him enter her and she gasped despite being ready for him. Her pulse pounded and she bit at his neck and face, her legs wrapped around the core of him, as the frantic rhythm rose to a crescendo of staccato breath and concordant gasps. She dug her fingers into his torn flesh as her body rippled and shuddered.

Tyburn felt drowned in her presence, his hands entangled in the briar patch of her hair and the year's separation and all his qualms fading into nothingness at the touch of her body and the caresses of her lips. He felt his fear flutter and vanish, and turned all his attentions to the solace found in her embrace.

The firelight was dying and the chill discernable, so eventually Clair teased the reluctant player into edging out from under the warm blankets to feed the fire with some additional chunks of wood and kindling. She sat in the bed, a mischievous smile on her lips as she watched Kit make his shivering way back to their bed and slide under the coverlets, pulling her close into a warm embrace, feeling the long lean heat of her against him.

"I think you should leave London," he whispered after a moment.

Startled, Clair sat up. "Leave London? Why?"

Kit reached up and pulled her back down into the bed, wrapping his arms around her, pulling her close. "Harlequin. This Suzanne Martaine, she's ... dangerous. And thanks to Chaucer's loose tongue, she knows you exist."

"One woman out of thousands in London." She scoffed.

"One woman, who is tied in some way to Kit Tyburn, actor and notorious wastrel. They just need to ask about Worcester's Men to find out your identity. It is only a matter of time before she turns up."

"Christopher, I am not some defenseless waif you need to protect." She reached over the edge of the bed and opened the bedside cupboard. With a slight grunt, she pulled out a leather-scabbarded wheellock pistol. There was a clatter as the cleaning kit fell out onto the floor.

"Coads," exclaimed a bemused Tyburn, "where did you fetch that hand cannon?" He reached out and took it from her grasp. Pulling it from the holster, he gave it a quick look. "Spanish." He looked at her, a speculative grin breaking his normally grim visage. "I should have been politer, obviously." The player checked the priming pan to confirm it was empty, and cocked the dog, feeling the tightness of the spring and the smoothness of the mechanism.

"I spend a great deal of time on the roads and with highwaymen and the usual rag and tag that lurks about the countryside, so I decided I needed to become more proficient. I've been practicing for almost a year. I have a matched set of two."

"How fast can you load it?"

"About a minute," she admitted, a rueful look visible in the firelight glow. "which is why I have two." She snatched the heavy wheellock from Tyburn's hands.

The Spanish weapon was shorter than the wheellocks that Tyburn had handled in the Low Country, decorated with an intricate pattern of whirls and lines adorning the long barrel. The handgrip had been wrapped with thin leather, giving the user a more secure grip than the carved wood and inlay. Clair hefted it and then slid it back into the scabbard.

"I still think you'd be safer out of London. She's got a long reach."

"I should abandon you to that bitch's mercies? I think not." She turned his face towards her. His grey eyes were worried. "I let you push us apart for a full year because you couldn't or wouldn't allow yourself to be happy or to let go of that damning guilt you trail about you like a ragged cloak. I will not permit it to continue."

"I told you, the work I do—"

"Is an excuse, nothing more."

"I'm more damned than you know."

Clair reached out and took his callused hand in hers, cradling it. "Then I share that damnation, because I won't let you walk that road unescorted. You think you've lost God's grace but you haven't, I would know it, I would sense it. You think I could be with someone who was anything like the blackened soul you think you have become?"

"Annika ..."

"Your Annika is dead. My husband James is dead. Alongside my father and my devil of a brother. We aren't. The dead don't matter! Only the living."

Kit reached out and stroked one finger delicately along a lock of her tousled hair. "Another reason to go. Never could win arguments with you." He took a deep breath. "We tried it my way for a year, and it was an emptiness I fear to repeat." He smiled. "So we will try it your way, for now." He pointed at the wheellock. "Doesn't do much good unloaded."

"I can't leave it charged," Clair countered, "the powder will get damp."

"Wad up some paper after you tamp the ball and powder. It will help keep the damp out, and keep the shot from rolling back from the charge. Empty it and recharge it fresh each day. Keep one with you, and put the other one someplace within easy reach." He reached up and cupped her chin, turning her face towards him. "You don't go to market. You don't go to church. Cloaked, armed, and escorted, anytime you leave."

"You think it necessary?"

There is nothing like Flanders. Tyburn paused for a moment, remembering the gleam of the Harlequin's eyes and the look hidden behind her visage when she had carded Chaucer's skin from his arm. "Yes. More than you can know."

"I suppose it would be wasted breath to suggest we leave London together?" She smiled at Tyburn's reluctant nod. "What rock do you turn over next?"

"Not much point staying dead, when the ones trying to kill you know you're alive. Time to make the rounds and shake the maypole. I think I'll start with Burbage."

"Burbage? Why would you waste time on him?"

Tyburn gave her a smile that, in the reddish glow of the fire, looked positively devilish. "Well, if I can't get Burbage to give Oldcastle and Worcester's Men their promised performance dates, Oldcastle won't be taking me back. I have a passing fondness for tramping the boards with the boys, so while it might not be as prominent a point as tracking down Stokely's murderers, I can at least bring Burbage to account for his delinquency." He paused for a moment, considering. "And for whatever reason, Burbage seems to have a line into the Castle now, so anything I crack with him ought to drift back to the Harlequin with undue speed. I need to delve into whatever is between the Harlequin and that Spaniard. He might have been some trader or foreign mercer, but his accent was Castilian. A well-spoken Castilian Spaniard roaming about London ale-bushes is a rare as an honest Frenchman."

"You think there is some link betwixt the Spanish and the Harlequin?"

"At a guess, I would ask what the Spanish want from Stokely's account books? Stokely clerked for Rutledge, and Rutledge, from what I'm told, has his fingers in a great many pies. And, as a complication, he was meeting with Walsingham when I first was dragged into this squalor."

"Mayhaps you need to speak with Master Walsingham?"

Tyburn snorted in derision. "The Moor made it fairly clear I was to make myself scarce and not darken his doorway until he sends for me."

"He trusts you."

"He uses me. When the time comes that it is more useful to have Christopher Tyburn bound to a hurdle and hanged from a gibbet, he will be the one to lay out the hemp."

Clair scowled at him at this, a mocking scowl belied by the smile that lurked behind it and the bright spark of her eyes. "He likes you," she said in a flat tone. "You are one of his most prized agents."

"Where's this coming from?" Tyburn asked, his frown tightening his scarred cheek.

"He told me."

"When were you speaking with Walsingham?" Tyburn was startled.

"Last summer. At a fête at Somerset Place. I seldom attend court events, but I am oft invited. In this particular case I took care to encounter Master Walsingham, as I was seeking news of you."

"And did he provide any insight?"

"Indeed he did! We spoke at length." Clair closed her eyes and pulled the warm coverlet upwards, snuggling into the bed.

"Well?" Tyburn asked, piqued.

"He said you were abroad, on the Queen's business, and that he would inform me upon your return."

"That's why you were in London on my doorstep instead of Warwickshire."

"Yes." She opened her eyes to see him peering down at her. "He said that while many could dabble in secrets, rather fewer could be trusted with honour. You were in the latter group." She tilted her head. "He trusts you, Christopher. God in his heaven only knows why, the way you blunder about." Clair gave him a smile he could feel to his very bones. "Now sleep. Let the morning's problems be dealt with in the morning."

With reluctance, Kit lay back in the bed, staring up at the flickering patterns of shadow and light the fire cast on the bed canopy. For the first time in a very long time, the player felt calm. He closed his eyes and let what was left of the night steal him away.

Chapter the Twentieth

THE INKPOT SHATTERED against the decorative painted wallboard. Covington suppressed a snarl as he felt the dark ink spray across his shoulder and left side of his face.

"Three God-cursed weeks I've been paying this Danegeld, listening to your benighted excuses and pitiful attempts to end this farce. By the light, you set of turds can't even manage to track these blackmailing miscreants back to their lair and return my accounts. And now you miss the opportunity to cut the head off the snake?" The Earl of Rutledge spun about, eyes darting as though seeking some other breakable object to throw in his fury. His pale mien red with rage, a look more common than not these days, Covington thought.

Rutledge glared at Covington, his ruddy face inches from the ex-soldier's. "What's your excuse this time? What squeaking, pathetic pretext is going to pass your lips now? I wanted him dead!" Rutledge roared.

Covington reached up with one gloved hand and dabbed at the wet spot of ink on his cheek, holding his finger up for brief examination. The gesture had the effect of silencing the earl for the moment. Covington looked at the dark splotch, watching the ink blot through the pale cheveril of his gloves, and waited. Covington let the silence stretch until he saw the earl take a breath to resume his tirade, and then he spoke. "It was never the plan to kill him. The objective was to frighten him, to drive him back to his protection, to whomever he was working with to place this press upon you, milord. And it worked. Killing an earl, a ward of the Crown, would be an affront that you can ill-afford. Walsingham and Leicester have already begun to question your role in these actions. Those inquiries would be far more pressing, if this affair had resulted in a dead Earl of Asquith." Covington kept his voice chill and matter-of-fact. "If you want Asquith dead," he continued, "then we can arrange that at a future date. He can pass away slow from some wasting disease or from an accident while hunting, or be stabbed by some harlot or hoaxed into treasonous conspiracy, like Norfolk. He's a fool and easily led, but what we must not do is allow ourselves to be herded like cattle into some precipitous action where we cannot proclaim our innocence."

"I want him dead." Rutledge grated.

"And dead you shall have him, but not before we retrieve your accounts and extirpate this nest of wolves. Him dead and the accounts unsettled leaves the blackmailers at liberty, or worse, the accounts loose in the hands of some know-nothings who pass them on to the Crown."

That thought made Rutledge pale and settle back on his heels. "We cannot continue to do nothing!" he snapped.

"We aren't doing nothing. We've traced the payments and Asquith back to the Saracen's Head and that bitch Harlequin twice now. We know she's his mistress and he's using her as the go-between. She's the wheel we use to turn Asquith's world asunder."

Rutledge picked up a crystal decanter of wine from the sideboard and poured himself a liberal quantity, gulping it down. "Time is of the essence. I can ill-afford a scandal. Too many things are coming to fruition. Burghley and Leicester have conceded that I should be taking over a parcel of Walsingham's portfolio of foreign duties. I expect the Moor to be boiling by now." He laughed. "That cold, dour fish thinks himself immune, but I have a long arm and many unexpected friends, as he will find to his detriment."

Covington merely nodded, used to Rutledge's preening talk. He wondered how much of the decanter Rutledge had punished before sending for him.

"Lady Howard is still playing the willful bitch. She's ignored my entreaties and proposals. That rutting bastard seems to have turned her head with promises of coming into his patrimony. I've heard nothing but empty wind from Audley. He is loath to step too visibly in holding his ward in check." Rutledge fumed. "A marriage to Lady Howard would bring the largest dowry in England. That could settle my debts, cover the tariff books, and provide high patronage in court through the Countess of Lennox." He drummed his fingers on the table, ending with a clenched-fist slam that made the glassware and decanter recoil with a glassine crash. "Bring that bastard in."

Covington was startled. "You think that wise, milord? We've already spoken with him."

"Do it. I'll hear it for myself."

Covington nodded, opened the door and spoke briefly to a liveried man waiting in the hall. Several minutes passed, while Rutledge grew steadily more red-faced and unsteady.

There was a polite tap and Covington opened the door. Bristow and another man wearing the crossed poleaxes and collared unicorn badge pulled a prisoner into the room.

The man was unkempt and stank of urine and smoke fumes. He was rail-thin, the heavy oversized fetters on his hands giving him a stooped and hangdog posture. He kept his eyes downcast.

Rutledge drained his glass and set it on the side table with an unsteady hand. "You work for Asquith?"

The man kept his head and eyes down, though his breathing was fast and nervous.

"Tell him." Covington said, giving the thin man a prod in the ribs.

"Yes, milord," came a voice in a strangled whisper.

"What do you have to tell me? If it is useful, I will reward you with coin."

"Yes, milord." The man gave a darting glance up and Rutledge took a half-pace back, grimacing at the rotten smell of the man. "My master … Lord Asquith … commanded that we make preparations for a grand celebration."

"A celebration?" Rutledge asked. "Celebration of what?"

"The end of his wardship … and an announcement of his impending nuptials."

Rutledge turned away. Covington could see his skin getting ruddy and a thin vein throbbing in his forehead.

"The Crown has given assent?"

"Not yet, milord." Covington noted. "If the Queen had assented, it would have been formally announced. Asquith is merely trying to lay the groundwork and move the issue to the forefront. He dare not defy the Queen, but if the Countess of Lennox intervenes and asks for the Queen's blessing, then it could force her hand on the release of his wardship."

Rutledge said nothing but Covington could see him clenching his fists in rage.

"Tell him the rest," Covington said.

Rutledge swung around, glaring at the fettered man. "What more do you have to say?"

The thin man flinched and muttered. "The Harlequin is upset. She won't brook no rivals and she … she likes the steady coin coming in through his hoaxing yer accounts."

"What do I care about some Newgate whore?"

"She's hurting for men. Some play-actor crossed swords with 'em and she's down five of her best. Worried the Roaring Boys will push her out of the Saracen's Head and take over the western dunnage."

"Play-actor." Rutledge gave a sidelong look at Covington who shrugged. "That sot Tyburn?"

"Like as not," Covington said in agreement.

That brought a thin, humourless smile to the earl's face. "And you want to play up to the Harlequin," he said to Covington. He drained another glass.

"Might be worth bandying about. She likes coin, doesn't want to lose her position as Asquith's mistress. If she has access to the accounts, mayhaps we get them without having to go through Asquith, for less gelt."

"She's a whore." Rutledge said dismissively. "Pretending to be some kind of thief-queen. Unimportant. She will do what she's told."

"An ally," said Covington suggestively.

The earl snorted and poured another glass of wine. "At best, someone we can use to put the wind up Asquith's tail."

"She's no whore." The whisper from the fettered man was tentative.

"Did it speak?" said Rutledge. He stepped forward. "Did it speak? I don't recall giving you leave to open that toothless hole and spew your thoughts forth." The earl reached over and yanked Covington's slim poniard from his belt. Rutledge waved the blade under the man's chin, his face bathed in drunken rage. The prisoner flinched back, stepping into the liveried guard, who promptly shoved the man hard back into line, unseeing, directly into the blade. The long, razor tip of the poniard sliced deep into side of the man's throat, catching him just under his left jawline, severing the jugular in one neat cut.

The carmine spray shot out, making Covington curse and leap aside in sudden horror. Rutledge stepped back and gaped, the reddened blade still clutched in his hand while the prisoner shrieked in terror and tried to clutch at his torn flesh with his fettered hands. The fetters clanked as Covington yanked the prisoner's hands down to see the extent of the damage, and he cursed again as he watched the man slump to his knees, rocking and keening as the blood spurted out with every heartbeat. Covington snatched the blade from the earl's hand and said in utter astonishment, "By Christ! What did you do?"

The earl, his face now pale and surmounted by a mixed rictus of fear and amazement, stepped back, staring at his blood-drenched hand. "I ... I ..."

Covington grabbed the liveried guard by his collar and yanked him forward. "That man attacked the earl. You saw it, witnessed it before God. The earl was merely defending himself."

The guard, stunned by the sudden unexpected violence, stammered out an agreement. Rutledge stumbled back to the side table and, with an unsteady hand, poured himself another full glass, gulping it down like water. He set the empty stemware down carelessly, not even noticing as the delicate Venetian glass toppled and shattered on the blood-covered floor.

"Jesus." Covington muttered as the slumped prisoner toppled with a thump, landing in the growing puddle of gore staining the expensive parquet floor, his legs thrashing and kicking, drawing out thin ribbons of red across the neat squares.

"The man attacked me."

Covington turned and Rutledge was drawing himself up to his full height, looking down at the supine figure on his drawing room floor. "You saw it Covington. The man tried to kill me. I merely defended myself."

Covington caught a short breath and nodded. "Indeed he did, milord." Covington turned to the guard and said in a low voice "Remove his fetters, then go fetch the coach house guard and a wrap to remove"—he gestured in disgust—"this."

Rutledge was breathing hard and staring at the dead man, slowly resuming his usually assertive posture and aggressive mien. "Defended myself. Unwarranted assault on my person by some alleyway filth." He nodded to himself. "Acquitted myself well, in the face of a violent attack." He glared at Covington. "You should have stopped him. Careless of you, Covington, almost reckless, bringing him here unfettered. You're lucky I killed him. He might have had you in an instant, had I not snatched that blade at the last second."

Covington was barely listening. How could such a thin wastrel hold so much blood.

"Covington!"

The ex-soldier looked up.

"Did you not hear a word I said, you purblind fool?"

"Milord?"

"Have my seamstress sent to my chambers."

"Your seamstress ...?"

"To be sent to my chambers immediately. And see to this mess." Rutledge turned and left the room with an attitude of such haughty indifference that Covington had to glance down again at the corpse on the floor to reassure himself it wasn't all in his imagination, that his patron hadn't just ordered him to bring his resident whore to his chambers after killing a man in his drawing room.

"By Jesus." He muttered to himself. "You poor bastard ..." he said to the body on the floor. "Poor bloody bastard. I guess I'd best go fetch his whore." Covington looked at the long poniard, now stained with blood. He wiped it fruitlessly on his now blood-drenched sleeve and slid it back into the scabbard with a hard click.

Chapter the Twenty-first

THE FRAGRANT SCENT wafted upward in a small curling jet of steam, escaping the edges of the silvered lid.

"Marvelous!" exulted Don Bernardino de Mendoza. He breathed in the aromatic smell of the *sopa castellana*[7] as his servant deftly removed the rounded silver cover. The Spanish ambassador tapped his heavy silver spoon twice on the table, as was his habit, and greedily ladled a mouthful, pausing to purse a delicate blow over the surface to cool it. "Sebastián, this new chef you found is excellent. One would not think to find such skill among the heretics."

"Apparently he was long in the employ of a wealthy Andalusian mercer, based in the Canaries. The man had him trained in Seville, no less, as he missed the flavours of home. When the mercer passed away of some wasting disease, the cook returned to

---

[7] Garlic soup

England." The ambassador's aide smiled in insincere sympathy at the thought of the poor, deceased mercer dying so far from Spain.

"Exquisite. And you said *capon armando*[8] for the main course?"

"With *arroz en cazuela al horno*[9] and *adobado de carnero*[10]."

"Mutton." Mendoza scowled. "Sheep and cows. It is all these bastards know to eat."

"I assume," Sebastián said, "the man is one of Burghley's or Walsingham's spies. But nonetheless he is the best cook we have been able to find."

"So we keep him! We keep him! Let him prattle gossip to his handlers, as long as he stays in our kitchens, where he can be useful."

A discreet knock sounded at the door.

"The ladies cannot have arrived this early," observed Mendoza. He pointed at the door with a quickly flung hand and spooned another bite into his mouth, savouring the smooth bite of the roasted garlic. A peasant dish indeed, but still, this cook gave it a subtle, buttery texture that made it exceptional, he thought. Portolà opened the door and conversed with one of the doorwardens. He turned to Mendoza.

"My lord, an emissary from *arlequin*, with news."

"See him in."

Portolà nodded to the doorwarden and waited. The warden returned with the visitor. Portolà ushered Bent into the room. The man gazed about, unfazed by the expensive table settings and furnishings. Mendoza continued to savour his soup, refusing to even acknowledge the man standing to one side until he had

---

[8] Armored capon – roasted rooster, coated with pine nuts and almonds

[9] Rice casserole

[10] Marinated mutton

finished the last spoonful. He belched and wiped his lips and long mustache with a silken cloth and waved for the servant to remove the silver bowl.

"Speak." Portolà gave the Englishman a nudge, a move that earned him a baleful look in return.

Bent tore his glare from the face of the supercilious aide and gave the ambassador his attention. "We might have a problem."

"A problem?" Mendoza responded. "A problem? I pay you—you and that heretical bitch you serve—to solve problems, not to bring them to me."

"He escaped."

"Who?" the ambassador asked, at the same moment Portolà hissed in frustration.

"The play-actor."

Portolà interrupted with a quick spate of explanation in Spanish. Mendoza leaned back, the relaxed look that had been on his face tightening into a fearsome scowl. Portolà snapped at Bent. "He was supposed to be dead. He should have been dead within minutes of my leaving the building."

Bent shrugged diffidently. "What can I say? Harlequin likes to play with her food."

"What damage," Mendoza asked, "can some lowly play-actor cause to our plans? He's street offal, a vagabond scavenger, a freebooter at best. That bitch should have killed him and been done with it."

The aide interjected. "Milord, the description of this player is very much like that of the English agent that lured and kidnapped that English exile Story from Bergen op Zoom six weeks ago."

The slow turning of Mendoza's head and the look in his eye sent a shiver down Portolà's back.

"Explain."

"Walsingham has many agents, both here and abroad. This player, Tyburn, matches the description we received from the customs agent that survived the kidnapping. Dark-haired, with a hooked scar on one cheek."

"You think a man of Walsingham's resources would employ an actor for such a position?"

Portolà shrugged. "It is entirely possible. Play-actors move in all circles. He apparently was a former soldier and fought with the heretics in Walcheren and Brill."

"But a play-actor? Even for Walsingham, it is unlikely." Mendoza looked mournfully at the empty soup bowl, irritated at the disruption of his meal.

"I told her. Kill him, dump him and be done, but she ... she's got her own way." Bent shook his head in exasperation. "She wants what she wants."

"To her own detriment, I fear," Mendoza noted. "I fear we are reaching the end of this particular chess piece's usefulness. I think the Castle could use new leadership, stronger leadership. Leadership that knows how to achieve results."

Bent shook his head. "The Castle won't follow me. Not yet. Not till this plays out. Once they're all in coin, yes, then we can pitch them, but not unless she takes a misstep. I wouldn't last a turn of the glass."

"Does she still hold the ledger with Rutledge's accounts?"

"Yes, milord."

Mendoza frowned. "I would feel better if those ledgers were in dependable hands. Our hands, by preference. Can you arrange it?"

Bent thought for a moment. "Possibly."

"Then do so, Master Bent, and you will be amply rewarded."

"And the play-actor?"

"We do not want any additional complications nosing about. It is best that he exit this stage."

Portolà spoke up. "I have two men that can find him. They will deal with the player." He glared at Bent. "They aren't dancing to the tunes of some wayward bitch."

Bent bristled and began to turn before Mendoza's icily polite voice cut through the moment. "Let us focus on the ledger, Master

Bent, and your mistress's next steps. We must move swiftly to bring this galliard to a finish. Walsingham out, Rutledge in, and Asquith—well, he is our goat. I will pray for him."

Chapter the Twenty-second

THE LONG RED and yellow pennon cracked and fluttered in the brisk wind. Tyburn squinted against the cold breeze, his eyes watering, noting the livery of the Earl of Leicester's Men dancing in the lively air.

An animated crowd was flooding out of the entrance doors to the Theatre, pushing and shoving past Tyburn where he stood by the muddy ditch at the edge of the road. A cheap printed playbill was affixed to a small signboard. "The excellent Comedie of two the most faithfullest Freendes, Damon and Pithias. As shewed before the Queenes Maiestie, by the Children of her Graces Chappell, excepting the prologue that is somewhat altered."

The player gazed at Burbage's new creation. Now complete and gleaming under a fresh coating of plaster and paint, it rose more than three stories, encompassing a broad, octagonal structure topped with a tile and thatch roof. The entrance was a narrow, double-doored gate, roofed with a small tiled decorative peak to provide a minuscule shelter from any downpour. At present the entrance was crammed with spectators pouring out of the interior open yard and galleries. Tyburn waited patiently for their numbers to disperse, and then pushed his way through the chattering throng, like a salmon thrusting itself upstream. As he stepped into the gateway, a beefy hand thrust out and caught his arm.

"Here you wastrel, the play is done. Begone!"

Tyburn looked up at the bearded face scowling down at him. "Here to see Burbage. Where can I find him?"

The gateman grunted in reply. "Burbage's in the tiering house. Pass through the galleries to the left and on through the door." He turned back and resumed chivvying out the slower patrons, chanting "Push off. New performance tomorrow. Performances every day excepting Sunday. Push off!"

Tyburn stared at the completed interior. Burbage had been up and running now for near two weeks and the playhouse was the talk of London. The graveled interior yard was smoothed with crushed limestone, its dull white and grey colour speckled with flecks of orange peels and the broken shells of nuts. The surrounding viewing galleries had been decorated with swatches and swathes of colourful fabrics, denoting each section. Directly opposite the stage was the Lord's Gallery, a well-appointed collection of cushioned seats and rich, decorated hangings. Tyburn marveled at the stage. Burbage, for all his braggadocio, had not been parsimonious with his setting. The once half-completed sky vault and its supporting columns were carved with entwined vines and leaves, flaring roses and flowers. The stars and carved planets on the interior of the sky vault shone with gilt-edged brightness against a brilliant deep blue, with long silvery trails demarking constellations and comets. The faces of Roman and Greek deities peeked out from corner posts like grinning children peering from above.

"Jesu," the player muttered with a sense of awe. Leicester's Men now had a performance forum worthier than any seedy inn-yard. It was glorious.

"Best close those chops, Kit, before something decides to nest in that space." The laughing voice came from a tall man wearing an expensive oversized doublet that hung on him like rags on a scarecrow. Tyburn grinned back in recognition. John Lanahan was one of the leading players in Leicester's Men. The man's hooked nose and slanted grin were a welcome sight, despite the purported rivalry between Worcester's Men and the more richly appointed troupe supported by the Earl of Leicester.

"Quaint location you boys have found. Always figured you more for a nunnery than a priory."

"We've been getting a better draw than the church, so I expect we'll be hearing some nonny-nonny from the aldermen soonest. Precisian bastards can't touch us in the Holywell liberty, though." He laughed, a straight-up malicious cackle. "Not their jurisdiction, but it don't stop their prosing. Just last week, some sermonizer claimed 'dicing, dancing, vain plays, and interludes were idle pastimes.' Next they'll want to ban bear-baiting, fornication, or bowls."

"God forbid. Where do I find Burbage?"

"He's in the tiering house. Probably in the count room."

"Making good coin?"

Lanahan snorted. "Ain't like an inn-yard – passing round the hat and hoping fer a penny. No one gets through the gate without paying. Two pence for the yard, another penny for the low galleries, four pence for the uppers. The Lord's Gallery is more still. Penny for a cushion, half-penny for ale or oranges. Kit, we're pulling near six hundred or more watchers for each performance. You couldn't mint that much coin in a month of inn-yards."

"How'd Burbage free up his funds? Last I heard, he was near done."

Lanahan gave Tyburn a broad wink. "You know Burbage, always with the scheming and close packings. I heard he's mortgaged to the hilt and tussling with Brayne for the expenses. There's the sharp edge on that blade for certain. Grand place like this means lots of coin paid out. He's watering the ale for sure, but Burbage is a canny bastard, he'll pull it through."

Tyburn nodded in agreement, gave Lanahan a quick wave farewell. He ducked through the narrow doorway into an equally narrow passage. A reinforced door lay to the right, which Tyburn guessed was the counting room. Muffled voices could be heard within. Tyburn tugged on the door latch and stepped in.

The counting room was small, dominated by a tall, well-fitted wooden lockbox secured against one wall. The lockbox had a round opening in the top, just large enough to allow the clay coin pots used to collect the gate payments to drop into the box. In theory, the cheap clay containers, which had no opening except a slot permitting a thin coin, would shatter at the bottom of the lockbox, leaving their small collection of monies safely deposited away from light, filching fingers and empty-pocketed gate wardens. It was a tried and true method to collect entrance fees, similar to systems used at the bear- and bull-baiting rings to minimize pilferage.

Burbage turned at the interruption, a fixed scowl permeating his ruddy brown beard. Brayne and his usual apprentice shadow stood in front of the lockbox, both with their arms crossed. Tyburn sensed he had interrupted a well-practiced disagreement.

"Tyburn! God mend me! You oaf, you handless geck! No monies, no letters, no Stokely! Where have you been hiding?"

"I found Stokely."

Burbage's face was a slow simmering bluster of red and violet. "Yes. Yes, I heard. With steel through his gullet and no account books or writs to be seen."

"The tale being spread in the alehouses is that you killed him," Brayne interrupted. "You were supposed to deliver him to us, we didn't pay you to …. we didn't pay for any killings. This affront is on you! And we will happily speak of it to the bailiffs, so don't even try to threaten us!"

Kit cocked his head, keeping one wary eye on the grocer's apprentice, who seemed content to lean against the wall and shrink away from the potential discord. Tyburn let the two men's imprecations and accusations sputter to a halt before speaking.

"I didn't kill Stokely. I fished him out of the Clink for you, but we were interrupted. Whoever killed the poor bugger knew aforehand I was checking out the Clink. They were waiting and I marched him right to the shambles, like a sheep for the slaughter. You want to dun someone up for your writs? Be my guest. It was the cozening bastards that paunched him you'll have to lay suit to for your redress. In the meanwhile, I have questions of my own, namely who'd you noise off to about Stokely's location?"

The question elicited another round of mixed imprecations, declarations, and side-insults. At another time, Tyburn might have paused to admire some of the more colourful asides that Brayne tossed so freely at Tyburn and his business partner, but at this point, the headache that had haunted him since his venture through the sewers began to resume.

"We did nothing of the sort." Burbage declared, his voice cutting through Brayne's muttered comments. "I expect that drunken cupshotten Oldcastle opened his fool mouth. He's a besotted, wine-soaked knave who would sell his own mother to the Spanish."

"The keyword is sell. Drunk or sober, Oldcastle wouldn't sell naught for naught and the only ones in coin at the moment, strangely enough, are you two. Oldcastle was stringing along for those performances, not for pennies or a poor man's groats. You knew that, you made him promises. And now sudden as a spring rain, your coffers are full. You've finished your theatre. Who paid that bill? You told me your own self, all your coin was tied up with Stokely. You couldn't pay a penny, and now, like the turn of the Wheel, you're mint. Who bought you your cathedral, Burbage? What did you sell Stokely's blood for? What did you sell mine for?" Tyburn dropped one hand onto the hilt of the poniard on his belt. Burbage took an abrupt step back, catching his heel on the edge of the lockbox while Brayne finally closed his mouth with an audible clomp, his now pale face suffused with perspiration beneath his thick mane.

"I assure you…" Burbage began.

"It was him." Brayne pointed emphatically at Burbage. "He told me, by God's Word, he told me!"

"Told you what?" Tyburn asked, beginning to regret having ever broached the subject.

"Shut it, you purblind fool," growled Burbage. Tyburn caught the apprentices' eye-rolling response to Burbage's command. The player held up both hands in front of Burbage and Brayne, cutting off their mutual spate of denials and accusations.

"Another breath of wind from either of you and I'll start slitting tongues." He pointed at the silent grocer's apprentice, leaning against the lockbox. "What's your name?" he asked.

"Simon Ashclough," the dark-haired young man replied.

"You know who spilled the news of Stokely's whereabouts?"

"Aye," Simon said, giving both of them a glare. "That one"—he pointed at Brayne—"told one of the Castle's filchmen that you had a line on Stokely. Then that one"—he pointed in turn at Burbage—"made an agreement on the details with a fellow named Bent, who came calling. Deal was that the Theatre's funds would be advanced if the information led them to Stokely. That one"—Burbage again—"told them the when and where, and tol' them about you, like who you were and a description." He paused and then grudgingly admitted, "Burbage did say you weren't to be harmed if possible, but he didn't insist on it. Didn't care about Stokely, said Stokely's judgment would come from on high, but as long as his writs freed the funds, he daren't care. And then they both stiffed me again for me pay, third week in a row. I got a little 'un at home ta feed and you bloody curst spavined bastards are too cheap to pay me a tuppence. Plenty of coin to gilt up some fancies for yer stage, or to spend on those painted doxies and Winchester geese, but nought fer Simon." He spat and pulled a stout iron key from his smock and waved it. "I be helping myself to my God-anointed pay and taking my leave of you."

The dark-haired apprentice turned, unlocked the front of the lockbox, and scraped a handful of copper and silver coins mixed with clay scraps into one hand. He gave them a careful count, tossing the shards back into the open lockbox. He threw the key to

Burbage, who caught it reflexively. "And just so you know, Brayne's got another copy of the lockbox key so 'e can open it without yer presence and filch extra coin." Simon gave Tyburn a curt nod and pushed past the sputtering theatre owners with a muttered curse.

The player paused, taken aback by the sudden flood of information. James Burbage was glaring daggers at his partner, whose face in turn was mottled and stormy. Before the two men could resume their angry tirade, Tyburn thumped his open palm against the top of the lockbox, making the hollow space ring with a resounding bang. Both men froze, remembering the presence of the play-actor.

"I don't care what folly you two bandy about between yourselves. I don't care if you decide to draw steel and settle it. I care when you prose off about business you hired me to handle and get me killed. Stokely's dead, and the reason he's dead is your blowing off about it to Thieves' Castle." Tyburn gave the two men a thin-lipped smile, a grim promise devoid of any trace of humour. "Mayhaps you didn't realize the consequences of your actions. Or maybe you did. You two are canny men, you know your way about. I have trouble thinking that this came about as a surprise, rather than something close laid and planned."

James Burbage was ghost pale under Tyburn's steady grey eyes. "I assure you we—"

"Don't care. Your assurances don't mean rot to me. You are going to pay me double my requested fee." Tyburn tapped one finger on the hilt of his poniard, cutting off the reflexive sputter from Burbage. "You are going to pay it because I fulfilled my contract and you owe me my earnings. You are going to double it because if you hadn't interfered, I wouldn't have been dropped off bloody London Bridge. Lastly and most importantly, you are going to pay it because the cost of your funerals is higher than what you owe me."

Burbage and Brayne nodded in unison.

"Now the next time the Castle comes calling ..."

"Not a word, not a spill of wind shall pass from our lips. Silence will be our mandate!" Brayne promised.

"Tell them I'm coming for them."

Chapter the Twenty-third

"THE ROPE IS around his neck. Everyone is staring, waiting for the drop. And there's that terrible silence, the one that flows over the crowd in the last moments, just before Death can stride forward and claim his due ... but Ratsey leans over and mutters something to the sheriff." Oldcastle waited a beat, just long enough for a voice to chime in and ask the inevitable question.

"What?"

The gnarled play-actor rubbed his red-veined nose and scowled at the circle around the table. He took a deep draught from the pewter goblet, emptying it. He gazed into its depths, a mournful expression hanging on his face, until one of his listeners proffered a bottle of malmsey.

As the man poured a respectable measure into the cup, Oldcastle continued. "Ratsey asked the sheriff if, in the name of God the Almighty, he could take a last moment and speak some words of caution and wisdom to any that might be considering taking the unrighteous path that he himself had followed. The sheriff, being a God-fearing man, did rightly agree, and so the hemp was removed for a moment and Ratsey was given leave to speak. And so he held forth, spinning a long and unfortunate tale of woe and fate to all who would listen. And on, and on did he prose, while the sheriff waited patiently." Oldcastle surveyed the circle of expectant faces and nodded. "The skies were not so patient, for shortly after he began, rain started to fall, and indeed, the sky opened and it began to pour, like unto the very Flood, and the sheriff, in his finery, was soaked and ruined in the downpour, as were the watchers, the bailiffs, and the hangman. When everyone was thoroughly drenched and swimming in their garments, Ratsey admitted that in truth, he had naught to say, but had noticed the gathering storm clouds in the east, and wished one last revenge upon the sheriff."

The circle of expectant faces burst into laughter and a flurry of toasts were hoisted to the unfortunate highwayman who had foxed the sheriff with his last breath. Oldcastle smiled in turn as another listener topped up his tankard with wine.

"That's a story I've only heard you spin once before. Unusual," Tyburn observed as he pushed his way through the dispersing throng.

"Yes," said Oldcastle. "But thinking about poor Gamaliel Ratsey dangling always makes me pensive. Poor bastard. Worst highwayman you ever saw. Tried to waylay some scholar once, but the man had no monies. Ratsey forced him to do a learned oration instead. Almost got trampled by the man's horse. But," he observed, "a right witty bully rook in the end."

Tyburn had found the troupe in their usual haunt, a run-down drinking establishment called the King's Head off Fenchurch Street, just within the confines of Aldgate. Oldcastle dragged the troupe to the seedy tavern mainly as part of his half-hearted romantic pursuit of the widowed proprietress who, despite Oldcastle's continuing leering propositions, had taken a liking to the play-actors. Abigail Goode had run the King's Head for almost ten years after her husband had died of the flux; still she remained a remarkably beautiful woman, despite the daily rigor of brewing, cleaning, cooking, and serving. Oldcastle was well-smitten.

"The boys are in good spirits." Tyburn watched the players shouting down a red-faced Motely as he tried in vain to catch the eye of the server.

Oldcastle snorted in derision. "That wastrel drunkard Colle passed dead away before time. Had to have Motely cover his lines … Motely! Can you even fathom it? I thought Alleyn was going to burst out laughing at every pause. The good news was the groundlings was so deep in their cups, they didn't pick up on anything. *Titus and Gisippus*. Bloody hate that tripe, but histories seem to be the thing." Oldcastle glared at Tyburn as he raised his cup, his eyes fierce over the rim. "Don't be thinking you're back on the boards. I'll keep that staggering drunken geck until you fulfill your bargain. How are you in with Burbage? Last I heard, he was cursing you for treachery and murder, on account of his goldseller turning up paunched on the Bridge."

"Burbage sold me to the Castle. Found out they were hunting Stokely, so he kindly pointed them in my direction. I led them right to him and served him up cold, on a plate. Burbage got his coin for delivering Stokely. So I doubt he'll be giving you your performances."

Oldcastle stared and then grunted and drained his cup. "Guess I'll have to work around that bastard Colle, then. Pity. Got a court performance coming up. You might have been useful."

Tyburn frowned, making no attempt to disguise his annoyance. "You'd squander your troupe just to teach me a lesson?"

"Performances, cully, performances." Oldcastle waved a chiding finger. "We had an agreement. You square us with Burbage, and you get to throw Colle in a laystill and rejoin our superlative ranks."

"Bastard."

Oldcastle shot Tyburn a sharp glance out from under his heavy brows. "You think this is games, cully? Worcester's hasn't the pull at court to give us the edge we need. Cutting the boards well don't guarantee us performance dates, and between the London aldermen, the Master of Revels squeezing us for permits, and the bloody plague, we can't make this work. If we can force a Theatre performance, I can get leverage with Bowes, the Bear Ward, and mayhaps we can access the Paris Garden for future performances. It would beat an inn-yard foresquare! It's in Bankside, so the London aldermen and Leicester's Men can go fuck themselves. 'Only theatre in London!' Codso!"

Their argument was interrupted by the arrival of Meg, a round-faced, sharp-eyed serving girl that always left Motely stammering and red-faced whenever he needed a refill. She gave Oldcastle a curt, disapproving nod and granted Tyburn a shy smile. "You not been about much lately. Given up play-acting for greener pastures?" she asked, pouring a healthy measure of thin red wine into Tyburn's purloined mug as he handed her some coppers.

"Occupied." Tyburn said, while simultaneously Oldcastle chimed in with "Kicked 'im out."

"Mam favours him." Meg noted archly to Oldcastle, "Says he reminds her of my da, when he was young and troublesome." Oldcastle snorted in derision and drained his cup, shooting a quick glance across the room at Abigail, who was spooning a trencher full of pottage for a customer.

"See what you can do about Burbage," he growled at Tyburn. "We need the performances." He shoved back the bench, picked up his mug, and sauntered across the room to lean on the counter where Abigail toiled. Tyburn watched as Oldcastle smiled winningly. Abigail waved her hand at him in mock dismissal, but the smile and the bright pink cast to her face belied the actions.

Jacob Willens and Edward Alleyn, both long-standing members of The Earl of Worcester's Men, wandered over, bringing a tall flagon of wine and a set of cups. "Any luck shifting the fat bastard's mind?" Alleyn asked with a malicious grin. He was the troupe's new lead actor, stepping into the role after Alec's untimely death the year before in Warwickshire.

"What do you think?" Tyburn responded.

"I think the fat bastard wants to swive the daughter as well as the dame. And I think he wants you back in the troupe on the reason that Colle is a useless sot. You know he was versing lines from the wrong bloody play the week before last." Alleyn rolled his eyes.

Jacob tutted, his long face and silvered hair giving him a deep and sonorous gravitas. "Of course he wants to swive the daughter as well, Oldcastle is nothing if not ambitious in his sins. But Motely has nothing to fear. Meg can't stand Oldcastle." He leaned over and topped up Tyburn's mug. "Our wayward friend here though, won't be back in the troupe unless he can find a way to let Oldcastle collect his victory, so either grant him his performances or beg most keen for profound forgiveness."

"You two aren't helping," noted the play-actor. They laughed.

"It's your own fault you know, Kit. All you need to do is, like a Tower raven, continually squawk how absolutely correct he is in all things." He leaned over and tapped Tyburn on the forehead. "Even Motely does a better job assuaging our troupe leader's sour belly than you do."

Tyburn drank a healthy measure of the Madeira in his cup and held it out for a refill. "*Ab uno disce omnes*—that means 'from one, learn all,' for you ignorant louts."

"All the Virgil in the universe won't get you as far as a bended knee and some humility. Wait," Jacob said with a smile. "Humility. Your pardon, I forgot to whom I was speaking."

The door creaked open and two more men entered. They glanced around, then hesitated and pulled out a bench on the far side of the common room, waving for Meg. As the girl poured them a healthy measure, the newcomers glanced about the room until one spotted the saturnine play-actor seated with two of his fellows. The hooked scar on one cheek confirmed their prey's identity and the two men settled in, content for the moment to observe as the play-actor laughed and conversed with his compatriots. They could wait.

--

Clair Carey sighed as she carried the basket of bedding into the bed chamber. The work, whether in the city or the country, was relentless. She had inherited the Warwickshire estates on her father's death, alongside the Carey holdings and dowered lands she had received after a long court battle when her husband had passed. Once the legal niceties had been finalized, she had become crushingly aware of the burden of managing the various lands, rents, enclosures, and permissions. She was determined to cope with the many varying interests in a fair manner but was constantly being pulled into the contending interests and handling the manors, cottagers, artificers, rented freeholders, and leased lands.

The room was dimly lit, the fire having died down to low, smoldering embers and the low clouds of the early evening cloaking the diminishing rays of the sun. She sighed again in exasperation and set the basket on the edge of the bed. Old Richard was supposed to have tended the fire but obviously he had sloped off to drink again. She turned to go fetch more wood but froze at the sight of a shod foot sticking out from behind the length of the canopied bed. Heart pounding, she edged around the bed to see Old Richard stretched out face-down between the sideboard and the bed. A carmine puddle of blood was pooled around his head.

"Sorry. Didn't mean to mess your floors. Thankfully no blood on the sheets though." The voice came from a figure seated on a settee in the far corner. Leaning forward, the shape tossed a handful of kindling onto the fire, which flared to life. Clair stood frozen in shock as the growing light illuminated a dark-haired woman who leaned back again, her stretched legs encased in a pair of leather boots and tight-fitting hose and breeches, topped with an embroidered, silver-buttoned doublet over a silk shirt. A long blade hung from one hand, casually and loosely gripped.

Clair was not sure how she found her voice. "He was harmless."

"More harmless, now."

Clair stepped sideways, back around the edge of the bed, so her left side faced towards the dark-haired woman. Unseen, her right hand slid down under the edge of her kirtle, her fingertips tracing the smooth carved edge of the grip of the wheellock that Tyburn had insisted she cart about.

"You are the infamous Suzanne Martaine," Clair stated.

"Suzanne Martaine died in Paris four years past. The night the *Hellequin* was born." She smiled, a chilling sight. "Your play-actor tell you that?"

"He wasn't specific. He said you were mad."

The Harlequin laughed. "Mad? I suppose I am. To your eyes. I'm Hell's emissary on this earth. I would have to be mad. It would well suit, to wear that cloth."

"Are you here to kill me?"

"I came for the dead man, your Tyburn. He slipped my bonds, but strangely enough, still hasn't run." She shook her head in mock puzzlement. "Most would have fled London by now, but he keeps hanging about, pushing at my corners."

"He isn't here."

"You are. Bird in hand and all that." She laughed again. "I think you and I are of a kind. You seem to have a touch of the dark demonic blood coursing in your veins. No fear. No hesitation in the face of death. Methinks you've killed before?"

Clair shivered, her hand slipping around the carved grip. The Harlequin slid her booted feet underneath her and rose in a fluid, smooth motion. Clair drew the wheellock from the pocket of her kirtle and leveled the heavy weapon. She cocked the dog with her left hand and held the weapon steady, the dark hexagonal barrel pointed at the Harlequin's head.

"To answer your question, yes, I've killed before." Clair's voice was level and firm.

The dark-haired woman tossed her head back and gave a full, melodious laugh that in normal circumstances would have turned heads and drawn smiles. "I like you. You and your play-actor are very akin. Neither of you turn and run when you should." She took a step forward, the silvered blade in her hand rising a fraction.

Clair lifted the gun slightly, giving the Harlequin the barest shake of her head. "Why are you doing this?"

"Why is a foolish question. Fate propels us all. My fate was written four years ago in the blood of my mother, the indifference of an Englishman, and my father's treachery. Your fate drew you to your play-actor. His fate pulls him to me, the dead man to the *Hellequin*, like a moth to the flame." She raised the blade and delicately wiped a speck of dust from the gleaming edge. "You know who made me what I am today? Two men that used the tools at hand for their own aggrandizement. My father was one. He shaped me to be a weapon to use against the Duke of Guise. Taught me the arts of seduction, how to kill with poison and blade and the wetness between my thighs. When *la massacre* came in Paris, I watched my mother die before me, raped and sodomized by a dozen men before they slit her throat and tossed her in the Seine. The one that took me, I made sure, found his satisfaction and pleasure. I whored myself to him, using all the skills my father so painfully taught me, to escape my mother's fate and seek my vengeance. He wanted to keep me for himself, so he took me away from his compatriots, to enjoy proper." She smiled wolfishly. "I tore his throat out with my teeth."

"I'm sorry," Clair said after a moment's hesitation.

The woman's face twisted with anger. "Sorry? Sorry? Save your pity. I'm the black-faced demon. I pull the damned into Hell's fires and bathe in their blood as I choose. For myself. For vengeance. You think your powder and shot can even slow me? I will find your play-actor and pull his entrails out, if I decide that is the fate he deserves." She glared across the room at Clair and the force of it was such that Clair took a step backwards. The Harlequin took a deep, shuddering breath and seemed to pause. "But I like your dead man. Perhaps I will keep him for my pleasures. Or you. Would he shiver with fear or relief if I took you from him and kept you for my own desires?"

"If you touch him again, I'll kill you," Clair said flat and straight, barely recognizing the person that voiced it. She hadn't felt this way since that blood-drenched night in Warwickshire that saw her father and brother dead, washed in the red light of the blazing fireplace.

"So be it." The Harlequin stepped forward and the shot at point-blank range hammered out in the room, clipping the edge of the sword and spinning it out of her hand. Clair dropped the gun and dove for the sideboard, yanking open the drawer. Grabbing the second wheellock, she whipped it up and pulled it down in line. The powder smoke was dissipating, but the Harlequin was gone. Cold air was flooding in through the opened window; Clair cocked the dog on the gun as she ran to it. The Harlequin had dropped into the enclosed yard and was strolling to the barred gate.

The dark-haired demon turned when Clair shouted. She saw Clair with the leveled wheellock and paused for a moment, a warm smile across her lips. Clair leveled the weapon, took a steady aim, and fired. The wheellock mechanism spun, sparked the powder in the pan, the second hammering blast bucking the weapon in her hand. She could have sworn that the shot made the curly tendrils of hair atop the Harlequin's head flicker as it passed.

The Harlequin gave Clair a grave nod of her head, pulled back the locking pin on the gate, and vanished into the London twilight.

Chapter the Twenty-fourth

THE SMOKE WAS harsh and raspy, but with a hint of sweet fragrance that hung in the nostrils with irritating persistence. Tyburn waved his hands to clear the air. "Leave off, Motely. It stinks like fox piss."

"It is considered to quicken the mind and the acumen, to give strength and good health." Motely protested, waving the long, thin hollow wooden tube. The end of the tube was packed with a dense roll of burning dried fragrant leaves. "It's very efficacious and—" The claims were interrupted by an immediate spate of coughing and spitting from the young actor.

"Yes. Very," came the usual caustic response from Alleyn. "Who showed this to you?"

"That mercer, the one from Bristol."

"Dear God, Motely, you paid for this nonsense?"

"It's"—he wheezed in response—"healthy. Cures the pox! He told me his own self!"

"The only decent thing about your tobacco leaf is it covers your usual stench," observed Jacob. "Where are you off?" he asked as Tyburn stood and slid out from his spot on the bench.

"Got to go pluck a rose," Kit muttered in response, "and get a breath of air fresher than what's served around yon Motley fool."

Tyburn pushed his way past and exited through the side door leading to the alleyway, the customary location in which to relieve a full bladder. A few seconds after Tyburn left, one of the two men seated at the far table also arose and followed him through the door.

The play-actor stood in the narrow alleyway, fishing at the ties to his breeches. The sky was grey and fading, the alleyway narrow and caked with refuse. It was cold and getting colder, with light snow floating down and melting as it lit upon the warmer ground. Tyburn heard the side door open behind him and he threw a glance over one shoulder, recognizing one of the tavern customers. The man gave him a quick nod and shifted down the alley to relieve himself.

The faint soft crunch of a footfall squelching in half-frozen mud was the only warning.

Tyburn heard the noise and the corner of his eye captured a brief glint of drawn steel. Kit threw himself backwards as the man lunged with a short blade.

"Coads!" Tyburn cursed and scrambled away as the man whipped the blade a second time through the space he had vacated, a vicious slice that, had it landed, would have opened his throat in an instant. Tyburn felt his back hit the alley wall and he spun sideways along the bricks, yanking his own dagger free of it's sheath.

Time seemed to hang slow and fine as Kit drew his weapon. He could see every detail as though it was etched in ivory. The man was grinning, his face a rictus of fear and excitement, the sinews in his wrist drawn and tight where they held the knife. He stabbed again. Tyburn slapped the man's extended arm aside and flicked his own blade inward with sudden and implacable precision. The blade tore through the man's coat and doublet, catching no flesh but ripping a long rent in the heavy fabric. The man grunted in surprise and backpedaled for a moment before driving in with a rapid flurry

215

of stabs and cuts. Tyburn's feet slid in the muck as he retreated down the alleyway, his own blade weaving and making quick stabbing thrusts to keep the attacker at bay.

The man drove the blade forward and Tyburn slapped his own gloved hand down to catch the man's extended forearm. The player dropped his own blade, reached across with his right hand and clutched the man's arm in a two-handed grip, locking the man's arm, wild fear lending strength to his hold. The player set himself in the muck and yanked the man forward. The attacker's feet slid helplessly in the alley waste as he tried to pull the weapon back to strike but it was too late. Tyburn stepped in, pivoted, and rammed his right elbow into the man's face, slamming his head back. The man slouched, the grip on the weapon loosening as Tyburn hammered his elbow in again and again. The man slid down into the half-frozen mud, the knife falling from nerveless fingers.

The side door to the tavern was shoved open and Kit backed in, dragging the unconscious, mud-caked body of his attacker behind him. The player ignored the shouts and queries as he hauled the now quiescent man into the common room. Tyburn bent and lifted the man's head by his lank hair, giving them a look at his face.

"Anyone know this one?" he asked, surrounding by a circle of astonished eyes.

"He was seated over there."

A sudden crash and a screech of pain parted the crowd, revealing the second man gripping a bloodied hand. Meg, the serving girl stood beside him, one arm raised, a heavy pewter flagon still held in it. She brought it down a second time, slamming it into the man's skull, and the man screeched again, flailing at her.

Motely leaped forward, snatched the pewter flagon from Meg, and crashed it into the man's head again. He paused, raising it for another strike, but instead watched as the man sank slow into the bench and crumpled into the rushes on the floor.

"A pistol!" she shouted excitedly, her eyes wide and her breath coming in throaty gasps. "A pistol!" she repeated. "He was going to shoot you," she said to Tyburn. "Had it up and leveled. So I hit 'im! Twice."

"Well done, Meg!" called Alleyn. Motely gingerly picked up the weapon off the floor and handed it to Tyburn. It was a wheellock, which was not unexpected. It was hard to shoot from ambush with the slow-burning match cord used for flintlocks.

"Loaded. Pan primed, lock back," Tyburn observed, clicking the dog back to a resting position.

"Abigail!" Oldcastle called out. "Bolt the door." He gave Tyburn a sly look. "Any thoughts on who these brigands be? Or do we call the catchpoles?"

"No." The player's voice was grim and determined. "I need to know who sent them."

Oldcastle snorted. "Sit your arse down and drink. Leave this one to Jack and me." He gestured to the tall play-actor who doubled as the troupe's collector and enforcer. Jack reached down and hauled one of the unconscious men over to the far corner near the kitchen entrance, propping him up against the bench. Tyburn watched as Abigail held a long, tense conversation with Oldcastle, who made a series of soothing conciliatory gestures. Meg, on the other hand, was marching about the common room with Motely in tow, pewter flagon still clutched in her grip, looking, Tyburn thought, as though breaking a few more heads would be good sport.

The play-actor forced himself to down another cup of sour wine while carrying on a desultory conversation with Jacob Willens and Alleyn. The slow mutter of voices interspersed with Oldcastle's cajoling tone could be heard from the far corner. The other attacker was still sprawled insensate under a bench, being watched over by the two troupe servants, Much the Younger and Robbie Hobson, a former London draw-latch turned carter. Robbie cheerfully rested both feet on the downed man's head, on occasion giving him a hefty jab with his worn heels.

The shriek from the corner made Tyburn raise his head but Jacob smiled, a thin humourless grimace, part sympathetic and part reassuring. "He won't kill him."

"I don't care if he kills him, but I need answers," Tyburn responded. "Oldcastle's not known for his subtlety."

"You aren't the only one that's ever smelled powder or clashed steel. Oldcastle went north with Hertford in '44, with Henry's campaign. St. Mynettes, Leith, and Edinburgh. Learned enough tricks from the Scots guaranteed to make a man voluble. Just be patient."

A second shriek was muffled and smothered. Tyburn glanced over to see Abigail fussing behind her counter, ignoring the noise through sheer force of will. The three play-actors traded small talk until Tyburn glanced up to see Oldcastle threading his way through the tables and benches carrying a bottle. The ruddy-faced troupe leader caught Willens' and Alleyn's eyes and gave them a quick toss of his head to send them shuffling to another table, talking inconsequently. Oldcastle hooked out the bench with his foot and sat down with a hefty sigh and an audible thud.

"Dons." He set the bottle down and gestured for Tyburn to pour himself a measure. Tyburn gulped the last of his wine and poured himself a drink from Oldcastle's bottle.

Brandy, he noted. Not a good sign.

"Dons?" Tyburn replied, his voice credulous.

Oldcastle nodded. "Dons. Bastard Spaniards. How you can turn over a rock hiding some spavined goldseller factor and send the Dons scurrying out is beyond my judgment. You must be cursed." He squinted at Tyburn. "You cursed, Kit?"

"Sometimes, yes," the player replied under his breath. "Why in God's light are the Dons sending some London curtails to put me down?"

"Why do you think? I'm not stupid Kit, I know you do knifework for that cold wastrel Walsingham. You set the wrong foot on something the Dons might want you for. They're vengeful Papist bastards, and you've done them no end of harm in your day, in

Flanders and elsewhere. Mayhaps they're getting a bit of their own back, setting you about, putting your arse into a bloody laystill."

"It might explain a few things as to why the Castle is so intent on having its hooks in Rutledge."

"Rutledge? The Earl of Rutledge?"

"You know him?"

"By reputation only. Hard man to get paid by, in all accounts. One of those in whom petty ambition and mediocrity swived with arrogance and a God-birthed right to do what they please." Oldcastle shook his head. "By my troth, best not to get mixed about, when the great men clash. That's when poor fools like us are trampled underfoot in passing."

"I don't have that option."

"No. But we do." Oldcastle poured another measure of brandy into Kit's cup. "You drink that down and shift yourself. I'll not have the boys yanked into another of your malfeasances. We already lost Alec to it, I'll not lose another."

Tyburn was silent but he could feel his face burning. He still blamed himself for Alec's murder in Warwickshire the previous year. In one quick gulp he tossed back the brandy, feeling it scorch its fiery way down. He nodded.

"What are you going to do with them?" Tyburn asked, nodding at the supine forms of his attackers.

"Jack and I will have a long conversation with them about how it is best for all involved and their own reputations if they not sound off about how a playing troupe and a barmaid put them into the dirt. Can't say they won't speak about you, but then, I'm not caring so much on that aspect, am I?"

"I need the name of that Spaniard," Tyburn stated.

"Portolà. Some bastard fancy. Part of the embassy to court, as I understand it."

The player nodded at the troupe leader. "Thanks. I'll keep clear of the boys."

"You do that."

Tyburn turned and headed towards the door.

"Good hunting," Oldcastle called out after him. "Kill some fucking Dons for us."

Chapter the Twenty-fifth

THE ENTRANCE TO the Saracen's Head was no different in appearance than that of any other London inn-yard, although from the endless prating about the Castle that Covington had endured, it should have yawned like a hellmouth. Instead it was crowded with the usual relentless stream of mercers, factors, clerks, law students, printers, and unwashed apprentices that haunted the western reaches of the city. The blond swordsman pushed his way through the drinkers and the dice-tossing apprentices and up the main staircase. Near the top, several armed men lounged with careless aplomb.

"You take a wrong turn, cully?" one grated, giving Covington a careless glance.

"I need to speak with your mistress."

He snorted. "And who might that be? I don't know what you're banting about."

Covington paused. "Suzanne Martaine, the Harlequin. Now you can either go fetch the bitch, or I bleed you out and your replacement goes and fetches the bitch."

The guard stiffened and dropped his hand to the hilt of his sword but froze at the gimlet stare of Covington's cold eyes. Instead he turned and mumbled "Fetch Bent" to the other guard, who nodded and vanished through the closed door. Several minutes later the door reopened. A wide, battered-looking man emerged, a long, silvered sword that Covington recognized hanging by his side. Tyburn's, he thought to himself.

"Well, cully? You dropped some names and I'm the best you're going to get. What do you want?" Bent growled, his eyes sweeping Covington up and down in a quick assessment.

"I've come to have a word with the Harlequin."

"Have a word with me, cully, or bing a waste."

"The Earl of Rutledge would speak with her."

"You the earl?" Bent asked, amused.

"No."

"Come back when you've got that whoreson wretch in tow, and maybe the Harlequin will see you."

Covington hesitated, then turned away with a grimace. Bent made a grunt of amusement that ended abruptly as Covington spun, pulling a wheellock pistol out from his heavy open coat, cocked it and shoved the muzzle hard under Bent's whiskered chin. His other hand drew a wicked poniard seemingly out of nowhere and pointed the blade at the pair of shocked guards.

"As I noted, the Earl of Rutledge wanted to have a word with your mistress."

Bent reached down, and as his fingers touched the curved, embossed rapier hilt, he heard an amused voice in his ear. "Stand wary Bent, I think the man is serious. You would look embarrassingly short without a head." A dark-haired woman stepped into the hallway, a crooked smile on her lips. "You wanted to meet the Harlequin? Here she is."

Covington shifted his gaze to look at the woman. "You're the Harlequin?"

"Underwhelming, aren't I?"

"More the opposite." The blond swordsman muttered, his eyes taking in the well-used rapier she carried at her belt and the shorter, lethal hooked knife on her other side.

"Put up your dag and speak then, Master Covington."

"You know my name." Surprise coloured his voice.

She held the door open and gestured him in. "I know a great deal about you, Master Covington. I think you and I, we can help each other in … so very many ways." The Harlequin smiled and led the pale swordsman into the hallway. "So very many ways."

The door closed behind him.

--

"You found Tyburn?" Walsingham's voice was even and unhurried, but Charles thought he could detect the barest edge of relief. "I had assumed by now that he was dead."

"Apparently alive and well and engaging in his usual proclivities," Walsingham's assistant said with a grimace. "The story is that there was some set-to in the King's Head, near Aldgate. Tyburn and Worcester's Men were involved. The Watch found two men, beaten, naked, and bound, in an alleyway near Ironmonger's Hall."

Walsingham started to frown but paused as his assistant continued. "According to the report, these same two men are associates of our Spanish friend, Sebastián López de Portolà. Spanish-paid ruffians the court embassy and Mendoza use for knifework and back-alley persuasion."

That information brought one of Walsingham's eyebrows up, the equivalent in a normal man of a shout of acclaim. The spymaster leaned back in his chair, steepling his fingers and staring thoughtfully into the distance. "I would have thought, in the wake of Antwerp, our Spanish friends would be a more restrained presence. Our play-actor seems to have unearthed something of note. Something the Spanish have seen fit to bury, alongside anyone that could possibly speak of it. Where is Tyburn now?"

"Willens thought the player was staying at the ... uhm ... Carey House, in Chiswick, past Cripplegate. I queried Oldcastle, who confirmed the identification of the Spanish paymasters and admitted to dealing with the two curtails, but, in his usual colourful manner, had nothing helpful to say about Tyburn or where to find him. His exact words were 'Keep that purblind lackwit away from my troupe. He's a lodestone for trouble.'"

Walsingham's thin lips curved in a grim smile. "That purblind lackwit seems to have pulled the end of a very long thread, one that may tie our friend Rutledge back to the Spanish. Given that Burghley and Leicester are due to grant the Queen's approval of his appointment as principal secretary alongside myself, it has ... implications that do not bode well for the Crown." The thin smile lapsed into a brooding silence. "Second another two men to Milles. Use Master Jones, he's rapacious enough. If the Spanish break wind in the street, I want to know about it. And we need take a closer look at our friends Rutledge, Asquith, and that lot, and determine exactly what devil's brew is being concocted. My ears are itching, so something dark is afoot. What else is stirring?"

"Nothing since the attack on Asquith. Though he apparently will be announcing a betrothal to Lady Arabela Howard."

"Asquith or Rutledge?"

"Pardon me, milord. That would be the Earl of Asquith."

Walsingham winced. "That will set Rutledge afire, for certain. Asquith best look to his backside."

"He is expected to announce at his Christmas revels. He is holding a pageant at his warder's London manor."

"Lord Audley?"

"I believe so. I would assume that Lord Audley has arranged to receive some substantive remittance in exchange for permitting Asquith's wardship to be annulled. Perhaps the Countess of Lennox ..."

"An investment, Charles." Walsingham observed, pushing his chair back from the long desk with scraping force. "To wed the most landed woman in England will position Asquith for a multitude of other remittances and honours. And," Walsingham noted with a glum tone, "he has a good leg, which will draw the Queen's approval. She always has a weakness for a dancing fool with a good leg. We are between Scylla and Charybdis. Either Rutledge's petty ambitions and dangerous connections rise in court, or that petty, pretty, willful, wayward fool positions himself in power." Walsingham's brown eyes were level and biting. "I've a note for our wayward player, and instruction, however much he may not appreciate it. Have one of our couriers ready within the hour to carry it to Lady Carey's. I need to know what he knows, although he may settle all these problems for us if they cross him. I would feel better with our wolf on a chain."

Chapter the Twenty-sixth

"A REVEL. HE wants me to attend a revel." Tyburn crumpled the letter in his hand and waved it for emphasis. "I'm hunted by assassins and curtails across London and Walsingham wants me to attend a celebration."

Clair plucked the crumpled letter from Tyburn's grip, smoothed the paper, and read the precise, crabbed handwriting. She smiled. "It's worse than you thought. It's a pageant masque."

The play-actor threw up his hands in exasperation. "And how does he think I'm to attend such an event? Just stroll inside?" He stood and began to pace the length of the room while Clair watched in amusement from her chair by her writing table. "I assume they must have some entertainment planned—Lord Howard's Men, or maybe Strange's. Alleyn knows them. Maybe he can talk them into letting me in with their troupe. Or musicians. They must have a wait of musicians to play for them." He shrugged. "It's that, or disguise myself as a cook. Damn Walsingham anyway." By this time Clair was laughing outright.

Tyburn frowned at her. "What's amusing?"

"You, Christopher."

"This is serious."

"Straight to the skulking and the disguises." She shook her head in mock rueful amusement. "Have you never considered entering through a door?" She fished a small square of parchment out of the piles of correspondence neatly arranged on the desk.

"What's that?" Tyburn asked, puzzled.

"That my love, is what's called an invitation."

"You have an invitation?"

"The wealthiest widow in Warwickshire, heir to the deBarge estates, esteemed at court and related by marriage to the Carey family and the Baron of Hunsdon? You think I would not be invited?" She looked annoyed. "Just because I do not attend court, that does not make me some spinster, locked at her wheel." She leaned back, fanning the air with the invitation. "Of course if you wish to sneak about like some thieving filchman by preference, then I can toss this on the fire."

Tyburn made a hasty but still elegant leg and a deep bow. "Nay, my lady. My apologies for expressing any semblance of doubt. Of course a woman of your renown would be invited to all court affairs. Your presence alone would bring them a level of quality and prestige hitherto unknown."

"That's better," Clair observed.

"I still have my doubts that they would let me in, despite being accompanied by your grace."

"Nonsense! The heroic Captain Christopher Tyburn, but lately returned from battling the infernal Spanish in Flanders. They will be beside themselves."

"I doubt it. And according to Walsingham's letter, the infernal Spanish are also invited, so best they don't encounter the 'heroic Captain Tyburn'. My God. The Spanish, Rutledge, and

Asquith, all under one roof." He snorted. "Nothing can possibly go wrong.""

"Then you can be my second cousin, Thomas Swinton. He's in York presently, so no one is expecting his presence, and no one here knows him, so it should go unremarked."

"No one would know his face?"

She shook her head. "It's a masque, so it matters naught."

"A masque?"

Clair shrugged. "A costumed party. All the attendees wear disguises and masks."

"I can ask Oldcastle if we can raid the troupe's store. He'll charge a hefty sum but ..."

"No need. I have two costumes here."

The flat tone in her voice made the player pause. "What's wrong?"

She hesitated and then spoke. "Just before James died, we were to have attended a masque. Three years ago. We arranged for the costumes and then he fell ill. They were never used." She looked up, her eyes steady. "It just reminded me of him, for a moment."

"I'm sorry."

She reached out with one warm hand and grasped his. "No matter. The Fates rule us all. The Wheel turns, and God wills. James would be pleased to see them go to use." She straightened up and one hand dashed the slight, glittering tears that had emerged from the corners of her eyes. "So. Fox and hare."

"What?"

"The costumes. A fox and a hare."

Tyburn gave a smile. "I've always been partial to foxes."

She laughed. "Oh no, don't you know? You're the hare. Best keep watch for the cony-catchers."

--

Audley House was located beyond the western reaches of the city, bordering York House, and tucked gracefully in the confines between the Strand and the Thames. Though it lacked the grandeur and scale of its immediate neighbours, the manor house was a stolid mass of carefully dressed stone, resplendent with tall glass windows, etched and crossed with diamond-shaped panes and surmounted with decorative carved lintels. The building soared three stories above a thin sward, its high, sharp-angled roof cutting a wedge out of the darkened sky. Carved corner posts decorated each crook of the façade, twisting heavenward in perfect symmetry, interspersed with the wider and broader brick chimneys. Every window of the entrance façade sparkled with the warm and inviting glow of dozens of blazing candles that shone with a vibrant, luminous radiance, driving back the sallow light of the evening.

The gatehouse was crammed with porters and liveried doorwardens, bustling back and forth to manage horses, coaches, and the occasional more decorative and expensive carriages. The Strand was lined with waiting grooms and drivers, whiling away the hours tossing dice and drinking from surreptitious wineskins and alepots purchased from canny street vendors that carted barrels and hot food down from the inn-yards that populated the area around St. Clements.

Christopher Tyburn alighted from the hired coach, pausing to glance up and down the broad, heavily rutted avenue. He turned and handed Clair down, careful to avoid catching any of the wide spread of lavish fabrics of her dress on the coach steps. He nodded to the groom, who whistled and whipped up the horses and moved off at a brisk trot.

"Audley House, milady." Tyburn gestured with a grandiose wide sweep of his arms, a theatrical movement ruined by the sudden shift it caused to the half mask perched atop his head. The rabbit mask was problematic. Despite the fact that the decorative rabbit ears were swept back to run alongside the head, it prevented Tyburn from successfully wearing a hat, so the player was bare-headed in public for the first time in memory. Clair had spent some considerable time combing, rinsing, cutting and shaping the play-actor's hair into something that at least loosely resembled a fashion, instead of the usual rat's nest of tangles and sweat he wore under his hat. In addition, she had rifled through her late husband's trunks, settling on an elegant, but somewhat somber collection of a fine worsted doublet and velvet hosen, accompanied by a long German-style cloak trimmed with prickly fur that Tyburn reckoned had been selected for its itchiness alone. A loose ivory ruff, open in the front with both ties dangling down, encircled his neck, alongside a thin gold chain that hung invitingly among a field of silver buttons. A silver buckled belt and a painfully dull short sword completed the ensemble.

Clair herself was resplendent in a rich embroidered russet cloak that hid an apricot gown layered over a pale green kirtle, the colour bright across her upper chest and in vivid splashes along the length of her laced Spanish-style sleeves. She wore her hair in a tumbled, resplendent pile, surmounted and held in place by a pair of silver and pearl combs. She wore no hat or coif, as that would have marked her as a married woman. The fox mask she wore was decorated with thin traceries of gilt and reddish enamel that gave it an expressive and almost wistful air, rather than the traditional sly character of the animal.

Every time he looked at her, it was if the air had been stilled and held immobile, frozen in a single moment, stealing his very breath.

Every time.

The doorwardens at the gatehouse ushered them through to the short limestone graveled path that led to the main entrance. The sounds of music and laughter drifted through the air, clear and sharp despite the heavy paned windows and the broad oak doors. The entrance swung open as they approached, held by two liveried doormen wearing colours and emblems that Tyburn recognized as the Earl of Asquith's rather than Lord Audley's. It looked, he mused, as though Asquith had received the long-sought royal assent to the annulment of his wardship, and this celebratory Christmas revel would be the first of many to come. He wondered how much money Audley had pocketed to unleash his hold on his young ward, or if Asquith had successfully harnessed the power of a more influential patron, like Leicester or Burghley or perhaps even the Queen herself.

Clair paused in the doorway, holding Tyburn's left arm, enjoying the unusual sensation of being out in public with a man, however brief the moment might be. She gave the play-actor a look. He was intent on the crowd in the hallway, that familiar, measured, half-skeptical look visible on his face despite the mask. She felt a brief flutter of anxiety. She knew he still punished himself for what he saw as his guilt for the events in Flanders. Tyburn's failed attempt to salvage Annika and her daughter from the siege of Haarlem had been cut short by a vicious Spanish ambush and a random harquebusier's ball. She suspected the memory of that day still haunted him, marching alongside the long procession of death and unspeakable violence that the war had wrought. As much as the player felt himself damned and condemned for his actions, she thought that under all the pain lurked a decent man—but one, she feared, so irrevocably anchored by his guilt that he would abjure his own happiness and future. Clair drew a deep breath. She would not allow it, she decided firmly. Christopher would not be permitted to push her away once this was settled.

The couple moved along the broad entrance hallway and through a set of ornate doors into the great hall. The room was blazing with hundreds of tall white candles and crammed with the buzz and hum of conversation and laughter. A quartet of musicians was tucked into one corner of the broad room, where they played a spritely and invigorating tune. A set of long tables, groaning under the weight of their largesse, were piled high with savouries; spiced breads lay alongside sculpted marchpane decorated with gold leaf and azure trimmings, along with an array of glistening fruit tarts and carved wheels of hard Dutch cheese. One table was laden with succulent roasted meats of all types encircled by a sea of preserved fruits. Cherries and strawberries were piled high; crystal bowls were heaped with oranges from the Canaries, sliced in half and sprinkled with sugars and cinnamon. A steady procession of liveried servers entered and exited from the far doors, carrying bottles of wine, silver serving trays, and platters.

At first glance, the room was a glittering confusion of people, rich swaths of fabric and lace, aglow with gold and colour. Some wore ornate masks, feathered like peacocks and edged with gilt and ivory, above broad coloured ruffs with lace cutwork that extended outward like so many butterfly wings. Gold chains and the gleam of jeweled rings, combs and seals adorned many of the guests. Tyburn spotted a decorative diamond-edged gorget that, he mused, would have paid for Burbage's Theatre fivefold. After several minutes, he began to make more sense of it. The wide room was crowded, but at various locales the crowds had coalesced into eddies and tighter groups, clustered about the ranking members of court. Tyburn easily spotted the Earl of Asquith, his mask clutched in one hand, daintily nibbling on some fruit, a dozen obsequious hangers-on laughing and calling back and forth.

Clair gave Tyburn a nudge and whispered in his ear. "You said Walsingham wanted you to observe the Spanish ambassador, didn't you? There he is." Clair tugged on Tyburn's arm, steering him away from Asquith towards the far corner of the room. The Spanish were easy to spot, as none were masked and most bore the same mixed look of genial boredom and supercilious contempt. Only Mendoza appeared to be animated, speaking closely with a tall, hatchet-faced elderly woman that Tyburn did not recognize until Clair whispered, "The Countess of Lennox."

"Wasn't she sent to the Tower?" Tyburn asked.

"Yes. Two years ago. For marrying her younger son, the Earl of Lennox, to Elizabeth Cavendish, step-daughter of the Earl of Shrewsbury. Without Crown permission. The Queen saw this as a threat to the succession."

"What succession?" Tyburn muttered, well aware that the lack of any clarity on the succession was a massive point of political contention for Walsingham and the Privy Council to manage. It made the imprisoned Catholic monarch Mary, Queen of Scots, believed by many to be the legitimate and true heir to the throne, a lodestone for conspiracy and plots.

"She was pardoned last year after her son died."

"She's on Walsingham's watch list," Tyburn observed. "Her second son was Lord Darnley in Scotland. Married to Queen Mary. Walsingham's secretary told me about it. Supposedly the Earl of Bothwell arranged to blow up the house he was in with gunpowder, but missed, so they strangled him afterwards and left him a field. There's Scots for you." He shook his head.

Clair winced. "You move in such exclusive circles, Christopher."

"They were all courtiers. Not too many of my friends deal in murder and mayhem at that level."

"Her niece is now betrothed to Asquith."

"Wheels. Wheels. Wheels. Too many warring factions and cross-purposes. They are making my head hurt. I'm not sure who's dancing to what tune, or whether it's a volta or a morris. I've got the Spanish allied with the Harlequin, the Harlequin blackmailing Rutledge, Rutledge crossing with Asquith, Asquith's soon-to-be-mother-in-law chatting up the Spanish, Rutledge pushing on Walsingham, and far too many of them wanting to kill me."

"Poor Kit," Clair said.

"Aye. Poor Kit indeed." He peered around the room. "Why don't you find your court friends and see what they can tell us about Rutledge and Asquith. I'm going to take a turnabout and see what mischief I can find on our Spanish friends." Clair nodded but froze as Tyburn put one cautionary hand on her arm. "Keep your mask on and your guard up. We don't know who might be about, and I'd just as soon not take any more chances. I think we've both stretched our luck to its breaking point on this one." Clair gave the player a dazzling smile beneath the fox visage, and stepped off lightly into the throng. Tyburn watched her glide through the crowd, pausing momentarily to speak to acquaintances.

The player completed a long, slow circlet of the great hall, gently sidling through and past the various clusters of costumed courtiers and perfumed ladies. He recognized a handful of courtiers, including the superbly arrogant Philip Sidney who wafted past on a billow of incense, wearing a heroic-styled mask that failed to disguise either his carriage, good looks, or overwhelming sense of self-worth. The Earl of Worcester's Men had encountered Sidney the previous year at a court performance carried out on behalf of Walsingham. The man had sniffed, disdained, and prosed in loud asides through the entirety of the troupe's performance. Oldcastle had his revenge, though, by having Robbie quietly rifle the man's carriage, lifting some cheap jewelry and an ornate jeweled poniard. The troupe had drunk for a week on the proceeds.

Tyburn paused. Striding through the entrance hall, masked in gold as a smiling, benevolent Sun God, was the Earl of Rutledge. An unmasked and grim-looking Covington accompanied him. The ex-soldier looked drawn and edgy, his eyes moving, constant and tight, over the crowd, his blond hair even paler than normal in the bright light of the candlelit room. Kit was surprised. He would have thought the Earl of Rutledge would never been seen dead at his rival's function, but, the player supposed, perhaps Rutledge had felt the social necessity of maintaining appearances and not allowing his young irritant to claim even the smallest of victories.

From his position near the tables, the player could also see the small group clustered around the Earl of Asquith and the sudden flurry of activity that Rutledge's arrival had stirred. It seemed to presage some sort of response. Tyburn saw one decorative fancy detach himself from Asquith's group, slowly waft his way through the parting crowd to ostensibly greet the Earl of Rutledge. The court minion danced his obsequious bows and greetings, to which Rutledge did not even deign to glance, but wafted past like galleon under full sail.

"Point and match to the earl," muttered Tyburn to himself, watching the minion turn scarlet and spin away on his heels. The player continued his slow circlet of the hall, angling back to resume his watch on the Spaniards but keeping a close watch on Covington.

Tyburn wanted a quick word with the cold swordsman. At this point, he thought, comparing notes would be valuable. At least he might be able to find out what Rutledge was up to in coming uninvited to Asquith's celebratory triumph.

"Master Player." The voice in his ear might have sent him jumping except that Tyburn had spotted the man's approach an instant before.

"Thomas." Tyburn responded without turning his head. "You're looking well." Thomas Phelippes was another of Walsingham's agents, a slender, short man, with tangled, dark blond hair and a face pocked and scattered with scars. He wore a servant's livery and carried a heavy silver tray in one hand.

"Heard you were busy in Flanders. Dr. Story?"

"Nothing grand or notable. Just the usual dung heap shoveling," Tyburn responded.

Phelippes gave a thin smile. Tyburn had spent several weeks with him when he first joined Walsingham's brigade of irregulars, brigands, and intelligencers. A scholarly man, Phelippes had run Tyburn through his paces in code-breaking and letter-drops. "You want to watch the one in the blue ruff. That's our Spanish friend Portolà, the one that sent those curtails after you at the King's Head."

"Marvelous," Tyburn noted, his tone caustic. "I'm not allowed to kill him, am I?"

Phelippes smile broadened and he turned away. "I'm all for it, but I fear Master Walsingham might be put out by that much directness." He disappeared into the crowd, silvered tray held high. Tyburn eyed the man in the blue ruff. Portolà was young, dressed in what Tyburn assumed was the height of Spanish style. He spent most of his time dancing attendance on Mendoza, who, having completed his conversation with the Countess of Lennox, had resumed his customary look of genial boredom, sprawling in a thin decorative chair and nibbling on some crusted tarts.

Clair slid through the crowd with ease, despite the broad skirts of her gown. Court revels were as familiar an environment to her as the stage was to Tyburn. She had gone to court at sixteen, prompted and promoted by her ambitious father. Even at that age, she had recognized the inherent dangers in the endless dance of favour and faction that court represented, particularly for a young woman in the full flush of marriageable age. Her father had insisted on careful and cautious approaches, designed to garner appropriate suitors and to avoid and discourage the rakehell bloods intent on deflowering and seduction. It helped that her older brother, also in attendance at court, had a dangerous and unpredictable reputation as a man quick to affront and fast with a blade. Nothing like having an unpredictable sadist in the family to keep the wolves at bay, she thought. She shook her head sadly and then turned her attentions to the matter at hand.

The crowd shifted back as a small stream of liveried footmen cleared space in the centre of the room for dancing. The quartet in the corner had been supplemented by a consort of viols, flutes, and lute. The opening sounds of a pavane, a processional dance, echoed through the great hall and Clair turned to watch as the lines of dancers whirled past, dancing one of the newer, faster pavanes that had begun to become popular. Clair recognized the trim figure leading the first dance: Arabela Howard, her dark hair swept up and pinned back, her face covered by a beguiling mask of some Roman or Greek goddess. She was dancing and laughing with her matched pair, the Earl of Asquith himself, wearing a mask recognizably of Apollo. The two led the long, brilliant dressed procession in the pavane, showing a smooth and elegant grace born of long practice. Clair herself hadn't danced since her wedding and felt no desire to chance her ungainly steps on the floor this evening, even if, she mused, it would be wonderful to have Christopher whirl her about. She doubted the player knew too many dances, aside from the stamping joy of the morris, often performed by the playing troupes, or the chaotic reeling and brawling of the soldier's dance. Still, it might be worth trying, she thought, peering over the procession, trying to catch a glimpse of the tall player in his hare mask.

The knife point in her ribs took the breath from her lungs.

"What a wonder to see you out and about, my Clair." The masked face of a stylized Moor was level with hers. One hand gripped her left hand tight, while the other held a short, thin knife, the tip placed judiciously between the bones of her corset, angled up below her heart.

Clair tried to shift away but the blade followed and the voice of the Harlequin in her ear was one touched with amusement. "I just have to lean in, milady. The flicker of a moment and you are dead in my arms. I call out, 'she faints' and gently lay you down, and as help surrounds you, I melt away into the crowd while your life's blood stains the dance floor."

Clair found her voice and was surprised at its steadiness. "What do you want?"

"A telling query to which I have no answer, though long have I searched. At this particular moment in time, I will settle for a dance. Mind you, if you call out or flinch, I will have no choice but to gut you like a steer, but I will swear, by all the Lord's light, you will not be harmed and I will release you from this upon completion of our coranto."

"You'll find me a poor partner."

"Your play-actor does not incline to dance?"

"I don't know. The occasion has not arisen."

"But he is here, is he not?'

"Probably watching as we speak."

"Ohhh. How thrilling." The Harlequin chuckled beneath her Moor's face. "Let us give him a performance, then. And return you to him educated and unscathed."

The pair moved out into the open area of the dance floor as the musicians began a lively air, suitable to a coranto. A dozen dancers were on the floor, and the group spun about in a disorganized chaos with the younger men kicking out and spinning with exuberant energy, while the few older dancers, moved in a slower, more paced style. Clair watched the Harlequin with wary eyes as the masked Moor took her left hand and began to dance around her. Clair spun, trying to keep herself facing towards her assailant.

The Harlequin danced like any of the young men, kicking high and frequent, and spinning with unseemly grace. In a coranto, Clair knew, the lady was expected to emulate and keep up with her male partner, but in reality, such kicks and spins were regarded as indecorous by ladies of good repute so it was a practice often ignored. Clair kept shooting looks into the crowd, searching for Tyburn or any other possible point of salvation. Each time she turned her head and her eyes raked the crowd, she could see the edges of the Harlequin's curved lips beneath the concealing half mask curl upward in a malicious smile. The Harlequin switched hands, spinning her in for a close embrace, and flashed the knife in front of her, hilt cupped in the hand, blade tucked upwards, as a quick reminder of where Fate had positioned her.

Clair felt the flare of anger. She watched the masked Moor dancing and spinning. To be trapped like this, forced into this charade, brought the old anger simmering to the forefront. She had always hated the relentless manipulations of her father and brother and now, free of those at long last, this masked madwoman had decided to put her in the position of a temporary plaything, to be dangled and pounced upon like a lure in front of a cat.

She waited for the precise moment.

As the music reached a crescendo, the Harlequin gave another high kick and began a shuffling spin. Clair reached down, yanked up a handful of her skirts to give herself freedom of movement, and kicked out her leg with perfect timing, catching the spinning Harlequin on her standing foot, hooking it out from under her with one smooth, elegant thrust. The masked Moor crashed to the parquet floor, while Clair stepped back and turned away, as though in embarrassment. Laughter and raucous cries and catcalls sounded from some of the drunker bloods circulating through the crowd as the dance spun and clapped its way to a conclusion.

Clair started to move away through the crush of watchers but the Harlequin, extricating herself from the mob of exiting dancers, shoved through the bystanders and grabbed Clair's wrist. Clair pulled back, and the Harlequin was suddenly close, Moorish mask pushed back, dark eyes and smooth skin only inches from her own.

"I could have ended you in blood," she said, her voice breathless. "Remember, when the time comes, that I did not. Mayhaps the demon's blood runs less deep than I thought." The Harlequin's lips pressed hard against hers, locking them in a ferocious kiss. Clair stepped back in shock, feeling the quick flicker of the Harlequin's tongue on her mouth. The malicious smile vanished as the Moor mask dropped down like a gate, and the Harlequin vanished into the throng.

Clair's breath was panting and her heart pounding in her chest, though whether it was from the woman's kiss or the unpredictable, predatory nature of any interaction with the Harlequin she couldn't be sure.

She had to find Kit. The Harlequin would be hunting him next, and she doubted it would end with a kiss.

--

Tyburn finished his third slow circlet of the great hall and blew exasperation through his teeth. He wasn't sure what Walsingham had expected him to be able to unearth at this type of celebration. He had watched the Spanish contingent closely but had seen little indication of any connection with either Asquith or Rutledge. Neither man even deigned to glance in Mendoza's direction. The Spanish themselves seemed more preoccupied with working their way through an immense quantity of wine than in pursuing any nefarious schemes. Tyburn was now looking for Covington, but the blond swordsman seemed to have a knack for vanishing. For once, he was not dogging Rutledge's heels and was nowhere to be found in the contingent of obsequious hangers-on that surrounded the earl. Tyburn himself steered well clear of the masked Sun God, not wanting to chance any interaction with the man, who still held Tyburn to blame for the loss of his factor and his accounts.

Clair darted through the dense throng and grabbed Tyburn's hand. "She's here."

"Coads." The player hastily scanned the room. He didn't even need to ask who *she* was. "Are you alright?"

"I managed myself." Her face was flushed.

Tyburn gripped Clair by the elbow and began steering for the relative safety of the edge of the great hall, feeling an edgy, tingling sensation in his exposed back. Too many unknowns, he thought, too many potential points of attack. "What the hell is the Harlequin doing at a court revel anyway?"

Clair shook her head. "She didn't say, but I don't think she is here for us. We are just pigeons. She's hunting boar."

"You spoke to her?"

"Oh, yes," said Clair, with deliberate dry aplomb. "We had a long conversation during our dance."

Tyburn stared at her and then shook his head. "I'm fair certain I don't want to know."

"She's masked as a Moor, in case you wondered."

"Probably discarded by now. The Harlequin knows her way around this type of work, a little too well. Damn her father anyway for all that training. This is a fallow field for her—all masked and disguised. She could sidle up on just about anyone." His head felt like it was on a swivel. He turned back to Clair. "I need to find Covington. He might be able to shed some light on the connection between Rutledge and the Spanish, if any, and that's what Walsingham wants me to unearth."

"Go then." She waved one hand at him. "I can look after myself. If the Harlequin wanted me dead, she could have killed me a dozen times over. As I said, we aren't her focus tonight. I'm perfectly safe."

Tyburn nodded reluctantly, leaned in, and gave her a quick kiss that left her flushed and gasping. He pressed the rounded pommel of a small, sheathed short-bladed knife into her hand. "In case there's more dancing. Keep your back to the wall." He turned and eeled away through the crowd, coursing like a hunter, looking for Covington.

Tyburn found the blond swordsman emerging from the serving hallway, threading his way through the steady flow of liveried servants carrying drink and food. The pale eyes were alit with suspicion as Tyburn moved towards him and his hand crossed to grip the hilt of his long rapier until Tyburn flipped up his hare mask. The man's relief was visible.

"By Jesu, play-actor, you are a sight for sore eyes. I thought you were dead." He reached out and gripped Tyburn's hand. "Glad to see you still among the living. But what in the name of God's bowels are you doing here? Rutledge didn't see you, did he?"

"No. Rutledge upset?"

"He's been cursing you steady since Stokely turned up dead on the Bridge. Blames you for the loss of his account books." Covington gave Tyburn a sidelong look. "He wants us to geld you, and then let you bleed to death. Slowly. In public. Preferably in the stocks."

"Always inventive, our Lord Rutledge."

Covington grunted. "You don't know the half of it."

Tyburn led Covington to one side. "I think I know who has the account books."

"If you mean Harlequin and Asquith, we've figured that out." He gestured around the room. "Where do you think the monies for this little celebratory banquet came from? I suspect Rutledge's payments are funding our appetites tonight and were used to pad Audley's purse and purchase an end to his wardship."

"What you might not know is the Harlequin isn't conducting the music for this dance. Our old friends the Spanish are."

"The Dons?" Covington's normally controlled face fell in astonishment.

"There's some kind of connection between the Spanish and the Harlequin."

"And you think the Spanish are using it to influence Rutledge?

"I think those accounts might give the Spanish some undue influence. How bendable is Rutledge?"

"Eminently," Covington said in a grim voice. "It might explain why our blackmailing friends Asquith and Thieves' Castle are pilfering his lordship at such a slow and steady pace. Anyone just out for coin would have pocketed a few thousand and run from his vengeance. The Dons want a well-set hook, they want him broken. And they're paying—first in coin, later in influence and information."

"So Asquith's just a distraction. A bendable pawn they can dance in front of Rutledge to keep his attentions."

"Maybe. But also a threat—to his prestige, his honour, his reputation. He'll move heaven itself to keep those pristine."

"Shite." Tyburn's mind worked furiously. "Rutledge is on the Privy Council but mainly focused on trade and commercial holdings—tariffs, correct?"

"He shits gold with those wool tariffs. It's why Stokely's disappearing had him in a dither," noted Covington

"Wool? Broadcloth? Kerseys? Jesus. It all goes through Antwerp." Tyburn felt a shiver ripple down his spine. "Antwerp is a smoking, sacked ruin. The Spanish Fury just shredded the cloth trade. All that is buggered now, and so is Rutledge's purse ... and he was meeting with Walsingham when I met him."

"He's angling for a new position."

"What position?"

"Taking over some responsibilities from the Moor. I don't know what it is, but Rutledge said it's a position of stature. High-up role, garners attention from Burghley, Leicester, and the Queen. An opportunity for that lickspittle to arse-kiss and parade with the best."

Tyburn felt the chill rippling through his spine spreading. If Rutledge could take over or sideline Walsingham, he would have his hands on one of the most widespread and efficient networks of informants, spies, and intelligencers in Europe. Bendable to his will. Or more accurately, to the Spanish. Burghley and Leicester had their own informants and agents, of course, but they were mainly focused on domestic issues, Catholic recusants, and the court. Walsingham, by contrast, had a net spread across the capitals and courts of Europe, from Paris to Geneva to Rome to Constantinople, providing a steady flow of letters, conspiracy, scurrilous gossip, military information, trade, and rumor. If the Duke of Alva's whore was ousted in favour of another, you could bet that Walsingham would know it almost as quick as the whore.

Sever that network, and it would be as if England's own eyes had been gouged out, the player thought. Take over that network, and you could topple the throne. Manipulate to your heart's content. "The Harlequin is here. The Spanish are here. Asquith and Rutledge are both here. All the players on stage under one roof, but I still don't know why," Tyburn muttered to himself.

"Rutledge is here to parade himself for one last time in front of Arabela Howard. And to shove Asquith's nose in it." Covington shook his head in disdain. "From everything I've heard, the Countess of Lennox favours Rutledge for his coin and influence, but Asquith is prettier and Lady Howard has romantic delusions of his chivalry. Odds are on the cot-quean but Rutledge might be able to curry favour from the Countess. We didn't even know the Spanish ambassador was here."

"Harlequin wouldn't be here without a purpose."

"Go check on your Spaniards. I have to keep watch over Rutledge." Covington gave the player an airy wave and moved back down the serving hallway. Tyburn stared after the blond swordsman, something nagging in the back of his mind. He shrugged it off and turned back into the great hall. At least he had some answers now. Answers, but no proof. Whether that would satisfy Walsingham was anyone's guess.

Chapter the Twenty-seventh

C LAIR STOOD NEAR the far wall of the great hall, watching
the steady procession of dancers flow and ebb on the dance
floor, while more guests drifted over to the sideboards piled
high with food and drink. She had no appetite, and after fending off
several masked bravos, who gravitated towards an unescorted
woman with unceasing optimism, she decided to ignore Tyburn's
advice and move about the celebration.

She crossed the great hall, circling the dance floor, and
moved down to the main entrance hall. Audley House was less
grand than some of the other manors located along the Strand, but
the earl had little to learn from anyone about ostentatious display.
The main hall was replete with carved inlaid wood and elegant
woven tapestries, included several astonishingly bright Turkish
works, adorned with intricate plaited designs. Clair walked past
this grandeur without a glance, intent on the figures she spied at the
far end of the busy hallway. Lady Arabela Howard was strolling

arm in arm with a man. Clair drifted closer; something about the man's posture and walk was tickling her sense of recognition.

The two strolled around the far corner, and Clair pushed her way past the various people idling in the hallway. Clair reached the end and paused by the corner before daring a darting look. The secondary hallway ran the length of the house, with at least six or more closed doors interspersed along it. The hall was empty.

Clair grimaced. Strolling down the empty hall and opening random doors would not be an easily explainable act and one almost certainly to be caught, given the number of servants and guests.

The noise of a door opening sent her back around the corner with panicky speed. After a moment, she leaned out just far enough to see Lady Arabela and the man resume their slow stroll. Clair froze for an instant and then squinted at the pair. "That's impossible," she muttered to herself as she stared at the pair's retreating backs.

The man in question had gained at least two stone and several inches in height during his visit to the room. Clair looked again and noticed that Lady Arabela's dress had also changed. The colours were identical, but the cut and the material were not.

They were neither Lady Arabela nor the original escort.

Clair lifted her heavy skirts and ran, albeit at a measured pace, back into the great hall. She pushed her way through the guests, frantically looking for the familiar hare mask.

"Christopher!" she shouted, as she spotted him speaking with a pock-faced blond serving man.

"Clair, what is it?"

"I think I know why the Harlequin is here. I think she's taken Rutledge and Asquith's little prize."

The player looked confused. Clair whispered, "Arabela Howard."

Tyburn gripped her arm and said, "Tell me."

Clair outlined what she had seen in the hallway and the switch of the strolling couple. Kit frowned. "You think it was the Harlequin walking with Lady Arabela?"

"Yes. She escorted her into that side room and not twenty seconds later a different couple emerged. They were wearing the right masks, but her dress was wrong, the cut was different. And the man was taller and heavier."

"And you're sure of this?" Tyburn asked dubiously.

"Christopher, trust me. I might not know the intricacies of subterfuge as well as you, but I know the cut of a dress far better than you or any man ever could."

"Show me." Kit gestured and the two left the great hall and moved past the decorative tapestries down the secondary corridor to the corner.

"It was the second door."

Tyburn nodded. "You up to damaging your reputation in a good cause?"

Clair grinned. "I don't have much reputation to damage, thanks to my father. Lead on!" The player moved down the hallway and paused at the second door. It was unlocked. Tyburn eased his short sword in its sheath to ensure it wasn't caught and then whipped open the door.

Covington spun at the sound of the door, one hand dropping to the rapier hilt at his belt.

"Covington. Codso, what are you doing here?"

"I might ask you the same." The blond swordsman said in a grim voice. He held up a broken enamel mask, similar to that worn by Lady Arabela. "Rutledge ordered me to find Lady Arabela, but the one I found wasn't her. I found this."

"I think the Harlequin has her."

Covington looked unsurprised. "Figures. She thinks to hold the prize and dangle it in front of Asquith or Rutledge as another inducement. But they still need to get her out of the manor and away, and that's a trickier process." He looked at Tyburn and then over to Clair, giving her an appraising, chill look that made her uneasy. "Can you cover the carriages and coaches out front? I'll duck around back and check the stables, circle the house, and send some men down to the river. They may be waiting for the guests to leave or trying to hide her in the crowd."

Tyburn nodded, and he and Clair hurriedly returned to the great hall. Covington tossed the broken mask to one side and watched as the shattered fragments skittered across the polished tiled floor. He nodded to himself and moved out through the open door.

--

Suzanne Martaine enjoyed wearing men's clothing. It was far less confining and restrictive than women's dress, and more important, it gave her a delicious sense of independence from anyone's control. And she was the spawn of the black-faced demon, the emissary of the Hellmouth, answerable to no one. Why shouldn't she enjoy all the freedoms that men seemed to claim from the world? She gave her captive a gentle push forward down the path, hearing the muffled panting and gasping from under the black hood she had placed on the woman's head.

All in all, she would have preferred to take Tyburn's woman. She found Clair a far more satisfying conversationalist than this vapid broodling of the Howards. But, she sighed, one had little choice. This one was a useful means to an end, while the Carey woman would have been mere pleasure.

"Move, bitch." Bent pushed the hooded woman down the stone-lined pathway. They had passed through the garden and were nearing the river bank. The dark chuckle of the Thames flowing past was loud in their ears, and the heavy scent of the cold, damp, ice-tinged air hung in their nostrils.

The sudden sound of running feet on the path behind them made the Harlequin straighten and pause.

"Lanterns now, I think, my Bent."

The flare of the hooded lanterns that Bent's man had been carrying chased back the enveloping darkness like a brand startling a flock of crows.

"Guards," Bent muttered.

"Set one down, that's a good Bent."

"You want me to kill them?"

The Harlequin laughed. "Bent, you always want to take the most enjoyable jobs away from me." She reached across and tugged the long, silvered Spanish rapier he had liberated from the play-actor out of his belted sheath. "You go on to the boat. This won't be but a moment." She stood in the light of the lantern, one sword in each hand, and waited.

The two liveried guards jogged down the path, sliding to a halt at the sight of the unmasked Harlequin. "Stand aside, bitch."

The Harlequin smiled, a warm, inviting smile. She stepped forward, rapier tips both held low, in a casual stance. "Two new souls for my lord and master. How grand."

"I said move." The first guard batted at her left-hand rapier contemptuously with his sword, at which she spun the weapon around, pivoting it upwards in a quick, slicing cut.

He bellowed and leaped back with a shout of pain, his left hand clutching at his ear, gloved fingers stained with blood. "Bitch cut my ear!" he said, astonished.

"Best stand aside, you fucking cunt, or we'll carve you up." The other guard said in harsh voice, his breath hanging in the frost-thickened cold. His sword was up, and his eyes hot with anger.

"I'm going to cut your pretty little face clean off." The first guard cursed and stepped in with a swinging stroke aimed at the harlequin's throat.

The woman laughed and sidestepped the thrust, giving the man's blade a light caress with her left-hand weapon and encouraging the direction of his heavy swing before ripping her right blade in a stinging cut across the man's upper back. She spun with elegant and studied grace, her left blade flicking out in a crisp, effortless parry as the second guard attacked. The sound of the steel blades touching was almost drowned out by the mocking, joyous laughter that rose from her lips.

The cuts were smooth and languid and drew a red line of blood with every blurred, silvery movement.

And then the screaming began.

--

The coach house and gatehouse were quiescent. Tyburn spun slow on his heel, eyes raking the shadows up and down the pebbled driveway. Small clusters of coach drivers and grooms stood, gossiped, and gambled in the cold night air, while others tended their beasts. Carriage horses stamped and blew in the cold evening air, listening to the distant buzz of conversation and music that arose from the manor house.

It was quiet. The player enquired of several of the doorwardens about any sudden or hasty departures, but none were evident. Tyburn cursed and ranged back down the drive, looking for any sign or hint that the Harlequin and her minions had passed. Something isn't right, he thought. The Harlequin is too canny to not have her departure well planned. Trotting out to a coach house and driving off into the night with the richest woman in England barring the Queen herself bundled up like a rolled carpet was unlikely. He paused, thinking.

"Rot it," he whispered to himself. The Harlequin had taken a cue from Tyburn's own playbook. Kidnap and then leave by water. The river. The player turned and ran for the corner of the manor house.

Tyburn sprinted past a narrow colonnade that ran the length of the western edge of the house and into the garden. The player dodged through the intricate layout of winter-wrapped hedges, following the graveled path that led towards the manor wharf with its small boathouse. He could see the yellow flickering glow of a lantern beyond the next set of tall hedges. He dropped one hand to his sword as he spilled out onto the narrow sward that lay between the river and the garden.

Two guards lay crumpled on the barren grass, both laced with cuts and thrusts, their dark blood staining the frozen ground. Covington stood several feet away with a drawn sword, cursing to himself; the player could see a slow-moving lighter gliding away into the night. A faint laugh that Tyburn recognized drifted across the open water.

"They're both dead." The blond swordsman's voice was flat and bleak. "She sliced and carved them up in turn. Put them both down. Couldn't stop her. She was in the boat and away before I even realized what had happened." He turned and looked at Tyburn. "I don't think I truly realized just what she was, until I heard them screaming. She took Lady Arabela."

"We'll have to take her back."

"How?" Covington said in dismissal. "That's a fool's errand."

"They'll go to the Saracen's Head. Thieves' Castle."

He snorted. "We can't reach her there. Not even with twenty men."

Tyburn shook his head. "No. She's made a mistake. She thinks the Castle is safe. She thinks it's her fortress but she's wrong. It's a trap, a cul de sac."

"We'll not get past the door. How do you think we can pry her out of that rattrap? What makes you think we can succeed?"

Tyburn smiled, for what felt like the first time in ages. "Because I know where the back door is."

Chapter the Twenty-eighth

"THIS IS A fool's errand," Clair observed.

"So I've been told."

"Back down into that hellish tunnel? You barely escaped the last time, and now you are strolling back into her lair?" She reached out and turned his face towards her. "This smacks too much of pride and vengeance and too little of sense. You know better."

Kit took her hand. "I know what I'm doing. She won't expect an attack from this quarter. She won't even know we are there until it's too late. Her men will be spread out, watching the entrances and exits. We slide in, pluck Lady Arabela from their clutches, vanish how we came. Quiet, neat, clean."

"Assuming you can find your way through that maze you wandered out of. Assuming you don't choke on fetid air or end up trapped in some sunken passageway. Assuming you don't draw their attention the moment you enter the Saracen's Head ..." She stopped. "Assuming you don't end up with her sword through your throat. What then? You think she'll stop?"

"I can't worry about what the Harlequin will or won't do. If I stop to worry about catching a blade, I end up doing naught but waiting for Fate to throw me asunder."

"Don't trust to Fate or God. Trust to your skill and wits. What does it tell you about the Harlequin?"

Tyburn reached out and pulled her into his arms, holding her tight. "It tells me that I need to upend her plans, force her to react instead of always finding myself on the sharp end of the sword." He tilted her head up. "I'm coming back. Whatever hellfire bars my way, I'm coming back." He leaned down and kissed her. "You still have two more books worth of Italian poetry to torture me with. I have to come back. Besides," he noted with airy confidence, "I'll have Covington, Bristol, and two of his picked ruffians alongside. For once, I'm not hip-deep in this mess alone."

"This Suzanne Martaine is clever. Do. Not. Underestimate. Her. She hasn't survived *la Massacre* or the London thief lords by chance. Don't make the mistake everyone else has made, in treating her light because she is a woman. She's dangerous and utterly devoid of scruples."

"I suspect I'm one of the few that haven't made the mistake of treating her lightly, ever since our encounter on the Bridge," Kit replied, his voice grim.

Clair watched him with steady eyes. "I think you pity her."

"Pity her?"

"Yes. I think you see a reflection of yourself in her. Both of you, the spawn of war, bereft of faith, lost in a greater world."

Tyburn felt his face flush. He nodded a terse acknowledgement. He scrubbed his face with his hands, and then spoke. "I could have gone down that road. Vengeance. It would have been simpler. When I returned from Flanders, I had lost everything that mattered—Annika, family, friends ..." He snorted. "Faith in God and a greater promise. I had nothing left. Just a sword. A damned soul."

"But," Clair countered gently.

Tyburn gave her a half smile. "But. It was chance, not thought. The Fates, not will. I turned left instead of right. Went down Mark Lane instead of up towards Fenchurch, ran into Peter Norlande, whom I hadn't seen since Cambridge, and he brought me to the Moor. Fate tugging on her strings."

"No, not fate," Clair insisted. She reached out and grasped his arm. "You chose. Walsingham was a door that you elected to pass through. The Harlequin made her choice when she chased revenge and death."

Tyburn shrugged off Clair's hand and reached over to pick up a knotted canvas bag off the bed. The contents clunked with ominous weight.

Clair left her hand suspended in space for a moment before she recognized that Kit wasn't going to be drawn down that path any further. She drew a guarded breath, pushing down her instinct to lash out in simmering anger at the man's stubborn refusal to change. Instead she gestured at the lumpen canvas bag, trying to shift his mood away from the brooding, self-destructive anger that seemed to surface unbidden. "I can't believe Oldcastle let you take those."

Tyburn laughed, the sound forced and tight. "He didn't. I got these from Willens. The boys will suffer along without them if they need to, and Willens will have to find some excuse when Oldcastle shouts and rants."

"Just be careful. Don't do anything ... reckless." Clair's eyes voiced deep concern, even as her lips pursed in a smile of rueful acceptance. She knew Tyburn well enough to know how unlikely it was that she or anyone could dissuade him from a set path, once his mind was made up.

"We will be back and drinking malmsey by midnight," he promised, slinging the heavy canvas bag over one shoulder. He leaned down and gave her one last parting kiss before exiting the door. She listened to the heavy tread of his boots descending the staircase and closed her eyes for an instant in silent prayer before busying herself with the endless stream of manor correspondence.

--

The sun was fleeing westward, edging the buildings and fields in a fitful pale light, casting a sickly illumination over the steadily thickening clouds. The sky was darkening faster than the late-afternoon hour dictated, with a brutal cold wind cutting along the laneways and up from the river. The chill scent in the air coupled with a flitting curtain of fat snowflakes augured the arrival of a storm.

Tyburn and Covington had arranged to meet by St. Bride Church, which sat prim and upright near the intersection of Fleet Street and Shoe Lane, in the ward of Faringdon Without. Covington and Bristow, accompanied by two hired curtails, were warming their hands over a small brazier outside a run-down set of tenements and almshouses on the eastern side of the street. The door lintel of the building displayed the carved symbol of the Goldsmith's Hall, signifying their ownership of this particular slum.

"You fetch your toys, play-actor?" Covington asked as Tyburn approached, his footsteps crunching through the layer of frozen mud and thin snow that covered the alleyway. The blond swordsman was acerbic and tense, wrapped in his cloak against the cold.

"You bring the lanthorns?" the player countered, giving Bristow a nod as he stepped past the mute ex-soldier.

Covington nodded. "Brought you an extra dag as well." He handed the player a heavy handgun, a handful of shot, and a belt of apostles filled with powder.

"A snaphance," Tyburn noted, examining the weapon. Rather than using a burning matchcord to ignite the powder charge, a snaphance used a flint striker, similar to the spinning one of the wheellocks that Clair favoured.

Covington grinned. "Acquired it in Bruges. Hard to come by here, so try not to lose it. There is nothing like Flanders." He laughed.

There is nothing like Flanders. The words echoed grim in Tyburn's head as he led the small group down the lane to Fleet Street, across the bridge and along the eastern bank of the river. The cold wind whipped past, pushing the usual miasma of the Fleet away, much to Kit's thanks, diffusing the stench through the maze of suburban tenements and decaying buildings that surrounded the Fleet Prison. The prison itself sat, quiet, dingy, and foreboding, adjacent to the river, its unassuming façade hiding a surfeit of debtors and a glut of despair, avarice, and fear.

Tyburn peered up and down the riverbanks, eyes searching for a sign of the location where he had exited the sewers. He knew it was only a short distance from the Fleet Bridge. After several minutes, he spotted the narrow, dark passage through the now whipping snow, the iron and wooden grating that covered it having been levered off when the player exited.

"There it is." He pointed.

"Jesu, you expect us to go in there?" One of the curtails spoke in shock. The other surreptitiously crossed himself.

"You'll go under and in, or I'll be carving my initials in your backside. You've been paid good silver for your service by the earl, and service is what you'll provide, or bigod, I'll take it out in a pound of flesh." Covington's voice rang harsh and cold. The two hired men gave the blond swordsmen a wary glance and a meek nod of acquiescence.

Tyburn led them down the steep bank, splashing through the shallow water puddled at the entrance of the sewer. Covington looked distastefully at the cold, dark water but waded through it nonetheless, while Bristow gave it a bare glance, intent on keeping his burden of lanthorns balanced in his hands. The group paused at the entrance to light the lanthorns and then Tyburn took a deep breath, staring at the yawning darkness that lay before him. Steeling himself, he entered the void.

The tunnel was as narrow and unpleasant as the player remembered it, only marginally better now that it had steady illumination. He led the small party through the long straightaway that angled upwards in a barely perceptible slope. Covington followed closely behind the play-actor, trailed by the two curtails, who Tyburn was told were the Smythe brothers, Edward and Abel. Both men were paid retainers of Rutledge that Covington had pressed into this escapade. Bristow brought up the rear, stolidly trudging through the dank confines of the sewer system with the same unreadable expression he sported on the uncaring streets above.

Their progress was slow and cautious once they moved past the straight tunnel and into the narrower confines of the older passages. Tyburn had to pause and think, trying to recall the myriad turns and confusion of his lost hours in the dark, recalling the feel of the passage as much as his memories of the turns for guidance. He remembered where the walls were rough and where the low ceiling had scraped his head and hunched shoulders. One positive aspect of the lanthorns and their bright gleaming presence was that the haunts that had blighted his previous journey had apparently been chased away.

They stopped to rest at one of the intersections. The left-hand tunnel echoed with the splash of distant falling water, and Tyburn was certain this was the location where he had lost his glims and flints in the fiery blast that had tossed him asunder.

"What's this?" Covington asked, his attention caught by a deeply etched, carved graffito adorning the intersection.

"It's a Solomon's knot," Tyburn replied absently, intent on recalling through which tunnel he had first entered the water chamber.

"A what?" Covington replied, puzzled.

"Solomon's knot. The story is that King Solomon was given a ring emblazoned with that design. It gave him power over demons. Demons are curious. They follow the line to see where it

THIEVES' CASTLE

leads, but it's an endless knot, looping perpetually, so they are trapped in the confines of the design, never able to escape."

"Who in God's name would carve that down here?" Covington said, irritated.

"Every maze has its minotaur. Maybe someone knows the Harlequin is at the end of these tunnels."

"You're too educated for your own good." The blond swordsman growled. "Let's get moving. I want out of these cursed tunnels."

They circled the chamber, ducking to avoid the torrents of cold water and effluent that poured out from one of the upper passages. Abel Smythe slipped on the grim-coated stone and slid into the cold, dank water for an instant before rising, dripping and coated in thin skeins of muddy slime. His cursing echoed through the chamber until Covington snapped and told the man to hold his tongue or he would duck him under the next torrent until he drowned.

Tyburn looked at the selection of tunnels and clambered up the two-foot shelf into the opening. He lifted up the lanthorn and checked the walls. A set of ragged, thin scratches was evident on the brickwork. This was the path, he thought to himself. The random scratchings he had etched on his way out should serve as his own little ball of twine to lead him back to the minotaur. "Come on. Darkness waits." He beckoned the party into the looming tunnel and they continued onwards.

Chapter the Twenty-ninth

THE WOODEN HATCH made an eerie squeal as the player levered it upwards. Tyburn paused and took a quick glance around, listening for any presence.

"Give me the glim," he muttered softly to Covington. The small rush candle cast a fitful light over the room as Tyburn raised it higher.

Nothing stirred.

"We're in." Tyburn whispered back down the passage. The play-actor set the glim onto the dank stone lip of the hatch and clambered through the narrow confines. Tyburn winced. He had forgotten the stench. Nothing had changed. The dank, filth-crusted walls were undisturbed. Despite Tyburn having departed through the sewer entrance, no one had bothered to close off the passage. He guessed that, at the time, no one had imagined he would ever emerge alive from the depths, much less worry about someone coming back in through that perilous route.

Tyburn edged over to the closed wooden door. It sagged on its hinges, never repaired after Tyburn had kicked his way out. He shoved it open and held the glim high, washing the room in a flickering light. It was unchanged, except the door to Thieves' cell was now barred with a sliding wooden deadbolt. Tyburn checked the staircase. The barred metal grate was still locked in place.

Covington entered the main room. "What a squalid little lair," he muttered.

"It's prettier in the dark," Tyburn replied. He walked over to Thieves' cell and slid the deadbolt open. Taking the lanthorn in his left hand, he drew his dagger with his right and gestured to Covington to open the door.

"Monsieur Thieves?"

"The dead man has returned to his grave. I would say 'why do you darken my door,' but down here you lighten it by necessity. Otherwise how would you find it?" He laughed and then groaned. "You *fils de pute*. You know you cracked at least one of my ribs when you left? Bastard."

"Always making friends," Covington observed.

"It's resurrection day for you, Thieves. You want to see sunlight again? You give us the layout of the Saracens' Head, and we'll leave you a knife and a clear walk to the exit."

Thieves levered himself off the midden of straw and torn blankets he slept on and limped his way into the light. Covington took one look and took an inadvertent step back at the sight of Thieves' torn, scarred face. The prisoner spoke again. "Dead man, you are forever an optimist. What are your intentions towards my lovely Suzanne?"

Tyburn gave him a tight smile. "Avoidance. We're here for some stolen property and a lady, not to go to war."

Thieves snorted. "You're a fool, then. Your war has already begun, and if you don't recognize it, she will cut out your kidneys and serve them to you."

"The layout." The player persisted.

Thieves shrugged. "You may die on your own terms." He gave them a quick verbal sketch of the building. The vertical hoist shaft led direct to the inn's main kitchens, but the lift had fallen out of use in the last few years. The upper reaches of the shaft were blocked with thin wooden door latches, but the pulley system had been removed. Thieves used to be able to sit at the bottom of the shaft, listening to the kitchen gossip echoing down from the rooms above, his only outlet for news of the outside world.

From the locked staircase, doors opened into the main floor, with access to the inn common rooms, privies, kitchen and pantries. The stairs continued past the first floor, rising another three stories in a tight, twisted climb. Each floor was connected to a long, jinked hallway, linking the upper wings of the inn-yard. These rooms overlooked the enclosed yard, much of which had been overbuilt in recent years with extensions and additions, contributing to the chaotic, jutting appearance of the building. Side passages from the various hallways joined the Saracen's Head to its two immediate neighbours: a decrepit brothel and a grime-encrusted tenement house, home to the Castle's resident beggars and filchers.

"Where do we find the Harlequin?" Covington asked, tired of listening to Thieves' endless circumlocutions.

Thieves shrugged and waved the hand with its truncated digits in the air. "The fourth floor was reserved for me," he noted, "when I called this place home, rather than a prison. My lovely daughter has doubtless usurped that for her pleasures."

Tyburn nodded. He tugged open the knotted cord that bound his canvas carrybag closed and fished around. He pulled out a thick metal rod, tapered and bent at one end into a blunt, flattened hook. He handed it to Bristow. He pulled out a corkscrewed piece of metal with a wooden handle long enough to grip with two hands. He gestured for Bristow to position himself beside the locked iron door grate, fitting the tapered hooked end of the metal rod the mute held into the thin space between the grate and the frame. Inserting the edge of the corkscrew by the locking mechanism, Tyburn began to twist the screw. The corkscrew shaped piece of metal slid into the narrow gap and, as he twisted, began to push the grate away from the frame. The player grunted at the effort, the wooden handle slippery in his hand.

The metal bent and gave a soft ping as the screw began to push the pieces out of alignment. As a gap opened, Tyburn whispered, "Push, and then lever it. Sharp now!" The flat, hooked bar slid into the space and creaked ominously as Bristow leaned into it.

A metallic crack sounded and the grate popped as the locking pin slid out of alignment. The metal grate swung open with heavy grace. Covington pushed the door back and peered up the stairs. He pointed at Bristow and made a quick, fluid hand gesture. The man nodded and drew a slim, wicked-looking poniard that must have been more than a foot long. He slipped away up the dark staircase, with a bare rustle of noise. Tyburn tucked the tools back into his bag. He had borrowed the thieving implements from Robbie Hobson, one of Oldcastle's servants. Prior to joining Worcester's Men, Robbie had enjoyed a thriving albeit brief stint as a house breaker, hookman, and draw-latch, and was not shy about sharing his knowledge when plied with coin or drink.

Bristow returned as silent as he had left. He gave a quick circle with his finger, indicating no guards or servants. Tyburn nodded. "We go as far as the first landing—the kitchens—and no further." He drew his own blade and started up the staircase.

"Dead man, you promised me a blade," Thieves growled.

Tyburn paused. He reached under the edge of his buff coat and pulled out a small, short-bladed knife. "Here. Wait five minutes. Then up the stairs, through the kitchens and the common room and out."

"And then straight back here in irons." Thieves said, his voice dripping with scorn.

The player gave the battered thief lord a grim smile. "The guards will be occupied elsewhere." He shrugged. "Or you can chance the tunnels. Your fate is your own." Tyburn tossed the knife into the room behind Thieves.

"Destiny has a way of biting back, play-actor," the scarred man called. "I look forward to the day it catches you in its maw."

The player made no reply and began to ascend the steep, twisting staircase as it wound upwards in a tight clockwise spiral. In a castle or fortification, such stairs were designed to provide an advantage to defenders, with the spiral stair impeding a climbing attacker's weapon hand, while providing space for defenders to wield their swords. Just why such a design was incorporated into a London inn-yard was a mystery. *How old was this place?* Tyburn wondered. Mayhaps the Saracen's Head was built on the bones of some ancient stronghold. He might not be the first to clamber these narrow stairs with murderous intent.

The player pushed the thought out of his mind as he reached the landing, Covington close behind.

"Now what?" Covington whispered.

Tyburn edged open the door at the top of the landing. It opened up onto a narrow hallway with two wide framed stone arches opposite their cellar doorway. The kitchen lay beyond the archways. Tyburn could see a broad, well-lit fireplace, surmounted by a metal rack suitable for roasting meats. A large preparation table stood in the centre, and the walls were lined with well-stocked shelves and latticed cupboards. A selection of tin and copper-tinged pots hung from hooks above the shelves. A tired-looking turnspit dog lay sleeping in its enclosed wheel.

Tyburn gently shut the door and tugged open the drawstring on his bag. He reached in and pulled out several round enclosed clay pots. "Hold these." He handed them to Covington, who eyed them with suspicion.

"Powder?" Covington asked dubiously.

"Saltpeter and sugar." The player replied. "Smokers. We use them onstage, along with fireworks and the like for explosions and mists. I liberated them from Worcester's Men and then had an apothecary pack in some additions. You wanted a distraction. These will fill the whole bloody place with smoke. Those that don't run outright for fear of a fire should be easy pickings."

"And how do we get out?" Covington observed.

"We hit one floor at a time, keep the staircase doors closed, so it's sealed. By the time we get up to the fourth and back down, the smokers on the main floor should have fizzled. If we can't exit on the main floor, we continue back down and go through the tunnels."

"They don't burn or explode then, like lantern oil or black powder?"

"Just smoke."

Covington grinned. "This should be fun. Harlequin didn't quite know what she was dealing with, when she crossed a play-actor."

"Let's try to avoid her. We want Lady Arabela and the accounts. The Harlequin can wait."

Covington nodded and Tyburn pushed the door open, stepping into the empty hall. He could hear voices in the distant common room, and singing drifted from the covered inn-yard which lay beyond the door at the far end of the hallway. The player stepped across and into the kitchen. He had thought it was empty, but a serving boy lay sleeping on a mat in the corner. A pot sat on the edge of the fire, simmering quietly. The air was redolent with the scent of herbs and steaming pottage. A second serving table was laid across a raised brick platform that Tyburn recognized as the open end of the lift shaft that led down into the Devil's Hole.

Tyburn lit the short fuse on the first smoke pot and pushed it under the kitchen table, where it was hidden behind the broad table leg. With an audible puff, thick cloying smoke began to billow from the open neck of the pot in a steady, rushing jet.

Covington lit a second pot and set it beside the edge of the fireplace, well clear of the flue. The third pot refused to light, so Tyburn tossed it into the open fireplace. Hopefully the heat would ignite the saltpeter and the smoke would at least contribute to the general chaos.

Covington was back at the staircase. Tyburn paused and opened the wheel cage of the now whimpering turnspit dog. The dog darted away and the player, choking on the thick acrid smoke, rolled his last lit pot down the hallway towards the common room door.

A bursting sound and a sudden flare of bright yellow flame from the fireplace indicated that the failed smokepot had ignited. A billowing cloud of smoke washed out of the kitchen, rolling across the ceiling in a roiling wave. Tyburn heard the choking yell of surprise from the waking pot-boy.

Tyburn ducked back into the staircase and closed the door. "Up. Fast."

The group darted up the stairs, weapons drawn and ready. On the second landing Tyburn stopped and listened. He could hear the distant shouting of the pot-boy in the kitchens below, but no general alarm or outcry yet.

Covington dug into the bag and pulled out five more pots. He handed two to Tyburn, passed two to the Smythe brothers, and took one for himself. "Bristow, with me. Abel and Ned, down the hall to the far end. Light 'em and toss 'em in some of the rooms, let's get the confusion spreading." The Smythe brothers nodded in acquiescence, grinning in anticipation. The long tunnel journey now behind them, they were primed for mischief and trouble.

Tyburn pushed open the door and stepped right into one of the guards that had dragged him down into the Devil's Hole as the Harlequin's prisoner. The man gaped in astonishment, mouth hanging open for a protracted instant before Covington's long poniard drove up through the man's chin and into his brain. The look of ineffable glee on the blond swordsman's face was palpable, but all Tyburn could see was the hurt, stunned look in the other man's eyes as his life faded away into darkness.

"You need to be quicker, play-actor, or we won't be walking out of here," Covington noted as the blade slid back out with nary a sound. The man slumped forward and Tyburn felt the hot wash of blood from the man's wound coating his hand as he caught the man by the collar. They dragged the body into the stairwell and dumped him unceremoniously on the landing.

"What are you waiting for?" Covington hissed in anger. "Go plant your pots." The Smythes nodded in unison and darted down the hallway, lit matchcords fuming the air around them.

Tyburn moved down to the far end of the hall and paused at a door. Distinct snoring could be heard from within. He moved on to another door. This one opened onto a small landing that led down to the common room below. He lit the pot and set it by the opening. If it was panic they wanted, then the common room with its drunken inhabitants and raucous laughter was an ample opportunity for confusion. The smoke pot lit off and began pouring a billowing cloud that churned and thickened like a thunderhead.

Tyburn closed the door behind him and continued down the hall, hearing panicked shouting behind him as someone below noticed the mounting cloud of smoke. The door at the end of the hall led to the brothel attached to the inn-yard. Tyburn lit his last pot and rolled it through the doorway, taking care to leave the door open to allow the smoke to spread down the inn-yard hallway. A few panicked whores added to the mix can't hurt, he thought. He turned and raced back down to the stairwell and the others returning. They continued upwards.

--

Benoît Thieves fingered the short blade dubiously. It wasn't much of a weapon that the player had left him, more suitable for cutting cheese than slicing throats, but no matter. It would suffice.

He began the slow, painful climb up the staircase soon after he heard the first thumping of feet and panicked shouts of alarm echoing down through the lift shaft. It was a slow climb on the narrow, curving staircase, with the sliced tendons in his foot forcing him into a limping, hobbled gait. He paused to rest several times. This brief climb up the stairs was the farthest he had journeyed in more than three years, since his imprisonment and crippling.

Suzanne.

She was above. Somewhere.

He levered himself back to his feet and continued his upwards climb, the truncated digits of his hand splayed against the curved wall for support.

"I am coming, my sweet," he murmured.

He pushed open the door to the first-floor landing and was greeted by a thick, boiling cloud of choking smoke. He coughed and thrashed at it with one hand, stepping across the hall into the glowing light of the kitchen fire. He paused, kneeling to breathe in clearer air. The kitchen pot-boy stumbled back into the room in a panic, colliding with Thieves. The boy glanced up at the scarred, crusted, ruined mess of Thieves' face and screamed. Thieves grinned and whipped the knife across the boy's throat, sending him toppling across the wooden floor of the kitchen in a flood of red that flowed across the floor in a widening pool.

Thieves laughed. He reached over and pulled a long, hooked poker from the rack beside the blazing fireplace. Reaching into the fire, he raked the burning logs onto the wooden floor. He kicked one out into the hallway and watched as the flames began to lick at the dry wood of the wall. He reached in and raked more coals across the floor, then yanked the contents of a pantry shelf down to feed into the growing conflagration.

He lifted a jug from the preparation table and unstoppered it. A quick taste and another sharp laugh saw him pouring the oil out into the flames before tossing the jug into the blaze with a shattering crash.

"Never forget—destiny, my friend, has a bite," he murmured, opening the staircase door and resuming his climb in pursuit of Tyburn and his party.

Chapter the Thirtieth

SHRIEKING GREETED THEM on the third landing as thick smoke rose up through the floorboards and thin walls of the Saracen's Head. Shouting and running footsteps echoed through the building as panicked inhabitants engaged in a frantic search for the exits.

"We need to check every room for Lady Arabela," Covington said to the party. Bristow nodded, his face calm and expressionless. The Smythe brothers looked excited. "Watch for guards, this is where we are likely to find them."

"You mean like those two?" said Tyburn. The player calmly lit his smokepot and tossed it down the hall in the direction of the two guards charging down the hallway. The guards froze at the sight of the rolling pot emitting a steadily thickening jet of smoke that rapidly filled the hallway. The hesitation was just enough time for Tyburn and Bristow to burst through the thickening miasma of smoke and slam into the two men. Both guards were armed with hardened wooden tipstaffs, tipped and weighted with iron. Tyburn caught his opponent's wrist as he drew back for a swing. He levered the man's arm up and back, gripping his wrist and elbow and then stepping in tight, spinning the man sideways into the wall. The player whipped his fist backhanded into the man's throat and watched him fall with a sinking choking sound. The player yanked the tipstaff from the man's nerveless fingers. One quick, vicious club downwards sent the attacker into a dreamless oblivion.

Tyburn turned in time to watch Bristow hammer his opponent into the wall face-first before dropping the limp, unconscious figure onto the floor with a gesture of contempt. The mute ex-soldier cocked one eyebrow at Tyburn and then pointed back down the hall. The Smythe brothers grabbed the two unconscious guards and hauled them down the short distance, dropping them into the stairwell with an audible thud.

Tyburn and Bristow moved over to flank the doorway. It was locked.

Tyburn gave Bristow an expansive gesture at which the mute nodded, gave a polite half-bow, drew back one massive leg, and gave the door a lock-splintering kick that sent it slamming back into the room.

The player drew his short sword and sprang into the room. A beautiful, dark-haired woman was lying on a well-appointed bed, her face streaked with tears, eyes wide and round in fear.

Covington pushed past Tyburn. "Milady, Lord Rutledge has sent us to free you. You need come with us!"

The woman froze and then nodded mutely as Covington lifted her from the bed and gestured to Bristow. "Take her down the back staircase, it runs past the brothel and opens into the street. Abel and Ned go with you, while Tyburn and I go for the account books and set off the rest of the smoke pots. Kill anyone that gets in your way, and then go straight to Lord Rutledge's once you are in the street. We'll follow."

Bristow made a fluid set of finger motions that left Covington shaking his head. "No. Go with Lady Arabela. The play-actor and I can handle the Harlequin."

Bristow tugged on Lady Arabela's hand and pulled her, unresisting, down the hall with the Smythe brothers in tow. The group turned left down the hallway, passed through the door at the end and headed down the opposite staircase.

"You certain that's a good idea?" asked Tyburn, his face etched in a dubious scowl. "They run into Harlequin or any guards, they'll have a hard time managing them."

"Bristow can handle himself. I want Lady Arabela out of here. She was always the priority and Lord Rutledge would skin me if I waited. Besides," he said with a grin, "now we can settle the Harlequin, grab her accounts and any loose coin we find, and be out of here before anyone is the wiser. Your smoke pots seem to be very effective."

"A little too effective, I think." Tyburn eyed the blackening haze thickening the hall and smelled the familiar acrid stench of woodsmoke and burning fabric. "I don't think that's smoke pots anymore."

Covington looked alarmed for the first time since they left the sewers. "You think the Saracen's Head is ablaze?"

Tyburn jogged down the hallway back to their stairwell. "The smoke from below should be thinning. That's one hell of a lot coming up! The pots only burn for maybe five minutes. The inn's on fire, before God. We'd best get ourselves out as fast as possible."

"Then let's be about it, you purblind wretch. Move!"

--

The smoke was pouring up the staircase, rising in a solidifying hazy wall, with a blast of heat licking behind. Somewhere, beyond the choking air, lay the red and yellow flames of a growing conflagration, a flaming pit that, fanned by justice and God's will, would bring the world itself down in flame, thought

Thieves as he hauled himself laboriously up the next set of stairs. Perhaps the fire had been a mistake, he thought. He might not last to travel four flights before the air clotted in his lungs and sent him spasming into unconsciousness. No, he smiled to himself, feeling the muscles tug on his scarred face. No just God would permit him to die before he had served vengeance on his sweet Suzanne.

His foot bumped into a body. The man stirred feebly, one hand grasping at Thieves' leg. The thief lord patted the man's hand in sympathy and then sliced down hard with his short blade, hearing the man's gurgling shriek cut short with finality. Thieves paused to rummage his truncated hand over the man's body and then discarded the short blade that he had obtained from Tyburn in exchange for a long, lethal poniard the man carried at his belt. "Much better," Thieves murmured to himself. "You are doing God's work," he said to the lifeless corpse staining the wooden stairs crimson. Thieves' laugh was cut short by the choking smoke. He coughed and grumbled his way up the next set of stairs, hearing panicked cries from somewhere behind him, someone trapped in one of the inn's many rooms or in the maze of corridors. A rosy glow shone through the smoke behind him, climbing even as he did.

--

Clair reread the letter from her Warwickshire estate manager for the third time, trying and failing to parse some semblance of meaning out of the man's accounting. She set it aside in frustration. She wasn't sure if it was the man's obtuse prose, his crabbed penmanship, or the late hour that was keeping her from comprehension, but it was a waste of time to continue to pretend she cared about the drainage in the eastern pasture. She glanced at the white beeswax candle she had lit. Beeswax burned at a very steady rate, so she was certain the hour was just before midnight.

No news.

Clair shook her head. She had known that her play-actor wouldn't let Stokely's murder go unanswered, although she had hoped to be able to pull him aside from his obsession. Once Christopher had a thread, he was compelled to tug on it, no matter where it led or what might lie at the end of the string. The Harlequin was not one to be trifled with. Clair could feel that in her very bones. The woman was a primed pan awaiting a striker. One spark, one flash, and nothing would be left but a red memory of fury and force.

The quiet knock on her door startled her. She wrapped her gown tighter and opened the door a crack. Her doorwarden stood in the hall, a small lanthorn in one hand.

"Milady, pardon for disturbing you. You did say you wanted us to let you know if anything unusual or strange was about."

Clair's tired eyes sharped. "What?"

"Fire, milady. Large 'un. Heard the bells summoning the Watch. Out past Smithfield, near Holborn."

"Jesu," she whispered to herself.

"Milady?"

She opened the door further and leaned out. "Have two horses saddled. I want Henry with me—armed. We're riding for Holborn in ten minutes."

"Milady? At this hour?"

"Go." She closed the door, feeling the anxiety growing in her stomach.

It had to be Christopher.

"Malmsey by midnight indeed." She gave a hollow laugh.

She walked over to the side table and pulled open the drawer. The two Spanish wheellocks, both loaded, lay within. She lifted the top one out, feeling the solemn heft of the weapon. She nodded to herself. That die was cast, she thought. "*Amor, ch'a nullo amato amar perdona ...*" As she whispered to herself she turned to change into clothing more suitable for shooting, whether it be masked clowns or demonic Huguenots.

Chapter the Thirty-first

"COADS" THE PLAYER muttered to himself. He knew firsthand how fast a timber-framed building could burn, recalling the ravaged towns of the Scheldt and Walcheren as the armies of both the Spanish and the Dutch flowed across the Lowlands. He had burned at least a dozen buildings himself to deny supplies and shelter to the relentless, advancing steel-clad Spanish *tercios*. They didn't have much time.

The landing on the fourth floor was a familiar one. Bathed in the pale yellow light of the lanthorn, a thickening veil of smoke was climbing one wall and slithering across the thick beams of the ceiling, pooling and eddying in the air like river water swirling past an outcropping. A heavyset set of double doors faced the staircase landing, surrounded by a dark, gorgeously carved wooden doorframe depicting a tangle of flowering green ivy and white and yellow flowers all of inlaid coloured glass set delicately into the wood.

Covington, with a grin that could only be described as malicious, stepped up and kicked the door hard, popping it open, scattering crystalline petals in all directions. The room beyond was a large set of apartments that Tyburn recognized from his brief visit.

The Harlequin was nowhere to be seen.

"We need to find that account book quick or we'll roast alongside it." Kit scanned the room quickly for likely hiding places.

"You have a gift for the obvious, master player."

Tyburn let Covington's sour sarcasm slide off as he pushed by a wide table, heading to the far end of the room where an ornate poster bed stood against the end wall. He began to rummage through the pile of books stacked on the side table. The books were French, a mix of some lurid popular tales and a fat cookery book.

"No accounts." The player yanked the thick pile of bedding aside to check the bed. Aside from a sharp, hooked blade he found dangling from a hook behind one of the supporting headboard columns, there was nothing. He peered at the tester above the bed, but it stood a good eight feet above the floor, so as a hiding spot it was inopportune at best.

Covington rummaged through the desk that stood against the far wall before stepping back with a curse and turning to bang open and empty a wooden trunk. Both men were coughing as acrid smoke billowed through the open doors behind them, catching in the back of their throats like barbs.

Damn it, Tyburn thought, there is no time. The player stepped back. The room was big enough to hide something as small as an account book almost anywhere. An extra wide joist, a hinged wooden side panel, a loose floorboard—there was no end of possible hiding places, and time was gone.

Tyburn paused. The Harlequin was not a trusting soul, he knew. She would want the accounts at ready hand and accessible to her. They wouldn't be locked away in some gated sacristy, but someplace where she could snatch them at a run. Tyburn grasped the small side table he had moved and dumped the remaining books unceremoniously onto the floor.

The table was unprepossessing, worn and unremarkable, with no drawers or storage space, but once Tyburn lifted it, he noted it was strangely heavy. And thicker than one would expect. With a satisfied smile, the player lifted it high and smashed it into the floor. The table legs snapped and spun away. He lifted it again and crashed it down onto the floor a second time. This time it split and cracked, and Tyburn slid one gloved hand into the splintered wood of the corner and levered the decorative facing off. It gave way with a crack and the player grinned as a fat, thick, leather-bound account book tumbled to the floor, alongside a cheveril purse heavy with coin.

Tyburn tossed the purse to Covington and straightened, Stokely's missing account book in his hand. *At last*, he thought.

The click of the pistol cocking made a statue of him.

"I'm thinking I'm a better thespian than you are, Master Tyburn." Cynicism tinged Covington's voice, and his blue eyes were like chips of glass. The hexagonal barrel of the snaphance seemed to loom larger in Tyburn's eyes. Covington gave the pistol a quick flick, indicating for Tyburn to move back. Tyburn shrugged the canvas bag containing the remaining smoke pots off his shoulder and dropped it on the floor. He stepped backwards around the fallen pile of books and the broken remains of the side table. Covington moved to the left and banged his left fist twice against the wall. The wooden panel clicked and swung open on a set of silent hinges.

Tyburn recognized the heavy tread and wary eyes even before he spotted his silvered rapier hanging at the man's side. Bent surveyed the room, sparing one contemptuous glance at Covington before stepping towards Tyburn. The instant Bent crossed in front of Covington's line, Tyburn reached back and drew his own snaphance with brutal speed. His left hand was cocking the dog back to fire even as the pistol drew level.

The dog clacked and sparked but no shot blasted forth. Bent grinned. "You don't think we're dotterals enough to grant you a loaded squib, are you?"

Covington stepped to one side, clearing his firing line, the pistol still leveled at the player. "It's been very amusing, watching you galliard about like a fool, but as this place seems to be genuine alight, it would be best if we finished our business and departed. Hand over Stokely's accounts without undue fuss and I'll make it a clean shot. No messing about, no dying by inches, flayed by the Harlequin. Just a quick trip to oblivion."

Tyburn gazed levelly at Covington. "When did this happen?"

The blond swordsman laughed. "Right after I realized how much I wanted to put steel through Rutledge's throat. That juking bastard made me clean up one too many of his messes." He gestured with the weapon. "He's no different than Morgan or Gilbert sending us into Sluis and Bruges cold against Spanish regulars. Right bastards!" he spat. "You were at Bruges. You saw what happened. Rutledge is more of the same—some monied, titled, pratting capon that thinks nothing of sending good men to die in some breach for nothing!"

There is nothing like Flanders. The words echoed in Tyburn's mind, a distant shout across a desperate field. Tyburn felt a flush of heat rising through the floorboards. More smoke occluded the hallway, a choking miasma that stung his eyes and rasped his throat. A door opened and closed in the distance.

"Rutledge is a dung-rattled whoreson. We can both agree on that. But why align with the Harlequin? Why ally yourself with Spain?" Tyburn drew out the last word as though it had an offensive taste that lingered on the tongue, a texture not easily removed. "You've seen what they do. You know what they want to do."

"Harlequin doesn't give a wet shit about the Spanish or what they want to achieve. They're a means to an end. Rutledge is the key to the biggest hoard of coin in England with his position on the privy council and the Treasury."

Tyburn rolled his eyes in disbelief. "She sold you on that? It's a load of shite. Rutledge is near penniless. He went sideways on the cloth and wool trade when the Spanish burned Antwerp. He's been cooking his account books for years, trading with Crown money on the sly. That's why Stokley's dead and the accounts are so valuable. Should anyone lay hands on these accounts, Rutledge is bound for the Tower or the block. The Spanish want him in play. They want him holding Walsingham's reins. Those accounts will go straight to the Spanish, not to pad your pockets."

"He's penniless, but Arabela Howard ain't. As far as she knows, Rutledge arranged for her rescue after that cockless sod Asquith had her grabbed. The Countess of Lennox will make sure of it, that's the arrangement. Rutledge will get one of the richest domains in England through his marriage, and we'll spend ourselves plucking him clean."

Tyburn nodded. "I thought it was an easy entry to her room. Just two guards. And you knew exactly where Bristow should exit. Strange for a man that hadn't been to the Saracen's Head before."

Bent grunted in annoyance. "Shoot the bugger and get it done."

Covington's response was a muffled gasp of pain. The pistol wavered in his hand as the long poniard slid back out of his side. The blond swordsman reached over with his left hand to touch the red wave that was spreading down his right side and across his expensive doublet. He choked, sending a spray of blood from his mouth as he toppled to the floor.

Benoît Thieves laughed, the long, bloodied poniard gripped in his one good hand, smoke coiled about him like a wide-swept cloak. Tyburn caught a fleeting glimpse of flame before he sidestepped Bent, who, seeing Covington topple, ripped Tyburn's long, silvered rapier out of its sheath and stabbed forward.

Tyburn hit the floor, rolling to one side. Even through the thick leather of his buff coat he could feel heat radiating from the wooden floorboards. He grabbed the canvas bag and tossed it as hard as he could into the still blazing hearth. The clay smoke pots shattered, spilling loose granular white powder and broken ceramic out of the open mouth of the bag. The stray powder ignited with a brilliant hissing yellow flame that filled the room with churning buttery light and sent a spray of burning powder arching through the air like a hissing flight of fireworks. Smoke poured out of the hearth, thickening the haze in the room, smothering it in a choking fog.

Tyburn drew his short sword and continued to roll to one side, head pivoting around, looking for Bent.

The man emerged from the dense cloud with a shout, whipping the rapier downwards in a vicious cut that caught Tyburn in the left shoulder.

He doesn't know how to use a rapier was the only thought that went through Tyburn's mind. The hard slicing cut, though it stung like fury, barely penetrated the thick leather of the buff coat. If the cut had caught Tyburn on exposed flesh, it certainly would have laid him open and bloody, but a rapier wasn't a bastard sword; it wasn't designed for cutting and chopping. Tyburn's Spanish prize was razor sharp along its edge, but a rapier was a thrusting weapon. You killed best with the point, not the edge.

Tyburn kicked out, catching the side of Bent's knee, grunting in satisfaction at the exclamation of pain.

"Come on, you pox-faced bastard, I'll send you back to your sty." Tyburn spun the short sword in his hand, feeling the balance and heft. It was a dull, worn, and unprepossessing blade, but Tyburn knew he could kill with it. That was all he needed.

Bent drove in again, properly this time, with a short flashing series of quick passes that drove the player back. The steel scraped and clashed, sending curlicues of smoke spinning away.

Tyburn spat, his mouth dry and empty of all moisture. Bent had the reach, with the longer blade of the rapier, but Tyburn knew the street curtail wasn't a swordsman. He was a brawler, all attack, slow to riposte and more tellingly, slow to remove his weapon from the attack. Tyburn decided to use that to his advantage.

The heat was intense. The player could feel the air, thick and pulsating, like a baker's oven opening and closing. He edged backwards, dropping the point of his short sword to the left, deliberately leaving an opening for a thrust.

Bent drove in.

With fearsome speed, Tyburn brought his short sword blade up and level. The blade caught the rapier thrust on the inside edge of the short sword, deflecting the point up. The player's left hand shot up and parried the rapier. Catching the blade in his gloved right hand and, using his own weapon as a fulcrum, he levered the rapier back and down, rotating it around his own leveled steel. Bent's face was a rictus of fear and anger that spun into astonishment as the silvered rapier was torn from his hand.

Tyburn plowed headlong, locking his elbow and heaving all his weight behind the dull blade. Bent tried to deflect the short sword as it rammed forward, crying out as the steel ripped through his gloves into his hands, slicing leather, flesh, and tendons. There was a moment of resistance, and then Tyburn was pushing forward, the short sword ripping into Bent's upper chest and pinning him to the wall. Tyburn leaned in. He could feel the curtail thrashing spasmodically, like a gaffed fish. Bent coughed, blood and phlegm spraying across Tyburn's face. The blood felt almost cool in the boiling, fiery smoke.

"Fucker." The whisper was faint. Bent slumped. The short sword pulled loose from the wall as the man's unsupported weight crashed to the floor.

"I did warn him."

Tyburn spun. The Harlequin stood in the doorway, a long, edged blade of her own held languid in one hand.

"He always was slow, recovering from a lunge. Tried to teach him better, but Bent was Bent. Stubborn. He should have stuck to knives. He always had a fondness for knives." She canted her head at Tyburn, a slow smile on her lips, like a liar's caress. A red glow flickered in the hallway behind her as flames began to lick up the walls. "I trust you won't play such an amateur trick on me, when the time comes." She gestured at the silvered rapier lying on the floor. "Go on. Pick it up. We need to finish our dance, dead man."

Tyburn reached out and hooked his fingers around the blade, sliding it into his grasp, feeling the familiar deadly heft, hearing the steel ring faint and clear as he lifted it from the floor. The air felt thick and substantial around the weapon, as though the sword carried a surfeit of haunts that clung to the edged steel like barnacles to a ship.

"I just want the book," Tyburn said. "I see no reason for discord."

"Aside from all the murder attempts?"

Tyburn gave a ghost of a smile. "Why help the Spanish? Can't be for coin, you'd bilk more out of Rutledge then you'd get from those cozening bastards."

The sword in her hand was rising. Infinitesimally slow, but rising.

"You think I care about Spain? Or gelt?"

"No," said Tyburn, side stepping, trying to ensure he had clear space to move. "I think you care about vengeance."

She smiled. "I am the Hellequin, the black-faced demon. I have a duty to take the corrupt and the sinful to their just abode."

"Who then, if not Rutledge?"

She spat in contempt. "Rutledge? Rutledge and Asquith are lap dogs. They aren't worth the effort to spill their blood. I hunt kings and gods and spiders, not mice."

Despite the growing heat Tyburn felt a cold chill slither up his spine. "You want Walsingham," he whispered.

The full lips widened into the purest of smiles. "I do. I will."

"Why?"

"Why?" The smile vanished, eclipsed by a snarling fury. "Didn't he tell you? My dear father was Walsingham's kept man in the admiral's court, betraying de Coligny's secrets to the English, playing his little games with both sides. Until de Coligny was assassinated and *la massacre* swept across Paris like a hot wind."

The blade tip was up and circling in a slow hypnotic rhythm, pointed at Tyburn's eyes. He watched her torso, refusing the blade tip, refusing to lock eyes with her. That way lay death. Getting tricked into following someone's gaze or their sword tip. Too easy to be tricked by a sidelong glance or a flick of a blade.

"Where was Walsingham then? When the streets ran red and the bodies clogged the Seine?" she snarled. "Where was he when my mother and I hammered on his embassy door for surcease? For refuge from the mob? What did the honourable Ambassador Walsingham do when my mother was raped and murdered at his gates? I'll tell you what he did," she shouted, "he locked his doors."

A crashing sound thundered outside the hallway as something collapsed. The floor shook and groaned. A roaring sound, like a thousand men emptying their lungs in one collective shriek tore through the room. The Saracen's Head was screaming like a live thing. The far wall by the poster bed was aflame, the heat palpable but the Harlequin stood unmoved. The smoke swirled and caught in their throats, acrid and harsh.

With barely a glance towards the flames, she continued. "The Spanish want Rutledge to take over Walsingham's spies, to assume control over his web of informants, spies, and traitors. They want Walsingham to hand over the keys to the kingdom. I am happy to take their coin. Coin is always useful." She shrugged, the blade now frozen in mid-air, level with Tyburn's eyes. "But I want him dead. I want Walsingham's blood painting the cobbles. I will taste my vengeance."

"And I want mine." The voice came out of the smoke at the same moment that Thieves did. Limping, hobbled, and snarling, the ex–thief lord plowed out of the fire-tinged smoke into the Harlequin. She spun with phenomenal speed, but Thieves was already inside the reach of the rapier and he beat it aside with his maimed hand, the long poniard clutched and stabbing out. The Harlequin screamed once before the cry turned into a shriek of anger and calescent fury. She hammered the hilt of the sword into Thieves' head, but he barely noticed.

"Come my lovely, we go to Hell's portico as one!"

The play-actor was forgotten and rooted as the pair vented their hatred, a noise lost in the rising ferocity of the fire. Tyburn watched as the Harlequin levered her father's head back with her elbow and then drove the point of her long rapier into his side.

Thieves didn't even pause. One hand was on her throat, the other holding the bloodied poniard, while the man shoved forward, crippled legs shuffling relentlessly towards the open doorway and the blazing hallway.

Tyburn leaped after the pair. The smoke stung his eyes and hot cinders floated past, bobbing in the heated air like corks in the ocean. Tyburn saw Thieves' body slump but his grip was relentless. The Harlequin pulled back her weapon to strike again but Thieves surged upwards, shoving her back.

Tyburn caught one quick glimpse of Thieves' scarred and crusted face, alight with a thick and sneering grin of triumph, and the Harlequin, for once, losing her customary composure and cold mien, a look of stark terror suffusing it, a look that he guessed had last been worn as a child. For the first time, Tyburn felt he had seen the real Suzanne Martaine lurking within the demon. Those terrified eyes caught his.

They fell.

The player hadn't seen it until the pair toppled, but the hallway beyond the turn was gone, collapsed under the relentless fire. It was a rising column of flame, almost like a flue, pushing the fire like a live thing, strident and clamorous, spreading out into the upper floor and the roof above.

Tyburn couldn't help himself. He edged forward and took a quick glance into the blazing abyss. Most of the flames seemed to be roaring up the far side of the opening but below it was a straight drop into the fire-strewn inn-yard.

Hanging from a charred and broken beam by one hand, peering upwards, was the Harlequin.

"Jesus." Tyburn flattened himself on the charred and shuddering floor, feeling the heat boiling up from below. He reached out without even a conscious thought, fingers just grazing the top of the beam where Suzanne Martaine clung. "Reach, damn you!" he shouted down at her.

The look of terror was gone. Suzanne Martaine was gone. Only the Harlequin remained.

The Harlequin's face was calm, almost placid as she stared upwards. Her face was grimed with soot and the short brown curls of her hair were crusted and charred black along one side. "The world has turned, dead man. You fell into water, and I into flame."

The Harlequin's right hand came into view, the long rapier still clutched in her fist.

"Damn you, just lose the blade and reach. I'm not going to drop you!" Tyburn snarled.

The rapier rose upwards, slow and relentless. Time seemed to slow and Tyburn watched as fire flicked about in eddies and churnings, one long tendril reaching out and arching along the shattered wooden beam that the Harlequin clutched with her left hand. The flames caressed that hand, curling around and burning her fingers.

They loosed.

Just as the blade sliced upwards, her grip failed and the Harlequin fell into the maelstrom of smoke and roiling fire. The sword tip slid past Tyburn's gaze, inches from a strike.

Gone.

The world slammed into focus and Tyburn jerked back, feeling eddies of heat and the choking grasp of smoke, tainting his throat and lungs.

There is no place like Flanders.

Tyburn crawled back into the room, peering through the thickening murk, gasping, tears streaming down his face from his stinging eyes.

The account book lay on the floor, the edges of the vellum curling in the heated air. If it hadn't been bound in leather, it would have burned by now. The player shoved it under his buff coat and doublet, feeling the radiant heat of the book on his chest.

A groan sounded to his right. He turned. Covington had pulled himself onto his side, his blue eyes peering through the smoke. He choked out a whisper and Tyburn moved closer to hear the blond swordsman.

"I'm a venal fool," he murmured. "Live through Flanders and Goes and die like a dupe in a London alehouse." He choked and spat blood onto his sleeve. "Let that bitch turn my head. She knew what strings to pull. Not sorry I chased that gold. Sorry I did it so badly." He grinned, his smile varnished in red. "Sorry I turned coat. Couldn't abide Rutledge, but I shouldn't have fucked you over."

Tyburn shook his head in dismissal but voiced no response.

"A favour?" The man paused to cough another fistful of blood. "Don't let me burn."

Tyburn froze for an instant and then gave the blond swordsman a short, careful nod.

"And look after Bristow, will you. He won't take this well."

Tyburn slid his knife out and gave the swordsman a reassuring smile. "A little ale cures many woes. In Bristow's case, it might mean a surfeit." Covington started to smile and laugh just as Tyburn slid the blade home. The blond swordsman stiffened for an instant and Tyburn watched as the muscles in his face relaxed.

"There is nothing like Flanders," he muttered, half to Covington's now slack face, and half to himself.

A thumping crash from the hallway pulled him back to the moment. It was past time to leave the Saracen's Head to its fate.

Chapter the Thirty-second

THE AIR WAS thick and blinding. Tyburn crawled along the edge of the wall, feeling for the opening to the stairwell. He could see nothing but churning black smoke, interspersed with red pockets of flame. His hand fell into open space.

The player slid down the wooden steps like an eel, keeping his face averted from the heat, one outstretched hand grasping the next step in a careful descent. For a moment, he flashed back in memory to the darkness of the tunnels, but the broiling heat and choking miasma of smoke almost made the comparison laughable. He felt the same stomach-churning fear though, rising with each inch he slid.

There is nothing like Flanders.

But Flanders had been cold and wet and effused with the scent of coppery blood, not this baking heat, coupled with acrid, sparing gulps of air, like sips of the finest wine.

No more steps.

Tyburn knew he had hit the second floor landing. The stairs resumed just past the landing, but he could feel the swirling heat and smoke rising through the stairwell. He ducked his head tight against the shoulder of his charred buff coat. It was no good. The heat was too intense. If he went forward, he would burn.

The player crawled out into the second floor hallway. Bright flame licked at the far end of the hall, illuminating a long, low bank of grey and black smoke that hung in the air about two feet above the floor.

A low moan came from the open doorway across from the stairwell. Tyburn slid across the hall and into the room, eyes stinging and tearing in the smoke.

A round-faced Lord Asquith was curled into a ball against the wall, his velvet doublet and silken finery crusted with soot and grime. Asquith was sobbing and rocking in a paroxysm of fear, a fact that made Tyburn feel better about the numbing terror threatening to rear up in his own mind each time he felt a wash of heat.

"Milord." Tyburn reached out and shook the man. "Milord!" The crying man ignored the player and curled tighter into himself.

"Milord!" The player repeated. Exasperated, Tyburn clenched his left hand into a fist and hammered the man's thigh.

"Ahhhh!" Asquith screamed. His pale, tear streaked face gaped at Tyburn in astonishment. "You hit me! Why did you hit me?"

"Milord! How do we get out? You know this place. Where do we go?"

The man stared at Tyburn as though he were a simpleton. "It's on fire. You can't go anywhere."

"What about the stairs?"

Asquith shook his head. "Burning," he whispered.

"The inn-yard? We could drop down."

Asquith looked at him as though he had just exited Bedlam. "Flames." He began to keen and rock, pulling himself tighter.

"We're going to burn." He sobbed. "I don't deserve to burn." He looked at Tyburn earnestly. "I'm a lord, you know."

Despite the circumstances Tyburn was tempted to laugh out loud. "Milord. Any windows?"

Lord Asquith gestured feebly. Just those. They don't open and I couldn't break them."

Tyburn was already crawling towards the far side of the room at almost the instant Asquith had finished speaking. The darkness was near absolute but he could see the dim outlines of a large, diamond-paned window, reflecting the red light that filled the open door of the hallway. His fingers traced up the edges, the cool, thick glass like a balm on his hands.

He stood, feeling his chest clench against the harsh smoke. He hammered the glass window with his open hand.

Nothing. Drawing his sword, he pounded the rapier hilt into the pane. Once. Twice. Again. The thick glass splintered and cracked, but was held tight by lead framing. Tyburn slumped. He could probably batter his way through eventually, but he could feel himself slipping. His heart was hammering in his chest, his lungs screaming for surcease, for clear air. He shoved the rapier blade under the window jamb.

The silvered weapon slipped and skittered along the window edge.

"God's bones," the player muttered to himself. I need something heavy. I need to smash through the window. I won't last long enough to pry it open or break enough panes. Even with the panes shattered, he would still need to push through the diamond-shaped lattice that supported the glass.

Something heavy.

The room was bare of furnishing, save for a thin broken table and smashed crockery. A fat mattress lay to one side, smoldering in the heat, but it didn't even have a wooden frame, which might have provided something. Tyburn slid down the wall, coughing and choking in the smoke, feeling the darkness beckoning.

There is nothing like Flanders.

Something heavy.

The barest edge of thought crept into his mind and darted away again, as he sluggishly tried to grasp at it.

Something heavy.

He could hear bells frantically ringing. Alarms, he thought. Summoning the Watch. For the fire.

Tyburn's eyes fluttered open. Something heavy.

Coughing, Tyburn scrambled back through the room and grabbed the huddled Earl of Asquith. Spitting black soot out of his mouth, Tyburn began to half-lift, half-drag the terrified earl into the room. "Come on, you fucker," he said, pulling and tugging. The earl shrank back in fear. Tyburn leaned in and shouted in his ear. "We're leaving this bousing ken right now."

Tyburn dragged Asquith over the window and stood.

"You can't break through," Asquith sobbed. "I tried. I tried and tried and tried."

"You need something heavy." said Tyburn with a grin. Asquith gazed up at him in confusion and Tyburn bent down, grabbed the earl under one arm, and took hold of his belted velvet doublet. Tyburn gave Asquith's pale, sweat-soaked face a reassuring nod and, muscles screaming in protest, raised the earl up and hammered him bodily into the window. Asquith gave a choking half scream of fear that transmuted into a shout of pain. Tyburn slumped against the window, feeling Asquith thrashing against him. "Maybe a bit harder," he said to himself.

He grunted and heaved up the squirming earl again, stepped back, and pounded him against the glass panes, hearing a distinct cracking sound from the splintering wooden jambs. The player felt his head clear as cold air blew in through a broken pane that had popped out completely. The roaring sound of the fire behind him was growing distinctly louder, and light was flooding the room as open flame licked through the doorway behind him. The earl tried to scratch and punch his way free of Tyburn's grip, but the player was beyond noticing, focused on the window.

Tyburn hefted the earl a third time. "Something heavy." He repeated, taking a few steps back and charging at the window, hurling the earl and all of his own weight against the sagging window and frame.

The jamb gave with a screeching crack that was rivaled by the pitched scream of pain from the Earl of Asquith as he and Tyburn crashed straight through the shattered remnants of the window and fell from the overhanging jetty into the hard, cobbled street below.

Compared to his plummet from London Bridge, the drop from the second floor of the Saracen's Head was but an instant, a single second of weightless spinning descent followed by a crashing stop on the inflexible paving stones of Snow Lane.

Tyburn felt his eyelids flutter and blink open. He was staring down, Asquith's unconscious body sprawled beneath him in boneless repose. Tyburn groaned and levered himself over, wincing as his head cracked the uneven slope of Snow Hill Lane. He felt like he had been kicked by a horse. The player was lying in about two inches of light snow covering the cold stone cobbles.

He stared upwards, watching the fat, thick flakes drifting down around him, lit by the flickering flames from the Saracen's Head burning behind him. He heard a thumping, hammering sound and a pair of booted feet stopped beside him.

"You alive?" The voice growled.

"I think." replied Tyburn.

"Then get the fuck outta the way, you prat. We've work to do."

Tyburn forced himself up, stifling a groan. He was sprawled on the cobbles of Snow Hill Lane. Above him, the overhang of the second floor of the Saracen's Head was afire, sending a slow rain of hot cinders and burning ash into the verge of the street, where it landed and sizzled briefly in the snow before extinguishing. Asquith lay unconscious and smoking, one arm bent at an improbable angle that made the player wince inwardly.

He scrambled to his feet, staggering back like a drunk in the early morn. "God's teeth," he hissed to himself, feeling the collection of pain reverberating through every parcel of his being. Tyburn peered around, shielding his eyes against the flames which shot high into the night.

The street was thronging with activity. A man on horseback was directing a loose line of people passing buckets in a steady, though fruitless, effort to reduce the blaze. Another more organized group wielding long metal hooks was industriously pulling down the ramshackle neighbouring constructions and buildings, even while a steady stream of residents, occupants, and thieves exited the various doorways clutching furnishings and personal property. A large mattress was pushed out of an open window from a building two doors down from the burning inn-yard to land with a soft thump and a billow of loose snow. A dozen terrified horses were being led away from the conflagration, freed from the inn-yard stables before the walls went up in flames. The grooms were gaping in horror and astonishment as one wing of the Saracen's Head collapsed with a roar and a flaring burst of sparks. A man wearing the colours of the London Watch was haranguing the crowd to keep well back, but the onlookers ignored him, edging forward to gape at the spectacle.

In truth, the lack of wind and the steady fall of fat, wet snow was the most effective factor containing the blaze. Fires were not unknown to London; indeed they were a regular, if terrifying experience, one the city aldermen spent much time and effort in railing against but expended little in practical effort that went beyond pulling down the worst offenders and insisting on tiled roofs. It was neighbourhoods that policed and fought fires, as it was usually the locals' possessions and properties at risk if a conflagration spread.

A couple of men busily dousing burning scraps of construction that had fallen into the street paused to drag Asquith's supine form away from the fire. They left him with a set of wardens who began to pilfer the unconscious man's pockets. Tyburn grinned. Asquith was alive at least. He clearly had one broken arm and, judging from the impact, probably two or three broken ribs. He wouldn't be happy when he awoke, thought Tyburn, but the player doubted if the earl would have any recall or remembrance of who had thrown him through the windows of the burning inn-yard.

Tyburn sat heavily on the far side of the street and watched the Saracen's Head burn. His head ached, along with most every part of him. A small group of liveried horsemen milled about to one side, carrying on an angry conversation.

"Have the pumps been fetched from the yard yet?"

"They are expected momentarily, Sir John. Do we continue to pull down these neighbouring houses?"

"Bigod of course! I would let the fire burn out these pestilential tenements, except that the flames might spread to St. Sepulchre and we can't have that! Pull them down!"

"About my horse, my lord..." The speaker was a well-dressed man who stood, arms akimbo, in front of the small group of horsemen. Tyburn caught sight of the double dragon and crossed shield livery of the Lord Mayor of London, glittering in silvered thread in the blazing firelight.

The man on horseback visibly sighed. "Very well. What about your horse, Master Wolstan?"

"Stolen, sirrah! Nefariously stolen! In the very charitable act of helping some poor soul."

Tyburn was half-listening, gauging the energy required to walk back to Clair's abode and half-torn with the need to watch the inn-yard funeral pyre burn itself out.

"... came out of the fire and hit me!"

Tyburn sat up.

"Hit you?" the lord mayor said in dubious tones.

"Indeed! Before God, it happened. I dismounted to help this poor benighted soul that came staggering out of the conflagration and the boy struck me and took my horse! My prize bay!"

Tyburn limped over to the group and grabbed Wolstan's arm, spinning him about. "This boy," he commanded, "What did he look like?"

Startled by Tyburn's vehemence and his charred and smoking appearance, the man stammered a reply. "Dark, almost curly hair, partially burned away. One arm and the hand were burned, and certainly the boy looked worse for wear."

"What did this boy do? What was said?" the player demanded.

Wolstan coloured. "He … he kicked me. In the … uhm … the leg. And then took the horse." The men on horseback laughed.

"Did she say anything?" Tyburn repeated, shaking the man for emphasis.

"No. Well maybe …"

"What?" Tyburn was practically shouting.

"Something about one last soul … but it was hard to hear over the noise of the flames."

"And the high-pitched wailing," muttered one of the horsemen in a cheerful aside. The mayor snorted in amusement.

Harlequin.

The player pushed the pains and aches in his body aside. "One last soul," Tyburn muttered. It was either Clair or Walsingham. He had best not choose wrong. Tyburn spun away as the horsemen laughed and asked how long Wolstan's "leg" was.

The player forced himself upright and pushed his way through the gawping crowds, up the rising slope of Snow Hill Lane to the intersection where the rescued horses from the inn-yard had been gathered into a string.

Tyburn grabbed one of the young grooms. "I need a horse."

The groom growled back, "These ain't yours and they ain't for hire."

"I didn't ask." Tyburn hauled the boy away from the string of horses. "I've got to ride to see the principal secretary, so I'll take the dun. Now." The groom looked up at the play-actor's scarred and begrimed visage and shrank at the expression. Within minutes

Tyburn was aback his chosen horse. Peering down at the frightened groom, Tyburn called, "I'll leave him at the Three Tuns on the morrow." The player fished out a silver coin and tossed it to the boy. "Sorry!" The player started off in a flurry of snow, the flickering, burning pyre that was the Saracen's Head behind him, as he pounded through the open Newgate, heading for Cheapside, the cold winter darkness cutting into him like a knife.

The *Hellequin* was loose in London.

Chapter the Thirty-third

THE BROTHEL NEXT to the Saracen's Head was well aflame when Clair arrived. The team of men with metal hooks had succeeded in pulling down the neighbouring tenement, which toppled with a resounding crash that startled her horse and sent him skittering sideways, kicking up the fallen snow and frightening the watchers edging the side of the street.

The new fire break seemed to have worked, as the blaze had not been able to bridge the gap between the fallen tenement and the stony splendor that was St. Sepulchre. The bell still rang with urgency but the blaze seemed at last to settle down, content to burn in one place like a tall candle, sending a short, truncated pillar of flame into London's night.

Clair maneuvered her horse deftly through the milling crowd, looking for a badge or flag of authority. She spotted the small cluster of men on horseback by the intersection, recognizing one with the badge of the Lord Mayor of London, surrounded by aldermen and functionaries. She turned the horse and trotted up to the group.

"My lord mayor!" she called. Sir John Langley, the Lord Mayor of London, turned at her call.

"Milady Carey, isn't it? By the troth, what brings you out on such a hellish eve?" He gave her a low bow.

"I thank you, milord. I'm seeking a friend whom I believe might have recently escaped this conflagration. A tall gentleman, dark-haired, with a scar on one cheek?"

"I'm afraid you just missed him, milady. He was present, but last I saw he departed in haste on horseback, heading to Newgate."

"Indeed!" The mayor rubbed his hooked nose and sniffed dubiously. "He had many a question for our poor Sheriff Wolstan, who had his horse stolen by some ruffian."

Clair leaned forward. "Tell me everything."

After several minutes, Clair spurred her horse away from the lord mayor's group and returned to where her groom, Henry, patiently waited.

"He's gone. Bare minutes, according to the lord mayor. Gone to see the principal secretary—that's Walsingham—according to the boy. We'll go ourselves. Walsingham's house is on Seething Lane, near Tower Hill."

"Tower Hill? Milady, it's full dark and you want to ride clear across London?"

"No," she replied with asperity, "I want to gallop clear across London, so cease complaining and start riding."

--

It was a slow ride. Tyburn, unaccustomed to horseback, felt every jolt and uneven hoof-fall as they trotted down the icy and now snow-crusted surface of Cheapside. The steady thickening curtain of snow, the relentless darkness, and the nervous horse had slowed his headlong rush. The player felt a frisson of fear over his slower pace, but reassured himself with the fact that, mad as she was, even the Harlequin couldn't navigate a horse down a darkened London street at speed without the creature balking or breaking a leg. He was, at best, mere minutes behind her.

He nudged his mount into a more rapid pace, peering ahead into the snow-flecked night, the cold wind a welcome respite after the scorching heat of the Saracen's Head. He coughed relentlessly, the thick taste of soot clogging his throat and nostrils. The sides of the street were cloaked in darkness except for a handful of thin candles that flickered in various windows. At one point a small contingent of the Watch raised a lanthorn from a doorway, calling out a slurred and drunken challenge as Tyburn trotted past. The player ignored the men with their long poleaxes and they proffered no additional questions or demands. A man on horseback doubtless was of so high a rank that it was beyond their measure or authority to challenge. Had Tyburn been afoot, they would have caused him no uncertain amount of grief with their petty larcenies and perverse sense of authority.

Tyburn peered into the darkness, looking for some sense of where he was. He had passed the Cheapside Cross some minutes before, so it was with relief he recognized the familiar square shape of St. Mary Woolchurch looming in the snow. He angled the horse down the street that arched off to the right, following the slight slope downwards. This neighbourhood, at least, he knew passing well even in the darkness. His old set of miserable rooms was a bare few blocks away, though as Clair had informed him, it was doubtless let out to some other pitiable occupant by now. He followed Fenchurch's rutted length through the cold wind that coursed down it until he saw the familiar worn sign of the King's Head. Tyburn yanked the bridle and steered the horse past the tavern and down the narrow street.

He was close.

Seething Lane ran roughly north-south, anchored at each end by the churches of St. Olave in the north, and All Hallows Barking at the south. Tower Hill, with its grim scaffold and execution block cloaked in fallen snow and darkness, lay just beyond. The torch-lit expanse of the Tower battlements and the dank, still moat surrounding the castle were hidden by the tall homes lining Seething Lane. The player dismounted a block short of the Lane, tying his horse to a convenient cart that was canted against a side alley. Tyburn peered down the street, feeling the cold flecks of snow settling in his hair and melting on his bare forehead. Walsingham's house lay a bare stone's throw from the corner, tall and imposing, even in the midnight gloom.

Nothing looked untoward.

Tyburn cursed inwardly. If the Harlequin's "one last soul" had referred to Clair, and the demon-bitch had gone to Cripplegate and the house on Chiswick, there was nothing he could do.

An imposing carved stone archway led into the main entrance of Walsingham's home, with a small offset alcove set to one side. A doorwarden was posted in the alcove at all hours, keeping watch over Her Majesty's Principal Secretary. Though Walsingham was lacking in titles, properties, and visible honours, his influence and position on the Queen's Privy Council was significant, holding the ears of both Burghley, the Lord Treasurer and Robert Dudley, the Earl of Leicester. The spymaster never travelled without the protection of a small coterie of loyal and very skilled guards.

Tyburn could see the casual bulk of Walsingham's doorwarden, leaning back in his usual alcove by the doorway, arms crossed in a relaxed demeanor, a small candle flickering in the window beside him. The player breathed a short sigh of relief and strode towards the entrance. He caught sight of a dark ribbon of glistening liquid trickling down the small stone step leading into the street, and his blood ran cold.

Tyburn darted forward. The doorwarden's eyes were open, his face twisted into a sightless smile, propped against the corner of the alcove. The front of his jerkin and overcoat were wet with blood.

"God's teeth …" Tyburn muttered. He checked the man's pulse. Dead, but warm. This had happened maybe within the last five minutes.

The Harlequin was here.

Tyburn drew his poniard. In close quarters, his rapier would be an impediment. He stepped past the alcove. The heavy oak door was closed, but at his touch, it yawned open like a gaping maw. Tyburn slipped through it and down the familiar hallway leading to Walsingham's set of offices, clerk rooms, file rooms, and parlors. He slid his feet with care on the parquet floor, gliding in absolute silence past the quiet offices piled high with letters, books, accounts, and missives, the flood of paper, ink and the avalanche of correspondence and messages that defined the role of the secretary and his staff. He paused at the anteroom, spying the tumbled shape of a body sprawled across one of the desks.

It was Robert, the secretary who had been so reluctant to part with Tyburn's salary arrears. His face held a look of open astonishment. His torn throat had been opened almost to his backbone. Tyburn winced at the sight. He had been irritated by the man's petty thievery, but he wouldn't ever have wished the Harlequin's gentle ministrations on anyone.

Voices.

The door to Walsingham's office was closed, but Tyburn could see the bright gleam of light edging along the base of the heavy door. The conversation was muffled but to Tyburn's ready ear, it sounded strained.

He reached over, clicked the handle down, and stepped into the room.

"Slow." The click of the gun cocking was loud in the sudden silence. "So very slow." The Harlequin shook her head in exasperation. Francis Walsingham was standing carefully behind his desk on the far side of the room, both hands flat on a desk stacked with correspondence, the same dull, beatific tapestry hanging still behind him. His thin, bearded face was tight and expressionless.

Tyburn glanced from Walsingham's grim visage to the smiling expression on the Harlequin's face. Despite having fallen through an inferno of fire, the woman was surprisingly intact. Her hair was scorched away on one side, and a thick, dark grime of soot masked her clear skin, flaring upwards past her left eye, like some savage's war paint. The remainder of the dark, short curls were intact, and despite a string of red, blistering burn marks, she seemed to have emerged relatively unscathed. The right hand holding the pistol was unmarred but the left hand was fiercely burned and raw, the scalded flesh melted and crisped in places, but she ignored it, letting it hang by her side as though the burned limb was irrelevant and a minor irritant.

"You are a poor horseman, dead man. If you had been quicker, you might have arrived soon enough to warn them." She smiled. "But that would have meant I simply had to kill a few more."

"You are acquainted with this woman, Master Tyburn?" Walsingham's voice held an untold amount of scorn and an undercurrent of lambent anger.

Tyburn moved slowly across the room, his eyes locked on the woman, who held the heavy pistol in a rock-steady grip leveled at the player. "Her name is Suzanne Martaine, also known in certain circles as the Harlequin. You employed her father in Paris."

The Harlequin flicked the muzzle at the poniard clutched in Tyburn's hand. "Lose it." Tyburn tossed the dagger to one side. His chest was tight, his nerves taut as he watched the woman and the looming barrel of the weapon.

Walsingham gave the Harlequin a skeptical glare. "I employed dozens of informants, news-gatherers, and petty street urchins in Paris. You will need to be more specific."

"Benoît Thieves." His name was a distasteful hiss on her lips.

Walsingham's lips thinned. "I had assumed he was long dead."

"Living in London, one of the Roaring Boys. Ran Thieves' Castle. Before the ... current proprietress," Tyburn said in a quick summary.

"Bastard pretender to nobility, rapist, thief, murderer, informer and your man with de Coligny's party," she said into the silence that followed.

"I recall," said Walsingham, his voice toneless. "His reports were highly fictionalized. Unreliable."

The Harlequin smiled. "He was a born liar. But I'm not here for him. I'm here because you refused us."

Tyburn slid one foot to the side and the muzzle of the weapon twitched in his direction. The Harlequin threw the play-actor a derisive glance and stepped back so she could cover both men. "Move to your left again, dead man, and our conversation comes to a very abrupt halt."

Tyburn gave her a tight nod and threw Walsingham a warning look. He slid into the space in front of the desk, beside a skeletally thin wooden chair reserved for visitors.

"Refused you? I don't even know you." The Moor scowled at the woman.

The Harlequin smiled, a familiar, predatory, and seductive curving of her full lips that sent shivers of warning down the play-actor's neck. "No. Of course you wouldn't. You see, you had shut your doors. Barred your gates. Stationed armed men to hold back the crowds." She cocked the weapon. "You remember them? All those crying, screaming, desperate people? The ones begging you for your help, pleading for a tiny ounce of mercy and grace in a slaughterhouse? *La Massacre*."

Walsingham stared, his face pale at the memory. "You were there?"

"Both of us were there. My mother bled to death holding on to your gates. An Englishwoman. Gone to you for protection, yet you bolted your doors and let us scream." The Harlequin's mad smile widened. "They chopped her fingers off, where she clung to your iron gates. And she still begged and called and pleaded. When the others ran to die in the streets or drown in the mercy of the Seine, she stayed. They beat her to the cobbles. She said that you—the English ambassador—would protect her. Not because my father was your agent, your spy, your provocateur, but because you had a duty to protect her."

Walsingham was still. Tyburn, long-versed in his employer's often expressionless mien, could read the emotions chasing across the Moor's long, bearded face. At last he spoke. "Before God, I am sorry for what your mother endured. But I could not open my gates. The mob would have stormed through and slain everyone, including my own wife and child. The king's guards that were sent to the embassy were the sole reason the mob didn't kill us all. I had not power to open my gates nor to protect any within my walls."

"Liar!"

"I couldn't even protect Seigneur de Briquemault, who took refuge with me the night of the massacre. They dragged him out of the embassy itself and hanged him. How could you expect me to protect your mother, when I daren't even stir for three days for fear of slaughter?" Walsingham stared at the Harlequin. "The memory of those days haunts my rest. I will hear that chill screaming in my ears for eternity, but if it is vengeance you seek, you should go to the source. Foist yourself upon the Duke of Guise, or that conniving bitch Catherine d' Medici. They put the Huguenots of Paris to the knife, not me."

She was shaking her head. "No, my father told me that he wrote you. He warned you that de Coligny was to be assassinated days before, that the Huguenot nobles were to be destroyed, but you did nothing, because it suited you and England to have the de Guise and the Catholic League destroy the Huguenots of Paris to strengthen your political hold here, to support your Protestant rabble and your heretic Queen."

"Your father was a thief, a drunk, and a liar," Walsingham said, his voice flat and cold. "He lied for monies, he lied for advantage, and he lied for prestige. He betrayed de Coligny and everyone he cared about. Why do you think he still lives while almost everyone else is dead and buried? Why do you think he concealed himself in London's underbelly?"

Tyburn winced at the Moor's tone and held his palm out in warning.

The Harlequin stared, her face blank as she weighed Walsingham's flat statement. Tyburn could almost see the thoughts sifting through her mind, reflected on that expressionless face. Her eyes shifted, edged as blades. "Probably true. He betrayed everyone he touched, why not de Coligny? Well. It changes nothing. You still left my mother to die on the streets." She shrugged and lifted the pistol. "I'll kill them next."

Tyburn stepped in front of the secretary, one hand raised, the other dropping to his sword hilt. "No."

She laughed. "Really, dead man? You fall through water, darkness, and fire, slip Death's fetters again and again, and then decide to place yourself between Hell's wrath and this spavined trickster? Why? What mortal debt do you owe him?"

"I could have walked your path when I returned from the Low Countries." *There is no place like Flanders.* It rang like a distant bell in his mind, an echoing refrain that rose unbidden. "But I owed other debts, carry too many ghosts. Walsingham" — Tyburn gestured at the saturnine bearded man standing behind him — "offered a path to ...redemption, of a kind."

The Harlequin gave another laugh. "More fool you then! You think he cares whether you live or die? You serve his immediate purpose, like my father did before you. You are as valued as the last piece of natter you collect, or for your skills at placing edge of blade on Spanish throat. You're a pet dog to chase his rats and wastrels. His little hunting kestrel, to fly on command." Her smile broadened. "Loose your jesses! Join with me. *La Hellequin* and her dead man, cast loose upon a sinful world. Think on the possibilities."

The player and the Harlequin locked eyes. Somewhere, far, far below the Harlequin was that hidden, terrified woman that had suffered in Paris. He had glimpsed her for a bare instant in the fiery

Saracen's Head. But she was long gone. Torn and burned to cinders and wind-blown ash.

There was nothing of her left to save.

Tyburn shook his head. "No. I'll stand where I've always stood. I cannot do other."

She shrugged and her finger whitened on the trigger. "*C'est bon.* You die by shot, him by steel. It's best."

Tyburn gave a half turn, his right hand tearing at his rapier hilt, his left hand hooking the back post of the wooden chair, sending it careening across the room.

The shot bellowed in the small room, and the Harlequin was snatched back as though by an invisible hand. Tyburn flinched involuntarily as the woman's pistol discharged with a spinning hiss of the wheellock mechanism, a flare of sparks, and a roaring blast. The ball shot high above the player's head to bury itself in the wall tapestry. The player, realizing he wasn't shot, turned his head.

Framed in the doorway, wreathed in powder smoke, one hand holding a fuming wheellock, Clair Carey stood glaring into the room. She dropped the pistol and yanked another from the holster on her belt.

Tyburn heard a low scrape and a quiet, pain-filled laugh. He turned. The Harlequin was sprawled against the thrown side chair, her burned hand clasped to her chest, the other twitching hand vainly trying to raise the empty pistol. Her grin was laced with blood, and her eyes were locked on Clair.

"I told you what I would do, if you touched him ever again," said Clair.

The Harlequin laughed, hollow and wet, and spat a mouthful of blood onto the floor. "You did. You did indeed. Well shot, my lady." Her burned fingers probed nerveless at the wound, and she winced. Walsingham stood, grim and reflective, watching.

She laughed again, a bubbling sound that ended in a spasm of harsh, bloody coughing. "Don't be"—she sucked in a deep, labored breath—"too pleased with yourselves, though. *La Hellequin* returns, again and again, in whatever vessel suits. We will dance this dance anon ..." Her eyes flicked over from Clair to Tyburn with an almost audible snap. "Should have taken my offer, dead man. It would have been ... entertaining. Now," she breathed, "your fate lies with the turning Wheel." Her flint eyes glinted in the candlelit room, reflecting a moment of red pain before fading into emptiness.

The three watched as she slid the rest of the way to the floor, blood pooling and staining the polished parquetry beneath her. The only sound was the click of Clair releasing the cocked dog on the weapon.

Chapter the Thirty-fourth

THE INN-YARD COMMON room was crammed with people, thick with the cacophony of conversation and laughter. The air was a mélange of smoke, baking bread, rich roasted beef, spilled ale, and sour wine. Christopher Tyburn and Clair Carey had squeezed into a corner table under a low ceiling, trying to hold an audible conversation over the din.

Clair glanced with a dubious eye at the wine in her cup. It was supposed to be an osey, a sweet Alsatian wine, laced with honey and spice, but it tasted of sour apples. Tyburn laughed at her expression. "I did tell you to drink the ale."

"I'm not fond of ale." She pushed the cup to one side. "Next time perhaps a decent canary."

Tyburn laughed again and gave her a mock toast. "No worries. They'll empty out into the yard as soon as the performance starts. We'll threaten the ostler until he finds something upright in his cellar."

"The last inn-yard performance for a time." She observed.

"Yes. The Earl of Worcester's Men will shift over to the Theatre for their next sets. Ten days, according to what Oldcastle and Burbage agreed. I thought Oldcastle was going to burst his head when I told him. Never seen the man get that red except when he's angry."

"And he still won't let you rejoin?"

Tyburn sighed exaggeratedly and nodded. "No. He refused to be moved. Claimed that Colle is better as Vice, now that he's sober."

"But you had an agreement!" Clair burst out. "You settled your half of the bargain—found Stokely, helped Burbage, and now Oldcastle's reneging."

The player shrugged again, inordinately calm about the situation. He reached out and grasped her hand, feeling the warm skin, fingers tracing her palm. "Things could always be worse. Look at poor Rutledge."

She laughed. The Earl of Rutledge had been selling off most of his properties and remittances over the past two weeks and had resigned from all his Crown posts. He was withdrawing from public life and service, retreating to his ancestral manor, such that remained.

Walsingham had made certain of that.

The charred account book that Tyburn had retrieved from the Saracen's Head had provided the spymaster with an in-depth and eye-opening look at the earl's financial dealings, partnerships, and investments, one that Walsingham was now applying with needlelike precision. The earl had withdrawn his suit for Lady Arabela Howard's hand and had stepped back from his concerted efforts to assume control over the principal secretary's portfolio of responsibilities. In addition, Walsingham's normally constrained purse was now filled to bursting, though he still paid it out with his customary parsimony.

You could call it blackmail, the player thought, but he preferred to think of it as a just turnabout. The thought of Rutledge's public discomfiture made the player smile. Walsingham had even grudgingly parted with monies for his wayward intelligencer, so for a time, the play-actor was freed from his usual penury.

Tyburn heard a voice calling his name through the dense and raucous crowd. He looked up in surprise to see Oldcastle plowing his way bodily through the throng, like a bullock squeezing through a too-narrow gap in a fence. Tyburn cocked one eyebrow and took a quick drink.

"Tyburn, you scurrilous … your pardon, milady Carey." The man gave her a quick leering nod that managed to be both polite and skin-crawlingly lecherous at the same time.

Tyburn leaned back against the canted wall beam and waited.

Oldcastle tugged a bench out and sat down heavily. Without preamble, he spoke. "I know we've had our differences, Kit. I know you think, at times, that I'm unfair or harsh on you, but it has been done solely to help you tread the boards with more confidence and ability." Oldcastle avoided meeting Kit's amused gaze. The troupe master took a deep breath. "I'm prepared to welcome you back to your role as Vice, provided," he temporized, "you agree to certain conditions."

"No." Tyburn gulped another mouthful of hoppy ale.

Flustered, Oldcastle sputtered, "What? No? Coads!"

"No," the player repeated, enjoying the choleric glare that Oldcastle radiated. Clair looked down, trying to hide her amusement.

"Mayhaps you didn't understand."

"I understood you perfect. You want me back in Worcester's Men. I said no."

Oldcastle flared. "You perfidious wattle. You know we need you back."

"Colle drunk again, is he?"

Oldcastle glared and then gave a sharp single nod. "He's beastly drunk. Sunk. Sodden. Wretched." The play master reached over, snatched Tyburn's mug, and drained the remaining ale in a single gulp. And sighed. "We need you." The words were reluctant, but to Oldcastle's credit, he spoke them anyway.

Tyburn rubbed two fingertips together and gave Oldcastle an evil grin. "I brought you your Theatre stage performances with Burbage and you … you reneged."

"I was mistaken."

"Reneged." The player repeated. "That's at least a ten-shilling remittance right there. And I want the same wages you pay Alleyn and Motely, not the tuppence you toss to some for hired dross."

Oldcastle's brow knitted. "Done," he said in a grudging voice. He stood. "Get yerself stirred then, Jacob's got the line notes and he'll walk you through it. Another bloody history play, sod it." Oldcastle gave Clair a sketchy bow and shoved his way back through the crowded common room, with Clair's open laughter trailing behind him.

"Damn that man," she said with a breathless smile. "But he does make me laugh."

Jacob Willens and Edward Alleyn sidled up to the table from out of the throng, both with wide grins. Jacob was rubbing his hands together in mock malicious amusement.

"You back in?" He cocked a sideways smile at Kit.

"Indeed I am. Gentlemen, I thank you for your conveyances," Tyburn replied, waving to get the pair some drinks from the ostler.

"What am I missing?" Clair asked, eyeing the new arrivals with suspicion.

"Just the degree to which this pair of reprobates plied Colle with wine." Tyburn muttered.

"You didn't? You horrible men."

"Don't fuss. Colle will go back to working for his brother at the cordwainers. He wasn't sober a single day on the boards anyway, and that was before we bought him a bottle. Only reason Oldcastle didn't lay him out weeks ago was to give Kit trouble." Jacob gave Tyburn a nudge. "Welcome back to the wars."

A loud bellow came from the front of the common room. "You gecks! Codso! Get out here, you board dogs!"

Tyburn, Willens, and Alleyn all winced in unison and cocked their heads like a group of pointers. Clair stifled a laugh. Tyburn leaned over and gave her a quick kiss on the cheek. "Time to tread the boards." He smiled, turned, and vanished into the multitude.

Clair sipped the remains of her wine and then followed, her laughter trailing along with her, out into the bright inn-yard, one thought on her mind: the play awaits.

-Fini-

Author's Note

ANYONE THAT HAS studied the history of London is well
aware of the critical impact that the twin destructive events
of the Great Fire (1666) and the German Luftwaffe (1939-45)
inflicted on the city's architecture and infrastructure.

Very few London's Tudor-era buildings survived relatively
intact into the twenty-first century, so the visible bones and
foundations of the old city are, at best, fragmentary and disjointed,
providing only a tantalizing glimpse of the era and its inhabitants.
The majority of Tudor-era buildings, residences, inn-yards,
guildhalls and workhouses, palatial homes, hospitals, and markets
have been burned, toppled, overbuilt, or consumed in the 415 years
since the end of Elizabeth's reign.

Trying to reconstruct or recreate a sense of the rhythm, the
pace, the sense of place, and the feel of London for that era is a
challenge for any writer. There are any number of reference books,
contemporaneous writings and historical sources to draw upon—
too many to cite here, so I limit myself to the essentials. Anyone
looking at Elizabethan London needs to acknowledge the incredible

contribution of John Stow and his work *The Survey of London*, first published in 1598. Stow's *Survey* offers up an indelible picture of the city, its populace and commerce, and the often intricate threads that permeated the social and economic structure.

What the era lacks in physical remains, it more than makes up for in documentation. The Tudor era witnessed the start of two major innovations: the printing press and the rise of a robust structural bureaucracy, the combination of which led to a broad range of historical documentation ranging from personal letters to legal and court documents, coroner's rolls, property surveys, legal disputes, writs, recipes, plays, lurid newsheets and polemics, religious tracts, guides to gentlemanly behavior and a robust review of the London underworld.

It does not lack for sources.

I will note, for the record, that any errors or misrepresentations found in this work are entirely mine. Some exist on purpose, while others may be outright errors. I ask for fictional indulgence on the former and forgiveness for the latter.

Dr. John Story was, as noted, kidnapped from Bergen op Zoom by English agents after being lured onboard a ship for a purported inspection for heretical publications. Story was transported to Yarmouth, imprisoned, tried, and later executed in 1571, having the dubious privilege of being the first person to be hanged, drawn, and quartered on the new "triple-tree" gallows at Tyburn. For my own selfish fictional purposes, I shifted Story's kidnapping by five years from 1571 to 1576 in order to give Kit Tyburn a mission of note that would correspond to the Spanish destruction of Antwerp.

Also shifted slightly downstream in history was the opening of The Theatre by James Burbage in Shoreditch. I moved the circumstances of the Theatre's initial opening to the tail-end of 1576, again purely for the convenience of my tale. In reality, Burbage leased the land in April 1576 and opened The Theatre in the fall, probably about two months earlier than I've indicated in my fictional account.

The arrival of The Theatre heralded a new age for the London troupes. Within a year, a rival facility, The Curtain, would be opened nearby, followed by the Rose (1587), the Swan (1595), the Globe (1599), Blackfriars (the first indoor theatre, opened in 1598), the Fortune (1600), and the Red Bull (1604). Almost all of the theatres were located outside of London proper—Shoreditch and Southwark being the most popular locales—beyond the reach of the Puritan-controlled Corporation of London. But not beyond their disdain and distaste.

Sir John Spencer, Lord Mayor of London in 1594 described the theatres as "places of meeting for all vagrant persons and maisterles men that hang about the Citie, theeves, horsestealers, whoremoongers, coozeners, connycatching persones, practizers of treason and other such lyke." The London aldermen's dislike for the players was deep, long-standing, and well practiced.

Despite the Precisian opposition, or perhaps because of it, Londoners flocked to the playhouses. The Lord Admiral's Men are documented as having performed 38 plays in 1594-95. The Globe Theatre alone was estimated to hold almost 2,000 people per performance, so the economic scale of the theatre industry in Elizabethan London was considerable. These early days of The Theatre paved the way for the rise of William Shakespeare, Christopher Marlowe, Ben Jonson, and their peers. It heralded the crowning achievement of the English Renaissance: the early Elizabethan theatre and a set of plays that remain a brilliant testament to the era and its peoples.

The Saracen's Head Inn, as a home to Thieves' Castle and the nefarious Harlequin, is entirely fictional; however, the real Saracen's Head inn-yard was located as noted and was a popular stop for travellers, merchants, and visitors. If you go seeking it today, you will find naught but a plaque commemorating its demolition in 1868. The location is now home to the City of London Police.

Lastly of note is Sir Francis Walsingham, who though fictional in this work, is a fascinating and deeply gripping historical personage. Walsingham served as principal secretary for Queen Elizabeth from 1573 until his death in 1590. He sat at the centrepoint of countless plots, schemes, and subterfuges, serving as Elizabeth's spymaster, intelligence agency, and advisor through one of the most dangerous and fraught eras in English history. He did, as noted, serve as Elizabeth's ambassador to France and was, also as noted, trapped in Paris during the St. Bartholomew's Day Massacre in 1572 that saw more than 10,000 Huguenots slaughtered.

The response of Pope Gregory XIII to the Paris massacre was telling. He sent a golden rose to the King of France, had a commemorative medal struck honouring the event, and considered it equivalent in significance to the Spanish victory over the Turks at Lepanto. He commissioned three frescos of the event to decorate the Sala Regia (Regal Room) in the Apostolic Palace in the Vatican.

When informed of the Massacre, Philip II of Spain reportedly laughed, one of the only documented records of such an occurrence.

While James Burbage and John Brayne are actual historical personages, the Harlequin is strictly fictional, as are Rutledge, Asquith, Christopher Tyburn, Clair Carey, Oldcastle and most of the members of Worcester's Men (although the troupe itself did exist).

Not fictional was Gamaliel Ratsey, the wayward highwayman cited by Oldcastle, although he was active from 1600 to 1605 rather than the timeline cited in the book. The account of his hanging is also lifted from that of another real-world hanging but was too good of a tale not to tell, so I gave it to Ratsey as a tribute to a character too unique for actual fiction.

Kit Tyburn will return, as there are still tales left to tell.

Dean Hamilton
Toronto, Ontario, Canada
www.tyburntree.blogspot.com
Twitter: @Tyburn__Tree

Glossary

Abraham-man   - Vagrant or beggar that feigns madness

Adobado de carnero   - Spanish, marinated mutton

Amor, ch'a nullo amato amar perdona   - "Love, which absolves no
                                    loved one from loving" – Dante

Angels   - Gold coins, each valued at ten shillings

Arroz en cazuela al horno   - Spanish, rice casserole

Autolycus   - In Greek, 'the wolf itself.' A character from
                        Greek mythology, Autolycus was the son of
                        Hermes. He possessed a helmet that rendered
                        the wearer invisible and was usually
                        portrayed as a thief and a trickster.

Bales   - Dice

Banting   - Fooling about with

Bartholomew Fair   - Ironic nickname for poorest section of the
                        Fleet prison

Bate	- Strife or discord
Beadle	- Constable
Bedlam	- Informal name for Bethlehem Royal Hospital, also known as St Mary Bethlehem, located near Bishopsgate, which served as London's psychiatric hospital. The hospital was one of London's most famous locales.
Bene bouse	- Literally "strong or good liquor"
Bene	- Good
Bing a waste	- Go you hence or bugger off
Blood	- A fast or foppish man
Boot-halers	- A freebooter or a brigand.
Bousing ken	- An alehouse
Bull-beggars	- Bogeymen
Burghley	- William Cecil, 1st Baron Burghley served as Secretary of State and chief advisor of Queen Elizabeth I. He was appointed Lord High Treasurer in 1572.
By the troth	- A "polite" oath
Cacodaemons	- Evil spirit
Canary	- Wine from the Canary Islands
Cannikin	- Plague or illness
Capon armando	- Spanish, armored capon – roasted rooster, coated with pine nuts and almonds

Capon	- Specifically a castrated male chicken; however, used as a common derogatory or insulting description.
Cheveril	- Soft kidskin leather
Cittern	- Musical instrument similar to a guitar
Clapperdudgeon	- Chief beggar
Close packings	- Secret plans
Clyster	- Irritation or infection
Coads	- Emphatic oath, probably a variation of "God's Own"
Coal house	- Dark, lightless dungeon
Cobs	- Water-carriers. Their business was to deliver water to various households and customers, commonly carrying a large tankard or wooden tubs hanging from a shoulder-yoke.
Codso	- "God's Own" an impolite oath
Codso	- Emphatic oath, means "God's Own"
Cogging and foisting	- Cheating at cards & dice
Coif	- A white cap worn by lawyers, symbolizing their profession
Cony-catching	- Slang for fraud, thievery, and con games. A cony was a rabbit.
Coranto	- A court dance for couples, which originated as an Italian folk dance.

Cordwainer	- Leather shoemakers, specifically makers of new shoes, as opposed to cobblers who were only permitted to repair shoes
Cot-quean	- Effeminate man
Counter	- The Wood Street Counter, one of 14 prisons in London. The Counter was known for housing debtors, among others.
Cozenage	- Fraud or confidence schemes
Cozening	- To trick or deceive
Cross and pile	- Coin-tossing game
Cullion	- A contemptible fellow; a rascal.
Curtail	- A vagabond or criminal, of lower status than an upright man.
Cushions	- Seated playgoers in cushioned chairs, benches or stands.
Dag	- Pistol, small gun
Doddypol	- Fool
Doublet	- A padded jacket, usually close-fitting and ending at the waist, worn over a shirt or jerkin.
Draw-latch	- Petty thief
Fie	- Expression of disgust or anger.
Fluyt	- Dutch ship, similar to a galleon
Foists and draws	- Pickpockets

Foliots	- Imaginary mythical creature or imp
Galliard	- An athletic Elizabethan dance, characterized by multiple leaps, jumps and hops; a favourite of Queen Elizabeth.
Gasters	- Terrifying spirits
Geck	- A fool
Gorget	- A piece of armor protecting the throat. It was reduced to a more decorative role with the arrival of firearms.
Groat	- Four-pence silver coin
Groundlings	- Common playgoers that stand in the inn-yard or theatre open space for the performance.
Holborn Conduit	- London's conduit system brought fresh water from local springs into the City where it was held at large neighbourhood cisterns called conduits.
Hookman	- A thief who uses a hook on a line to reach over fences or through open windows, also known as a hookman, curber, or hooker.
Huguenots	- French Protestants
Humours	- Temperaments believed to affect basic aspects of bodily health; sanguine, choleric, melancholic, and phlegmatic
Jennet	- Small Spanish or Moorish horse, often favoured by the nobility across Europe for its smooth gait and distinctive spotted pattern

Juking	- Chirping, as a bird.
Knight's Side	- The "nicer" area of a prison where prisoners of quality could pay for private rooms, better food, bedding, and luxuries.
Laystill	- Manure pile or sewage pit
Le Balafré	- "Scarface," nickname for Henry I, Prince of Joinville, Duke of Guise, Count of Eu. He was the eldest son of Francis, Duke of Guise. He was widely suspected of instigating the murder of Admiral de Coligny, a noted Huguenot leader, in August 1572 and supporting the subsequent St. Bartholomew's Day Massacre that saw up to 3,000 people killed in Paris and another estimated 7,000 in the provinces.
Leicester's Men	- Leicester's Men were a playing troupe supported by Robert Dudley, the Earl of Leicester.
Lex talionis	- Latin, the law of retaliation
Lour	- Money
Malmsey	- Fortified sweet Madeira wine
Mandelion	- Type of overcloak
Marshalsea	- Prison for debtors
Melite	- According to Greek mythology, Melite was a river naiad, daughter of the river god Aegaeus, and a lover of both Zeus and Hercules.

Mercers	- Grocers and merchants, dealers in food and merchant goods, incl. fabrics and cloth
Models	- Small dolls or manikins wearing copies of the latest clothes and fashion styles
Monchance	- Gambling card game
Morisco / Morris	- Dance. A morris was a more popular dance spectacle, akin to a jig, based on Moorish dancing; in particular it was a staple used in the various theatre performances and at public events.
Mudlarks	- Children & poor scavengers looking for salable or lost items on the tidal mudbanks of the Thames
Noblesse de lettres	- Noblesse de lettres was a purchased nobility in France, for non-noble holders of a noble fief.
Non sufficit orbis	- Latin - The world is not enough – Philip II, King of Spain's motto
Nonny-Nonny	- A term of indelicate allusion, based on the practice of using these words to render rude Italian songs. A modern equivalent would be Seinfeld's "yada-yada-yada" in reference to sex.
Numini Cæsaris provincia Britannia	- Latin, "To the deity of the Emperor, set up by the province of Britain"
Obs	- From obolus, a half-penny, small valued coin

Ordinary	- Common drinking or food establishment
Osey	- Sweet Alsatian wine, laced with honey and spice
Paunched	- Stabbed in the belly
Pavane	- Processional dance
Perinades	- Catamites, "rent-boys"
Petard	- Explosive charge used by sappers
Pluck a rose	- To urinate
Poniard	- A dagger
Precisians	- Puritans / Protestants
Primero	- Card game similar to poker
Punk	- Prostitution
Queans	- Whores
Rapier	- A long-bladed sword characterized by a protective hilt and a thin blade designed for thrusting attacks.
Robins	- A French man of the law or a magistrate
Sarsenet	- Fine silk
Shambles	- A butchering yard
Shove-groat	- Coin-tossing game
Slip	- A coin
Sopa castellana	- Spanish, garlic soup

Spada da lato	- A precursor to the rapier, the spada da lato was a one-handed sidesword, akin in design to a medieval arming sword, albeit with a thinner blade and designed more for cutting than for thrusting.
Star Chamber	- The Star Chamber (Camera stellata) was a court made up of members of the Privy Council and senior judges. It was a secret court often utilized to try political or influential parties. The name was derived from the painted stars on the ceiling in the meeting room they used at the Palace of Westminster.
Starlings	- Pilings supporting London Bridge
Steelyard	- The Steelyard, the Stalhof, was the London premises of the Hanseatic merchants from High Germany. It consisted of a private wharf, warehouses, homes, and offices in a walled community on the north bank of the Thames in Dowgate, west of London Bridge.
Swinge-bucklers	- Bold fellows
Tallman	- Professional fighting man or thug
Tempus fugit	- Latin, "time flies"
Tercios	- Spanish military unit, a company
The Hole	- Poorest section of the Counter prisons
Upright men	- An "upright man" was someone with authority in the Elizabethan criminal underworld, someone who held command or

authority over a group. They typically carried a truncheon or staff to mark their position.

Veritas lux mea — Latin, the truth is my light

Vice — A stock villain. Many playing troupes used recognizable stock characters such as Vice, the Virtuous Youth, the Lord of Misrule, etc., so audiences could easily identify the various characters. Often specific actors were associated with these roles and played them regularly.

Viol — A six-stringed musical instrument held vertically and played with a bow.

Volta — Dance. La volta (vault) was a popular Elizabethan dance involving lifting the female partner in the air. Puritan Philip Stubbs was strident in his condemnation of the dance, noting "what filthy groping and unclean handling is not practiced everywhere in these dancings."

Wait — Musical troupe using wind instruments

Warwick's Men — Earl of Warwick's theatre troupe

Watergausen — Sea Beggars – the name assumed by the Calvinist opposition to the Spanish rule of the Netherlands. They mostly operated as coastal pirates, raiding the Spanish, until they captured the port of Brill in 1572.

Winchester Geese	- Southwark whores. The brothels operated on property owned by the bishop of Winchester.
Without Newgate	- "Without" was a geographic descriptive term used to refer to locales outside the various London gates and wards. In this case, in the area beyond Newgate.

Kit Tyburn will return

in

Sorcerer Street

www.ingramcontent.com/pod-product-compliance
Lightning Source LLC
Chambersburg PA
CBHW031342070726
47496CB00017B/1421